I0679756

Riders Up
Book One

Cassie's Hope

by

Adriana Kraft

Riders Up: Book One
Cassie's Hope
By
Adriana Kraft

ISBN: 978-0-9894693-8-8

B&B Publishing
1970 N. Leslie St. #560
Pahrump, NV 89060

Cover by
Rebecca Poole
Dreams2Media.com

Riders Up

Book One: Cassie's Hope
Chicago, 1996
Available now

Book Two: Heat Wave
Iowa, 2000
Available now

Book Three: Willow Smoke
Chicago, 2002
Available now

Book Four: Detour Ahead
California, 2004
Release Date: January, 2015

1996

"You must know your heart. Trust your blood."

The setting sun cast a warm glow on the reddish clay hills of eastern Utah. Resting one foot on the lowest corral rail, Clint Travers paid close attention to the soft words spoken by his grandmother. She stood patiently, hands clasped at her waist, gazing at the eastern horizon.

Clint loved the bent old woman whose dark hair hung in a single braid over a heavy shawl. He'd fight mountain lions barehanded for her. But she wanted him to see the world as she saw it, and that wasn't entirely possible.

"You are a good grandson. Listen carefully. A red ball will rise from a great lake in the east. Those flames will make for you much joy and much pain. Do not be afraid. They are your destiny."

"What do you mean, Grandmother?" Scowling, Clint pushed away from the fence. "I've never been good with riddles."

"I speak no riddle. I speak of your future."

1

CHAPTER ONE

"Dad, I've got a life. I want to live it." Arms folded and shoulders squared, Cassie glared at the tired old man slouched in the battered arm chair.

"Now, Cass. I'm not askin' much. Six months. You can manage that for old time's sake, if nothin' else."

Cassie dropped her gaze. Before his stroke, Tug O'Hanlon had been such a vibrant man, full of unstoppable energy and everlasting dreams. Now her father sat with blankets draped across his thin shriveled frame, his energy sapped. Yet, somehow he was still able to dream.

She shook her head. "Old time's sake." Her voice strained from remembering. "Maybe we recall the past differently."

She paced slowly. "Broken down trucks, rusting horse trailers, rundown hotels — if we could afford them. Watching you chase rainbows from one racetrack to another. I don't know about old times, Dad. As I recall, they weren't so grand."

"They weren't so bad, girl. You saw a lot of country most kids don't ever see. You got to dream. Many folks don't never dream. You know horses inside and out, better than most who make a living with 'em." The old man paused to catch his breath. "And we always had this place to come back to." He squinted. He choked. "Could've been worse."

Cassie winced at the sudden ache behind her eyes. *Not now. Don't give in now.* But she found herself kneeling by her father, holding his wrinkled hand. "I know. We had a lot of good times. I'm sure it could've been worse. And through it all, you never gave up this land."

Gruffness returned to his voice. "You sell your land, and you risk having nothing left."

How many times had she heard that aphorism in her twenty-seven years? Scenes raced through her mind's eye, each one tumbling into the next. Spending summers on the road with him when school was out, getting caught up in his dreams, mucking the stables, exercising horses, cheering wildly when their horses ran well, and wondering where the next meal was coming from when they didn't. And coming home to the farm and Aunt Lizzy with little to show for their efforts. He'd always said he wasn't looking for a derby horse, just a consistent stakes contender. So many risks taken—but never the farm.

He'd lost so much. Even her mother, who deserted both of them before Cassie was two. Abigail O'Hanlon wanted more out of life than chasing dreams from one bush track to another. Apparently, her mother also wanted more than a chubby red-headed baby girl.

Pressing a fist to her mouth, Cassie stared hard at the man with shocking white hair and skin as fragile as paper hunched awkwardly in his chair. She'd nearly lost him—but how much did she owe

4

him? She bristled. "And now you want me to give up my life so you can have one more shot at your dream?"

"I didn't say give it up. Put your career on hold for a few months. That group home you slave at will always take you back." Again, he coughed. "You got to go look at the horse, Cass. I tell you, she's somethin' exceptional. You look at her and you'll know. She's got class and desire. Work with her. If she don't pan out, you can go back to your social work job, and I'll grow weeds from my rockin' chair. I just got to know how good she really is. And the clock is ticking—hers and mine."

And what about my clock? Cassie wanted to scream at the shell of a man. She'd turned her back on horses nearly a decade before. Instead, she'd done college with Aunt Lizzy's help, and then graduate school. Now she held a steady job as assistant director at an inner city group home—not lots of money, but far more predictable than horses.

Damn horses, anyway! They were as cantankerous, beguiling and seductive as men. She'd done her best to swear off both.

Her father played on her emotions like a skilled flutist.

"I'll go take a look at the filly." Her voice faltered. Her shoulders sagged. "But I'm promising nothing."

"That's okay Just look at her. Maybe I'm slippin'."

Cassie saw the edge of a smile creep onto his

lips but chose to ignore it. "Which paddock is she in?"

"Second one on the east end of the barn."

"It won't take long. Don't get your hopes up. I'm just gonna look at your latest rainbow." She hesitated. "You know, you could sell off just a little land and retire like a king. You're sitting on a gold mine, being this close to Chicago."

Tug blinked. "I know, but I ain't done yet. Now go look at Cassie's Hope — she's a real looker, has a lot of spunk, and gleamin' chestnut hair. No wonder I named her after you."

Cassie picked her way through the familiar barn, reacquainting herself with ancient smells. Until her dad's stroke three weeks earlier, she'd made a weekly trek out from Chicago's Northside to see him. Yet she'd adamantly refused to have anything to do with the horses. They were part of her past.

Her dad could spin a web of intrigue and hope that would seduce a concrete statue to blink. Most people liked Tug. He was friendly, loyal, and could be counted on for a loan, even if he had nothing to lend.

"Well, where is this damn horse?" she groused, striding briskly through the barn.

"Ah," she whispered as she reached the paddock. "So you're the cheese in the trap he's set." The filly nickered softly and stepped forward to sniff her visitor. Cassie scratched the animal's neck and the horse nodded.

"Oh, you really are a lover, aren't you? Damn, you're a beauty. Straight legs, tall but compact, a good chest for lungs, and that indescribable fire in the eye. Yeah, you've got promise."

Cassie waved her arms, encouraging the filly to dash to the other end of the paddock.

"Oh, my. You've got poetry, too," she groaned, assessing the chestnut's smooth gait. *Don't get hooked on his dream.* "Okay, I don't want to do this. But if I'm to be fair to Dad and you, I'm going to have to feel you under me."

After Cassie returned with a bridle, saddle blanket and saddle, Cassie's Hope stood rock solid still for tacking up. Cassie led her charge out of the paddock to the small half mile track her dad maintained for training. Then she hefted herself into the saddle for the first time in years. She sat a little timid. The filly shied and skittered.

"Okay, gal, so you're not the pony that little girls dream about," Cassie muttered, regaining her seat and control of the horse. "Now we're not gonna do anything stupid. We'll just trot a bit and then gallop out a half mile or so."

"Golly, you love this, don't you? Your trot is as smooth as glass. Okay, let's see how you like to run."

With hardly any encouragement, the filly tucked her chin to her chest and easily moved into a controlled gallop. After a half mile Cassie settled the filly back into a trot. "I'm sure you could go miles, but not me."

Back in the paddock area, Cassie brushed the

chestnut, checked her hooves and let her cool down. "Damn it, Hope, I was wishing you'd be just another nag that Dad fell in love with — beautiful, but over-rated. Girl, you're a lot of horse. You got your grand-daddy's genes. Seattle Slew was a runner. Could you be it? Dad would be so thrilled." Suddenly she could hardly see through her tears. "He's lived his whole life for you, and now he can hardly lift a pitchfork."

"She's a nice filly." Cassie cast a cautious glance at her father, who hadn't moved from his rocking chair during her absence. "A pleasure to ride. But a race horse — who knows?"

"I know." He paused. "And you know, too. You never were able to outfox your old man."

Letting out a sigh, Cassie sat on the arm of a chair opposite her father. "Yeah, she's got a hell of a lot of potential. But you know better than I, there's a lot of room between potential and being a bonafide stakes contender."

"Of course I know. That's why I need you, Cass." His hands balled into fists. "It's why the filly needs you."

"You've got her nearly race ready. Why not just send her to another trainer? There must be a dozen who owe you favors and would be more than willing, especially now, to continue her training and get her started racing."

"No. No." Tug's voice rose. "I've gotta be part of it. If I send her away, I'm out of it. You and I, we can work together." His voice became crisp and clear for the first time that afternoon. "Develop strategy. Pick the right spots for her. You can train the horse, but you'll need help at track management, pick'n the races and so on."

Cassie stood and absently wiped some dust off one of her old riding trophies that sat on a display shelf. "Even if I wanted to do this," she said, "and I'm not saying I do, I can't just walk away from a paying job."

"They'll hold it for you. You know that. And I've got six other horses who'll be runnin' and trainin'. Was trainin' eight more, but their owners moved 'em to other barns. Can't say I blame 'em much, but they coulda waited a little longer. You'd take in the trainer's percentage on whatever we make."

"I don't have a license," she said, knowing that was no gigantic hurdle.

"No problem, you'd be my assistant. Besides, you'll pass the exam standin' on your head."

"I'd have to live out here," she mused. "Too far to commute daily. Maybe I could sublet my apartment for six months. That would help a lot."

"You'll do it then?" His voice squeaked.

Guilt, excitement and fear washed over her in such quick succession that Cassie couldn't sort them out. Was she yielding? Hell, it'd been a done deal before she'd left Hope in her paddock. "Yes, I'll try. Six months. No more. She is a very promising filly. I still don't know how we can afford to do this."

"We can afford it." Tug's eyes twinkled. "I got

somethin' else to tell you. Didn't wanna till after you made up your mind. Didn't wanna influence you too much...I've agreed to sell eighty acres to Mr. Dillingham, who's been after that land for the last five years. After taxes and everybody's fees, we should net a little over a million dollars." Nodding softly, he said, "For once, I think we can afford to chase this dream."

"Holy shit!" Cassie shrieked. "You did what? Why now?"

"There's plenty of farm left for horses. Thought maybe I've been too stubborn for my own good. This may be my last chance, Cass. Holdin' on to land is an important principle. But bein' land poor probably don't make much sense either. It's yours, you know. I'm just gonna share some of it with you for awhile."

"Oh, Daddy." She bent down and kissed him on the cheek. "I don't know what to say! We could go out and buy contenders. Horses that could be competitive stakes runners right away."

"I know that."

She saw a quick flash of that familiar stubborn streak set deep in his cat-gray eyes.

"Nope. The key is to raise a big horse — not just buy it. Any rich fool can buy into a good race horse. That's what baseball owners do when they ignore their farm teams. It takes skill to raise a contender. Later, we might upgrade our broodmare stock."

"Broodmares! Now hold on." Catching a glimpse of her father's long range dream, Cassie stiffened. "Money or not, I've only signed on for six months. I've got a life. People depend on me."

- o -

"You're going to do what?" Dirk Johnson exclaimed, his jaw dropping.

"Like I said, I'm taking a six month leave of absence to train some horses for my dad," Cassie said. "I'll be at our farm out in McHenry County."

Cassie doubted if the short dark-haired man had been out of the city twice in his life. Dirk worked in the financial district by day, but lived for the night: for opera, ballet, theater and fine restaurants. She'd met him when he was seeking help for a younger brother. They were friends. He might see that differently. But they were just friends. She'd been clear she wasn't looking for an intimate relationship.

"It's...it's just such a shock," he said. "I can't imagine you working with those huge beasts. And how can you be away from the city that long? You need to be where life pulsates, where things happen. My god.. McHenry County?"

Cassie flushed. "Not all of life takes place inside the city limits of Chicago. There's no moat keeping me from going back and forth. You could even come out and visit."

"Fine for you to say, but the city is my life. I know where I'm going," he said, peering with disdain. "I love it here."

"And I don't?"

"It doesn't appear so. I thought you would tire of working with screwed up kids soon enough. That's not surprising," he hurried on. "But I hoped you would develop a nice lucrative private practice. Then we could see what the future held for us. You'd be done playing around...but now?"

"Playing around!" She spat the words out, then felt her cheeks burn, horrified that people at nearby tables were staring. "I'll have you know, Mr. Has-It-All-Together," she whispered, "I've not been playing around with those screwed up kids. And I have no desire for a lucrative private practice. I'm sorry I'll never be worthy of you."

Briefly she hesitated. "Hell no! I'm not sorry at all." Jumping up from her chair, she flung her napkin at him. "You can pay the bill, asshole. Goodbye and have a good life. Try not to choke on your fortune cookie."

Grabbing her own cookie, she stormed out of the restaurant without looking back. On the sidewalk, fighting back tears, she ground the cookie in the palm of her hand until she could read its contents: "Changes will lead to hope and romantic intrigue." Right!

Crumbling the paper, she flung it in the gutter. "You're full of shit, too."

- o -

Her three best friends sat in Cassie's North Side apartment stunned, not knowing quite what to say after hearing her news.

Traci Steele, the tall dark-haired lawyer, flashed her a smile and spoke first. "You can count on me, Cass. Let me know when you have a horse running and I'll try to be there. Haven't been to the track in ages. Should be lots of fun."

"Fun? Hanging out with gangsters? Taking money from the poor? No way I'll go to a race track," Susan Jackson declared adamantly. The tall blonde looked down her nose with shocked disapproval.

Cassie shrugged, smiling. "You don't have to come if you don't want to."

"Well, I don't. And I can't imagine you dumping Dirk Johnson. Have you totally lost your mind? He would've been such a catch."

"You can have him if you want," Cassie said cheerfully. Susan's reaction had not surprised her at all. Now that she thought about it, Susan and Dirk would make a fine match. Traci's more tempered response had also been expected. Cassie knew she could count on Traci no matter what. But there was one more friend to hear from. "And what about you, Ashton? Do you think I've lost all my marbles?"

The attractive thirty-something African American woman, Ashton Drake, beamed. "Well, you're not likely to find me nuzzling up against a horse, but I admire your guts and your loyalty. I'll come watch your horse. As far as Dirk goes, I think you should've dumped him months ago."

"Well," huffed Susan. "I guess I don't belong here anymore."

"Nonsense," interjected Traci, standing to fill their tea cups. Her ebony hair swung about her chin, punctuating her words. "Just get off your judgmental pedestal. You know we love you. God, we've been together since grad school days. Cassie's decision to make time to help her dad shouldn't break us up. We can still get together once a month, either in the city or somewhere out in the burbs. And how many guys have you gone through in the last year?"

"Yeah," Susan replied, haltingly, reaching for the sugar cubes. "I'm sorry, Cass. My strict parents saw horse racing and gambling as works of the Devil. Sorry I shot from the hip."

"No harm, no foul. We all react too quickly at times. I do want to thank you all for your support. It means a lot to me. This is a temporary thing, but it's still scary." She hugged herself briefly, wondering what she was getting herself into.

Six weeks later a cacophony of April sounds greeted the first rays of dawn on the O'Hanlon farm. Cardinals, robins and mourning doves sang to each other. Young foals whinnied, seeking attention from their mothers. A light, bright mood greeted the rising sun, except for the storm brewing on the front porch.

"I can't do it. I proved that already." Cassie kicked at a corner porch post.

She'd been so hopeful. She'd allowed herself to be bitten by that same damnable bug that had infested her father for years. That bug carrying the *dream of the big horse* disease.

Hope had responded well to the training regimen. She'd worked hard. Nothing seemed to bother her until the day of the race. Then things just fell apart. One race might've been excused, but two races back-to-back?

And Cassie had no answer — *not true*. The answer was to fess up to being a social worker, not some damn magician with horses.

She stopped her pacing and stood before her father. Quietly, with hands clenched tightly behind her back she announced, "I quit. I'm sorry, Dad. But I'm not good enough."

"Sorry?" her dad spat out. "Not good enough? Quit? Hah, I never thought I'd see the day when the daughter of Tug O'Hanlon quit anything…just rolled over and played dead."

Cassie recoiled. Tears filled her eyes. She knelt and rested her head on his knees. He held her. She sobbed.

Her mind whirled. She never cried, especially in front of her dad Why couldn't she stop crying?

Damn, Cass, put on your social work hat. Was it just because she couldn't rescue her dad's dream? Or did it reach farther back — losing her mother, who they'd never talked about, not wanting to get hurt again? Was she just afraid of the lure of adventure horses had always held for her? His fingers continued massaging her shoulder muscles like he used to do when she was a child.

At last, cried out, Cassie rocked back on her heels and accepted the blue bandanna her father

15

proffered. She laughed weakly and blew her nose loudly. "Sorry about that unexpected display. All of this is getting to me."

Tug managed a smile. "You know running horses has more downs than ups."

Cassie nodded. She couldn't take any more downs.

"You haven't given the horse a chance yet. Cassie's Hope deserves more than bein' dumped after two poor races." Cassie cleared her throat to speak. Her father raised his hand to quiet her. "I know you think somebody else, maybe someone like Ed Harrington, coulda done better with her."

"I didn't say," she blurted out, "that Harrington would do better."

"Anyway, I don't want you to give up on the filly or yourself so quickly. Remember, you signed on for six months. There's still over four months left."

A chill raked Cassie's body. Surely, he wouldn't try to hold her to the agreement. He wouldn't expect her to endure the pain of losing that long — but why not? He'd endured a lifetime of losing. *Unfair!*

"It often happens in young horses, after a bad start or two, they just lose confidence in themselves. They train well till the day of the race. Then they remember bein' bumped around or whatever and really want no part of racin'. Honey, what we gotta do is help Hope get her confidence back."

Cassie's heart lurched and her mind scrambled

16

to keep up with her father. She felt like a kitten being lured by a string dragging across a floor.

"Sometimes horses need to get away from the track where things went wrong. They need a change of environment. In the old days, we'd take such a horse to a track where we could run against a poorer class of horse, increasing the odds for a win."

Cassie listened intently. So far everything he was saying made sense. After all, he had years of experience.

She watched him admire the yearlings running their own impromptu races in the nearby pasture. He sighed, turning his attention back to her. "I wish I could do this, but I can't. Only you can do it. I want you to take Cassie's Hope to Wyoming Downs. They have a stakes race comin' up May seventeenth — that's saying a lot more than it is — but it's a decent race."

"Wyoming Downs!" Cassie squealed, her eyes rounding. "Where the hell is that?"

Tug cackled. "It happens to be in Wyoming."

"The state?"

"The state."

"You want me to haul a horse half way across the country to find her confidence? Why not Prairie Meadows or Canterbury?"

Cassie saw the cagey glint dancing in her father's eyes. Every horse trainer, every horse player had to have an angle. She was about to hear one more.

"Altitude. If we train the filly in the mountains,

17

she'll have a tremendous edge when we run her back here."

Before she could voice her skepticism, he hurried on. "Olympic athletes do it all the time. Horse trainers do, too. If this don't work, Cass, if the filly is simply a dud, so be it. We tried. We can feel good about that. You can go back to your old job. I won't even try holdin' you to your commitment."

"How long would I have to be gone?"

"Probably two weeks. It'll take at least a couple days to haul each way. You'll want to be out there a week so the filly can train and get used to the altitude. When you get her back, I'll have her entered in a cheap allowance race. Then we'll really see what we've got."

This was too much! Wyoming? Hauling horses alone?

She searched for words to tell him he'd gone too far and discovered she couldn't find them. Her excitement mounted. New scenery, adventure, a chance to make it up to Hope. "I wonder what Cheyenne has to offer. Bet it's real cowboy."

"Not Cheyenne." The corner of Tug's mouth turned up. "Wyoming Downs is in Evanston. That's in southwest Wyoming. You'll be a lot closer to Salt Lake City than to Cheyenne."

"Oh my god, are there people where you're sending me?"

"I'd be surprised if you don't meet at least one or two along the way," Tug cracked. "Thanks." His eyes shone with mist, his hands trembled.

"Thanks. Cassie's Hope and I both owe you."

"You better believe that. Guess I ought to start packing my bags."

Looking around her new surroundings, Cassie decided she liked the duck pond in the infield of the Wyoming Downs seven-eighths-mile track. Otherwise, she couldn't tell if the place was sterile, or subtly exquisitely beautiful. Dust swirled in the dry wind. Grasses were already turning brown. Mountains crowded the distant southwestern horizon like so many sentries.

Shaking her head, she grabbed a hoof pick from her back pocket, lifted one of Hope's front hooves, and began extracting dirt and pebbles.

"Nice lookin' filly."

Cassie groaned at the strange deep voice and the too-familiar line. Couldn't men anywhere be a little more original?

Dropping the hoof, Cassie glanced across Hope's back and gasped. The deeply tanned hunk behind the voice had shoulders that stretched taut a pale yellow polo shirt covered, in part, with a thin buckskin vest. The wide cowboy buckle appeared unnecessary to hold up well contoured Levi's. A sweat-stained brown Stetson, tipped low, cast a light shadow across his facial features. His worn boots were those of a working man. This was no drugstore cowboy.

He stepped closer. She could make out a scowl. Dark eyes snapped a foreboding anger. Raven black hair framed chiseled features, searing them into Cassie's brain. Her toes curled involuntarily. She rubbed Hope's coat vigorously. Who the hell was he? And to top it off, he didn't even seem to notice her. His eyes appraised only the horse.

"Thanks," she mumbled, ducking down by Hope's flank.

The handsome stranger walked around the horse. "Very nice," he drawled at last.

Cassie kept on grooming, doing her best to ignore the man.

"You're gonna wear a hole in that horse with all that hand rubbing," he commented dryly.

Cassie straightened. Her lips flared. Her cheeks burned as if on fire. Her eyes bore into the man. "And just who the hell are you? And what gives you the right to criticize how I groom my horse? I've been tending horses since I was big enough to walk."

"Whoa there, don't get all bent out of shape. I'm Clint Travers." The stranger rested a hand on Hope's withers. "I run some horses here from time to time. Didn't mean to impugn your horsemanship, ma'am."

"Well, fine." Cassie pushed stray hair from her eyes. "Maybe I overreacted some."

He ignored her attempt at apology. "So, this is the filly that's created such a fuss around shedrow."

"What do you mean? I didn't know anyone noticed."

"Not notice! You got to be kidding — or incredibly naive."

Cassie clenched her teeth and glared at the stranger.

"Strike that last comment," he said quickly. "I seem to be putting my foot in my mouth."

"Apparently you've a large enough mouth for it to fit, with plenty of room to spare."

"Okay. Guess I deserved that. The fuss is simple. Most people who race here at the Downs are working stiffs who run horses because they love them. Very few of these folks win enough to keep their horses in oats."

"So." Cassie dragged the toe of her boot through the dirt. "I love my horses too. And there's nothing wrong with expecting they might earn enough to pay their own way and then some."

"Be that as it may, bringing a well-bred horse in here from Chicago doesn't go down well. If you win, which is highly likely on class alone, you'll have denied someone here the kind of check that can make a real difference in maintaining a string of decent horses. Yet it's unlikely the purse will even cover your expenses of traveling and staying here." He glared and anger crept into his voice. "You're just trying to get a cheap win for your horse."

"That's horse racing, isn't it?" Cassie's voice rose. She boldly returned his hard stare. "And the favorites win only a third of the time. So?"

"Uh, huh. Unless someone ships in a ringer, this filly will go off three to five. The bettors aren't gonna be very happy with you, either."

"Well, hot damn. I didn't come here to win a popularity contest. I came here to win a horse race. And that's what we're going to try to do." Cassie abruptly turned her back on him.

"Okay, but don't expect everybody to roll out a red carpet," Clint barked at her back.

Cassie's ponytail did a hundred and eighty degree turnabout as she declared shrilly, "I don't expect any western hospitality from the likes of you. Who the hell started this conversation anyway? Not me! And if you don't mind too much, I have other things to do."

- o -

Clint Travers turned away, hiding a grin. He heard the sputtering fireball whisper soothing sounds to her horse. Stuffing his hands in his back pockets, he strolled back down shedrow toward his own horses.

Later he saw the woman ride the filly out onto the track for a mid-morning gallop. His experienced eye followed filly and rider. Damn, he'd thought *poetry in motion* was a cliché until now. "She's as good as she looks," he grumbled, grading the horse. Could the same be said for the rider?

Reluctantly, he had to admit he liked what he saw. Damn it. He'd been prepared to boot the invader back to Chicago where she belonged, but he hadn't counted on her coming in such a nice package.

Now, she might as well stay at least until he had a chance to see that long fire-burnt hair hanging loose. The ponytail stuffed through a Cubs hat had cast a sexy and sensual spell bobbing with her hand movements, but he'd rather see that gleaming hair unencumbered, blowing in the Wyoming wind.

The snug indigo blouse she wore obviously had all it could do to contain shapely breasts; palm sized, no doubt. Not too small and not too big. And, the young woman was graced with an extraordinarily tempting rear end.

Clint shook his head. The horse was trouble enough. The woman would no doubt be a disaster. It wasn't exactly like they'd started off on the best of terms.

- o -

At 5:30 the next morning, Cassie swore she was soaring on the wings of Pegasus. While her body complained loudly about a 4:30 a.m. wake up call, and some of her muscles had not recovered from the long road trip from Chicago, nothing — absolutely nothing — could compete with dawn at a track. And Wyoming Downs was no exception.

The thermos of very hot coffee might have been her physical lifeline at a time of day when only a few months ago she had been accustomed to sound sleeping; the sun poking up over the dusty foothills proved to be her spiritual lifeline. Cassie sighed deeply, taking in the familiar scents of horses, liniments and hot mash.

She welcomed the sounds of creaking leather and neighing horses. Here and there were human sounds: trainers giving quiet instruction to exercise lads, riders clucking to their mounts, and cuss words spoken in frustration at a balking horse or human.

Cutting the strings on a bale of hay, she glanced over to check out Hope, exercising on a hotwalker. Hope appeared to have no trouble adjusting to her new surroundings.

Cassie had to be careful not to be taken in by the charm and subtle allure of the track. Making the racetrack a way of life was kind of like joining the circus or the carnival. And she wasn't about to do either. She'd experienced more than enough of that growing up.

Horse people worked hard, putting in long hours and crazy schedules. And horse people stuck together. They competed with each other, they fought each other, they played together, and they stood by one another in their isolated world.

Cassie mucked out Hope's stall. Her gear was stored along with feed in an adjacent stall. She'd arrived so late in the night on Sunday she'd simply made a bed of straw in that stall and slept until dawn. It turned out her motel room wasn't much larger.

She guided a wheelbarrow loaded with straw and manure toward the dump pile. What would her Chicago friends say if they could see her now? She laughed out loud.

"Must've found your sense of humor."

"That damn voice," Cassie muttered, taking her time to empty the wheelbarrow before turning to face the man.

"Thought you might like to hear the latest scuttlebutt."

"I doubt that very much." Cassie folded her arms and awaited whatever news the *stable crier* had to offer. Too bad he didn't look ugly to match his disposition.

"Sounds like one of the other barns based here is shipping in a California horse for your race. The horse ran fairly well at Golden Gate — we may yet see a horse race come Sunday."

That news certainly popped her reverie, but she wasn't going to let Mr. Travers know. Her lips thinned and then she brightened. "Good. I'm not the only one shipping in from out of state. And it will make Hope's victory more meaningful."

"You might not be so cocky after the race. The horse they're shipping in has won three out of four lifetime races. Granted, they were cheap races, but at least the horse has won." Clint removed his Stetson long enough to run his fingers through thick jet-black hair. "Pulled up your horse on the internet last night. She's bred a hell of a lot better and looks a lot better than she's performed. Guess I know why you're here."

"Why I'm here is none of your business."

Clint breathed deeply. "Look it," he said, more slowly, "I'm not saying you don't have a right to be here. It looks like you've got a troubled filly. If she wins, it may prove worth the effort. I admit I don't like people shipping in classy horses from around the country to compete with the locals. But now that the California horse is coming, the fact that you're here doesn't make much difference. One of those two horses is bound to win.

"That filly of yours walking on the hotwalker," he gestured toward the chestnut, "is the best bred horse we've seen here in several seasons. She looks the part. Even on the hotwalker, she's up on her toes prancing. Anybody here would love to have her in their barn." He smiled at the quizzical look on Cassie's face. "Yes, including me."

"Well, thank you," Cassie sputtered. "I just hope she's up on her toes come Sunday."

"So what do you do when you're not at the track?"

Cassie swallowed. Did he know she wasn't really a horse trainer? She wasn't about to tell him she was a social worker.

"Evanston, Wyoming isn't the most lively place."

"Oh." Cassie blushed slightly. "I've read a lot of novels. It's pleasant enough. Say, don't you have a place to belong? Or is the track your home?"

The deeply tanned trainer laughed. "Actually, I have a ranch in eastern Utah. During the racing season here at the Downs, I may spend a week or two up here at a time."

"What about the running of the ranch?"

"Others can handle that while I'm away," he said, turning to walk away. "Well, guess I best be getting about my business."

Cassie was left with her mouth ajar wondering why he'd walked off so abruptly. His questions were more personal than hers. Maybe he'd stay away from her from now on.

She shut down the hotwalker and went to get Hope. She was here to race a horse. And that was it.

Still, the man intrigued her...against her better judgment. Was it his looks? Was it the sparks that seemed to always fly between them? Maybe she was she just bored.

- o -

Clint eased into his truck to head toward his motel. He would be eating alone again, then going over pedigrees or reading a novel. There were those connected with the track who partied hard every night. He wasn't one of them. Apparently neither was the redhead.

What would she have done if he'd invited her to dinner? He pressed his lips together tightly. No doubt she would have given him a tongue lashing. Damn, she was a hard woman to get close to.

She had piqued his curiosity. It certainly was unusual to see a woman haul a horse halfway across the country to race—and a damn pretty woman, at that. She had to have a lot of guts. He'd give her that.

He was looking forward to the big race. And he was looking forward to seeing how the big-city

27

tigress would handle victory or defeat.

He turned his truck toward Evanston. What would she do if he showed up at the café next to her motel around dinner time? It hadn't been difficult to obtain that information from a secretary in the track office; they needed to know where folks stayed in town in case there was an emergency at the track.

He'd stay away from her, though he liked the way she blushed every time she got her dander up. Which seemed quite often. Would she have as much fire in bed?

CHAPTER TWO

By Saturday, the dark haired cowboy hadn't pestered her for days. She'd often felt more than seen his brooding gaze around the stable area. A few times she'd returned a nod of greeting, but no further words had been exchanged. She figured her world was safer for that.

With only Hope to care for, she had far too much idle time. Her motel room was small to begin with; now it felt like a cell. How many novels could she read?

The sights of Evanston had taken about half a day to explore. The old railroad station was quaint. Initially, seeing live buffalo was exciting, but they so seldom moved she'd decided watching them for any length of time wasn't much more appealing than watching grass grow. A couple hole-in-the-wall restaurants had proven to be excellent hangouts for observing local culture. But if she hung out in them long, she'd be fat.

At least there would be horse racing later in the day. That would give her something to do. Then Hope would run in the featured race on Sunday. And then she'd sit on her hands for a week for Hope to soak up the benefits of altitude. Not fun.

But this morning she could feel the anticipation and excitement of race day. There was a stirring on shedrow that was the same at any track on race day. Trainers and grooms were more alert, eager and anxious. The early morning hours dragged for some. For others there never seemed adequate time for last minute adjustments. There was a lot of well wishing. But everyone wanted to win, and few would.

After exercising Hope, mucking the stall, and brushing her, Cassie did a last check of the hay and water before tidying up the work area. It was already mid-morning. She'd have to hurry back to the hotel to get changed for a day at the races. She looked forward to being a spectator and fan, for a change. Wyoming Downs wasn't Hawthorne or Arlington Park, but it was horse racing.

- o -

Clint grimaced at the redhead striding rapidly toward her truck. He stepped around his own truck to confront her. "I see you continue to mess things up for us."

Cassie scrunched to a halt. Her glare could've killed lesser men. "Now what the hell did I do to earn your praise? Well, get on with it," she sputtered. "As self-appointed guardian of Wyoming Downs, what do you want now?"

"You can pull in your claws, lady. I'm not going to bite your head off."

"It's hard to tell." She folded her arms across her abdomen and waited.

Two flashy magpies landed ten feet away in the middle of the dirt road, pecking at unseen things.

Clint sighed. Why did he want to confront this delightful filly who seemed more likely to be found in a board room than at a horse track? She irritated him, that was why. It was pure and simple. Coming in here like she belonged. She annoyed him, the way she carried herself.

Never, as far as he knew, had she asked for help or about how she might better fit in. No. She was too damn proud and combative. Always coiled like a rattler, she was ready to strike at a moment's notice. Well, truthfully — he smiled inwardly — he did have something to do with her shaking those rattles.

Keeping his face expressionless, Clint said, "Well, just wanted you to know that I don't like it when my regular jock switches from my horse to anyone else's, especially yours."

"Oh." Cassie clearly wan't trying to hide her smile. "Do you own him? I asked around to see who was the best jockey at the meet, and then asked him if he wanted to ride for me."

"Did he ever look at the horse, or was he merely taken with the filly's bewitching big city owner?" Clint caught Cassie's wrist before her hand collided with his chin.

"Damn, you are a feisty one. I didn't mean that you shouldn't try to get the best rider." Feeling the tension ease from her, he released her hand. "Actually, I'm more angry with the jock than with you. Thought he had more loyalty than that. Guess that's another reason they call 'em pinheads."

31

Cassie laughed. "I don't expect they like being referred to by such an endearing name."

"Yeah." Her throaty laugh spurred him on. It was good to hear the woman laugh. "Well, I imagine they have some precious endearments, as you call them, for trainers and owners, especially those of the female gender."

Cassie nodded. "You're probably right about that."

Clint shoved his hands in his pockets and looked toward the Uinta Mountains. Maybe he had been riding her too hard. Why? Others had shipped in horses from the east and west. He usually ignored them by taking care of his own business.

How could he ignore the auburn ponytail, the green eyes, and the cockiness of the woman from Chicago? He'd been behaving like an overzealous idiot, and he knew it. He should walk away and be done with her.

"There's a rodeo in town this weekend." His words betrayed him. "Don't suppose you've ever seen one. I'd be willing to escort you, if you'd like to go."

Clint winced at the shock registering in the woman's eyes.

"You got to be kidding," she said, "or brain dead."

Damn, there she goes again.

"I've seen more rodeos than I care to remember. We raised rodeo horses along with thoroughbreds and a few quarter horses when I was a kid. If the road didn't lead to a second-rate track, it went to a fourth-rate broken down rodeo. No thanks, Mr. Galahad. I don't want to go to a damn rodeo. And if I did, I wouldn't need you along to protect me."

Clint nodded and spun on his heel. He tried to amble nonchalantly toward his pickup.

What the hell got into him to ever ask her about the rodeo? What the hell got into her? She'd swat away an olive branch if he held one out to her. Well, no matter — he'd be going back to eastern Utah come Monday.

Ms. High-and-Mighty could cool her heels in Evanston until hell froze over, for all he cared.

- o -

By the start of the Saturday afternoon races, Cassie sat in the grandstands dressed in a clean pair of jeans, a new blouse, boots and her Cubs hat, and watched as people of all stripes and ages cheered on their favorite horses and jockeys. Clearly, racing at the Downs was a family affair; there were almost as many kids as adults. Gifts were raffled away after every other race. Barbecued beef simmered in a large pit area at the end of the stands. A country western band entertained before the races began and would return for more at the conclusion of the last race. The mood of the place was not unlike a Midwest county fair.

The afternoon proved entertaining and a decent change of pace from reading in her motel room.

Cassie won a little money betting thoroughbreds; she stayed away from wagering on the quarter horses. *Bumper cars on legs*, her dad called them. They often ran any which way but straight, and she found it impossible to handicap them, so she didn't.

Between the sixth and seventh race she went downstairs to use the ladies room and to fill up again on popcorn and pop. Hurriedly rounding the corner leading to the ramp back to her seat, she caught herself just before barreling into the wide back of Clint Travers.

She recoiled. Her stomach tightened and her blood pressure rose. A tall blonde dressed in tight black shorts and a white blouse knotted to show off plenty of midriff hung all over Travers' muscled shoulders. The two of them might as well be making out in public. Didn't they know there were little kids about? Cassie swore she saw the blonde's red lips slobbering across the back of his neck.

"Excuse me, lady! I'd like to get by and see another race yet today," said a large man behind her juggling hot dogs and drinks.

"Oh. Excuse me," Cassie whispered, reddening. She turned quickly to escape any more accusing eyes.

- o -

She wasn't quite quick enough. Clint Travers turned to see what the commotion was behind

34

him and groaned when he witnessed Cassie O'Hanlon dashing down the ramp scattering popcorn all over the concrete floor. Damn, she had a butt that'd drive men crazy.

Very carefully he reached behind him to remove Gretchen's arms from around his neck. He knew she'd had too much to drink while sitting in the hot sun. "Come on," he said patiently, "let's see if we can find your husband. He's got to be around here somewhere. I've got other things to tend to and other places to be."

After finally depositing the woman with his friend, Clint retraced his steps. He looked everywhere but could not locate the woman from Chicago. Giving up, he figured she'd gone back to her motel. Wyoming racing probably didn't measure up to her standards. "

- o -

Cassie jammed the gears in her truck in her effort to get out of the Downs parking lot before anyone else could notice her. What the hell did she care if he had women draped all over him? Mr. Know-It-All probably had drooling women lined up like so many widgets.

What a spectacle she'd made of herself! She was supposed to be a sophisticated Chicago social worker. Whenever she was around Clint Travers, which was far too often, she felt like a klutz. Somehow he did it to her on purpose.

Well, she certainly hadn't come to Wyoming to

35

get involved with a man. And never would she find such an arrogant philanderer attractive or appealing.

Pulling to a stop in front of her motel, Cassie rested her head against the seat. "Who am I kidding?" she grumbled. "Travers is the most gorgeous man I've ever come across. He exudes sexuality."

What would it feel like to run her fingers through his shaggy black hair? Would his touch be rough or gentle? Why did she act like some half-baked adolescent whenever she got near him? She wanted to go home. *Damn Dad and his dreams.*

Cassie dozed off in her truck dreaming of a dark haired cowboy coming to the aid of his fair skinned cowgirl. With one arm, he hoisted her up to ride in front of him. Together they rode off toward the setting sun.

It was race day. It might as well have been Judgment Day.

In the post parade, Hope was up on her toes, full of vigor, certainly more eager to run than in her previous races. Checking the odds board, Cassie grudgingly acknowledged that Travers was right. Her filly had been bet down to even money. She didn't bother going to the betting windows. No horse, not even her own, deserved such short odds. Too many things could go wrong in horse racing: stumbling out of the gate, a bad step, blocked by other horses and so on. No, even odds were not justified.

Sitting alone in the grandstand area designated for owners and trainers, Cassie worked at calming her gnawing stomach. A couple acquaintances wished her horse a safe trip. Most folks ignored her for the interloper she was.

The California horse looked good, but didn't appear nearly as classy as Hope. And its breeding was second or third rank. But that horse had proven it could win — more than she could say for Hope, or for herself.

She took a deep breath trying to steady her nerves. She glanced down at her twisted program. When working with a troubled kid, she was long on patience.

Waiting for a horse race was quite different. Everything was in the hands of the jockey now. She'd given him instructions in the paddock and then hurried to her seat.

She saw a familiar brown Stetson near the rail. From that vantage point, Clint Travers was watching the horses load into the gate. Cassie scowled. Maybe she displayed even less patience with that man.

"They're all in," the track announcer said. Then the clang of the gate opening penetrated the stillness. Cassie watched her filly break cleanly and move immediately to the front. The California horse broke well but couldn't keep up with the pace Hope set.

It seemed too easy. The horse who had struggled to compete at Arlington led by six lengths on the back turn. She crossed the finish line ten lengths ahead of the second place horse.

"My god, is she that good?" Cassie mumbled, hurrying down the stairs toward the track. With a beaming smile, she attached the lead rope to Hope's bridle and led the victorious filly into the winner's circle. She was handed a small trophy, and a red and white blanket was placed across Hope's withers. She felt the eyes of the crowd: the pleasure of bettors who made the right choice, the awe of some horse people, and the resentment of others.

- o -

Clint prided himself on not being the jealous type. Still, he hated being bested by this woman. But then his horse had struggled to finish a badly beaten fourth. Damn, the woman looked stunning, almost radiant when she was overjoyed. Her crisp white blouse contrasted with the blue Cubs cap and that damn sexy ponytail poking out of it. Blue jeans seemed molded to her tight rear. Was he the only one who noticed? Or did every man there have his tongue hanging out? Most maddening was the fact that Ms. O'Hanlon seemed totally unaware of him and of her own sexual allure.

He'd offer his congratulations. It was only the polite thing to do. She might think him a chump, but he didn't want her to believe he was a sore loser.

After stopping at the test barn where winning horses provided a urine sample to be certain no illegal drugs had been used, bathing Hope, walking her, and placing her back in the stall for a much deserved rest, Cassie stood back with a smile of satisfaction watching her father's dream eat a victory dinner. She couldn't wait to get back to Chicago and see how the filly would do against stiffer competition.

She sensed his presence before he spoke.

"Congratulations, Ms. O'Hanlon. There was no doubt about that victory. Of course there never was any doubt."

Cassie nodded. She wasn't even going to let her nemesis break her festive mood. "I didn't think she would win by that much. I just hoped she'd win. For her sake."

"Don't know what went on back east, but this filly's got real potential. This lady blew that California horse away." There was a trace of awe in his voice. "So what do you plan to do with her now? Don't expect you'll hang around here long."

Cassie wasn't sure she liked the way her horse nuzzled up against the annoying man.

"We'll enter her in an allowance race," she volunteered, "two weeks from now. We'll keep her here for about a week and then haul her back. Dad wants the altitude edge."

"Clever move. It should give her an edge, but from what I saw today, she shouldn't need it."

Cassie said nothing. That was the longest unruffled conversation she'd had with the ubiquitous trainer.

Suddenly, he turned away from Hope and faced Cassie directly, peering sharply into her eyes. She took a halting step backwards. She hadn't said anything to earn his ire. Then she saw his eyes soften as he began to speak.

"On behalf of the jockey colony, I want to thank you for donating your portion of the purse to the local jockey insurance emergency fund...that was very thoughtful."

Cassie's eyes misted. "Being here was never about money." Without saying another word, she stormed off toward her truck.

Kicking at the rising dust-devils, Cassie wanted to throttle herself. Why did she feel so vulnerable when Clint Travers tried to be nice? She'd been more comfortable, more in control when the galoot angered her.

Back in her hotel room, Cassie spoke haltingly to her father. "She won, Dad. Just like you said she would...by ten lengths, going away. Can you believe it? I never saw her look so good on race day...Thanks. Yeah, now I get to twiddle my thumbs for a week...Yes, it does feel good to win. I can hardly wait until the next one...No, I said six months. No more than that. Take care, Dad. Love yah. Bye." Cassie tapped the off button on her cell phone, pleased with her father's glee and unspoken pride.

Too keyed up with winning to sleep, she grabbed her jacket and headed for the rodeo grounds. It was something to do.

Sitting on a backless wooden bench with a thin windbreaker tugged snugly about her torso for warmth, Cassie oohed and aahed with the rest of the fans. It had been years since she'd been to a rodeo under the stars. It was much more refreshing than watching in an enclosed arena that a day later would house a rock concert or an antique show.

After the last cowboy was thrown by the final bull, she strolled through the small carnival area, stopping along the midway to buy some cotton candy, which she hadn't eaten since she was a teenager. She laughed at grown men trying to knock over wooden milk bottles with three baseballs to impress their female companions. She watched the Octopus spinning and jerking up and down and listened to the girls scream as guys bent over to whisper in their ears. Didn't sound any different than the teens she worked with. Same bravado, jeers, and cheers. "Oh well," she yawned, heading for the parking lot. She must be getting old.

Nearing her vehicle she frowned and slowed. Three young men slouched haphazardly against the hood of her red pickup.

A tall wiry blond-mustached cowboy stumbled toward her, slurring his words as he spoke. "Well, if ain't the fancy lady trainer from the east.

Welcome to our town." The tipsy stranger doffed his hat, mocking her. Without moving, his two friends smirked.

"Did you spend all that purse money yet?" the first man asked. "Or are you gonna save it for a rainy day?"

Cassie stood stock still, poised on the balls of her feet with arms hanging loosely at her sides. If necessary, she expected she could out run these jerks back to the lighted carnival area. But she really wanted to get back to her motel.

"Bet she's like all women. She'll spend that money on frilly things," said a burly man, pushing himself away from the truck. A cigarette dangled from his upper lip as he spoke. "Silk panties, soft bras, peek-a-boo nighties. Bet you'd look damn good in 'em, ma'am. All dolled up and ready to play."

"Maybe we can convince her to model for us," the smaller third man piped. He lurched unsteadily forward. The men formed a semi-circle between her and her truck.

"Cat got your tongue lady?" the tall blond man asked. "I know where I'd like your tongue."

He lunged for her. Cassie kicked her booted foot firmly into the man's crotch. He wailed a piercing sound, doubling over on the ground. His friends froze for a moment, and then began edging toward her with more determination. She was about to turn and sprint toward what she hoped would be safety when she heard a familiar low voice slice through the dark shadows. Her heart skipped a beat in recognition.

"That's about enough, boys. You congratulated the lady. Now it's time to move on." Clint Travers stepped into the diffused light. His firmly fixed stare and straining muscles served due warning.

"Aw, shit," the stocky man complained, "we was just gonna have some fun. Wasn't gonna hurt her none."

"Yeah," his partner whined, "she didn't need an Indian raid to save her."

"You may be right about that." Clint scowled darkly at the man struggling to pull himself up off the ground. "But I'm here now. You have two of us to deal with. What's it gonna be?"

Cassie winced, but was pleased that Travers had included her when counting the odds.

Letting out a deep breath, the stocky man ground his cigarette into the dirt and grumbled, "Not a damn thing. Come on, boys. Think there's a beer waiting for each of us down at Randy's. The chief can have his cowgirl, for all I care."

The injured man wrapped an arm around each of his companions and limped away.

When they were out of earshot, Clint whirled on Cassie. "What the hell are you doing out here by yourself?"

"Son of a bitch," she spat out in return. "And a good howdy-do to you, too. I'm a big girl. I'm used to being on my own—even in the city. Didn't you see that bastard dragging his ass out of here?"

Clint grimaced. "Every place has its danger and its scum. You've encountered some home-grown

43

kind here tonight."

She nodded. Unable to fuel her anger at the man who had helped her out of a tight fix, she mumbled, "Thanks. So what were you doing here?"

"Thought I'd see what was happening." He offered no further explanation, but his features softened. "I better take you back to your motel. Your truck will be here tomorrow."

"I said thank you, but I think I can drive myself back safely," she declared hotly. "I'm not that frazzled by a few overgrown juvenile delinquents."

"You might want to look a little more closely at your transportation, Ms. O'Hanlon," Clint replied dryly. "It's not usually a good idea to drive on rims."

"The dirty bastards!" Cassie shrieked, racing around the pickup. All four tires were flat. Each had been punctured with a sharp object.

"Afraid you can't prove it was them."

"Son of a bitch, I can't believe they did that." She was reeling. If they could slash her tires…"They invaded my space. They violated me. My god." Her hand flew to her throat. "What might they have tried if you hadn't come along?"

Clint shrugged. He looked uncomfortable. "Don't know," he drawled. "I've seen those boys around, but don't really know them. I don't think they were as drunk as they made out to be. Or maybe your toe sobered them up quickly."

"Oh my god," Cassie cried. "I'm so prepared in

Chicago, but here, I thought I was safe for some reason. Thanks," she said, throwing herself into the security of Clint Travers' arms.

She trembled. She cried. She clung to him, garnering strength. A shock of energy emanating from her loins raced like a runaway horse through every fiber of her body. She pulled herself up short. Oh no, that was more than comfort — that was raw sexual desire. Hers. She didn't know about him. Actually, his hardness pressing against her belly allowed for little doubt.

Embarrassed by her momentary lapse, Cassie staggered away from him. "Sorry for being such a blubbering idiot," she muttered, wiping tears away with her knuckles. "My kids would laugh like hell right now if they could see me."

"Kids!" Clint said, taking a step backwards. "Didn't know you were married. You don't wear a wedding ring."

"I'm not married," Cassie said. "Oh. Not *my* kids." Why couldn't she speak coherently around the man? And why was it so important that he understand? "The kids I work with. Troubled kids, delinquents."

"Ah, you're one of those liberal do-gooders."

She bristled immediately. "I'm a social worker. If that means I do some good, so be it. But I'll have you know I'm damn good at kicking ass."

Clint bent back his head and howled. "I never doubted that for a moment. There's some guy limping around here wishing that was all you kick."

45

"Oh," she sputtered, stomping the ground with her foot, "you're impossible!"

Why did this man get to her so? He was a hunk—no question about that. But hunks had never mattered before. He was conceited and always bothering her. Well, he had been helpful tonight. Why did her muscles tense and then turn to mush whenever he smiled, which wasn't often, but still?

Damn, he looked good. Her brain seemed to do a double click. It had been a while. Had she forgotten the alarm bells? Could her body be telling her it was ready for a safe, out of the way fling? No muss, no fuss. Just good uncomplicated sex. Clint stood with hands on hips grinning crookedly at her as if he were inside her head. Never mind, she told herself, it wasn't a good idea anyway.

"Guess we might as well go," she fumed, kicking at a flat tire. "Maybe it won't look so bad in the morning."

"My truck's right over this way," Clint said, leading the way. "Is it okay with you if we stop by shedrow? I've got a horse to medicate yet."

"Sure," she agreed. "That's fine. It wouldn't hurt for me to check on Hope's knees again." Being with her horse might help take her mind off the night's events and off her escort.

Once in the truck, Cassie couldn't figure out what to say. Maybe she was coming down from the adrenalin rush caused by her would-be tormentors. The silence hung between her and her driver like a heavy quilt.

At last, Clint asked, "I've been wondering — is Cassie short for Cassandra?"

She laughed easily. "No. I'm not a Cassandra. It's short for Cassidy. My dad was a huge Hopalong Cassidy fan."

Clint looked sharply her. "I'll be damned. Cassidy. I like that. Your dad must be quite a character."

"That, and more. He's the reason I'm here. For his whole life he's chased the dream of having a stakes contender. Hope came along with a lot of potential." Leaning her head back, Cassie relaxed. "In March, Dad had a pretty bad stroke."

"I'm sorry."

"Yeah, well, that's why I got recruited for this job. When Hope had troubles in her first two races, Dad encouraged me to bring her out here so she could regain her confidence."

"I think she found that today. So you're doing all of this as a favor to your dad."

"Mostly. I doubt any of us always understand our motivations for doing things."

"True enough. But what you're doing requires a kind of courage and loyalty that's rare. Don't suppose many social workers trade in their desk jobs to be at a track at five in the morning until who knows when."

Cassie didn't respond to this sudden praise. She was struggling to control the toasty feeling rushing through her veins. She hadn't predicted that he could be kind and gentle. Powerful. Sexy.

47

Demanding. But not kind and gentle.

"Well, here we are," Clint said, pulling to a stop in front of a row of horse stalls. "Let me change a poultice on old Storm Jet, and then we can see how Hope is doing."

"Okay," Cassie concurred, aware that without saying so he didn't want her walking shedrow alone. Given her earlier evening experience, she swallowed whatever pride was left and waited. Besides, she enjoyed watching the tall tough cowboy speak tenderly to his horse. His fingertips moved gingerly up and down Storm Jet's foreleg, feeling for anything hot or out of place.

Cassie had seen many men and women do the same thing to horses hundreds of times, if not thousands. Why were his movements so erotic? She felt as if he were touching her leg, her thigh, her breast. She shivered.

Clint glanced at her standing in the doorway. His nostrils flared. He looked quickly back his work and continued rubbing his hands over the leg and knee.

She thought she heard him say, "Damn, you're tempting." Which didn't make sense at all.

"What did you say?" she asked.

"Just talking to my horse. There." He stood and looked at his handiwork. That should hold her until tomorrow. I'll stop by in the morning before I head home. Guess we ought to check in on your winner."

Cassie nodded, grinning broadly. "Winner —

that's an intoxicating word!"

- o -

As they walked to Cassie's horse, Clint felt her tug at his arm to stop him. She scanned the starry sky. She seemed to stop breathing for a long moment.

"Damn," she said in a hushed tone, hugging herself, "we don't see a sky like that in Chicago. Looks like you could pluck your own personal star."

"Yeah, it's fantastic. I never tire of watching Father Sky change hour by hour and season by season. Here, put this on," he offered, taking his heavy jacket and draping it around her shoulders. "Wyoming evening air can get nippy."

"Thanks," she said, shuddering. He watched her breathe deeply. He'd swear she was savoring his scent. Abruptly, she scurried toward Hope's stall.

Clint lengthened his stride to keep up, painfully aware of her sensuality. While unable to read her thoughts, he sensed the electricity pulsating between them. He'd been attracted to the firebrand since he first saw her rear end sticking out beside her filly as she bent over a hoof. But now he was having second thoughts. She had *beware of danger* written all over her. He doubted she'd had many casual relationships.

If he didn't watch it, he was going to willingly fall into a snare large enough for any man, and he

49

didn't even know who'd set the trap. Was it her? Was it him? Was it the universe? This woman wouldn't be satisfied with just sex. And he certainly needed no emotional entanglements, particularly with a temperamental woman from the big city.

After running her hands up and down Hope's front legs and knees, Cassie announced, "They're cool. That's a relief."

She stepped out of the filly's stall and turned toward him. "Oh, I've been meaning to ask. What did that guy mean tonight when he talked about me being saved by an Indian raid?"

Clint glowered at her. Her blank look told him everything. He spun as if to bolt.

She caught him by the arm. "What did I say wrong now? I can't ever seem to talk to you for more than five minutes without one of us getting upset."

He grimaced. "I don't mean to insult you, but you are beyond naïve at times. Did you think this skin was created by the sun? I'm half Ute. My mother is a full blood. My father was a mixture of all those things whites tend to be."

"Oh." Her eyes widened. "I hope I didn't offend you. I work with people of color all the time — guess maybe I'm sort of color blind."

He had a difficult time believing her, yet he knew intuitively that the outspoken, fiery Cassidy O'Hanlon did not lie. She might have many faults, but he was sure lying was not one of them.

Narrowing her eyes, Cassie quipped, "You

know, tonight I think I'm very pleased to have been rescued by an Indian raid rather than by the local cavalry."

Clint smiled at the mischievous woman. One moment she hissed at him and the next she tempted him. She never ceased being provocative. He could almost feel her surging heat. When she was busy he took the opportunity to rearrange his erection, which had become incredibly hard and uncomfortable.

- o -

Cassie stepped into the next stall, bent over, and rummaged though a pack. Finally she emerged with a tube of ointment.

She turned and fixed her green sparkling eyes on his. "Caught you gawking at my butt. See anything you like, Mr. Travers?"

"I've wanted to see your hair down," he said softly, "since I first saw you. Do you always keep it in a ponytail?"

"No," she responded weakly. She wet her lips. Was this it? Was he going to kiss her at last? Was she ready for him? She didn't do flings. But she was a thousand miles from home. So, why not? Her nipples hardened. She felt the sure sign of wetness in her pussy. She had her answer—she was more than ready. Her fingers trembling slightly, she removed the band holding her hair in place and shook out her long tresses, letting them fall loosely over her breasts. Smiling, she arched her back and thrust her pelvis forward in silent invitation.

"Sweet Jesus," Clint muttered, closing the distance between them. Gently, he ran his fingers through hair, grazing her breast in the process.

Cassie's eyes went wide and she bit her lower lip.

He smiled and bent his neck, leaning toward her.

She stood on tiptoes, raising her lips to meet his. Their lips brushed. His tongue sought her mouth and she opened to him, chasing his probing tongue with her own. Suddenly overwhelmed, Cassie slid off his lips gasping for air. She shook her head trying to find clarity. Spasms of desire raced from her toes to her most private place. His arousal pressed against her tummy; his hands clutched her buttocks. Thinking was a nearly impossible task. If she wanted to change her mind, this might be her last chance.

He held her tight as if he feared she'd run. He seemed to be smoldering just as much as she was. Were they ready to chance a wildfire?

She was certain of only one thing: she'd not had enough. Not hardly. Crushing her lips against his again, she tried to swallow his tongue as it searched her mouth. They fell to their knees. She slipped a hand inside his shirt and massaged his rippling chest muscles.

Clint cupped a breast. She moaned softly. Quickly, together, they unbuttoned her blouse, giving him more access. Her bra fell away, an easy victim before their quest.

"My god, you're beautiful. Your breasts are so exquisite," he whispered, cupping one in each hand and tapping the nipples with his thumbs.

His words enthralled her. His caresses sent a jolt of fire straight to her loins. "Not too small? Most guys seem to prefer big tits."

"Perfection," he murmured, lowering his head.

She looked down to watch him surround her nipple, then felt a jolt of electricity as he began to suckle. Her hands ruffled his thick black hair while she muttered unintelligible sounds. Her body was no longer her own. There was only an urgent demand for fulfillment. Her pussy throbbed with need. Her panties were already sticky from her juices.

Cascading her hair over her face as if attempting to hide would make things easier, Cassie let her thumbs pop open the buttons holding her jeans together. Determinedly, she pulled the zipper down. She stood and he helped her step out of boots, jeans and panties.

He remained kneeling before her. His gasp thrilled her. Only dimly could she see him through the fall of her hair, but she felt his ragged breath as he covered her mound. His fingers explored her heat. Would her rubbery legs give way? She leaned into him for support.

His tongue grazed her clit. Her hips swayed under the onslaught. Her fingers tightened around his head. His fingers, his tongue drove her to the brink. She rose on her toes and arched against him driving his fingers and tongue deeper.

"I'm coming," she squealed. "Oh god, yes."

And then her juices spilled over. His mouth covered her. She felt him swallowing and purred his name softly. Her muscles seemed like just so much loose powder.

Keeping his mouth in place, coaxing even more from her, he clasped her torso with both arms, or she would have certainly fallen.

She smoldered, savoring his touch, his strength, and his protective instincts. Shattered, but not lifeless, Cassie gradually came back to him. She traced his neck cord with her tongue silently thanking him.

"You are something else, Cassidy O'Hanlon," Clint groaned, his voice laced with awe.

She chuckled. "Me? You're the one who made me fly among the stars. This horse stall may not be the most romantic setting one could imagine, but it seems to be doing just fine."

"Uh huh. More than fine."

"I do believe there is some unfinished business though," Cassie said, smiling as seductively as she could. "We need to set you free," she whispered, unbuckling his belt.

- o -

Gently, Clint laid the beautiful trainer from Chicago on the thick straw-covered floor. He took his time admiring her trim body. He'd been right. Her breasts were perfection, large enough to fill a hand yet small enough to fit into his mouth. Her bare pussy was one of the tiniest he'd ever seen. Its swollen lips remained wide open from his tonguing. Its redness and scent attested to Cassie's recent orgasm and her anticipation of more. He gripped his cock and grinned a devious smile. "I'm sure you're used to a bit more luxury than this, but this will have to do. There's no time for waiting now."

"No, this will do. I'll probably have red blotches tomorrow, but that's tomorrow and this is now. No more waiting, please. Hurry. I need that big thing you're holding in me. Protection?"

Quickly, he reached for his billfold and extracted the necessary preventive foil. Cassie looked impatient watching through half closed eyelids as he roughly pulled the condom over his rigid cock. If he'd ever been harder, he couldn't recall such a time.

He ran the tip of his shaft up and down her wetness. Cassie grabbed his arms and pulled him forward. Slowly, he penetrated her sex, feeling her moist heat enfold him.

"You're filling me," she moaned, not taking her gaze off of his.

He nodded, seating his entire length in her. "You're incredibly hot. And this bed seems to work quite nicely."

"Oh, yes."

He moved hesitantly to and fro.

She wrapped her legs around his ass. "No need to go slow."

Silently he agreed. Slow would be okay later, but not now. He picked up the pace.

She matched his efforts thrust for thrust. She thrashed about under him, resisting and then embracing another orgasm. She howled into the night.

Clint swallowed hard trying to keep pace with the woman beneath him. Her squeals of delight echoed from some far off place: from the present and the past, from the past and the future. Spinning out of control, he pumped and pumped. His hips strained. Cassie's fingernails dug into his back. His breathing stopped and then he erupted. His howls echoed hers. He didn't stop pummeling her until he was completely drained.

His brain froze and then slowly melted, allowing a thought or two. What in the hell had happened? She was no reluctant lover. She'd overtaken him. Some of his questions were answered. She did indeed emit fire when making love. He held back a chuckle. And she made delightful sounds when on fire.

He shook his head. *Be careful. This one could be habit forming. Don't get burned.*

- o -

Cassie huddled in the warmth of Clint's jacket as they neared her motel in the predawn hours. Awareness of all they'd done on the bed of straw flooded her mind. She still found bits of straw in her hair. *Now what? Oh my. Oh my. Oh my. It's okay.*

Great sex for a week, if I'm lucky, and then back home. It's okay. Oh my! Oh my!

He parked the truck. She grinned shyly at him. "I'd invite you in, but we both need to get some sleep."

Clint nodded, laughing softly. "To do that, I got to get away from your burning flesh. Damn, woman, you could devour me if I let you."

"I just might," she said, leaning over to kiss him.

Breaking away from her, he paused, obviously considering his next move. Cassie waited patiently. Although sated for a week, she would like to see him again.

"I have to run down to the ranch and check some things out later today. I'll try to be back by Wednesday or Thursday at the latest. Maybe we can pick up where we left off then."

Cassie hesitated. That didn't sound too promising. If that was the way it was, she could play it cool too. "Sure, why not?"

All day Monday, Cassie had expected a call from the man who had helped her soar to such heights on shedrow. She'd fumed and sputtered about having second thoughts about the entire trip to Wyoming, especially that tryst in the stall. Her body might still be humming, but that didn't soften her total feeling of rejection.

By late Monday night she'd made her decision. It was time to go home. Her dad would be upset with her for returning early and not giving Hope the entire altitude edge, but she wasn't about to wait around for some damn cowboy who had left her hanging. He could've asked her to go with him to his ranch. She could've gotten someone to tend Hope for a day or two. But no, the big jerk just dashed off and left her. So be it.

Early Tuesday morning, Cassie had her tack and horse loaded and headed east on highway 80. With any luck, Chicago and sanity were only two days away.

- o -

Tuesday evening, Clint stomped up and down shedrow. The damn redhead had left him high and dry. He'd come rushing back early to hook up with her and have a fun week. He'd planned on taking her to Salt Lake so he could treat her like the lady she was. Or at least the lady he'd thought she was.

Instead, she'd run out on him.

CHAPTER THREE

"Don't know why you had to come back so soon," Tug groused at Cassie. "But it's good to see you and the filly in good health."

"I wish you could've seen her," Cassie said, not bothering to hide her grin. "She was so fluid. Unbelievable. We haven't seen anything like that performance here."

"Hope she was out in that mountain air long enough to help her next time. So did you meet any interesting folks? I haven't been at that track for years, but the locals were usually quite hospitable."

Cassie nearly spilled her coffee and then glanced out toward the pastures near the barn before answering. "A few. Stayed in my motel mostly. Wasn't a lot to do other than make sure Hope was doing okay. Got a lot of reading done."

Would she ever see the Utahan again? Did she even want to see him again? Yes. No. Yes. Why was she so ambivalent? All her friends envied her for always being so decisive. The man could only bring her disappointment and broken dreams.

She'd done the right thing by leaving. Cassie brushed dirt from her knee. Had she run away, like her mother did? Nonsense. It was a fling. A one night stand. Granted, a long, heated night.

Standing in the shower in the studio loft apartment over the barn that served as her temporary home, Cassie could hardly believe she'd been back for nearly two weeks. It seemed like months since the Wyoming wind had left her breathless — since she and the cowboy had quenched their lust in the straw.

She'd quickly gotten back into the routine of training horses. Still, she worried about her father. She worried about Cassie's Hope. She worried about herself. She worried about a dark handsome man, far, far away.

What was he doing? Why hadn't he called? Did he think about her as often as she thought about him? Damn, why couldn't she just erase those erotic images from her mind? Too many memories of him touching her skin, of his feel under her fingertips, of exquisite raw sex.

She shuddered and rinsed her hair quickly. She had less than hour to finish showering and drive to the little Italian restaurant in Arlington Heights to meet her girlfriends for dinner. They hadn't been together as a group since before she'd left for Wyoming.

Would she tell her friends about him? She thought not. Clint Travers had only been a brief happening of little consequence.

Toweling dry, Cassie blushed as she remembered teeth marks on each breast where the cowboy had marked his claim. She vibrated remembering lifting them, imploring him to take more. She grimaced. Maybe he had been more than a little consequence.

She tossed the towel aside and slipped on a light blue blouse and black shorts. As she left, Cassie tied her hair in a ponytail, poking it out the back of her white Wyoming Downs cap.

Her friends were seated by the time she arrived at Regalios. That was rare. She was typically punctual, if not early. After the waiter filled the water glasses and took their drink orders, the questions began in earnest.

"Tell us all about it, Cass. How was the wild, wild West? Did you meet any cowboys?" Traci asked, batting her dark eyelashes.

Cassie took a deep breath and looked around conspiratorially before whispering, "Well, it was really quite tame. I only saw six gunfights and two knife fights. Tame compared to Chicago." She smiled and leaned back in her chair. "It was a good trip. Cassie's Hope won her race easily. Now we cross our fingers that she can do the same here."

"What was Evanston, Wyoming like?" Susan asked. "I looked it up on the map. It looked pretty remote."

"Small town, USA, isn't much different in the west than it is in the mid-west. Not much happening. Good, decent folk. Country western, bluegrass, cowboy poetry on Friday night. A rodeo. And of course the track. And not far away was Bridger, the site of Fort Bridger from rendezvous days. That was interesting."

"Ladies, are you ready to order?" asked the waiter, his smile disarming.

No sooner than he was out of earshot, Ashton pointed her dinner knife at Cassie as if preparing for the kill. "Now girl," she intoned, "tell us about the man, about the lover."

"What?" Cassie gasped, at her ebony skinned friend who at times seemed far too clairvoyant.

All three women leaned in intently awaiting a response

"I said, tell us about the lover," Ashton reiterated. "The guy who put color back in your cheeks and a distant look in your eyes. Don't try to deny it. We know what we're looking at with envy — that's a well loved woman. Who is he?"

Cassie blushed. She groaned. Nodding her head, she told them of Clint Travers — her nemesis and one night lover. She concluded her story. "So you see — it was fine, but it's history."

"Fine!" Ashton squeaked. The half dozen bracelets she wore jangled as if they too did not believe. "You had some steamy sex with a hunk of a man. And that's history? Why?"

"I'm here, and he's there," she said, too quickly, rolling her napkin into a tight ball. Then glancing around the table at her stunned friends, she began to relax a little. If she wasn't so irritated with them, the picture they made would actually be comical. Ashton with her large gold hoop earrings swinging wildly, Traci with her reserved trial-lawyer fixed stare, and Susan — open mouthed Susan.

With a tiny smile, Cassie reached for her glass of water, "It was just a summer chance encounter. I'm glad it happened. Now it's over. That's all there is. End of story."

"You did it in a horse stall," Susan squeaked, shaking her head in disgust. "That must've been gross."

Cassie chuckled. "It may have been a lot of things, but gross wasn't one of them."

"Did they blow up all the bridges and airports between here and Utah? I hadn't heard if they did," Traci said dryly. "If he's as phenomenal as he sounds, why did you throw him back in the deep blue sea, or maybe I should say, leave him to dry up in the desert?"

"I already told you." Cassie lowered her voice trying not to draw attention to their table. "It was just good old fashioned sex. No expectations. No more, no less."

"Well, I for one think you made the right decision to dump him," Susan claimed, sitting straight, extending her already tall frame. "You don't know a thing about him, really."

"I know more than that he's well hung, if that's what you mean."

"You can go back any time, honey," Ashton whispered, placing her hand over Cassie's. "Your head may think whatever happened in Wyoming wasn't much but some good fucking. And maybe that's what you intended it to be, but your heart isn't buying any of that shit."

"Ashton," Susan complained, pursing her lips.

63

Holding up her hand to ward off criticism, the striking black woman continued, "What are you gonna do about him? It's gonna eat you up, if you let it."

Cassie shook her head, squeezing back tears. "Nothing," she sighed. "I'm going to do nothing. I'm a big city girl and he's...he's a man of the country."

"Hmm," Ashton replied pensively. "Like the city and country have never mixed before. Well, we can see you've had enough of our interrogation for now. Let's change the subject, ladies."

Cassie jutted out her chin. "So tell me, how are the Cubs doing?"

- o -

The phone rang shrilly in the small, drab walk-up. A brown sofa, two stuffed chairs, and a TV filled the living room. Pictures of horses and jockeys taken in the winner's circle covered the walls like wall paper. Several included an old friend, Tug O'Hanlon.

"Hello."

"Louie?"

"Yeah."

"Let her go this time. We'll let the old guy win one. It'll make the loss in the Capitol Stakes even more bitter. Got it? Don't do a damn thing. Let the horse run its race.

"I got it."

"Too bad he's got his daughter training for him. He could've gone with others, even you."

"Yeah.

"Saw your granddaughter graduated from U of I."

"Yeah. She's good."

"How many more coming up?"

"Plenty."

"That's good. You let me know when their tuition is due."

"You can count on that."

"Good-bye, Louie."

Louie Picard hung up the phone. Would bygones ever be bygones? Like many at the track, Tug O'Hanlon had his enemies. Most got even and went on with their lives.

Shaking his head, Louie had to admit he'd been suckered in at first. And then betraying his friend had become routine. Now his family depended on the financial support. No one before in his family or his wife's family had ever gone to college. He was proud that his kids had gone, and now his grandkids were going.

He'd get a call every time Tug had a horse that looked like a strong contender for stakes racing. He might have a claimer win five races in row. No call came. But on those rare occasions when he had a horse who looked like the possible big horse, the calls started up again until that horse faded.

And now there was the promising filly Tug's daughter trained. Picard reached for a beer sitting on the end table and stared at the images flickering on the TV. Screwing up Cassie's dreams left a bad taste in his mouth. He'd known her since she was born.

He'd helped Tug raise Cassie after her mother left. Cassie had been one of his best exercise riders. She'd done well for herself, real well. But she was now training a horse that had tons of promise. He'd wondered if he'd get the call this time. Tug wasn't doing the training; Cassie was. The call came anyway. At least he'd be able to enjoy tomorrow's race. He was looking forward to seeing how the filly would run without the drugs slowing her down.

It was a warm, cloudless Saturday morning, the day of Hope's first race since arriving back from Wyoming. Cassie sat back on her heels, running her fingers up and down the filly's legs, feeling for heat or any sign of puffiness. There was none. Hope appeared fresh and ready. Cassie smiled, yet was unable to keep the butterflies in her stomach from tumbling about. Would her dad's strategy actually go as he predicted? She wasn't so certain about the altitude edge. Had she stayed long enough?

"Well, if it's not the Chicago cowgirl returned."

Cassie cringed at the sound of Ed Harrington's biting sarcasm. She stood up and nodded a curt greeting. "I'm back, and we're ready to race."

"She does look more eager than I've ever seen her. Maybe your old man's onto something. I assume she won out in the boonies without difficulty."

"No problem — she won by ten lengths."

"Today will be different," he said flatly. "You're back in the big leagues."

"Right," Cassie replied warily. Her stomach cramped. She knew it could be very different.

Running his hand along the top of Hope's back, Harrington confided, "Say, if she wins, I'd like to help you celebrate by taking you out for a nice dinner."

Alarm bells rang in Cassie's head. Conversation with the man had always been punctuated with sexual innuendo, but she hadn't really thought he was seriously interested in her. Men! One fling for the summer was enough. One fling with a horse trainer was one too many.

"No thanks," she murmured. "I'll need to get back to Dad shortly after the race, win or lose."

"Some other time, then," Harrington replied with an air of cockiness.

Later that afternoon, Cassie watched Hope prove Tug O'Hanlon to be some kind of a horseman's wizard. The filly won her allowance race without much trouble. Just as she had in Wyoming, she held the lead from start to finish, winning by two lengths.

Cassie's spirits were sky high while cooling down her horse after the race. Even Harrington's congratulatory buss on the cheek outside the winner's circle hadn't bothered her. All was well.

She was proud of what they'd accomplished. Hope had a promising future. Her dad would be ecstatic and could soon look for another trainer to take over Hope's management as well as the rest of his small string of horses. And she, Cassie O'Hanlon, would be able to get on with her life. She looked forward to the comfort of her high rise apartment and to the challenges of her regular day job at the group home.

Wyoming seemed a long way away.

Would she miss the thrill of competition and the sweat of horses? Shake that nagging thought.

"Liked what I saw on the track this afternoon."

Harrington always turned up, like a lost penny. "Thanks," she replied evenly. "She ran a good race, all right."

"Yeah, your old man is a damn crafty trainer. I've got to give him that. How much do you want for her?"

Startled, Cassie backed away. "What?"

The tall sandy-haired trainer grinned. "Don't think I mumble that badly. How much money would you like for the horse?"

"She's not for sale! I didn't come here to sell her. Dad would have a fit."

"That must be who you get it from."

"Be that as it may, the horse is not for sale."

"Okay, doesn't hurt to ask, usually."

"Fine. You asked. And I answered."

"She is a nice looking filly."

Cassie leaned against Hope, watching the man amble off in the direction of his horses. Did he ever in his entire life experience a moment of self-doubt? Well, whatever. She'd have to watch out for him.

But Harrington was a damn good trainer. He had an excellent reputation on shedrow and typically was among the leading winning trainers at the Chicago tracks. *Up and coming* was a phrase often linked to Ed Harrington. And then there was the downside. Picking up track scuttlebutt, she'd learned he had a reputation for being a heavy drinker and a womanizer. No way was she going to let him add her scalp to his collection.

"Nice race, honey."

"Oh, thanks, Louie," she said, turning to hug her old friend. "Wasn't she great?"

"She's a racehorse, that's for sure. And looks like the Wyoming altitude advantage didn't hurt a bit."

"I didn't get to see today's last race. How did your horse do?"

"The old guy came in second." Louie shrugged. " That's not bad for a nine year old gelding."

"You ever going to retire Jasperson?"

"Probably the end of the year. Hell, I'm getting too old for this myself. How's your dad doing?"

"He's coming along. This race will do wonders for him. I'll be surprised if we can keep him from coming out to the Capitol Stakes."

"Maybe old Tug will be doing a jig by then."

Cassie shook her head. "I doubt that. Hopefully, he'll be able to come and watch Hope race."

Louie spat a stream of tobacco. "Yeah, well, I best be getting along. Pass on my hurrahs to your dad."

"I'll do that. You can count on it. Take care, Louie. Come on out to the farm when you get a chance."

The next morning, Cassie stood on the porch before her father with a smug look plastered on her face. She'd traveled three thousand miles by herself to further his dream. He'd been right, Hope looked spectacular in her win in Wyoming, and equally fantastic yesterday when she won the relatively minor allowance race against cheap but respectable competition. Next up, a mid-level allowance in two weeks.

She breathed in the fresh moist air. Thank god for humidity and all things green. Thank god for big old chestnut trees and oak trees. And thank god for a race horse who could run like the Wyoming wind.

"Don't get too high on your horse, Cass," Tug O'Hanlon cautioned with a scratchy voice. "She still has a lot to prove. And it's damn hard to keep a horse on her game for very long. We don't wanna peak too early."

"Me, high? I thought you were the dreamer in the family." Cassie scowled down at her father sitting comfortably in the old wicker rocker with a blanket over his legs.

"Dreaming comes with the Irish, my daughter," he replied, smiling ear to ear. "Ye can't do much about that now, can ye? Just try to keep your feet on the ground. Two wins in a row is good, but we're a long way from the Capitol Stakes."

"I know." She slumped onto the smooth boards of the worn porch swing. "It's hard to wait."

"One thing you gotta learn with horses is patience. You can't rush 'em. They seem to have minds of their own. Like women, I think." Tug began one of his coughing fits.

Every time he coughed, Cassie's throat clamped down with worry; would this be his last coughing bout?

After some moments, the wheezing stopped. "Cass, I really appreciate what you're doing," he rasped. "Know it's a hardship for you. Can't do it myself."

"You rest. I'll be out at the barn. Ring the buzzer if you need me." Covering his weathered hand with hers, she said, "I wouldn't be doing this if I didn't also share your dream—at least a wee bit. I love you."

His eyes fluttered open in acknowledgment and then closed. When his breathing returned to its normal shallow flow, she tiptoed down the steps. With sagging shoulders, she made her way to the barn, seeking solace from the horses.

- o -

"Let her go, Travers," Clint muttered, tossing about in his bed at the ranch. The old solid bed had never felt so large and superfluous. "Just let her go."

Sitting up, he combed his unkempt hair with tired fingers. His three day beard scratched like hell. His mouth tasted sour, like he hadn't brushed his teeth for ages. Cupping his hands over his eyes, he admitted reluctantly that he hadn't been doing very well in the self-care category. And it was that damn sassy redhead's fault. Why couldn't he shake the woman from the cobwebs of his brain like he had all the others? Because her scent clogged his nostrils. Her taste assaulted his lips. Her laugh echoed in his ears. Her fiery temper brought a smile to his eyes.

So what was he going to do about her? Nothing. How could he let her slip away as if all they'd shared was some earth shattering sex?

Groggily, Clint managed to get out of bed and shuffle to the bathroom. Looking in the mirror, he was appalled by what he saw. No woman had ever done that to him. He looked like he was a step or two away from being the skeleton in old man Granger's biology class.

The problem was clear; the solution was anything but. "No more sitting on your ass, Travers. Do something."

He picked up the phone and punched in the numbers on a piece of paper sitting on his night stand.

"Hello."

Clint smiled at her throaty voice. She was sexy just saying hello. "Hi," he said, "how did Hope do in her race?"

Her gasp was audible. He liked surprising her. "Clint. Oh, my goodness. Hope. Hope won by two lengths."

"That's great. So the altitude factor may have helped."

"Don't know for sure, but she won. Clint, it was great." She grew quiet. "I can't believe you called. I do owe you an apology for running off."

Clint sighed. "I didn't handle things well either, though I was back at the track Tuesday evening."

"You were?"

He swore she purred. "I should've stayed with you, but I really had to go take care of some things. Should've taken you with me." There was silence. "Would you have come?"

"Maybe."

"I guess that keeps me guessing. So when are you coming out for the second leg of the Wyoming Stakes?"

"What?"

"Didn't your dad tell you? Maybe he wants to skip it. The race you won was part of a series to determine the best thoroughbred horse racing at the Downs for the season. It may not matter to you. But it's a big deal out here."

"Dad didn't say anything to me about a second leg."

"There are actually three legs, but if you win two out of three you'll win the series. I've checked the dates of the Arlington Capitol Stakes you talked about—that's the same weekend as the third leg of the series here."

"When's the second leg?"

"Two weeks, on June fourteenth. It would be a good prep for the Capitol for Hope, and you'd have that altitude factor working for you again. Maybe your dad would like that."

"He'd love it. He's probably afraid he'll lose his trainer if he asks her to drive another three thousand mile trip."

Clint cleared his throat. "I have to be in California about the time you'd need to drive out, but I should be at the Downs by Friday. If we're still talking to each other by the time you return to Chicago, I could help with that part of the drive. My calendar is clear. I'll keep it clear from Friday until you leave, if you want."

He watched the red numerals flip over on the bedside clock. "I never knew silence could be so painful."

"Don't push me. I'm thinking. Or at least I'm trying to think. I told my girlfriends you were history, but you're not."

"I hope not. You've generated more sparks for me than I can remember—and not just in the stable. I'd like to show you my world, if you want to see it. I don't have any big ideas on where things will go. But I think we can have a good time while you're here."

"So I'd probably have to leave by the end of this week for Hope to have enough days at the Downs before the race."

"And then head back maybe ten days or so after the race."

"That would be about right."

Clint heard Cassie groan.

"Okay, I'll do it. I should be there by Monday or Tuesday at the latest." She chuckled. "I'll be sufficiently rested and bored by the time you arrive on Friday."

"Cassie."

"Yes."

"Are you doing this for the horse, or for yourself?"

"I'm not sure."

"That's good enough for me. I'll see you sometime Friday. Have a safe trip."

"See you."

There—he'd done it, and she'd accepted. Why were danger signals prickling the back of his neck?

- o -

What had she done? Cassie sat on her bed and hugged herself. Another trip to Wyoming! It would be good for Hope. The altitude should set her up quite nicely for the Capitol Stakes.

But she'd just agreed to much more than that. Much more. Where could she run, if she had to? She hadn't left herself much of an escape hatch this time.

Second and third thoughts nagged at Cassie as she sipped her second cup of coffee on the O'Hanlon farmhouse porch after feeding the

75

horses. Had her hormones driven her to this? It made good sense for Hope. But did it make any sense at all for Cassie O'Hanlon?

She'd only be there less than two weeks; it wasn't like she'd agreed to marry the guy.

"Didn't figure you'd want to trailer all the way back to Wyoming," he father said, breaking into her thoughts. "Thought you'd bite my head off if I suggested it. Should give our girl that altitude edge again. That'll be a bonus for the Capitol."

"Hope so. What about after the Capitol Stakes? Have you given any thought to that?"

"Oh yeah." Tug winked at Cassie. "We're nominated for the Land of Lincoln Stakes on Labor Day Weekend."

"The Land of Lincoln! A grade three stakes?"

"Why not? Doesn't cost much to nominate. The real money has to be put down closer to race day."

"That's heady stuff. She's only won a cheap allowance race plus the race in Wyoming."

"I know, but I've got a gut feeling. And I like this fellow's thinking you met out west. I'm not the only guy who has faith in the altitude angle."

Cassie lifted her cup to her lips and swallowed. "He thought you were pretty clever for sending Hope out there in the first place. So, what if we lose the Capitol—do we still move forward to the Land of Lincoln?"

"Depends on how we lose. If she just runs flatfooted, there's no excuse. If she gets knocked around a lot and has excuses for a poor performance, we'll probably move ahead."

"Plus we'll have another allowance or two for prep races between the Capitol and the Lincoln."

"Right. I figure she's strong and willing and can handle a race every couple weeks or so. Those first two races hardly took anything out of her. We'll probably give her a break sometime between the Capitol and the Lincoln. She'll let us know when she needs to freshen."

"I suppose she will. Sometimes I think she's talking to me. And there are plenty of times when I wish she really would."

"You'll hear her when she needs you to. You got a good ear for horses. So do you want to tell me about this Travers fellow?"

"Not really."

"Thought so." Tug coughed. "Nothing wrong with mixing horseracing and a little romance."

Cassie's cheeks burned. "Calling it romance may be too strong."

"Hell, call it lust, if you want. It's good for you. You've hung around stockbrokers and such for too long. Need to find a real man."

"Dad!"

"It's true. My health is coming back, slowly. Think I might make it a little longer. Sure would like to see some grandkids before I go."

Cassie scrunched further back in the wicker rocker. "Since when have you become so family focused? I don't mean to disappoint you, but I sure don't see any kids on the near horizon — or the distant one, for that matter.

Her father smoothed out the blanket covering

his lap. "I imagine near-death experiences are wake up calls for most folks." He turned to look at Cassie. "I'd like to see you settled and with your own family before I die."

"That sounds like another pipedream, Dad." Cassie swallowed. "I'm not sure it's any more realistic than dreaming that big stakes horse. And I'm not even certain I share the dream. I haven't had the best of luck with men. I thought I had a pretty good life going in the city. Of course, you and Hope turned that world upside down...for the moment. She shrugged. "But I don't know. I do like kids—maybe someday."

"A man comes in handy if you want kids. And you're not getting any younger."

Cassie laughed. "You're really on a tear this morning, aren't you? I should have plenty of child bearing years left. I'm only twenty-seven." Cassie scrutinized her father. He clearly didn't think *he* had that many years left. Sobered, she said, "I've even thought of being a foster parent. I see plenty of kids coming through the group home who need foster placements or permanent homes."

"Foster kids." Tug scratched his chin. "That's good. Doubt it's the same, though. They come and go. Just when you get attached, they leave."

A sudden chill niggled at Cassie. Being a foster parent appealed to her precisely because there was no expectation of permanency.

Her father had become quiet. Was he thinking about children—or maybe about mothers who abandoned their children? Soon he snored lightly.

78

He'd seldom talked to her about family. It wasn't a forbidden topic; it just wasn't talked about. The same was true of talking about her mother.

Cassie stood and tiptoed toward the screen door. Outside, she walked to the old tire swing suspended from a tall oak tree. The chain attaching it to the tree limb, although rusted, was still strong. This was a place she'd often done her best thinking and dreaming when she was a young girl in pigtails.

She climbed easily into the tire. The chain complained, but held. She hugged the old rubber treads.

There was no turning back. She would take Hope to Wyoming. But that was almost secondary. Taking care of Hope and preparing her for the next race would be a snap. Handling Travers might prove more difficult. She had no game plan for dealing with him.

Couldn't she have a two-week fling and be okay with that?

But he wanted to show her his world, if she wanted to see it. Did she want? That didn't sound so much like a fling.

Just maybe, she deserved an exciting adventure. When was the last time she'd taken a vacation? She was merely an adult female having an affair with a very sexy man in a very out-of-the-way place. And hadn't he said he had no grand designs? She'd peek at his world and then return to her own familiar world — hopefully unscathed.

CHAPTER FOUR

Where had this nervousness come from? One minute Cassie sat in the single chair in the motel room trying to read a novel; the next she was up pacing back and forth in front of the dresser. The trip had gone smoothly. Hope had settled in nicely and was well prepared for Saturday's race.

Well, okay, her anxiety had little to do with Hope and her race. It was Friday. Clint Travers was due any minute. He'd called from the Salt Lake City airport some ninety miles away to confirm that his plane had landed. Probably he'd called to confirm she'd made her way to Evanston without taking a detour.

She peeked at the clock again. They'd agreed he'd pick her up and they'd try a local restaurant. She'd dressed casually—that was really the only style appropriate in Evanston, Wyoming. She wore a denim wraparound skirt and a pink tank-top. Nothing too seductive, but he wouldn't mistake her for one of his cowhands, either.

So how was she supposed to greet him when he knocked on her door? Should she kiss him? Should she apologize again for running out on him the last time? What did he expect?

Clint Travers parked his truck in front of the Early Bird Motel. He rubbed his chin and combed his fingers through his hair before replacing the Stetson on his head. Now what?

The red-headed vixen of his night dreams was somewhere in the motel. What did she expect? Would she prefer a kiss, a hug, a handshake? Should he apologize for how he left so abruptly the last time?

Just go do it Travers. You're both adults. You'll figure something out. He picked up the flowers lying on the passenger's seat and headed toward the room number she'd given him.

- o -

Cassie jumped at the soft rap on the door. "He's here," she muttered. She moistened her lips and moved slowly. No need to appear too eager. She opened the door wide and Clint Travers stepped back into her life.

He was as commanding a presence as she remembered. She'd made the correct decision to return. "Hi, are those for me?" She pointed at the yellow roses squeezed in Clint's hand. "Come in."

Clint walked into the room and Cassie closed the door behind him. He turned and held the roses out to her. "Yes, they're for you—sorry." He grinned and cocked his head to one side. "You're even more beautiful than I remembered."

"You clean up pretty good yourself, cowboy. Let me get a glass and set the flowers on the dresser; they are quite stunning."

"Not nearly as stunning as you."

"My, you are full of compliments," Cassie teased, holding her arms out to him in invitation.

He took her in his arms. She tipped her head up to meet his lips. He tasted masculine. She chewed on his lower lip. His hands cupped her rear and pressed her body tight against his. His arousal didn't surprise. She was as excited as he was. It must have been caused by all the waiting. Cassie chuckled against his mouth. Maybe dinner could wait.

"What's so funny?" he murmured.

"I've been anxious about how we'd reconnect. Whether it would feel natural to kiss you when you arrived or if that might be better put off until after dinner."

"And?"

"We're doing just fine," she said, then slipped her tongue between his lips to greet his.

He worked a hand between them to cover a breast. She moaned her pleasure, then broke their kiss and leaned back, giving him more room to roam across her breasts. With both hands, he lifted them and grazed a nipple with a thumb.

"Oh my," Cassie moaned. "That feels so good."

Clint lowered his head and laved a breast through the light tank top.

Cassie jerked her head back and pushed her breast forward, wanting more, demanding more.

The fabric was getting in the way. She needed to feel his mouth on her skin.

She pulled away from Clint and smiled at his immediate distress. "Don't worry," she whispered. "I'm not going anywhere. The restaurant is open late. I checked." She tugged the tank top over her head and quickly dispensed with the bra. "There. Free at last," she said, fondling her breasts. "Nibble away, cowboy. And these are only appetizers, I promise."

"Damn it, you are a firecracker," he said, lowering his mouth to a breast and backing her against the bed.

She collapsed on the mattress and grinned as he worked to stay in contact with her breasts. They settled on the bed and he drew as much of one breast into his mouth as he could manage. Cassie shuddered. She ran her fingers through his thick, dark hair and down his back. His shirt needed to go, but she was enjoying his mouth too much to complain.

He continued to swirl his tongue around her breast at the same time she felt his hand working its way up her thigh. It caressed gently and moved slowly, never diverting from its target. She spread her thighs. His palm settled over her mound. She closed her eyes, silently encouraging him not to stop.

She lifted her buttocks slightly. He didn't disappoint. He slipped aside the bikini panty far enough to slide a finger inside her heat. "Oh," she moaned, opening her eyes to meet his steady gaze.

He shifted his angle until he could move freely.

She closed her eyes again and savored the sensations. Even the yellow roses paled in comparison to how he stimulated all of her senses. He plied her sex, clearly confident where he was taking her, and she followed greedily. Soon, too soon, she left him to race after that elusive rapture she didn't want to miss. There. There. She sighed.

- o -

Clint held her close, waiting patiently for her orgasm to subside.

Finally she opened her eyes and gave him a lazy smile.

"Welcome back to Wyoming," he said with a wide grin.

"You sure know how to make a girl feel welcomed," she crooned. "How set are you on dinner out?"

"Furthest thing from my mind."

"Thought it might be." She gave him a sly smile. "Why don't you get out of those clothes so I can give you an appropriate party favor?"

Nodding, Clint stood and reached for his belt. The woman loved to tease. He wasn't complaining. He shucked his clothes and watched her undo the wraparound skirt and skim the panties off, her gaze fixed on his straining cock.

"My, my, I thought maybe I'd exaggerated his size in my hazy memory. I didn't. You've done most of the work so far," she said, curling a finger at him. "Why don't you lie on your back and let me see what I can do to please you?"

He scooted up on the bed, lay on his back, and watched her auburn hair cascade over his chest, hiding her intentions from him. Her lips grazed his nipple and then her teeth fastened on it gently. Her fingers wrapped around his cock. They squeezed lightly and glided over its length.

His heart skipped a beat when he saw that mass of auburn hair moving lower. Her breath warmed him. He kept his hands by his sides, letting her stay in control. She lowered her mouth onto him, shifting her shoulders until she had the right fit. Waves of auburn bobbed up and down slowly. She took in half of his shaft before pausing. She swept her hair back from her face and winked at him before sinking further, taking nearly all of him in her mouth and throat. She cradled his balls in one hand and bobbed slowly up and down.

Clint clutched the sheet with both fists.

She stopped and dropped him. "Do you like?"

"You've got to be crazy. It's exquisite."

"Good. Then I guess you wouldn't mind a little more attention."

Again, her auburn mane kept him from seeing what she was doing. But every other part of his sensory system worked overtime. She bobbed. She twisted her hand. She left no doubt about her purpose. He felt her lips surround the base of his cock.

It started somewhere between his toes and his knees. His balls tightened, signaling the end was close. He heard her chuckle as she increased her pace. And then he exploded. He came and she never left him. In his climactic fog, he was surprised by that. But she'd never failed to amaze him before, so why should this be any different? She swallowed repeatedly, continuing to draw his essence from him until there was no more. Her warm mouth soothed him as he drifted.

Perhaps seconds, minutes or hours later. Clint cranked an eyelid open. Cassie was still there nestled in his arm. She played idly with his chest hairs.

"You're awake," she said, with a smile. "That must've been powerful for you, too."

"Amazing. You're an amazing woman."

"Glad you think so. I don't know about you, but this amazing woman is famished. How about I order some pizza so we don't have to go out at all?"

He laughed. "Sounds good to me. Make mine sausage."

She scowled at him. "Are you laughing at me?"

He leaned on one elbow and grinned. "Not at all. It's just that you are so expressive. You can be angry as hell. You can be depressed, almost vulnerable. You can be thrilled. And you can be a dynamo when it comes to sex."

"Are you complaining?"

"Not at all. Maybe I'm trying to explain it."

"Don't try." She chuckled. "It's simple. I enjoy uncomplicated sex. Always have, since I first discovered its potential. Don't mean to suggest that I'm highly promiscuous. I've had a few longer term relationships. When sex gets problematic is when guys want to make more out of it than it is. Can't a woman enjoy sex as much as a man without the guy immediately ringing wedding bells?"

Clint's felt his cheeks burn. "Don't get your dander up. As I said, I'm not complaining. And I don't hear wedding bells ringing in my ears."

"Good. That settles that." Cassie clapped her hands. "I'll order pizza and then we can consider a range of dessert possibilities. Right now my tummy needs filling to restore my energy." She winked and cupped her mound. "My pussy will need filling soon after, if you think you can get up for that."

His cock sprang upward. "Don't tease me, woman, or you may never get that pizza call made."

Cassie scrambled off the bed and reached for a robe and the phone. "Patience. I really am famished. You must be, too." She blew him a kiss. "My pussy's not going to evaporate in an hour or so." She nodded at his arousal. "Down, boy. You'll get your reward. Soon. Sooner, if I can make this call."

Less than twenty-four hours later, Cassie stood in the winner's circle at Wyoming Downs patting Hope's neck. Once again, she'd run a quality race. Two California shippers had dueled with the chestnut filly, but Hope prevailed easily.

Cassie beamed at the rancher from Utah who walked beside her as she led Hope out away from the stands and back toward the barns. "She couldn't have run better. Thought maybe she'd get hemmed in there at the top of the stretch."

"No way, she had another gear left," Clint said. "She's one smooth-running filly."

She appreciated Clint's admiration. Clearly, he knew a lot about quality horses. "At least with those two California horses in the field, the bettors got better odds on Hope."

"Two to one is not great."

They walked off the track onto the roadway leading to the test barn. "So why did you tell me about this series, if you were so uncomfortable with outsiders coming in for these races? If I remember correctly, you didn't exactly roll out the red carpet the last time I was here."

"No, don't suppose I did. This was different. We knew horses were coming in from California and Washington. The local boys weren't going to win anyway. By nominating for the first race, you'd nominated for all three even if your dad didn't explain that. So it might as well be you who won." Clint pulled his Stetson lower over his eyes. "Of course, that wasn't the only thing I was thinking about when I made that call."

Cassie brought Hope to a halt, looked up, and pulled down Clint's sunglasses. "Were you imagining some of the things that we did last night?"

"Could be. That and some more, maybe."

"Good. Once we have Hope bedded down and your friend has his instructions on what Hope requires for the next several days — maybe then we can explore some more of your imaginings without interruption. Maybe."

"Winning only makes you more saucy, lady."

"Of course." Cassie flashed her eyebrows. "Horny, you mean, don't you? What did you expect?"

- o -

"Wow!" Cassie exclaimed, sitting on the edge of the pick-up seat with her nose nearly touching the windshield. "It's so expansive. From this high it looks like the valley goes on forever."

"Yeah, if you look to the northwest horizon," Clint said, gesturing with a finger, "you can see the Salt Lake. It's that ribbon of blue." The Salt Lake Valley stretched out as far as they could see to the west, the south and the north. They'd just passed through the craggy canyon on I-80 that hid the panoramic view until the very last instant.

"Incredible. I've never seen anything like this."

Clint smiled at his passenger's awe-struck features. "If you think this is different, wait until we're a couple hours further west of here," he said. "I'm going to show you something you won't find in Lake Michigan."

"Amazing." Cassie said, shading her eyes from the blazing sun-scorched surface. "It's as flat as a parking lot and as white as a clown's face. I can't believe I actually eat this stuff."

"I believe they refine it some," Clint quipped, "before it gets to your salt shaker."

They had walked a good half mile out from I-80 across the Salt Flats. The sun baked everything in sight, even in the late afternoon. Foothills loomed miles away; in between was acre after acre of salt, overlaid with countless mirages.

"If we didn't have these shades and caps on, the glare could do damage to our retinas," Clint said. "That's how strong this sun is out here. It is a desert. As the Salt Lake rises from rainfall, it spills over into these outlying areas. Then as the lake recedes during the summer months, these flats dry up and the salt crystalizes and is harvested."

"Wow. This is one huge farm. As far as the eye can see."

"Actually, there are several, worked by different corporations. Over closer to those foothills," Clint said, pointing to the dark shadows on the northern horizon, "is where many of the ground speed records have been made. Bonneville Salt Flats attracts cars and dragsters from all over the world. You want to go look?"

"No thanks." She smiled at Clint, who was clearly checking her out. She knew her nipples hardened under his stare. She shrugged, shielding her sunglasses with the palm of her hand, not unaware of how such a simple gesture pressed her breasts tightly against her halter top. "Cars are simply a means of getting me from place to place. I do want to take a sample of this salt home, though. I doubt that any of my friends have seen raw salt."

"Okay. Let's take a handful each. I have a container in the truck we can use. But first things first."

Clint bent down and placed his lips on hers. It was a tender kiss. She felt the heat of his lips. She opened her mouth and deepened the embrace. Her tongue sought his. His hands cupped her bottom and she stood on the tip of her toes; her fingers dug into his firm shoulder muscles.

Lost in the kiss, she was struck by the image they must be making for the passing observer — two dark intertwined shapes, like a renaissance sculpture. Life, however, coursed strongly through their bodies. Although the heat was blistering, it could not compete in intensity with the fire generated by that simple kiss.

Breaking their embrace, Clint rubbed his face in her windblown hair. "We better get out of here," he groaned. "Wouldn't want to do anything rash. Our skin would be fried under this sun — and salt would be much worse for the body than straw."

She shuddered. "No way. Not here."

Dazed by a cacophony of sounds including bells, whistles, and falling coins, Cassie welcomed the air conditioning of the bustling glitter-laden casino. They'd driven only a few miles from the Salt Flats to the border town of Wendover, where on the Nevada side several casinos stood tall, beckoning any and all who were willing to risk a dollar in the slot machines or at the gaming tables.

Being a penny-pincher herself, she'd never stepped into a casino before. The place lured and saddened. The shrill yells of victory spoke clearly of those who were having a good day, some a *very* good day. Many more individuals sat glumly before the machines as though they could not move even if they thought about it. Their willpower appeared totally sapped. Cassie shuddered.

At least at a race track, people were able to disconnect and move around. And there were always the horses. Gambling had never been the primary draw to the horses for her or for her dad. They'd both lost and made some money at the betting windows, but raising competitive horses was the dream.

Cheers at the craps table brought her attention back to Clint and a game she expected she'd never understand. Craps moved too quickly. Chips were placed every which way on the lines and boxes on the table. Dice rolled. "Coming out," cried the casino man in a crisp white shirt and bolo tie. "Come seven, come eleven."

Many of the players' faces showed brilliant expectation while the dice were suspended in the air, only to droop in agony when the cubes stopped rolling.

"Snake eyes and out," the casino man declared. He used a long curved stick to remove the chips from in front of the players. Some placed chips down immediately, preparing to take on once again the odds of the game. Others grumbled and left.

Cassie watched Clint put his winnings in his pocket. He turned to her, placed a hand on her elbow and guided her away from the table.

"It's time to move on," he said. "The table was hot for a while; now it's turning cold. With craps, you got to know when to walk away."

"Expect that's true with any game of chance."

He gave her a puzzled look and then said, "It's getting late. How about grabbing something to eat and staying here for the night? We can spend the next day or two in Salt Lake and then head out to the ranch the morning after that, if you want."

"Sounds inviting to me," Cassie responded with a broad smile. "We might yet find a game I can play."

- o -

"So how come there's no serious man in your life?"

Clint appreciated the view of Cassie pulling at her unruly hair that showed the effects of a splendid, uncomplicated night of lovemaking. She sat in the middle of the large bed, her legs tucked under. No clothing marred his view. He hadn't

94

met a woman more comfortable with her own natural nudity.

Sitting in a large winged chair across from her, Clint waited patiently for her response to his question. He thanked the universe or whom or whatever for the opportunity to wake up just one morning with this beautiful creature.

She blinked. "Did I say there wasn't?"

"You wouldn't be here if there was."

She gave a coy smile and shrugged. "You're probably right about that. I enjoy playing, but I don't play around if I'm in a serious relationship."

She crossed her arms under her breasts, which only served to frame them even better for him. She appeared to ponder how much she wanted to share. He waited for her to make up her mind.

"There's no one now," she finally said. "The last serious relationship burned out and left a bad taste in my mouth for anything long term. I've been keeping an apparent dishrag of a guy at bay for the past six months or so. That's done. He thought I betrayed him by leaving the city to take on Cassie's Hope. He doesn't believe there is life beyond the Chicago city limits. He was someone to be seen with, but he never really fit. Dirk was safe. As long as he was around, I didn't have to deal with other men."

"Right." Clint sighed. He doubted he should ask, but he couldn't stop himself. "And where do I fit into this web of romance?"

Cassie responded quickly, perhaps too quickly. "In the short-run, you fit incredibly well." Her blush let him know that she was remembering just how well he did fit. "In the long-run," she said looking away, "you don't fit at all."

Clint felt a flash of anger and spoke before he could think. "My role in one week's time is to fill you up sexually for who knows how many years, but I'm not good enough for the sophisticated big city girl?"

"Whoa! Where did that sarcasm come from?" Cassie glared at him. "You've no right to be hurt. We're adults having a good time. That doesn't mean forever. I never suggested anything else."

Overstepped that one, cowboy. "Yeah, I know." Clint paused to regain his balance. "Doesn't mean my ego doesn't get in the way, though. I'm not looking for a wife anymore than you're apparently looking for a husband."

"Well, a husband would be okay," Cassie demurred. "But he'd have to be just right. And while you are a fantastic lover and I'm sure you're a great person, I've sworn to God and any who will listen that I will never ever marry a horse trainer."

"What?" She'd done it again, and he couldn't stop his words. "You mean you would throw me out of long term consideration just because I train horses?"

"Absolutely," she said, pulling her knees to her chest and covering herself with the sheet.

"That's ridiculous."

Before he could continue, Cassie broke in, "I've bounced from track to track. I know the life of the backside. I don't want to raise a family that way. I know about broken promises and broken dreams."

"Then why the hell did you come back to the Downs? And why are you in my bed?"

Cassie smiled ruefully. "You fail to remember that my first order of business is making Hope a stakes contender for my father. Cassie's Hope is probably his last dream of a big horse. After his stroke, I doubt he'll ever work again. It'll be a small miracle to get him to the track to watch Hope race."

"I'm sorry," Clint said frowning. "I forgot. Guess I've never been bitten by that big horse bug. Running around the bush tracks is good enough for me." He winced—he wasn't telling the entire truth, but then he doubted the redheaded minx had been entirely honest with him, either.

"Well, it shouldn't be!" Cassie said. She clamped her mouth shut, but then went on. "You have some good horses, but you're not giving them a chance. If you're going to be in this game, you should be playing to win. Why don't you take them to California to race? I've watched you, and I don't understand why you're satisfied playing around at tracks that can't pay horse owners and trainers enough to meet expenses."

"Well, well. You've been bottling a lot up, haven't you? For someone who can hardly wait to get out of the horse business, you sure are long on advice. Maybe I like to just play at horse racing." Becoming somber, Clint added, "Maybe I got other responsibilities that keep me close to home."

Cassie shook her head. "I'm sorry. I shouldn't have said all that. Christ, I'm in no position to judge how you or anyone else chooses to run a life."

Her eyes smoldered caressing his body. "As to your second question awhile back — why am I in your bed — that answer is easy. Because you are a terrific lover who dragged me off in his pickup to see his world."

Clint's cell phone rang.

"Yeah...Wendover. Right...Don't worry, I'll be there day after tomorrow...Don't nag me about it — I said I'd be there, and I will. Yeah, me too."

He put the phone back in its holder and scowled. "Let's get dressed and go down and have breakfast."

Cassie climbed off the bed and started getting dressed. With bra and panties on she turned and confronted him. "Hey, if you don't have time to show me around, I'll understand. You can take me back to Evanston and I'll be fine. Really."

"Don't even think about it. I cleared my calendar to spend time with you, and that's what I'm going to do." He laced his fingers in her hair and pulled her close. Her scent was intoxicating. "You got away from me once. Not this time."

Now what kind of questioning look was she giving him? He wasn't going to go after that, and apparently, for once, she was prepared to let things drop. He'd forgotten how much of challenge it was spending twenty-fours with a woman.

Should he really take her to the ranch? That was his safe house, his private life. He couldn't explain to himself why it was important to show her who he really was. Cassie O'Hanlon was a joy to be around, but she still was a high strung, complex woman—a woman who still had *danger* written all over her. He'd better keep his heart protected.

After two days poking around Salt Lake City, Cassie was pleased to be heading toward eastern Utah and Clint's ranch. She was more than a little curious about how he lived.

She was still high on adrenaline. How could life get any better? From the winner's circle to the last few days being with Clint—it just couldn't be topped.

They'd been traveling over a well maintained dirt road for the last twenty minutes. He'd announced when they'd entered his land. It didn't look any different than the landscape they'd been driving through for quite some time: reddish soil, dry and windblown. Mountains graced the horizon.

"There's the buildings," he said with pride, pointing ahead and to her right.

Several buildings were visible nestled among cottonwoods. The stable area appeared fairly new and well maintained. The house had that ever-evolving look of so many ranch houses she'd observed while traveling through the west. It looked like the original builders had only built for their current needs, then added on as the family grew or as owners changed.

As they got closer, she could see that Clint's house certainly wasn't ramshackle, but it was sprawling and low to the ground. Everything was on one floor, shaped in a U. That was another element it shared in common with most every structure she'd seen on their trip across Utah. People didn't build high. They didn't have to — they had plenty of space. And a lower structure probably caught less wind, which might be quite significant in the winter.

Clint pulled into the dirt driveway and stopped close to the house. "Come on," he said. "I'll show you around."

He headed immediately for the kitchen. Cassie followed, noting along the way what was likely his den and also glimpsing a wide open living room. What she could see was typically manly. Heavy furniture, bare floors and pictures of horses adorned the walls. The kitchen was surprisingly decorated in warm tones and was neat and looked quite functional.

Clint opened the refrigerator and grabbed a beer for each of them. He clinked his bottle against hers. "Welcome to Utah, Cassie O'Hanlon."

"Thanks. It's lovely. You have a huge place here. Do you ever get lost?"

"Let's go," he said, grabbing her hand and heading toward the entryway. "I'll show you the stables. That's much more interesting than the house."

Now who was nervous? It should be her, not him. This was his lair. But he seemed much more fidgety and much less certain now that he'd gotten her here. He hadn't bothered to give her much of a tour of his house.

As they neared the stable, she spied a beautiful black stallion prancing, rearing and then galloping off in a nearby pasture. "He's handsome," she said. A half dozen or so mares were in a paddock on the other side of the stable. And out beyond she could see over twenty colts and fillies of various ages mingling and grazing.

Squinting against the low sun, she breathed sharply. Some of those horses were like those he'd raced in Wyoming. But the majority of them were not. Definitely not. They were high class thoroughbreds that could rival many a horse at the best tracks in Illinois, Kentucky, New York or California.

She let Clint lead through the immaculate stable and came to yet another pasture with older mares. Leaning against the rail fence, admiring the animals, Cassie said. "You've been holding out on me, Travers. These aren't bush league horses. You do race at the larger tracks."

"Nope," he replied, shaking his head. "Told you I didn't. Some of my horses do, but I don't. Mostly, I sell well-bred racing stock to those who want to risk a lot more than I do for a dream."

"Really? Where do you get them?"

"I've picked up the breeding stock over the years, improving as I go. Sometimes I travel to the big sales at Keeneland or Barretts. Some call me a pinhooker. I'll buy yearlings, train them, and then sell them back as two year olds. There's good money in it if you've got an eye for horseflesh and the economy is doing well. I'd like to raise more from breeding stock. But I admit I find it hard to travel back from an auction with an empty trailer."

"But you don't race these horses in Wyoming?"

"Nope. A lot of things can happen when a horse steps on a track, most of it bad. I wouldn't want to risk a missed step or a collision with these babies."

"And you don't want to take the purse money from the small, local trainers."

Clint shrugged without responding. She saw the smile in his eyes.

"You are a very complex man, Mr. Travers."

"To bad you don't have the time to try and figure me out."

On the way out of the barn, Cassie waited for Clint to give instructions to an attentive, dark haired, dark skinned young woman who smiled at him, flashing pearly white teeth. Cassie felt her innards cringe when the woman's calculating stare swept up and down Cassie's body. Grimacing, not knowing quite what to do with her hands, she shoved them in her back pockets.

Seemingly unaware of the feminine byplay around him, Clint continued to talk with the woman about preparing some yearlings for a Kentucky sale. He would be back in plenty of time to oversee shipping them and last minute preparations at the auction. The young woman nodded, then briefly cast a menacing look at Cassie before heading toward one of the back paddocks.

Clint turned, smiling at Cassie. "My sister can be quite protective at times."

"Your sister! Oh." Why hadn't he introduced the two of them? Was *she* the secret, or was the sister?

"You may have a chance to meet her another time. Silver Hawk is not predisposed to be kind to whites—especially." he added, "women who might be interested in me."

Trying to ignore her rising anger and his implication, Cassie asked, "How many people do you have working for you?"

"Three, year-round. When things are really hectic preparing for sales, I may hire a couple part-timers to handle more of the menial work. By the way, Silver Hawk is damn good with yearlings and two year olds. The two of you would like each other, if we could get her to sit down and talk horses."

"That's our loss, isn't it?" Cassie regretted the catty remark as soon as it was out of her mouth.

"Women," Clint mumbled, walking rapidly toward the house.

Cassie hurried to keep up; did he expect his women to walk three paces behind him? Why was he so cross? She knew he wasn't like that.

Clint set immediately to work in the kitchen.

103

"Hope you like omelets? That's what I do best when it comes to cooking." Cracking eggs, dicing ham, cutting cheese and green peppers, he maintained a chatter that seemed uncharacteristic.

Again, he seemed out of sorts with her in his house. They'd made love on shedrow and almost incessantly in Wendover and at the Salt Lake hotel, but this was his home. Would it be that intimidating...making love in his bed?

"So how many women do you have over, Travers?" Cassie cracked, in an effort to lighten the mood. "You have enough supplies to feed an army."

"None," he responded. Clint turned to look into his guest's questioning eyes. "I have a large family." He laughed. "Hell, the entire community will show up unannounced. It's the way things are here. You have to be prepared."

- o -

Had he just dodged a bullet? Clint busied himself at the stove. Why couldn't he simply speak the truth to this woman? Why did he think he could bring her here without opening a large can of worms?

Turning over an omelet, he knew the answer to why he'd taken such a risk. He wanted her to know he was no cowboy drifter — he was a person of some substance. He wanted her respect. But that left a remaining question...why?

Minutes later, Cassie dug into the large omelet

he'd set before her. "This is delicious, Clint. Your kitchen may say down home, but this food is first class."

"Omelets are my specialty."

She pointed her fork at him. "You're just full of surprises, aren't you?"

He flinched, then gave her an easy smile. "Have to keep you on your toes, or you'll be getting so comfortable you'll want to stay."

She flushed. "No chance of that," she mumbled. "I've got a horse to run and a job waiting back in Chicago." She caught him grinning broadly.

- o -

Later that evening, they sat on a blanket watching the flames of Clint's fireplace dance about, leaping upwards as if to find new dreams and fresh hopes. Cassie sat between Clint's legs and leaned back against his chest. She sighed. His place was so comfortable. There were moments in life that deserved replicating, and this was one of those.

"A penny for your thoughts," Clint whispered into her ear.

Without pulling her gaze away from the fire, she said, "You can get more for your penny than that."

"Is that a threat or a promise?"

She laughed, turning toward him. "Whatever you want."

He rubbed his face in her hair and lifted it away

from her neck. His lips on her bare skin soothed and excited. She studied the fire again and let his hands roam freely over her body. They squeezed her jean-clad thighs, skimmed her crotch, and slid under her tank top, making their way to her breasts. She wore no bra to impede his efforts. His fingers played with her nipples until they quickly hardened.

She sensed his breath catch.

"You're an intoxicating lady."

She hummed, thrilled by his words and his fingers.

He tugged at the snap of her jeans. She smiled and helped him ease them off along with her panties. She tried to focus on the flames in the fireplace while Clint stirred her inner heat.

He eased a finger into her moist crevice and she arched her back against his chest. She covered his hand, guiding him, helping him with his exploration. He blew warm air on her neck and began a steady cadence with his buried finger. A second finger joined the first. The flames of the fireplace drew her; her inner flames gathered momentum. She brushed a thumb across her clit. She closed her eyes and leaned heavily against Clint.

"So sweet," she moaned. She felt his fingers curl up inside, searching. Leaning forward, she yanked her tank top off and settled back again, twisting her nipples as he found what he'd been seeking. "That's it. You're right on it."

"Come for me."

"I will. I am." She spread her knees as wide as she could while bucking against his fingers. "That's it. Almost. Keep going."

She arched forward and backward, panting with anticipation. "Now!" she yelped. "Oh god, yes!"

Her body went rigid and then collapsed against him. "No more," she whimpered. "Please. No more. Give me time. I'll be back. Trust me."

- o -

Clint eased his fingers out of her heat and held her close. Her body convulsed. It seemed to take forever for her breathing to steady. He wasn't certain he'd ever been closer to a woman's orgasm. She'd been so hot, so vital, so alive. Clint held her tight, not wanting to lose their bond.

"I need you in me," she whispered a few minutes later.

"Okay." He quickly shed his clothes and lay back down beside her.

"Can we just lie here and watch the fire?" she asked, turning onto her side and pushing her backside against him. Her voice seemed smaller than normal.

"Sure. That sounds fine." He cuddled her body until they were snug. His stiffness rested on the rise of her buttocks. They lay there like that for several minutes, each of them watching the flames, both lost in their own thoughts.

He inhaled deeply. He loved the smell of her,

the feel of her. He loved the fact that she could be wildly sexy at times and so quiet and comforting at others. She was so warm and toasty he was afraid he might melt into her like butter.

She reached a hand between her legs and sought him out. He shifted lower and she guided him to her pussy. He cupped her to him, seating himself fully in her sex.

She sighed heavily. "That feels wonderful. I'm not sure I can get enough of this. I'm yours, do with me what you want."

Her words washed over him. He eased back and then forward. He slowed and quickened. Her breathing changed to soft panting.

"I'm going to come again."

He smiled at her announcement—as if he couldn't tell. Steadily, he stayed the course.

"Oh god," she moaned. "So deep. Fuck me. So good."

Clint didn't let her catch her breath this time. His hips pistoned against her shapely butt until he filled her with his wanting and she called out his name in thanksgiving.

He held her. Remaining joined, they dozed.

Clint awoke still nestled against her body. Carefully, he withdrew his still semi-hard cock, retrieved a blanket, and covered his naked lover.

After getting a beer from the kitchen, he sat on the livening room couch studying Cassie as she slept soundly, seemingly fully sated at last.

He'd been startled by her words *I'm yours, do with me what you want*. Did she know what she was saying? Were they just words of lovemaking? Were they words intended for his ears? He doubted that.

How had he let this woman get in his blood so quickly? He truly loved giving her pleasure. She was so gloriously responsive. What they shared didn't happen often—he knew that for a fact.

What the hell was he going to do about it? And did she have even a glimmer of an idea what was possible for them? Probably not. She'd been so determined to define them from the beginning as a fling.

He'd had flings before, and this wasn't feeling like one of those. This woman was different. He liked the way she laughed. He liked the way she embraced new experiences. He liked the way she felt in his arms, like liquid fire. He even liked her saucy temper. Cassidy O'Hanlon was something else, and Clint wasn't sure he wanted to let her come and go as easily as she'd planned. Yet, realistically, what more could he expect from her than a fling?

Clint drained the bottle, stretched out on the floor, pulled up a blanket, and fell into a fitful sleep. Beside him Cassie slept peacefully with no awareness of the shadows chasing her lover.

CHAPTER FIVE

Should she be annoyed? They were driving out his driveway after breakfast and Cassie was aware she'd never made it to his bedroom. She still had no idea what kind of bed the man slept in. Of course, more importantly, she knew how he was in bed — damn good.

She watched the high desert go by out the passenger window. A row of green trees marked a meandering stream in the midst of dry grass and soil. The green string reminded her of an elongated oasis. For a short time, this arid land had been her oasis. But soon, too soon, she'd have to head east with Hope. She'd miss this land and the man it had come to represent.

He, too, had been an oasis of sorts. His softness surprised and comforted while his mysteriousness vexed and intrigued. The understated charm of the landscape and its occupants threatened to unravel her emotions, forcing her to look beyond the shadows. An unseen energy pulled on her, enticing her into its vortex.

Desperately, Cassie shook her upper body. Her life was already complicated as all hell. She'd have to work hard to retrieve her old life. Her dad had complicated things, and if she wasn't extremely careful, the man next to her could complicate things a great deal more.

They were headed into the small town of Roosevelt; Clint had to pick up some items from the feed store before they headed back to Evanston.

"Much of this area is reservation land," he commented. "The Ute people have done better than some Indian nations, probably not as well as others. Oil and natural gas have helped. Problem is, maybe for five years there's a real boom around here, and then it goes bust and people didn't plan ahead.

"Over there is a relic of a building. Never been used. A lot of money spent on a convention center, but no conventions. We might have done better to rely on the land more. There are some decent ranches in the area. Beef and horses. But there just aren't enough jobs to go around."

The countryside blipped by. Pockets of wealth alongside pockets of poverty were readily discernible. In that way, it wasn't too unlike sections of Chicago that she knew so well. There were many areas in the city where the wealthy and the poor rubbed shoulders on a daily basis. But she didn't comment. She wanted to listen to Clint share more about his land that seemed so desolate and yet so bountiful. She suspected that when he spoke of the land he was also talking of himself.

"It's a mysterious place in some ways. I've been to a lot of places, but none that quite compare. The air is clean. There's more space than you'd ever know what to do with. The people are fun loving, whether it's a boom or a bust. They may cry, but they generally find something to laugh about. Maybe it was something that happened generations ago, but it still tickles the funny bone.

"It's hard to explain. There's a spirit here that's hard to find everywhere. Maybe it's perspective. My grandmother likes to say *You must take life seriously, but not too seriously. Great Spirit didn't create all of this beauty just for you to ignore it.*"

Cassie twisted in her seat and smiled. "Your grandmother sounds like a very wise woman. I expect she and my dad would have a lot in common. One of his favorite sayings is *you got to stop and smell the flowers and the horses. A life without either is a life unfulfilled.* I think I'd like your grandmother."

Clint looked sharply at her. She wondered why her response had surprised him; his expression remained clouded and guarded.

Turning the truck into a parking lot, he announced, "Here we are. Why don't you come along? You'll see a feed store that hasn't changed much in fifty years or more."

He was right about that. It was clearly more than a feed store, though. Ranchers could bring their own grains in to be blended with others in the mill behind the main building. In the store, pre-mixed feeds and seeds were available in forty and hundred pound bags. One entire wall was lined with bridles, bits, halters, and saddles. Pitchforks and shovels were available, as were ropes of all sizes. Cassie paused and inhaled deeply the smells of leather and rope. She observed a cooler with cold drinks and shelves of snacks and many grocery items. There was even a small section toward the back of the store devoted to movie rentals.

Could the owner possibly know where everything was? Some aisles were neatly stacked, while others were haphazard, resembling a large grab bag. At the far end of the store, near the cold drink display, were a half dozen card tables with four chairs apiece. A few table legs rested on wood wedges.

Not one table was empty at ten in the morning. At each table sat four people, mostly men, but there were a few women. Cards flashed down quickly, matched by cheers and groans and occasional cussing.

Bending low to whisper in Cassie's ear, Clint said, "Welcome to one of our local community centers. People have played cards here since long before I was born." Catching the eye of one of the players, he said, "Hi Joe, how's it going?"

"Could be worse," groaned a man of indeterminable age. The man's weathered skin must be tougher than her favorite saddle.

Others soon took notice of Clint. They chose to ignore her. No one asked about her, nor did he bother to introduce her. An older man chatted briefly with Clint about the weather and then told him of a foal out of one of his stallions that had been born two days prior.

As Clint turned and guided Cassie down a

narrow aisle, one of the older card players shouted, "Hey Clint, you gonna make it to Luke's circle? Tuesday night around six. He'll feel a lot better if you're there."

Clint stopped and then retraced his steps. He appeared disturbed by the question, but maybe she was misreading him. He had proven to be nearly indecipherable at times.

"How's the kid been doing since the break-in?" he asked casually.

"Keeping his nose clean. If it weren't for you, he knows he'd be sittin' in jail rather than having a circle. He really wants to make amends and move on. Are you gonna be there?"

Clint sighed. "Guess I can go to California the following week. Yeah, I'll be there."

Cassie waited until he paid for his purchases, but as they carried them toward the truck she asked, "What was that all about? Luke and a circle."

"Oh, that," Clint said, placing the ropes and other items he'd bought into the back of the truck. He chuckled. "I forgot you were a social worker."

"Huh, thought you might have forgotten I was even there."

He ignored that jab. Why didn't that surprise her?

"Luke is a fourteen year old who can't decide how he wants to play the game. He's bright, but sees little future in being bright. He and a couple other guys broke into one of the local taverns. They were caught. Bright, but dumb."

115

"Yeah, I know the type. All too well."

"Anyway, instead of putting him in detention or giving him over to the state, the judge remanded him to a circle."

"So?"

As they climbed into the cab of the pickup, Clint continued, "It's a group of folks from the community along with professionals and of course Luke and the bar owner. Luke has admitted guilt, that's not the issue. Now he can apologize for his mistake, make amends—whatever the circle decides—and get on with his life."

"So where do you fit in?"

"I've sort of been a mentor to Luke and his family for the last couple years."

She flashed her eyebrows.

He shrugged. "It's part of what's expected in this culture. We try to help one another out, if we can."

Running fingers through her hair, she quipped, "Travers, I think you are a man of many secrets. I expect it'd take years to learn about all of them."

"Well, I guess I'm safe then, since you'll be headed back to Chicago soon."

Cassie said nothing, shading her eyes against the sun. She couldn't discern if his words were in jest or if they weren't tinged with anger. What the hell had she done to make him angry?

After spending much of the afternoon showing Cassie more of the area, Clint turned down a washboard gravel road. "I've got to make one

116

more stop before we head back."

The truck maneuvered haphazardly across and around ruts. Cassie felt like she was flying about the cab without a tether. Clint kept his seat as if he were riding a bronco.

After what seemed miles, Clint stopped the truck before a small old house. Its gray weathered clapboards hadn't seen paint in years. Its roof slouched a bit. Yet the building appeared quite sturdy. A variety of well kept roses, columbine, and honeysuckle provided color. Those and a large green garden on the south side of the house bespoke someone who enjoyed digging in the soil and watching things grow.

Before Cassie could complete her appraisal of the house and its surroundings, a middle aged woman came to the doorway. Coal black hair hung loose about her shoulders. Her dark bronze skin and oval face reflected her Ute heritage. The woman waited, not meeting Cassie's gaze as she and Clint got out of the truck.

"Cassie, I want you to meet my mother," Clint said, escorting her by the arm. "Mom, this is Cassie O'Hanlon. She's come from Chicago to race a horse at the Downs. I needed to stop and check on a couple things."

Trying not to act shocked, Cassie said, "Pleased to meet you, ma'am."

The older woman nodded, briefly glancing at Cassie, and murmured, "Me too."

Before Clint's mother could look away, Cassie saw mirth in the woman's eyes.

117

"Come in," Mrs. Travers said warmly. "Welcome to my home."

Clint had already disappeared inside. As she walked through the doorway, Cassie was struck by both the hominess and the neatness of the house.

"Can I get you some coffee?" the woman asked. "I always have a pot brewing."

"Sure," Cassie responded easily. "I'm not certain how long Clint plans on staying."

"There's always time for a cup of coffee. And I have some soup simmering." The woman smiled. "You may think it's too hot for soup, but the nights are sometimes nippy, and I like soup."

"I do, too." Cassie beamed with a sense of being in the right place. She liked the woman with twinkling eyes.

Noises of children running outside interrupted her reverie. She turned just in time to see a girl and boy knock each other about trying to wedge through the doorway at the same time.

Both righted themselves quickly and brushed reddish dirt from their clothes before being introduced. Clint's mother waited, giving the children time to straighten themselves out. Each child stepped softly into the kitchen, as if not to disturb. Each child smiled ear to ear, displaying pearly white teeth.

Cassie's heart did a somersault. What lovely children. So respectful, and yet full of energy and life.

"Ms. O'Hanlon, these are my grandchildren.

Lester, eight. And Samantha is six. Say hi to Ms. O'Hanlon."

"Hi, Ms. O'Hanlon," the two children chirped in unison, eyes bulging with curiosity.

"Oh, please call me Cassie," Cassie replied with a wide grin. Who did these impish children belong to?

Clint hurried back into the kitchen carrying several manila folders. When he saw the children, his face went blank and then lit up like a morning sunrise,

Samantha ran to him with open arms. "Daddy, you're back. I've missed you so," cried the little girl with two pigtails swinging about her face.

"How long are you back for?" asked Lester, stuffing his small hands into his pockets.

Clint ruffled the boy's hair. "I can't stay now, but I'll be back in few days. Then I'm home for a while. I promise."

Grabbing a hand of each of his children, he walked them over to Cassie. "Have you had a chance to meet this delightful woman? She lives in a very big city far from here. Don't think you've ever met anyone from Chicago before."

Both children beamed smiles that would warm the most frozen heart. Cassie struggled to breathe and maintain her composure. Responsibilities! He had implied that responsibilities kept him closer to home than he might wish. These were some responsibilities!

Before long Samantha was on Cassie's lap introducing her to two cute dolls. Lester asked

119

several questions a minute. What kind of horses did she own? Was she married? Did she have kids? Did she like his dad's place? Cassie kept her responses light and friendly, but she was beginning to wonder if the boy was his father's agent.

She overheard Clint speaking to his mother in low tones. "I thought they were supposed to be with Grandmother today. Is anything wrong?"

"Not to worry." His mother shook her head. "She woke up with a bad cold, so I said the kids have more than enough to play with here. I can go to town some other day."

Cassie's cheeks burned. She wasn't supposed to learn of these treasures. Was he ever going to mention them?

Her heart clinched. She would be driving back to Chicago in only days. It didn't matter. It had never mattered. If it had, Clint would have told her about his children. She found it hard to shake the urge to sob.

"Are you okay, Ms. O'Hanlon?" Mrs. Travers asked.

Cassie shook her head. "I'm fine. Just a bad memory there for a moment."

"Ah," the older woman said, moving back to the stove.

Turning to her son, she said, "Since you're going to stay for the evening meal, why don't you run over and check on your grandmother? If she's up for it, bring her back for supper."

"Didn't know we were staying." He cocked his

120

head to the side. "Suppose Grandmother never is going to get a phone." He scrunched his mouth one way and then the other. "Okay. Is it all right with you, Cass? We'll leave late, but we'll be back in Evanston well before morning."

Cassie hadn't missed his ambivalence, but she smiled. "No problem here. As long as I'm back to start working Hope in the morning."

"Thanks," he said cheerfully. "Grandmother wouldn't forgive me if everyone met you but her. It's a matter of honor."

"I know. I really do." Cassie's lips pursed. Had any of this been planned? Clint certainly looked innocent enough. He'd seemed flustered for a moment when he spied his children standing in the kitchen.

And now his grandmother. Yes, she knew about grandmothers. They could easily be bent out of shape if not included in what was happening. And Cassie guessed that at least for the day, *she* was what was happening. She had to admit it felt good to be included in matters of family.

"Children," Mrs. Travers said, after their father's truck disappeared bouncing down the rutty road. "Why don't you go out and play for awhile and give Ms. O'Hanlon a chance to breathe? You can talk with her some more later."

Cassie was now at the mercy of Clint's mother. She tried to steel herself for the inevitable grilling. "Can I help you, Mrs. Travers?"

"Sure, if you'd like. How about chopping some

vegetables?"

Cutting up carrots, radishes, onions and lettuce for a salad provided a pleasant distraction. Still, Cassie's brain and stomach churned. What had she had gotten herself into? And where were things going? A week-long summer fling was in danger of taking a twist or two. Two children. Oh, my god!

After what seemed a very prolonged silence, Clint's mother said, "You must be something quite special."

"What?" Cassie responded casually. "What do you mean?"

"Since Samantha's mother died giving birth, Clint has never brought a woman to this house to meet me or his children. I know through the grapevine that there have been some, but not in this house. So you see," Mrs. Travers said, "you have to be something very special."

"Oh," Cassie sputtered. "But he didn't really bring me to meet you or his children. Clint had to stop here for something before we left for Evanston," she explained. "He didn't even know the kids were here. You heard him."

The older woman stopped stirring the soup and stared at Cassie as if she believed her a fool. Finally, Mrs. Travers said, "You've been around my son. Do you really think he just happened to stop by? And I don't think he looked too displeased to find his children here."

"Oh," Cassie whispered. "Ouch," she yelped, as blood oozed from a sliced finger. Immediately, she placed it in her mouth and sucked on it.

Mrs. Travers laughed. "I'll be right back with a bandaid. I guess you didn't realize how special you've become to my son. If I'm right, you'll be in for many more surprises."

"Oh, hell," Cassie groaned, stepping outside to get some fresh air, her chest expanding with exhilaration, with pride, with an emotion she could not and would not name. What had happened to a simple, uncomplicated fling? And *this* would be a good time to have her own set of wheels.

Supper turned out to be a tasty affair. Cassie couldn't remember ever having a better vegetable soup. The homemade bread was delicious. And the salad she'd made was a hit. Conversation was light, prompted mainly by the children. They wanted to know about the city and the Chicago Cubs. She'd been surprised that even people out here knew about the Cubs.

Grandmother Littlefield turned out to be a different matter. *Taciturn* was a polite way to describe her. Seldom did she put more than three words together, and not often were there three. But she saw everything. Cassie hoped the woman couldn't see into her confused heart.

The slightly built elderly woman could no longer stand straight. Her eyes burned like coal. Her gnarled hands remained strong, her grip firm. Once she smiled broadly at her great-granddaughter. The old woman was missing several teeth. Cassie wondered if that was why she seldom spoke. Still, the woman carried herself with the unassuming pride of the wise.

As Grandmother Littlefield bade farewell before Clint took her back to her home, the wizened woman clasped Cassie's hands to her bosom. Staring intently into Cassie's eyes, she spoke solemnly, "Do not be afraid, Woman of Fire. You will do just fine." With that proclamation, she slipped into the darkness.

Cassie stood at the doorway watching Clint help his grandmother into the truck. Shivers dashed up and down her spine; goose-bumps fought for space on her arms.

Cassie played a board game with the children until Clint returned. Her spirits were up again. How could they be otherwise, with the energy of those two urchins? What one didn't think of, the other did. Their laughter filled Cassie's soul and made her heart lurch. Damn, she had to get out of here, and soon.

"We want Fire Woman to tuck us in," Samantha announced, when it was bedtime.

Starting to protest, Cassie saw the vulnerability so evident on the two beaming faces. They had seemed so, so strong and fun loving earlier. Now they seemed unsteady, nearly lost.

"If it's okay with your father and grandmother."

Both nodded assent.

The children slept in a small room off the

kitchen. Cassie pulled the covers up to tuck them under Samantha's chin. With a teddy bear in one hand, the little girl threw her arms around Cassie, nearly pulling her off balance. No peck on the brow was going to satisfy this child. Cassie hugged as strongly as she was being hugged.

Samantha whispered, "Thanks for coming to see us. I like you. And I know Daddy does too."

Cassie's eyes brimmed full with tears. She mumbled incoherently, "It was good to meet you. I like you too."

"What about my daddy?"

Cassie grinned. There was no getting off the hook with this one. "Yes, I like your daddy too. Good-night."

"Your turn, young man," Cassie said, taking a deep breath. Boys would not be as sentimental as girls. Right?

She brushed Lester's hair out of his eyes and kissed his forehead. "Good-night, Lester. I enjoyed meeting you too."

"Me too," he said, his eyes shining with intensity. "Can you promise me something?"

Cassie looked at the lad cautiously. "Well, if I can. What is it?"

"When you marry my dad, can we be at the wedding?"

"My goodness, Lester. Where did you get such an idea? We've not even talked of such a thing." Cassie clamped a hand over her mouth. She had to stop rattling on. This was an eight year old child she was dealing with. He didn't require a dissertation on why she and his father would not be marrying.

"That's okay, ma'am. Just when you do. Don't forget to invite us. Chicago sounds like a long way away."

Cassie hugged the boy. She tried not to sob, yet unwanted tears ran down her cheeks. "Okay," she barely managed to mutter. Slowly, Cassie stood, wiped the tears from her eyes and retreated from that tiny room overflowing with love.

When she re-entered the kitchen, she saw Clint watching her oddly. She couldn't decipher his emotions; he'd put on a mask again.

"Are you okay, Cass?" he asked. His concern was genuine.

Smiling weakly, she replied, "Yeah, I'm all right. You certainly have a couple livewires there." She sighed deeply. "Don't you think we'd better be going soon? It's already late."

"Yeah, let me gather my things."

"Thanks so much for your hospitality, Mrs. Travers," Cassie said, turning to face the woman pouring coffee into a thermos for them.

"I'm glad you could be here," said Mrs. Travers, glancing away. "Don't let the children upset you. They mean well. And obviously they like you a lot."

"Did you..." Cassie's hand flew to her throat. "Did he hear them?"

"The walls here are quite thin, I'm afraid." Shaking her head, the woman said, "Don't worry about it. No harm was done. If it's meant to be, then it will happen, and neither you nor my sometimes dunderhead of a son can do anything about it."

- o -

They were driving west on Highway 40 before Clint spoke, not quite sure what to anticipate from Cassie. He'd half expected her to be railing at him by now. "Sorry about that back there. Guess I should have warned you. Never know what's gonna happen when I stop there."

"Never mind. I had a delightful time," Cassie mumbled mid-yawn, dozing off to sleep.

He tugged on her gently. She slid across the bench seat and slept easily, with her head resting against his shoulder and his arm securely wrapped about her.

With one hand on the steering wheel, Clint drove on into the night deep in thought. There would be some serious explaining to do, but at least not right now.

Why had he stopped there? The papers he'd picked up regarding his mother's property taxes were important, but certainly not urgent.

And what about Sammy and Lester? Did they want a mother so badly they'd jump on the first woman he brought home? But she wasn't just any woman. She was his spitfire — well, at least for the moment. What was it his grandmother had called her? *Woman of Fire*. Wasn't that the truth. He never wanted to tame that fire, but neither did he want to be burned by it. Singed maybe, but not burned.

- o -

Cassie smelled his scent and savored it. She rested easily pressed against his body. There was much to talk about, but she didn't need to do that just yet. She wanted the whole afternoon and evening to just wash over her in its fullness.

Why couldn't life stay like this? She'd felt the love within the Travers family. And she'd felt the love they were willing to share with her.

She shuddered. That wasn't where she was headed. A horse trainer who couldn't even race his best horses where they might make some money. A strange man who she still knew so little about. A father. Two children.

Cassie slipped off into dreamland. Several sets of coal-black eyes moved in and out of a haze, comforting, beckoning, chastising, challenging, supporting. Their message was oblique; their message was clear.

CHAPTER SIX

The alarm clock clamored as if from a faraway echo chamber. Cassie moaned dreamily; one bare leg jerked out from under the covers. The noise didn't abate. With one eyelid slit open, she reached for the clock. It crashed to the floor with a bang, ringing as loudly as ever. Tossing the blankets aside, she dropped to her knees, blindly searching for the offending object. At last, she pushed the oppressive button. Silence. She sighed, grateful for small accomplishments.

Standing, disheveled, she raked her fingers through tangled hair trying to remember where she was and what she was doing in the small dank motel room. Ah, he'd dropped her off several hours earlier so she could get some sleep before heading to the track.

Memories overran her like so many unwanted bounced checks — memories of a slightly overprotective hunk of a man, of two impish children eager to adopt her as their own, of his mother, reserved yet welcoming, and of his grandmother peering into her heart.

Cassie shuddered. This she didn't need. A fling was one thing; a family was quite another. A fling wasn't even an affair. Family meant rings, promises, and responsibilities. And in this case, being a mother. "I've got more than enough responsibilities already," she snarled. "Thank you very much."

Who had poured concrete into her arms and legs? Everything she did preparing Hope for her morning workout occurred in slow motion. Her social outing to Utah had taken more out of her than she'd realized. Glancing around with more than a little curiosity, she could see no evidence of his blue pickup. He was expected at the stables, but then he'd driven all the way back to Evanston while she slept.

Where the hell was he? He had to come, because she had to tell him they were finished. And he had some tall explaining to do. When did he get the fantastic idea of taking her to his mother's house? And why hadn't he ever said anything about his kids? Clearly, he loved them. Didn't he think she was good enough for them?

Cassie forced bile back down her throat. No matter. She was leaving. The best thing about Evanston, Wyoming and all it represented would be watching it disappear in her rearview mirror. She kicked at an imaginary object; her horse kicked out a hind leg, barely missing Cassie's ankle.

"Better pay attention to business, or you'll find yourself in the hospital yet."

Cassie's heart sank. She whirled. "Why the hell are you always sneaking up on me, Clint Travers? Can't you ever make noise like the rest of us?"

"'Cause I love your reaction at being surprised, I

guess." He paused to watch a rider trot a horse toward the track. He smiled that lopsided grin, immediately sending Cassie's stomach tumbling, jeopardizing her vow to distance herself from the man. "Suppose we need to talk some about yesterday," he drawled, his tone turning suddenly serious.

"I don't," she countered, trying to appear nonplused. "I'm pulling out of here tomorrow after I've packed my gear and gotten some sleep. Yesterday was just one more crazy blip on this little weird journey of mine."

"Ah, so the ice queen re-emerges. You're right, it doesn't really matter. The people you met yesterday don't matter. It was a mistake to take you there. I hadn't planned it. I wish to God it hadn't happened." He spun about and walked stiffly toward his end of shedrow.

Tears burned Cassie's eyes. *Damn him.* Ice queen. She was no ice queen. She was merely being sensible. There was no room in her life for a man, especially a horse trainer fifteen hundred miles from Chicago with two incredibly cute kids. No way!

Two hours later, Cassie sat in the canteen sipping tea and trying to calm her nerves. She glanced out the window and saw Travers packing gear into his horse trailer. Was he going to leave before she could?

She stood up and tossed some coins on the table, then moved swiftly toward the exit. Damn if he was going to get away without her clearing up a few things.

- o -

Clint slammed the storage door shut. The woman had really gotten under his skin this time. Hell, he'd had affairs before. And some of those women were still among his best friends. But Cassie O'Hanlon had discounted him from the beginning—because he was a horse trainer. And then she'd rejected his family. That was the last straw. She might not like him, but...

He sat on the running board, took out his penknife and started cleaning the dirt wedged in the grooves of his boot.

Things would be better after she went back to Chicago. He wouldn't have to see her every day and visually undress the damn woman. He knew her curves too well. He knew her scent too well. He knew her taste too well.

She'd turned him inside out, and he'd done nothing to resist. Even when it was clear all she wanted was a fling, he had just blithely followed along, as if she was a female Pied Piper. The best thing to do now was ignore her. He didn't trust himself to get too close to her even now. He knew he'd never physically harm a woman, but he might burn her ass with words she'd never heard before.

He felt used...yet she'd been honest with him from the beginning. He was the fool for thinking there might be more between them. Maybe her declaration of having no future with a horse trainer had simply goaded him into trying to prove her wrong.

Clint folded up his knife and relaxed a bit. He'd bet that was it. She'd just provoked his competitive spirit. That was all there was to it. He could survive the resulting damage to his ego. My god, what would have happened if he'd won her over and she'd wanted more? He wasn't ready for another wife.

The best thing he could do was pack up his horses and take them back to Utah. He could skip the next weekend of racing. Besides, the kids would be thrilled to have him home for a couple weeks.

- o -

"There you are," Cassie said. "You're not going anywhere until I tell you a thing or two."

"Whoa, woman." Clint stood and leaned against the horse trailer. "I feel more comfortable facing your fire standing."

She stood with hands on hips glaring at him, trying to remember why she had to leave.

Clint smiled bitterly. "Okay, woman, spit it out. If you don't, you'll burst, and I don't want to be responsible for that."

That did it. Cassie pulled off her baseball cap and banged it against the trailer. Ignoring the resulting dust cloud, she said shortly, "You can be the most vexing man, Clint Travers."

"I imagine you're right about that."

"I just wanted you to know before I leave that what we shared this week meant a lot to me. I will always treasure that time in my heart."

"Right."

"Don't be an ass when I'm trying to tell you how I feel."

"Okay," Clint said guardedly.

"I didn't come here seeking a man in my life. I just got rid of one. You were different. The attraction was heated — mutually, I believe. And any relationship with you had boundaries. I was clear about that right along."

He stared blankly at her, neither agreeing nor disagreeing.

"So. I needed you to know how special our lovemaking, all our time together was. And it's terribly important to me that you know I'm not walking away because I didn't like your family. You have a warm, loving family. Your kids are treasures." Cassie shook her head, fighting back tears.

"Yes, you're a horse trainer and I've vowed not to get involved with any man in the horse world. But, to be truthful, I don't want to be involved with any man at this point in my life. There is too much going on with my father, with Hope, with my career. I don't have time or space for a man right now. I'm sorry, but that's the way it is. You need to find a woman who will be comfortable being the wife of a horseman and mother to his children. You don't need me."

Clint pulled on his nose and looked toward the southeastern horizon. He glanced back at her and tipped his hat. "I guess you're right, lady."

His cold words stung like windblown hail. She glimpsed the pain in his dark eyes before he spun on his heel, opened the door to his truck, climbed in, started the engine and drove off.

Cassie watched the truck disappear around the corner of the stable; tears coursed down her cheeks. What had she really expected? She'd said her piece. He'd listened. And then he left.

So be it.

The red-orange glow of the rising sun nearly blinded Cassie. Sunglasses hardly mattered. Fighting the glare, fighting a headache, fighting tears, she guided her truck and trailer eastward along the deep rock-cut banks of Rock Springs, Wyoming. The flaming orb appeared to be sitting atop I-80. She slowed down, letting braver or crazier drivers go by in the passing lane.

Anxiously, she cussed at the poor timing of having to travel through that particular part of the country at sunrise. But she'd wanted to get an early start to take advantage of the cooler morning hours and to avoid attracting unwanted attention to her departure. She'd pulled out of the Downs long before dawn.

I Only Wanna Be With You was blaring on the truck radio. Wrong song. She punched the *off* button, but the silence wasn't much better.

135

She hadn't been surprised to see the blue pickup that Travers called his road office parked among the few vehicles sitting in the lot that early in the morning. Had he come back to be certain she'd left his kingdom? As she drove her rig out of the parking lot, she'd felt his eyes boring in on her. He'd no doubt been buried deep in the shadows of the stables.

- o -

She'd been right. Clint had stood stoically in the shadows of shedrow and watched until the taillights of her trailer could no longer be seen. He'd wanted to leave for Utah before she left for Chicago—so much for determination. He'd changed his mind because he wanted to say something to her to erase the bitterness of his words the previous day, but he couldn't find the words to replace them. The woman made him feel inept and callous. Like no other woman he'd ever known, she'd turned him inside out, and he didn't like it a damn bit.

He stood there a while after she drove out, trying to appreciate the still burning stars of Father Sky. There was little room in his soul for thanksgiving. He felt utterly bereft and painfully alone. His eyes narrowed watching those taillights disappear in the darkness before the dawn. He wanted to put her behind him, but he was certain he wasn't finished with the red-headed minx aiming for I-80 and her escape route east.

The Chicago skyline stood out crisply against a clear blue sky. The strong tailwind that had helped Cassie make good time coming across the prairie had scoured the Chicago air of smog. Cassie knew it wouldn't last long, but it was beautiful.

She glanced in her review mirror. She hoped she hadn't made the biggest mistake of her life. She couldn't help but fume over him not telling her about his kids. She hadn't been prepared. They'd curled around her heart before she had a chance to mount a proper defense. No way could she be an instant mother. Good thing it was just a fling.

She was running scared, but that was okay. At least, she could still run. When would she be able to sleep again without feeling chilled because he wasn't holding her?

Turning off the Interstate, she left those thoughts behind. She had an important race to prepare for and she couldn't afford any distractions. Cassie's Hope needed her full attention.

Three nights later, Cassie wrestled in her sleep. There was no relief for a pained heart. She'd had no choice. She couldn't have stayed. Maybe he was more man than she wanted, and there was no room in her life for kids.

Why couldn't she convince her heart of that fact?

- o -

Fifteen hundred miles away, Clint Travers paced the living room where they'd made such beautiful music together in front of the fireplace. The hearth was now dark. He hadn't built a fire since she'd left.

He'd wanted to call, but she'd probably hang up. And anyhow, the phone couldn't help him with his need to run his fingers through her thick auburn mane. He wanted to hear her voice, but he desperately needed that tactile sensation of her fire singeing him every time he brushed up against her.

Would she even speak to him if he went to Chicago? Could he handle her rejection—again? Clint's cheek muscles twitched. Was she worth the risk? Were *they* worth the risk? If he went to her, he'd make it damn clear that he wasn't pursuing a fling. He'd be coming after the entire package—body, mind and soul.

What had his grandmother told him from the time he was a little boy? "Follow your heart, and you will be in tune with all that is."

"Follow my heart," Clint mumbled, chuckling. "Guess I got to get my ass to Chicago, 'cause that's where my heart is."

Louie Picard picked up the phone on the second ring. "Yeah."

"Louie, how's her filly look?"

"She's only been back a week. Filly looks sound and raring to go."

"Good. Her old man's probably got his hopes up real big."

Louie winced at the caller's snicker.

"Louie, you know what to do?"

"Yeah."

"Good. See that you do the job right."

The phone clicked in Louie's ear. He grimaced. What had he ever done to deserve this? "You wallow in shit long enough," he muttered, "you become shit like the rest of them."

- o -

Cassie sat in the owner's box fidgeting with the straps of her binoculars. She'd done all she could to prepare Hope for the big race. Now it was up to the jockey and the racing gods. Maybe the altitude switch would make the difference again. If it did, at least something good would've come from her Wyoming trip.

Eight minutes to post. The jockeys were jogging their mounts on the backside, loosening them up before entering the starting gate. Cassie tensed, suddenly aware that Hope didn't appear as up on her toes as she had in Wyoming. The horse was sweating more than usual, giving her an overall washed out look and no doubt depleting her energy.

Cassie sighed. Forlornly, she reflected for the hundredth time on her Wyoming trip. Had she made a mistake? He never called or wrote, but then neither had she. It was like they were on two planets in different orbits. She had to admit she missed his touch and his sensuous low voice. She wondered what kinds of troubles Samantha and Lester were attempting. And she heard again Clint's mother saying *You must be something very special.* And what did his grandmother mean, *Woman of Fire?*

The clang of the starting gate drew her attention back to the track. Her heart sank as Hope stumbled out of the gate. The filly did make up some ground on the home stretch to place a credible fourth. But that wouldn't be enough for her father; even second best wouldn't be enough. Cassie squared her shoulders. She wouldn't settle for second best, either.

Cassie retrieved her filly from the jockey and led her back to the barn area where she began rubbing liniments into Hope's ankles. She sensed eyes drilling holes in her back. She groaned, knowing that Harrington would be by to gloat. His horse had beaten Hope by six lengths for a well-earned victory. Hope had never really contended. Standing up, Cassie turned to take the abuse.

She was surprised to see concern registered on Harrington's face. "How's she doing? She had a pretty rough go of it out there today. Are you okay, Cass?"

"Yeah," Cassie acknowledged. "Ankles are still warm and tender to the touch. She should be okay in a day or two. Congratulations on your win."

"Thanks," said the tall, bulky trainer. "Maybe you should offer to take me out to dinner to celebrate."

Cassie winced. "I've got my hands full here and at home." She paused. Wrapping her arms tightly around her body, she warned, "Ed, don't be thinking that I'm part of your social life. I don't have time for one. So, please, find another woman to pursue. From what I hear, there are plenty who are interested."

"That's too bad," Ed countered. "Everyone ought to make time for play, now and then."

"I'm afraid I don't have the time."

"Oh well. Like you said, there are plenty other women lined up."

Cassie gave him a warm smile. "I'm sure you'll find more than one willing to care for your ego." His mouth twitched in response. "And I do appreciate the training advice you give me. I hope we can still be friends."

"Of course we're friends. You're a sexy looking woman, Cassie O'Hanlon but I'd much rather have you for a friend than an enemy." He doffed his hat. "Well, I better get back to my horses."

No sooner than had Harrington left than Louie

Picard stopped by to offer his condolences. "Don't mind Harrington. He's more wind than anything else when it comes to women. He thinks you're cute, so you should naturally think he was the best thing since sliced bread."

Although the news that Harrington thought she was *cute* made her want to gag, Cassie smiled faintly at her aging friend. Apparently, he'd overheard at least part of her conversation with Harrington. "That's all right. He's a big boy and should know he can't win them all."

"How's your dad going to take this loss?"

"He'll be okay, I think," she said. "I'm glad I talked him out of being here today. Dad warned me we couldn't win them all. And he's really pointing to the Land of Lincoln Stakes, and there are still two more preps before then. If we can win one of those, we'll be in good shape. If not, we'll probably still compete. That's horse racing. Right?"

"Yeah," the old man grunted, "that's horse racing. Well, I best be goin'. Got my own horses to tend to. Say hi to your dad for me."

An hour later, after taking Hope off the hotwalker and returning her to the stall, Cassie scratched the animal's neck. Hope nickered softly in response. Contact with the filly probably did more to soothe her own nerves than those of the horse. Hope snuffled, sensing that something was wrong.

"It's okay, Hope," Cassie mumbled, continuing

142

to rub both hands up and down the horse's long outstretched neck. "You did the best you could. That's all we can ask. You're a good horse, but maybe not at this level of competition."

"Giving up so soon? That seems to be a habit of yours."

The low dry accusing voice crackled in the late afternoon breeze. Cassie fought the urge to turn. Her heart leaped to her throat. Tears threatened to embarrass. Without looking at him, she complained, "How did you find your way out of Utah and Wyoming, Travers?"

Clint held his tongue.

Turning at last, she snapped, "And what are you doing in the barn area? Only owners and trainers working at this track are allowed."

"Well then, young lady, I guess it goes without saying that I'm not alone. Brought a few horses along to see how they might do against this rarefied competition." With legs spread slightly, Clint shrugged in his casual way. "From what I've seen, I might do just fine."

Folding her arms across her breasts as if to conceal them, Cassie declared, "Well, it's a free world." She squinted at him, determined not to show the tingling in her body. There were so many questions she was afraid to ask.

"Ah, Cassidy," he sighed heavily. "Put that Irish temper aside for a moment. It's good to see you. And you're happy to see me."

Fighting her irritation, she offered a small smile and let out the breath she'd been holding since

143

first hearing his deep voice. "Okay. I won't say I'm happy to see you, but it's good to see you." And he did look good, standing there in a fresh white shirt and jeans. His brown Stetson matched his boots. Yeah, Clint Travers cleaned up real fine. Cassie tried not to crumble before his overwhelming masculine presence.

"Well now, that is a start," he retorted. Walking around Hope, he scrutinized the filly and then ran his hands up and down the filly's forelegs. He stood to look in the horse's eyes. With both hands, he pried open her jaws and then gently probed the animal's tongue and throat. Hope pawed, her eyes flaring, not welcoming the unwanted intrusion.

Cassie waited patiently—he had to have a reason for being so thorough. She knew he wasn't just avoiding further conversation.

At last he turned to her. Shading his eyes against the late afternoon sun, his facial lines hardening, he said tersely, "I don't mean to alarm you, Cassidy, but I think this horse has been drugged."

"What?" Cassie shouted, her eyes widening in disbelief.

"The filly's tongue and throat are constricted; it's amazing she could run at all."

"How? Who?" Cassie threw her arms around her horse's neck. "My god, did someone try to kill her?"

"I doubt that," Clint said. She watched him take a step toward her. She shrank back. His face remained impassive. "If they had, she'd be dead by now. I expect they just didn't want her to win. By restricting her air intake passage, whoever drugged the animal was just about assured she couldn't win against the caliber of horses running out there today."

Digging her fingernails into her arms, Cassie railed at herself, "I'm so damn naive. Why couldn't I figure out she was drugged? You just stroll in here out of nowhere and have a diagnosis."

"You should confirm it with a vet."

"I'm not doubting your judgment one bit, Clint," Cassie said, her eyes closing. "It's just that I'm the trainer. I should have seen it. I should have protected my horse."

- o -

Clint fought to keep his arms from reaching out to cradle Cassie in his arms. He wanted to very badly. His muscles ached with wanting. But he would not take advantage of her vulnerability. When she was in his arms again, he wanted her there because she couldn't resist herself and couldn't imagine being anywhere else.

"You'd be surprised," he said. "Eight out of ten trainers would never suspect their horse was drugged. Guess I'm just a suspicious sort.

"Sometimes you see this kind of thing at high priced auctions. Not only do some despicable folks want to enhance the performance of their horses with drugs, others want to hamper it.

145

That's one reason the wealthy breeders buy so much security."

"What can we do now?" Cassie asked, stroking Hope with trembling fingers.

"Well, she's your horse," said Clint, edging closer to the woman. "I doubt that anyone will try anything until she races again. But if it were me, I'd take the filly back to your farm. Work her there, and then bring her in the morning of the next race while keeping tight guard around her. Many horses back home run after being shipped in the day of the race with very good results. It happens a lot with higher class horses who get overly excited by crowds and media attention."

"I'm certainly not going to leave her here alone for even one more night," Cassie growled. She frowned. "Damn, my trailer is parked next to the barn at home. I hadn't planned on needing it here yet."

"You can use mine if you like," Clint offered, trying to hide his interest in maintaining contact. Any kind of contact. "I could come by and pick it up later, if that seems okay."

"I couldn't help but overhearing."

Both Cassie and Clint turned to see the grim look on Ed Harrington's face.

He spoke directly to Cassie, ignoring her companion. "Do you really think your horse was drugged? That's pretty farfetched"

"Yes," Cassie responded, frowning at Harrington's intrusion. He was obviously

146

checking out the latest stranger on shedrow. She didn't want him around her or her horse. Especially with Clint Travers standing right there. "It would explain a lot that's happened over the last few months."

"And how do you suppose that could happen? We've got a lot of security. You should inform the stewards of your suspicions, if you really have any grounds." Ed looked sideways at the dark man peering at him through smoky eyes.

"Oh," Cassie said, "I should introduce you. Ed Harrington. Clint Travers. Ed runs a string of horses here. Clint is from Utah. He brought some horses to race here and raises some top quality thoroughbreds at his ranch."

Cassie was startled by the pride so apparent in her own voice. Clint looked pleased; Harrington looked annoyed. They shook hands warily.

Cassie thought two tomcats meeting in a dark Chicago alley would be more friendly than these two men. Smiling to herself, she had to confess that at times it was fun being female. Was she witnessing jealousy? The last thing she needed was each of them trying to protect her from the other. She had enough troubles without raging male hormones and runaway egos.

Looking back at Cassie, Ed said hotly, "Well, my hunch is you just have a very inconsistent horse that's often in over her head. But if you think there are other problems, then there are proper channels for dealing with it. Take your complaints to the stewards."

Cassie looked at him blankly. She knew Clint was taking the measure of the man.

Ed swallowed. "I've got to go, Cass. Can't hold your hand all the time. Got my own horses."

Before she could offer up a cutting response, Cassie felt a boot squeezing down on her own. Angrily, she looked up into Clint's solemn face. Almost imperceptibly he shook his head, encouraging her not to rise to Ed's bait.

"See you later then," Cassie said, scowling at his retreating back.

Turning to Clint, she asked, "Where's your trailer parked?"

Slamming the rear door of the trailer shut, she grunted, "That ought to do it. I'll have Hope in her own stall shortly. You've got the directions for finding the farm tomorrow."

"Got 'em in my pocket."

Cassie removed her work gloves. She was not at all pleased with the look he was giving her. It was a questioning look, almost accusing. "All right, Travers, what's going on in that deceptive mind of yours now?"

His stare softened. "Oh, I was just thinking of the competition. I didn't know you had a man stashed away here in Chicago interested in your favors."

"What? Oh. You mean Harrington." Men, they could make a competition over nothing. "Nope. Only in his dreams and in my worst nightmares."

"You," Clint replied coolly, "can be very

148

decisive at times."

Was he mocking her? She held her tongue.

"Some decisions are easier than others," he added, "I suppose."

"What are you trying to say, Travers?" Cassie demanded. His dark eyes filled with an intensity she didn't want to define. Her heart stopped beating. Well-conditioned muscles seemed incapable of holding her up. Leaning against the pickup, she breathed rapidly.

"I want to be honest with you, Cassidy." Clint paused, clearly studying her panic reactions.

"Yes," she whispered. Her emotions were raw, susceptible to every nuance, spoken or unspoken.

"I'm not here just to race horses." He pushed his Stetson up off his forehead.

"No," she mumbled, "I didn't suppose you were."

Folding his arms across his chest, he declared, "I've come for something you took with you."

"What? I don't understand." Although wary, she watched him carefully.

"I've come for my heart."

His coal black eyes filled with an indecipherable, haunting gleam. His words echoed in her brain. Cassie closed the distance between them with three halting steps. She moved into the warmth of his arms. He held her snug against his body. His strong arms felt good. She tried not to cry, but failed. Damn, she couldn't remember ever crying so much as she had of late.

Clint said no more. He waited.

The summer fling was definitely over, Cassie concluded. Could she open herself to the potential agony of another intimate relationship?

For an instant, she held their shared future in her grasp. He'd taken a huge step by showing up on her turf. Now it was her turn. Her mind whirled. She didn't want to go backward. Staying in place, in his arms, although desirable, was not an option.

She pushed herself away from him at last. "Clint, I am glad you're here, but let's go slowly. I'm not sure of myself. I need time to sort things out." She saw him go rigid. Fear clutched at her heart.

She ran her fingers through her unruly hair trying to find the right words. Would he reject her because she wasn't as ready as he was? "Can you give me some time, Clint? I know the road you want to walk. I'm just not sure I can go down that road. It can be such a painful journey."

Clint's neck muscles relaxed a trifle. "I understand. But it can also be the most joyful journey any two people can share. Take however long you need—just don't shut me out, because I'm not leaving you alone until I know where we stand."

"I wouldn't want you to," she said. Smiling at last, surprised by her own courage, Cassie continued, "Maybe we can take tiny baby steps. But not too many, and not too fast. Why don't you come by and pick up the trailer tomorrow, and then we'll take it from there."

Glancing shyly away from him, she said faintly, "I'd like you to meet my dad. I expect the two of you will find more than a few things in common to talk about."

- o -

Later that evening, Clint stretched out on the hotel bed weighing next moves. He didn't want to rush her. If she chose to be with him, then it would be for keeps. He wouldn't settle for an affair. She was a woman who could challenge him, who could love him deeply—who could be the mother of his children. He'd come to Chicago to pursue her, but he didn't want to scare her away. Obviously, she carried wounds of some kind—would she ever tell him about them?

He would bide his time. Waiting had finite boundaries--he just didn't know what they were yet. Probably things wouldn't be resolved before he had to return to Utah by the middle of the next week. Serious exploration of their future might be impossible until whoever was drugging Cassie's Hope was caught. He vowed to get to the bottom of that mystery as soon as possible.

CHAPTER SEVEN

While bathing a filly beside the barn, Cassie spied the familiar blue pickup wending its way down the long farm driveway. She inhaled the fresh morning air trying to maintain her balance. Could she really love this near stranger? Could they have a life together spread half way across the country? Could she be an instant mother?

Cassie shivered. *That* was where the rubber hit the road. She wasn't ready to think about it. Plus, there would be cultural differences. His Ute heritage. They hadn't talked much about it, but she'd seen some of it firsthand. His family was in some ways foreign, a little scary, yet very welcoming.

What about her father? She and Clint both had family with lots of needs. Responsibilities. They weren't teenagers trying to escape into an adult world. Perhaps they were adults envious of a carefree life—but that was no longer a possibility. Cassie shook her head, bracing herself for the roller coaster of emotions she experienced whenever Clint Travers approached.

- o -

Stepping out of his truck, Clint swept the horizon with his gaze. He liked what he saw. The

153

farm exuded comfort.

The old farmhouse could use some fresh paint on its green trim and white clapboards, but otherwise it was nicely maintained. Red, white, and yellow roses climbed trellises on the near side of the house. The screen porch looked well used rather than merely being a walk through or decorative space.

The yard had been recently mowed. He looked with appreciation at the two large chestnut trees in the front yard. It had been a while since he'd seen trees so full of foliage. Oaks and maples framed the far side of the yard. He wondered who handled all of the leaves in the fall.

His eyes moved toward the outbuildings. He chuckled. There was no question where the priorities were on this farm. The barn was in much better repair than the house. The barn appeared to be an old dairy barn remodeled for horses. Several horses of varying ages grazed in paddocks.

Whoever had converted the place into a working horse farm had done so with foresight and pride. A small half-mile dirt oval served as an exercise track. Not bad. Not bad at all.

At last his eyes settled on the woman with flaming hair bathing a young filly on a concrete slab at the side of the barn. With hose in one hand and a scrub brush in the other, Cassie looked as fetching as ever.

As he neared, he could see the pale blue blouse had been splashed by flying water in the most provocative places. He was immediately envious of her jeans molded against silky feminine skin. Standing in oversized rubber boots that appeared to be waders on her, Cassie looked like a misplaced waif. A waif he was more than willing to rescue from whatever terrible fate threatened her.

"Good morning, Cassidy," Clint said, with a hint of a smile. He chuckled nervously. "Once again I'm not sure if I'm supposed to shake your hand, hug you, or kiss you."

"Well, if you've come a courtin'," Cassie cooed impishly, directing the water hose away from them and rising on her toes to brush his lips, "I guess a discrete kiss is acceptable."

Clint used every muscle in his body to refrain from grabbing her and kissing her like he wanted to, like he hoped she wanted him to. "This isn't going to be easy," he grunted.

"No. It won't be easy," she snickered, squeezing his hand. "You caught me at an awkward moment. I'm just about done. I have to rinse this girl off and turn her out."

"No problem. I'd like to wander around, if you don't mind."

"Go ahead. We don't have any traps or land mines around."

He squinted, admiring the land mine standing before him. Without further comment he stepped into the barn. Again he was impressed with the workmanship that had gone into converting the building into a very functional space for horses. Stalls were solid and of adequate size. A separate area for feed and another for tack. In the tack room, surrounded by bridles, ropes, saddles, bits, and hackamores was a small desk with papers layered in every which direction. He smiled. The social worker horsewoman was not quite as organized as he'd expected.

A fairly new stairway led upstairs. He expected it was the way to the loft apartment that Cassie had told him about. Apparently, it had been used for a hired hand in the past. Now it served as her quarters.

When he walked back out into the sunlight, Cassie was leading the freshly bathed filly into a nearby paddock.

"You have a real nice set up here," he commented, leaning against the paddock fence. "This is obviously a place where people care about the well being of horses."

"Thanks." Cassie glanced in his direction and grinned. "It's certainly not nearly as large as a ranch, but it's big enough for us to raise some decent horses."

Clint heard the pride in her voice and smiled. Did she have any idea how happy she looked — or how happy she made him feel?

After giving the filly a pat on the rump, Cassie ventured, "Okay, I'll rinse out my bucket and then we'll go and see Dad. He's sitting on the porch, probably getting a kick out of spying on us. He always has set of binoculars close by so he can check out the horses in the various paddocks."

"That's handy."

"So…you're the fellow who's taken a fancy to my daughter. You don't look very damn Irish to me," chided the older man with more than a trace of humor.

"Yes and no to your questions," Clint said, suppressing a smile and glancing toward the kitchen doorway, where Cassie had scooted off for coffee after making the introductions. "I'm very taken with your daughter. And while I expect I have at least a speck of Irish blood in me, it's not very noticeable."

"Well," Tug said, thoughtfully studying Clint, "a speck will do, if you don't hurt her."

Clint took his time responding. Finally, looking directly at Cassie's father, he said, "I will do everything in my power not to hurt her, sir. You can count on that."

The older man didn't say a word. Clint wished he could read the fellow's mind.

"You better not," Tug countered at last. "I wouldn't want to have to hurt another horseman. At least I can see now why my daughter is in such a tizzy these days."

Clint cleared his throat. Was that an off-handed vote of confidence?

"Understand you think Hope's been drugged."

Welcoming the change in topic, Clint responded smoothly, "Yeah. I doubt it's the first time, either."

"That would explain a lot of things that don't add up, wouldn't it? Cassie's really had the horse trained right up on her toes till the actual race, and then everything falls apart." The older man ran his hand up and down the worn arm of the rocker. "I'm slippin', I guess. Should've expected it myself. Not as sharp as I used to be. Sure would like to catch the bastard who's doing it."

"We'll work on it."

"*We'll* work on it?" Cassie asked, carrying a tray of coffee and cookies out to the porch. "How long do you expect to be here? Thought you had responsibilities."

"I do," Clint acknowledged, accepting a cup filled with steaming coffee and two chocolate chip cookies. "I'll be here a week or so to see my horses settled in at the track." He shrugged, knowing there was no real need for him to stay that long just due to the horses he was leaving in her care. "Then I'll head back and make sure the two year olds we're taking to the Keeneland sales are ready. And I try not to be away from the kids for more than a week or two at a time."

"You sure were confident I wouldn't say no to training your horses for you while they're at Arlington."

"If you'd turned me down, I would've settled on another trainer. But happily, I don't have to do that. And you'll keep me informed of their progress."

"Then," she asked with a catch in her throat, "you won't be here for Hope's next race?"

"No, afraid not." The disappointment on Cassie's face tugged at Clint. He frowned, wishing he could stay, but knowing he couldn't. "I'll help you work out a plan to protect Hope. But I can't be here to help put it in place. Is there anyone else you totally trust?"

"Absolutely not," interrupted Cassie's father bitterly. "Somebody at the track is doing this. Could be anybody. Could be a stranger or a friend. Can't trust no one. It's just you and me, girl."

- o -

Cassie watched the sparkle in her father's eye. He was being revived by this mystery. He felt needed. But what could he do, nearly welded to his rocker?

In spite of her father's bravado, his words made her feel even more alone. Steeling herself, she resolved that Travers would not witness her fear.

She turned to the ever observant Clint Travers and chuckled at his furrowed brow. "We can handle it. Shouldn't be too much to it. I don't know how we can trap the culprit, but we can certainly keep Hope safe until the day of the race. She trains just as well here as there. I won't leave her out of my sight once we get to the track."

"Yeah, that ought to work," Clint said. "I'd suggest you might think about hiring some security for your shedrow barn a couple days ahead of race time. It may not be necessary. She's being drugged the day of the race. That seems quite certain. But if anyone thinks we're onto

159

them, their strategy could change."

Before Cassie could object, Tug agreed. "Sounds like a good idea. I know a guy I can probably trust to do that much. He won't have to know about our suspicions to do his job. But it does seem like a lot of trouble for someone to go through—drugging a horse that has yet to prove she can really do much of anything."

"I've been wondering and worrying about that," Clint said, nodding thoughtfully. "Seems likely there's more to this than the horse. Either one of you have enemies?"

Father and daughter answered in unison, "No."

"You don't think it's personal...?" Cassie asked, not liking the slight tremble in her voice.

"Could be," Clint hesitated. "Don't mean to alarm you. You do work with delinquents. How many of them have you alienated? How far might they go to settle a grudge?"

"Damn," she whispered. "That never occurred to me. But they wouldn't have access. You have to have a license to be in the paddock area."

Clint shook his head. "Come on. Access can be bought. Or people with access can be bought."

"You really have a suspicious mind, Travers," she said, sipping her cooling coffee. Her mind raced through all of her acquaintances at the track and at her work. She hated to walk through life being distrustful of everyone, but it seemed as if she had little choice.

"Well, I come by my wariness from experience." He shrugged, not offering any additional details. "Most often things aren't as simple as they appear. How about you, Tug? You can't have been around horse tracks for so many years without stepping on some toes here and there."

Tug's breathing was ragged. A cough sapped an attempt at laughter. Pausing at last, he scoffed curtly, "You're probably right. But that list would be so long it couldn't help at all. Still, I can't imagine anyone being so worked up that they would stoop to drugging a horse. And I'm not even training the filly."

"Just keep the question in mind, both of you. It just doesn't feel right that this is only about one horse," Clint reasoned.

Cassie nodded warily, wondering once again how much Clint was not saying.

"I've been to Chicago several times," Clint said, squeezing Cassie's as they walked along the lakefront, "but don't think I've ever seen Lake Michigan this calm."

"Seldom do we see it this peaceful," Cassie said. "I like it when it's like glass, and I also love it when it pounds waves across Lake Shore Drive. She has many personalities. And you never know which one she'll express on any given day."

"Sounds like a woman," Clint bantered lightly.

"Right," Cassie said, pulling them to a halt. "Any woman I know?"

"You might. I do like to watch the sailboats. At a distance they seem like toys and then as they

161

approach the harbor they take on real life form and you can see the folks trying to maneuver just so."

"Uh huh, and I think you just maneuvered out of a tight spot quite nicely, Mr. Travers."

Breathing in the moist lake air, Clint wondered if he'd ever be able to understand this woman at his side. He liked the warmth of her fingers interlaced with his. Her strength was evident. Yet her vulnerability was only a moment away. She seemed so sure and confident of so many things — but not about the two of them. Clearly she would try his patience. He had a deep reservoir of patience. He hoped it would be enough.

- o -

"If we walk up this little knoll, you can see my apartment building," said Cassie, leading him up a grassy rise. "There," she pointed, "that tall gray building, about one hand over from the John Hancock building."

"How long did you sublet your apartment?"

"Six months. Emily's an art history student taking classes at the Art Institute. So she doesn't have far to go." Cassie sat on the grass and looked back toward the lake. "I miss being surrounded by all my own things. Wish I could take you over and show you, but that feels like intruding."

"It's okay. There will be other times. What do you miss most about living in the city?"

Cassie sighed deeply and peered toward a new

shape emerging on the horizon. From experience she knew it to be a freighter. His question bothered her, more than she'd like to admit. It seemed like a simple question, yet it was anything but. In a way it was Dirk Johnson's question. It surprised her to realize she hadn't missed living in the city as much as she'd expected. But she was sure Clint's question was loaded with implications for the future, which meant she had to tread carefully.

Thoughtfully, she answered, "Mainly the ease of going down to a favorite corner restaurant. I enjoy being close to the theater and the symphony. Being around diverse sounds and people. The city pulsates. And I do miss the lake." She grimaced. "I know this should be easier than it is, but the city is simply part of my adult life. Oddly, it's stable. Every day people come and go in the city. Every day it changes. But every day Chicago remains the same."

Clint nodded. "Ironically, you could be describing eastern Utah." He chuckled. "Very different places, obviously. But that flavor of changing yet remaining the same...they have that in common. And I sense that you do like the country, too."

"Of course. The farm is almost idyllic. The smell of freshly cut hay. The sounds of robins and mourning doves. The stillness of the night. And then the chorus of frogs speaking their own incredible language. Sunsets and flowers. Sure, I love the country too. And I appreciate the hard work needed to make the farm go and the fact that it is so clear that we are not in control of everything. The farm keeps me in touch with the rhythms of the seasons in ways I'd almost forgotten." Surprised by her own fervor, she hastened to add, "I guess I need both city and farm."

Very quietly, she asked, "What about you, cowboy? Does the city offer you anything? Or is it simply a place to be avoided?"

Nodding, Clint said, "I'll be honest with you. I don't mind visiting. It has a pulse I find exciting. The city, like the country, has its own vibrations. I like to see a play or hear a symphony now and then. And you're right about the restaurants. I even enjoy watching the people scurry about. In my business, I actually spend a fair amount of time in cities. But I expect over time any city would wear me down. At some point, I have to see further than the next building or I'd lose touch with reality.

He chuckled softly. "And where would I put my horses in the city?"

She watched his lips curl into a half smile.

"Besides," he added quietly, "it would be pretty hard to throw my woman across my saddle and ride off into the sunset in Chicago."

Cassie laughed. "Would that be a western saddle you had in mind, cowboy? The saddle horn could be a problem."

"Yeah, well. For you, I would remove the horn. You know it's primarily handy when you're roping cattle. I don't expect you'd respond well to being roped and hogtied."

"You can count on that, mister." She poked him in the ribs. "I think maybe we ought to continue our walk before we get too carried away by your cowboy ways."

As she started to rise, Cassie glanced down at the grass and squealed, "Look what I found."

In her open palm, she held a four leaf clover. She felt her cheeks flush. "This is very special, Clint." Her voice cracked. "This is like receiving a blessing from the universe."

"I can tell," he replied "Guess if I didn't know you were Irish before, I would now."

A sudden chilly breeze picked up off the lake and Cassie, dressed in tank top and shorts, shuddered. She closed her eyes. She felt Clint's strong arm pull her into the protection of his warm body. She wondered if somewhere out there someone was trying to tell her something about her future. Certainly, her dad had spun many a tale to her as a child about the portent of four leaf clovers.

An Irish melody played a forlorn amorous tune in her head. How much longer could she refrain from inviting him to her bed? That would simply add more complications to an already uneasy relationship. He had responsibilities, and so did she.

Days sped by. Cassie and Clint spent much of that time together preparing their horses, talking about everything under the sun, learning more about each other, yet dancing around their own personal issues. Clint had come to the farm to see Hope one last time before heading back to Utah. He'd fly back the next morning, leaving his truck, trailer, and his horses in Cassie's care.

He watched her galloping Hope on the dirt oval behind the barn. What a sight. Did she have any idea what kind of picture she presented racing the chestnut filly full tilt with waves of rich auburn hair flowing in the wind over her back?

Clint moved out to greet her when she brought the horse to a halt and leaped off her back. "She sure looks ready. You've got her right where she needs to be a week before a race. You're good, O'Hanlon."

Was she flushed from her ride, or were those reddening cheeks caused by his words?

"I'm glad you think so," Cassie said, dismounting, "since you're entrusting the four horses you brought out here into my care. I'd like to think that's about more than friendship. God knows I've got the time. You know we lost five out of eight horses to other trainers when I was in Wyoming. Owners don't have much patience, particularly with a female trainer."

"I've got a lot of patience," said Clint, huskily, "especially with one particular female trainer."

166

"Yeah, I've noticed," she quipped, placing her palms on his chest, fixing her eyes on his. "Maybe we should do something special tonight. Go to a nice restaurant. Then back to your hotel and see what develops." Her eyes snapped with invitation. "Abstaining from making love was probably not a very good idea on my part."

"Ms. trainer, I accept whatever you have in mind. The race is in your hands. Very capable hands, I might add," he whispered, pulling her to him and rubbing his face through her hair. Damn, he loved her scent.

- o -

Later that evening, Cassie lay nude on the bed in Clint's room at the Palmer House, basking in the afterglow of raw lovemaking. They'd waited so long the buildup had nearly overwhelmed both of them. As soon as they'd entered the room, they'd attacked each other like two animals in heat. An inner smile warmed her body. They'd fucked...really fucked, hard and fast.

After catching their breath, she knew they'd be more sensuous, in some ways more intimate, and much more scary. Now that they'd worked off the tension from waiting, from denying themselves, he'd make love to her.

She inhaled slowly and cast her gaze about the luxurious space. A perfect setting for lovemaking. The decor was exquisite; she wasn't accustomed to such luxury. She could hardly remember their

167

dinner. It had been laden with erotic suggestion from the leg of lamb to the cherry tart. Both of them played the game and played it very well. Most precious was the adoration in her lover's eyes when he visually caressed every inch of her, anticipating that moment when he'd strip her and make her his again.

Lazily, she ran her fingers through his thick black hair as he leisurely explored her body with his. She loved the feel of his skin pressed against hers, that simple touch, so filled with promise.

"You have the most sensitive nipples," Clint murmured. He caressed first one taut nipple and then the other.

"Um," she breathed, thrilling at his caress, anticipating more. She arched her back, encouraging him to continue.

Extending a finger, he pressed one hardened nodule inward and smiled as it popped immediately back at him.

She shivered as his finger arched toward the other nipple.

"I love the way they bounce back, like they've a mind of their own. Pink on white. One of my favorite color combinations." Clint covered one breast with the palm of his hand while tenderly licking the underside of the other.

"They're not the largest tits," she said, her voice shaking, "but they sure do love to be played with."

"And I love playing with them. Damn, if those nips get any longer..."

Cassie flexed her lower abs as a stirring of latent energy began deep within her loins. She didn't know how her breasts could be so directly connected to her pussy, but there was no doubt about the connection. And Clint had found it.

Back and forth he went, delicately tongue-washing first one breast and then the other. Gently, he rolled a nipple between thumb and forefinger. Cassie again scrunched upward, seeking more attention for each breast. She watched him place a thumb on one rosy button and a pinky on the other. Lazily, he rotated each first clockwise and then counterclockwise. She moaned. The erotic torture sent more chills to her loins.

She rolled away, regaining ownership of her breasts. His tongue grazed her spine. She waited for the thunder within her body to complete its coursing from head to foot, from tits to loins, from eyes to fingertips. Clint's lips against her back assured her that he'd patiently await her return. There was no hurry. Conversely, the strong arousal pressing against her thigh was less calm, more urgent.

"That was amazing," she whispered, not sure he'd hear her.

"I've never been with a woman who orgasms when only playing with her breasts. You're amazing."

"Hmm. Like I said, my tits may not be huge, but they are incredibly sensitive. And," she guided his hand to her mound, "they are directly wired to my pussy."

"Damn, woman, you're sopping wet."

She chuckled. "What did you expect, Einstein? First, you fuck me senseless, then you tease my nipples, making me scale a virtual wall of sensations. I hope you don't think we're done for the night."

"That thought never crossed my mind."

Turning in his arms to face him, she felt as if her soul opened for him. She couldn't foresee the future, but at least in the moment, this was right. There was no doubt about that. Cassie kissed her lover's throat. She moved lower, flicking her tongue at each of his nipples until they tightened, reflecting the same kind of intensity hers had.

Straddling him, she took her time. She teased him by playing with her hair. Long wavy strands provided a see through veil for her nipples. Like an artist, she created a sensual picture. His appreciation for her display was evident in his smile and in his erection pressing against her bottom.

Neither partner hurried. This might be their last time together for quite a while. His eyes had a dreamy allure to them. Cassie tried to match his patience, but she was afraid if they put off the inevitable much longer, she would come unglued.

"You," Cassie chided, "like a woman to lose control don't you?"

"Of course, don't you like it?"

"More than I could ever say. It's just that I'm not sure you should take so much pleasure in my pleasure," she responded, pursing her lips. Her finger traced invisible lines from each nipple thorough his navel to a path of crinkling sable hair leading to the object of her keen interest.

Cassie rose to her knees and with one hand guided him to her entrance. Bit by bit, she sank down on his length. At last she had him fully encased in her heat. "You like?"

He nodded. "Oh, yeah. You're one hot woman. This could never become routine."

As if astride her favorite horse, she rode him, comfortable with her seat. She maintained a steady pace. Clint didn't move a muscle, letting her control their mating. She pulled on her nipples and maintained a steady tempo.

Clint grew taut beneath her. His groans fueled her concentration. She bore down with complete focus.

"Oh, god," he groaned. "Don't stop. Whatever you do."

"No chance of that, cowboy." She slowed her pace. "Got you right where I want you."

"Jesus, woman. Don't slow, either." He began to buck beneath her.

"And I thought you were so patient." She rose as high as she could without losing him and dropped down, slapping her bottom against his thighs, driving him deeper into her interior.

"Yes, that's it," Clint howled. "I'm coming."

In gleeful triumph Cassie rode on as he filled her until she was overtaken by her own pulsing convulsions. Boneless, without muscle, with no one in control, Cassie collapsed against his torso.

Sated, filled, Cassie basked in the afterglow of shared heat. Their comingled juices oozed from her while she lay cradled in his arms. Could this be love? Her eyes popped wide open. Fortunately, his were closed and did not witness the fright that must have been evident in hers.

She stayed the night.

Forgoing much sleep, they'd made love twice more during the night and wee early morning hours. Now they tarried over a late breakfast at O'Hare Field waiting for Clint's flight. Cassie had lost her appetite somewhere between the bed and O'Hare. What to do with him? He wanted more of a road map than she had available. How far would he push her? How long would he wait?

"So where do we go from here?" Clint asked.

Cassie averted her eyes. "I wish I knew."

"You got to know, woman, my feelings run deep for you. It's not just great sex."

"It is pretty good, isn't it?"

"Pretty good? Bullshit, you've never been so well loved, and neither have I. Let's stop kidding ourselves about that."

Cassie felt her face go pale. Picking up a fork, she murmured, "I know. But there's more to a long term relationship than even sensational sex."

He nodded, but said nothing, keeping his gaze on her face.

Damn, he wasn't going to give her any slack. "I have so many unknowns—I can't predict how they'll all fit together." She watched carefully for his reaction. "I'm not sure I'm ready to be with just one man. I don't know what I want to do with my career. I've got my dad to worry about. There's Hope." Could she say what she was most frightened of? She closed her eyes and opened them quickly. "I don't know if I can be an instant mother."

Clint covered her hand with his, a serious expression on his face. "Thanks for letting me know all that. You're right, there's a lot to work through. Just so you know, I think you'd be a great mother."

He paused. "It's like putting a puzzle together. We know how some of the pieces will fit. Others will fall into place as we go. The question is, are we willing to take the puzzle off the shelf and work at it?"

Cassie studied the placemat, trying to calm her nerves. She couldn't give him all he desired, but she sure wasn't ready to let him go. At least not yet.

Meeting Clint's gaze, she said, more calmly than she thought possible, "Okay. I'll agree for us to open the puzzle box together and see what we can build. To explore. But if either of us wants to set the puzzle aside and go our separate ways, then we need to say so up front, directly, with integrity. And no pressure. I don't want to get hurt again."

Clint's features softened for the first time since they'd sat down. "I accept those ground rules. I don't want anybody in all of this to be hurt. We both know there are more people involved in this than the two of us. I'll be in touch with you daily, and I'll be back as soon as I can.

Checking his watch, Clint frowned. "I hate to do it, but I've got a plane to catch. I'm going to miss you. Hope all goes well with the filly."

"Me, too." Cassie gave him a half smile. "And I'll miss you very much, Mr. Travers. Having decided to peek at the puzzle, I don't want you to take the box and go home with it."

He chuckled, rubbing his palms together thoughtfully. "I think we both have access to the puzzle pieces, together or alone."

CHAPTER EIGHT

A heavy mist hung over the mile long oval. Cassie could see the exercise rider working Clint's four year old gelding when they were on the near side of the track, but when they rounded the clubhouse turn and headed into the backstretch, horse and rider disappeared into the thick fog. Even then she could hear the rider clucking to his mount.

Normally such a gray morning would have taken her on a mystical journey back to Ireland. She'd been there only once as a small girl, with her aunt, but she would never forget the blending of slate gray and emerald green on those thick, soggy mornings. But not this day. Cassie sighed, seemingly weighed down by the fog and her troubles.

When Cassie left the farm at 4:30 a.m., Hope looked as fit as ever. Her race was only three days off. Cassie worried whether she could really prepare her well enough at the farm. Certainly other trainers did the same with flighty horses, but this would be something new for Hope.

Could she protect the horse from whoever wanted to do her harm? Could she figure out who was at the bottom of all of this?

Cassie took a deep breath. Hope was only part of her worry. What about *him*? Could she really open herself up to that kind of potential pain? She felt a knot develop in her stomach—she wasn't ready to lose him.

But two instant kids? How could she ever be a caring mother? She'd never had one. And what else would he ask of her—what about her career? Could she give up her life? Cassie shook her head. "That's got to be too melodramatic," she muttered. "My life would change; it wouldn't be over."

Hell, he might change his mind and not even come back. All she had to offer him was a set of insurmountable problems.

Hearing footsteps, Cassie glanced over her shoulder to see Ed Harrington striding toward her. His jaw was set firmly and determination shone in his eyes. Now what?

"Well, what a surprise. You're alone. Did your cowboy sleep in?"

Reining in her temper, she responded evenly, "No, he had to return to Utah."

"So when the going gets tough, he runs back to the ranch."

"Clint has other responsibilities," Cassie said, her back stiffening.

"I'll just bet he has," Harrington said, as if he knew a secret.

She glared at the man a long moment and then demanded, "What do you mean by that?"

"Nothing." He shrugged innocently. She knew he mocked her.

"What Clint Travers does or what I do is none of your business. I don't know why you should care one way or the other."

"No need to get bent out of shape," Harrington countered softly. "I'm just not sure I trust the guy."

"And who asked you?" The nerve of him. She was getting very tired of men looking out for her welfare.

"Did you ever have the horse checked by a vet? And I do care about what happens to you, whether you think so or not." Harrington leaned against the rail. Staring into the mist, he asked quietly, "Are you certain it's not Travers who's drugging your horse?"

His words hung like heavy blankets, suffocating the air between them.

Cassie stood flabbergasted; her mouth fell open. At last she stammered, "You've got to be kidding. He's never even been around when Hope had a bad race."

"Doesn't have to be. He's got money doesn't he?"

She nodded.

"Anybody with money can buy a guy to drug a horse or throw a race."

"Clint wouldn't do that!" she said. "He likes the horse. He doesn't have horses running against her here. There would be no reason."

She was annoyed that her own voice had faltered when uttering that last statement.

"Listen to yourself," Harrington said. "No reason? Humph, he wants you. That's reason enough. Without a successful contender, you'd be out of the horse training business in a minute. And our cowboy could ride in here and take away his damsel in distress without a lot of fuss and bother."

"Got it all figured out, don't you?" Cassie shoved away from the rail fence. "Well, I'm not buying it. It's too farfetched."

Ed Harrington didn't move. He just glowered into the rising fog.

"It could just as easily be you," Cassie said, going on the offensive. "You at least have horses running against me. You might think you have a better chance with me if Hope isn't a contender and if the blame can be cast on Clint."

Ed turned and faced her. "Fine," he said in a low, thick voice, "think what you want. For me, I don't trust a guy who runs out on a woman when she's in trouble."

Cassie placed a hand cautiously on his arm. "Ed, I am moved that you're trying to help. But I think you're absolutely wrong."

Letting out a deep breath, the tall trainer growled, "Okay, have it your way. Just don't forget what I said. You may not know who you can trust. I'll be watching, just in case."

Cassie heard Ed's last muffled words as he walked briskly away. She turned back to watch the first rays of sunshine filter through the mist, making thousands of shiny pinwheels out of the grayness. Try as she might, she could not prevent tears from sliding down her cheeks. Damn, she hated crying.

It couldn't be possible—what Harrington had suggested. Clint wouldn't do anything to deliberately hurt her or her horse. No way. She respected his loyalty to Lester and Samantha. If he had committed not to be away from them for more than a week or two at a time, then he needed to honor that commitment.

Was she only thinking with her heart? Cassie tried to massage the numbness from her brain. Was it possible he'd become so obsessed with her he'd do something so deceitful as drugging a horse?

She paused, trembling. Was Harrington simply trying to sow seeds of doubt and direct attention away from his own actions? Either way, she didn't like having to be suspicious about acquaintances, friends, and especially, her lover.

Who to trust? Even her dad had said it was just him and her. Cassie scuffed her foot in the dirt. Playing detective was not her idea of fun.

Damn, she wished Clint had stayed. But she was a big girl, competent and strong. She could do this. How could she stand up to six-foot-plus delinquents without batting an eye, and yet have her confidence blown away in the wind when it came to Clint Travers?

Travers. She cringed. What was really eating at her? Was it that emotion she didn't want to name? There was a difference between needing some good loving and needing love. Wasn't there?

- o -

"Louie."

"Yeah."

"Slow that filly down. Make sure she doesn't win."

"Again?"

"You heard me. Do it."

Louie glared at the phone and its annoying dial tone.

- o -

It was race day, again. Cassie's stomach churned like a clothes dryer. She'd done everything just the way she and Clint and her father had agreed to do.

She'd trailered the filly onto the track grounds two hours ahead of the race. Hope had never been out of her sight. No one had gotten close enough to touch the horse or her food. Of course, that had changed some in the paddock area.

Her assistant helped saddle the filly. And the paddock judge had to hold the horse's mouth open to read the tattoo on the inside of her lower lip, making sure it was the horse who'd been entered to run. And now she watched the jockey guide the horse onto the track, where he was met by an outrider.

That's it! Cassie gasped. It must be the outrider. Why hadn't they thought of that? She tried to watch closely. Reaching for her binoculars, she

180

quickly had the glasses focused on her horse. But even then, to her dismay, she wasn't always able to see the outrider's hands.

Had she gone to all that work protecting Hope only to have a nameless person, who blended into the track scenery so well that one seldom remembered they were there, bring her filly and their dreams down?

In contrast to her earlier walk from the barn to the paddock, Hope was not up on her toes. Her ears did not perk forward. Cassie could almost see the energy draining out of the horse. Something was wrong. There was no question about it. The horse had changed dramatically in the last five or ten minutes.

Someone somehow had gotten to her. Cassie put away the glasses. It was too late. Her balled fists ground into her thighs. Once again she'd let everyone down: her horse, her dad, herself, even Clint.

Why the hell wasn't he here?

The running of the race held no surprises. Hope ran a dismal sixth in a field of ten. Only able to pass a few tiring horses at the close of the race, Cassie's Hope did not appear to belong with these quality horses.

Dejected, Cassie led Hope back to the barn area to rub her down with alcohol and to give her some water before taking the defeated filly home. She desperately wanted to be back at the farm. She didn't want to talk to anyone at the track.

During the drive back to the farm, while she did her evening chores, and long afterward, Cassie railed at herself. She had failed. Maybe Harrington was right. Maybe she was in over her head.

Clearly, she wasn't good enough to train a horse and keep it safe from interference. Why had she ever left her secure social work world?

She wanted out. *Now!* To hell with six month agreements. Cassie paced wildly up and down the stable aisle muttering softly, cursing loudly, searching for a way out. Any way out.

If Cassie's Hope had a future, then someone else would have to step up and work with her.

Why the hell wasn't he here on the day she needed him most?

That's not fair. He has other responsibilities. She didn't want him to run out on his commitment to his kids. Her mother had done that—she didn't wish that on anyone, especially Lester and Sammy.

Cassie paused. Stepping into the small office tack room, she collapsed in the old swivel chair. Life seemed so confused. So cruel. Where did she fit?

In his arms.

No!

She laid her head on the desk and cried. Her body heaved and sighed. She had to make some decisions, and quickly. Things would be better if she could just be decisive.

Her father would be disappointed. Clint might be angry. But she had to regain some control over her life. She had to give up some of the baggage.

Mercifully, she drifted off to sleep.

Later that evening, Cassie slumped in the living room leather chair across from her father. He wasn't heaping blame on her. In some ways, that made matters worse. If he'd blame her, it would be easier to quit. Maybe she should get in her car and drive back to her apartment. She scowled. Even that wasn't an option — her sublease still had several months to go.

At least her dad acknowledged that Hope was probably doped again, although he didn't seem particularly moved by the outrider theory. He seemed more upset that his doctor forbade him from going to the track.

"Can't give up now, girl," he admonished, flashing an eyebrow at her. "We still have one more race before the Lincoln to smoke out the bastard who has it in for us."

Sinking further into the chair, Cassie nodded abjectly.

"Sort of wish Travers was here," Tug said, scratching his chin thoughtfully. "He's got a good head on his shoulders when it comes to deviousness. Wonder what he would make of this mess now?"

"I don't know." She hesitated. Should she share what she'd heard? "Ed Harrington thought maybe Travers was behind this whole thing, as a way to

183

get me to quit training and move out west with him."

"Humph. That's pure foolishness, if I've ever heard it."

"But..." Cassie struggled under a wave of mixed feelings. She had to say it. "He could certainly buy someone to do the job. What if I'm being played for a fool? You said yourself that it's only you and me we can trust."

She hadn't seen her father's eyes so sad since he was in the hospital. He shook his head. "I didn't mean to leave Clint out. Harrington is just trying to be a busybody and cause trouble where there's no reason for it."

"So you think we can really trust Travers?"

"Damn, love is blind." He laughed out loud.

She felt heat rise to her cheeks.

"Thinking Travers is the villain is ridiculous. You're mixing your personal stuff up with this. You're acting like some young green filly. You just don't want to trust your own gut."

Glaring at her father, Cassie sat up straight. "And what makes you such an expert on female-male relationships?"

He met her challenge with a cough and cackle. "I'm no expert about that stuff, and you know it, but I do know my own daughter fairly well."

"Yes, you do seem to know which buttons to push and which strings to pull." She rubbed the smooth leather arm of her chair. "I don't even know what I'm feeling. Something crazy is going on here."

She glanced over at his knowing look. "You're right, it's not all about horses."

"Promise me one thing, girl," he implored. "Don't give up on yourself. You've got too much grit in you to do that. You've got too much of me flowing through your veins to allow that to happen."

"You old sentimental egotist," Cassie chided with a giggle. She wasn't completely satisfied with staying on, but her dad had worked another of his miracles. He'd gotten her to laugh at herself and their situation. "I'll be okay. Don't you worry about that. The O'Hanlon fire hasn't burned out yet. We'll figure all of this out, one way or the other."

Sitting back in her chair, Cassie was pleased to see the relief in his eyes; she wished she was more certain of her own words. Who was right? Her father, or Harrington?

Could she truly trust Travers? From the beginning she'd questioned their relationship, but she'd never doubted Clint's integrity. Why now? Maybe her dad was right. Maybe she just had to trust her gut. But her gut was spinning in so many directions she sometimes felt like a top twirling out of control.

Get a grip, girl, there's a lot riding on your decisions over the next two weeks before Hope's next race. Now is not the time to panic. Now is not the time to cave in. Relationships would have to take a back seat.

In the small apartment loft over the stable,

Cassie sat on the bed with her back against pillows, sipping wine, pondering her future.

Surprisingly, talking with her father had helped lift her spirits. There was no way she'd allow herself to let him down. Six months she had agreed to, and six months it would be. But not a day more.

And he was right. There was no way Clint would betray her by sabotaging the horse. Furthermore, Hope had probably been drugged before she'd ever even met Clint. So why had she been so weak to even consider such a possibility? Was it a sign of how much he scared her? Damn Harrington, anyway.

It was good to hear her father express his confidence in her spunkiness and training skills.

But why did she feel splintered and ready to crumble? Nothing seemed clear. Nothing fit — whether it was evidence about the drugging problems, or her feelings about the handsome rancher from Utah. Perhaps there were too many puzzle pieces. Or maybe some trickster had stolen a key piece or two.

Cassie appreciated the simple pleasure of the flow of wine easing down her throat. Closing her eyes, she could envision that devilish look on Clint's face when he thought he knew something she didn't, or when he was about to play a trick on her. It was the same look she'd seen on Lester's face when he asked about being at their wedding.

Her cell phone rang, as she knew it would. She also knew who was calling at this hour.

"Hello," she said weakly. Her voice must sound like something disembodied coming from a dark cave.

Clint didn't hesitate. "Hello, Cassie. How are you? How was Hope today? How many lengths did she win by?"

Amazed at how many questions the normally quiet man could get off in one breath, Cassie answered somberly, "She didn't win. It happened again."

All was quiet on the other end of the line.

Finally, Clint said, "Tell me about it, Cass. What went wrong?"

She told him her story. It felt rote by now. That wasn't a bad feeling, given how the rest of her emotions were tumbling over themselves.

When she'd finished retelling the events of the day, she hugged her knees, pulling the extra-large Bears T-shirt down to her toes, waiting for his immediate analysis. To her surprise, there was none.

"I'm sorry, Cass." His voice cracked. "I'll be there next time we race. Maybe together we can figure this thing out. You did all anyone could do."

Cassie didn't know whether to laugh or cry. There was no accusation in his tone. No bravado suggesting that if he'd been there things would have gone differently. He seemed just as perplexed by the situation as she was.

"Dad wants to give Hope a little break, so we won't race her for three or four weeks. That will still give us two weeks before the Land of Lincoln."

"Good. She probably needs a rest. That'll give me time to get things in order here so I can be away. Not that I like the idea of being away from you that long."

"Do you have anything particular in mind to protect Hope?"

"Not yet," he allowed. "Don't know whether we can protect the horse, but I bet we'll find the bastard who's doing this."

His determination and confidence were reassuring, but she had her doubts. "If we don't catch him this time, it'll be too late for the Lincoln."

"I know. I think at the very least, we're going to have a number of eyes on that filly. Somebody is getting to her between the barn and the starting gate. That narrows things down a bit. So much for the horse. How are *you* doing, Cassidy?"

Cassie smiled at the concern caressing her ear. "I'm doing okay, now. Dad gave me an O'Hanlon pep talk. I'll survive. He wishes you were here, by the way."

"I do, too," was the immediate response. "What about you, Cass? Do you wish I was there?"

"Yes, I do. But," she confessed, "I'm not sure why."

"I'll get there three days before the next race. If I come much earlier, I'll need to be back here when you'll need me the most.

"I don't know about *need*," Cassie cautioned,

not willing to commit as much as he wanted to hear. "It will be good having you here race day. Another set of eyes can't hurt."

"I'd thought of bringing Lester and Sammy with me. Both of them have been arguing their case. They want to see Chicago. And they'd like to spend more time with you."

Had the room suddenly become smaller? Cassie found it difficult to breathe, never mind speak. Her muscles ached from fatigue. Those dark eyes, floating in her memory, were watching so intently — were they filled with accusation, with sadness, with laughter?

"Cass? Are you still there?"

"I'm here," she barely managed to mumble.

"Don't worry about the kids," he said cheerily. "They love you already. I won't bring them this time. If we're going to catch a crook or two, I don't want them in the middle of it."

This time. The words were imprinted on her brain. Would there be another time? Did she want another time? How could she be so afraid of two little kids? Because they could twist her heart just about as many ways as their father could.

"Cassidy?"

"Yes?"

"I'm not going to let you run away like some wild mustang, but I won't push you. I love your spirit the way it is. Please don't overanalyze us until there's nothing left."

"I'm trying hard not to," she said. "But you're so sure where things are headed, and I'm so uncertain. I don't see how it can work out."

"Just don't rush to that conclusion. That's all I ask."

"I won't, I promise...I have to go, Clint." Her voice wavered, surely giving away her emotional confusion. "I'll talk to you tomorrow."

"Okay. Oh, hold on. I almost forgot. Grandma has a message for you. She said *Tell the fire woman to trust only her heart. Not what she sees or hears. Only her heart.* Good-bye, Fire Woman. I miss you."

Cassie heard the distinct click at the other end of the line. She stared at the phone in her hand so long that it took the repetitive whine of the dial tone to bring her back to reality.

Listen only to her heart. That might be good advice for people who knew *how* to listen to their hearts. She was beginning to question her own ability to do so.

Then she smiled. How different was Clint's grandmother's advice from her own father's? She felt the blood stirring in her veins. That was Irish blood flowing. Certainly, the Irish could be counted on, when the chips were down, to listen to the heart. She'd never been afraid of passion before—but then, passion had never before threatened to unravel her entire life.

She'd be okay. She knew that. Now if she could only calm those feelings of lust. At that moment, she didn't want Clint Travers to be fifteen hundred miles away.

She wanted him right next to her, in her bed.

She wanted to feel his strong arms holding her, to feel his tongue licking her neck while he rolled a nipple between his thumb and finger. Cassie closed her eyes, welcoming the warmth flowing from her loins to her breasts. Even thinking of him had that effect.

But it wasn't enough. She needed to kiss his lips, to massage his taut muscles, to feel him responding to her need and to his own. Cassie's eyes popped wide open. Was this love? She sighed. "Maybe," she whispered, shivering, smiling weakly.

CHAPTER NINE

"It's been ages since we've been out here together," Silver Hawk said, glancing away from the expansive vista of high desert to eye her brother.

"Too long," Clint muttered, knowing his sister had much more on her mind than the beauty of the Utah landscape.

They'd ridden four miles from the ranch house to a place that had been special to them all their lives: Wild Horse Mesa. It was on this mesa table top where they'd shared dreams of places far away, of a horse ranch that would rival any, of a better life for their people. It was here where they'd come on special occasions to greet Great Spirit and to seek assistance when times were difficult.

"You're wondering if your fire woman could handle living out here, aren't you?"

Distracted from his remembering by her probing, Clint turned in his saddle to glare at his sister. The compassion evident in her eyes immediately eased his tension. They might be able to conceal their inner feelings from others, but seldom from one another. "I don't know. I don't think I could live in a big city all the time. I don't know about Cassidy—whether this ranch would be enough for her, whether she'd be satisfied here."

The woman frowned. "Have you asked her?"

"No. We haven't got that far. She's very wary about anything permanent. I think she's afraid she'll be like her mother, that she'd feel trapped and want to escape."

"That's a shame." Silver Hawk leaned over to pat her horse's neck. "But then maybe it's for the best. You two seem so different in so many ways. She's the sophisticated city person. A social worker, no less. That's all we need around here, another do-gooder."

Clint scowled.

"I'm sorry," Silver Hawk said, leaning over and placing a hand on his arm. "You know I can be too quick with my tongue, and too quick to judge." She paused. "From what mom and grandmother say, she sounds like a delightful person who may be just what you need. And Lester and Sammy can't stop talking about the red haired woman who read them bedtime stories. And she does seem to know horses."

"Yeah, better than she thinks." Clint noticed their mounts swishing tails at buffalo gnats and shifting weight comfortably from foot to foot, taking advantage of their respite. "There are moments when I believe she's the strongest woman I've ever met, and then there are times when she sells herself way too short. Like now, she seems to think she's totally responsible for failing to achieve her father's dream."

Clint relayed the saga of Cassie's Hope trying

to run while drugged.

"That's terrible. Who would do such a thing to a horse—and to an old man? And why?"

"I've never been so torn," Clint said. "I want to be with her to do what I can about the filly, and to convince her we have a future together. But I promised Lester and Sammy I wouldn't be away large chunks of time, especially in the summer."

"Why not take them with you? That's about all they can talk about. Going to Chicago. Seeing Ms. Cassidy in her place."

Clint chuckled. "I think they've lobbied everyone in the family. I'd take them, if it weren't for having to play cops and robbers. Thought about asking mom to go along with them, but she'd be like a fish out of water, and I doubt she'd consider leaving Grandmother at this time anyway."

"Of course not." His sister scrunched her face in several directions before continuing. "You haven't asked me."

"You? Why, you never leave the high desert. You don't even like her," Clint said, his eyes narrowing.

"Hah. I never said I didn't like her. I'm just doubtful it will work between the two of you. But I may be wrong. Certainly the kids want to go. And it's not like I've just stayed down on the reservation. I spent two years," she said, holding up two fingers, "if you will remember, at Berkeley. The city isn't a world that I want to make my own, but I can manage in it. Well, at least for a short periods.

"If this thing is going to work between you two," Silver Hawk continued, "the family is going to be a large part of it. Are you afraid I'll scare her away?"

"No, it's not that. I just never thought..."

"Sometimes you do too much thinking," she interrupted, "and quite often, your assumptions are totally wrong. So, what will it be? Will you take me along to Chicago? Or are you going to mope around here and make all our lives miserable?"

Clint shrugged, taking his time to observe a bald eagle soaring off to the east. "Okay, little sister, we'll see how you like the Windy City. But you are to keep a close eye on the kids. The more I think about it, we may be able to use you to lay a trap for whoever's drugging Hope. And I want you to watch your tongue around Cassie."

"Is that all, Master?" Silver Hawk pulled on the rim of her hat, trying unsuccessfully to conceal a smile.

- o -

While filling a water tank for the three yearling colts, Cassie heard the approach of a car coming down the long farm driveway. It was the Thursday morning after Hope's most recent loss. She wasn't expecting anyone; she didn't think her father was, either.

The rising sun blinded her, preventing her from

identifying their visitors. Shading her eyes, she saw a fairly new maroon sedan stop at the house. A man and woman were in the front seat. The first door to open, however, was a back door, and out tumbled two children, behaving as if they had been trapped inside for days.

Cassie's hand flew to her throat. The boy and girl running down the path to the barn suddenly skidded to a stop some thirty feet away to stare at her. Each looked shyly to her for some kind of recognition. Each had ebony hair. Each was dressed in jeans and a blue shirt and wore western boots.

Instinctively, Cassie went to her knees and held out her arms wide. Sammy and Lester raced to her beaming large smiles.

Hugging the children to her, Cassie tried to forestall the tears forming in her eyes. "My goodness," she said, "what a surprise! I didn't know you were coming."

"We just got here," Samantha explained, brushing a small hand across Cassie's cheek. "We flew on a big plane. We slept in a fancy hotel last night. I wanted to call you, but Daddy wouldn't let me."

"You wanted to spoil the surprise," Lester hissed, poking his sister. "We wanted to surprise you." The boy laced his fingers in Cassie's hair.

"Well, you certainly did that," Cassie agreed nodding. "My, I think you have both grown since I last saw you.

"Me, most," Sammy squealed.

"Now, I don't know about that," interjected a deep male voice. "Why don't you both stand up and let Ms. O'Hanlon breathe?"

Cassie closed her eyes briefly and took a deep breath before peering up into Clint Travers' dark face. His eyes were hooded, indecipherable.

"It's good to see you, Cassidy," he said, breaking the stiff silence.

Standing, she swallowed a laugh, recognizing his discomfort at being with her around his kids. He didn't know what to do with her. Well, why had he brought them, then?

Movement on the path caught Cassie's attention. She'd forgotten there was a woman in the car. At first she didn't recognize the stunning young female approaching them. Then Cassie felt a chill creep through her body as she recognized Silver Hawk, Clint's sister.

The tall, dark-haired woman dressed in a long denim skirt, white blouse with a turquoise necklace and belt reflected an understated beauty that made Cassie immediately jealous. The woman could have stepped right out of an ad for the southwest. Absently, Cassie brushed at the dirt on her jeans and faded blue work shirt. She remained wary as the other woman approached.

Reaching them, Silver Hawk offered a hand in friendly fashion. "Hi, Cassie. We were never formally introduced. I wasn't having a very good day when you were at the ranch. I hope there will be no hard feelings between us."

Surprised by the woman's directness, Cassie

responded quickly, although coolly, "Of course not. I'm just surprised to see you here." Looking around at all the faces, she said, "All of you, for that matter."

Silver Hawk stifled a grin. Turning to her brother she said, "Why don't I take the kids on a tour of the barn? Appears to me, big brother, you have some tall explaining to do. I believe this Irish lass is about to go on the warpath. And while I would love to stay and watch, it's probably best for little ears to be somewhere else."

"Funny. Funny. Yeah, take them through the barn. They'll probably find some cats to make friends with. Run along now," Clint ordered.

"But we just got to see her," Sammy complained.

Lester muttered, "Aw shucks," then grabbed his sister's hand and dashed toward the hidden treasures of an unexplored barn, with Silver Hawk trotting along behind them.

Once she saw the children were out of earshot, Cassie wheeled on the Utah rancher. "Now what are you up to? You said you wouldn't bring Lester and Sammy because of the situation with Hope. You didn't give me any warning, Clint Travers. You agreed to no pressure. Can't you let things take a natural course?"

He moved to her and pulled her to his chest. Cassie pounded his shoulders with open palms and then shuddered. It felt so good to be in his arms again. She loved his touch, his smell. Her head cleared. She sighed. She did enjoy the strength and the comfort this man brought to her life, but damn if she would be smothered or led down some devious pathway to bliss. Not that there was anything wrong with bliss—she just didn't want to be tricked into it.

"I didn't mean to startle you or burden you," Clint whispered. "No tricks. No pressure. This is the only way I could be with you. And I couldn't wait any longer."

Cassie moved back from their embrace, holding each of his hands in hers. She saw only honesty in his face. His ways might not be entirely her ways, but there was no trickery taking place.

Clint tried to explain. "Lester and Sammy wanted to see you again, like I said on the phone. I thought maybe my mom might be able to come."

Cassie shook her head. That would not have been a good idea.

"Then my sister volunteered."

"But she doesn't like me."

"That's not true," Clint corrected. "She doesn't know you, and she's is very protective of her family. I hope you'll try to accept her. Silver Hawk only wants what's best for her loved ones."

"We'll see," Cassie replied, realizing she didn't sound very convincing. "Why do I have this gnawing feeling in my gut that you're crowding me?" She glanced away, then turned back toward him. "I feel things for you I have never felt for any man, but I don't want to be stampeded."

"I don't want to rush you or me," Clint agreed. "But I'm convinced our destinies are intertwined and we will be together. I know that as certainly as I know that the sun will rise tomorrow."

Cassie stepped back and struggled to get hold of her feelings. "You're convinced? You're certain. Well, I'm not." She hated the hint of a smirk on his face.

"And don't think bringing the kids here is going to sway me. To my way of thinking, a man and a woman have to work out their relationship before being a family."

Clasping her hands tightly at her waist, Cassie continued, "I won't be railroaded into anything. Don't push me. Or I just might give you all the puzzle pieces back."

"Cool your fires some, lady," Clint said, none too gently. "I'm not pushing you. Just because I'm certain about the end doesn't mean I'm not a patient man. But you've got to realize that from my culture, family is very important. I wouldn't consider marrying a woman without having a good idea about how she'll connect with my children and the rest of the family. I'm not just one person in this relationship. I bring with me many others."

Cassie nearly collapsed under his intensity. "I'm sorry," she muttered, "I didn't mean to suggest the children aren't important. They're very important, and incredibly lovable."

She swallowed hard. She glanced toward the house. She struggled to hold herself in place. Family. What did she really know about being a family? Damn, she hated that word. She looked at

Clint, patiently waiting for her to say something. She shivered.

"I guess," she said, brushing a tear from the corner of an eye, "maybe I don't know much about family. We didn't have much of one. Yet Dad did the best he could, I know he did."

Then the tears flowed freely and she moved into her lover's arms. She didn't want to be pushed, but neither did she want to shove him away.

"He did a great job with you," said Clint, over her muffled sobs. "And this isn't some sort of test. The kids…my family already love you. They just want you to know them better."

"Even your sister?" Cassie chuckled against his shirt.

"She'll come around. You can trust me on that."

- o -

Clint appreciated Tug's beaming smile as he clasped Cassie's father's hand in greeting.

"I see you're back, young man. Couldn't stay away from my daughter, huh?"

"You're right about that," Clint confided, "but I also thought maybe you could use some help protecting the filly."

The older man led Clint to a group of lawn chairs in the yard. Cassie and Silver Hawk were raiding the refrigerator for pop. The day was too hot to remain inside. It pleased Clint to see Tug getting around better. Unsteady, but better.

"So who are these little ones, Clint?" Tug asked, after catching his breath.

Calling his children over to them, Clint announced, "I'm proud to introduce you to my kids, Lester and Sammy. Kids, this is Mr. O'Hanlon, Cassie's father."

"Just call me Tug," he said, reaching for the boy's hand. "So what do you two do for fun?"

"I ride as fast as the wind," Lester boasted. "And I catch toads and frogs down by the creek."

"Do you catch toads and frogs, too?" the old man asked Sammy, helping her settle on his knee.

"No," she warbled. "I play with my dolls and I chase the boys...I'm fast...and I ride my pony...he's not so fast." She paused and ran her finger pads across Tug's face. "You have wrinkles like my grandmother. But she doesn't have whiskers."

The old man howled. "You're something, little girl. I bet you can wrap Cassie right around your finger.

"Oh, no. Fire Woman lives too far away from me. Do you think she will want to live with me?"

Swallowing hard, Tug smiled at the girl. "I don't rightly know. She'll have to decide about that, but I can't imagine anyone not wantin' to live with you. And what did you call my daughter?"

"Fire Woman. That's the name my grandmother gave to her. She thinks Fire Woman is a good name for Ms. O'Hanlon, because her hair catches fire when the light shines on it."

"Sounds like your grandmother is a wise

woman. My daughter has a lot of fire, that's for sure."

Becoming very serious, Sammy responded, "I bet you're a wise man, too. I think that's what wrinkles mean."

Tug laughed again, but before he could utter another word his young new friend hopped off his lap and dashed toward the house. Cassie and Silver Hawk were coming down the steps with trays of drinks and food.

"Sorry, Tug, my kids aren't very shy," Clint said. "Good to see you getting some color back."

"They're good kids. The girl's observant. That's good. And she's already learning how to chase boys." Tug's eyes filled with mirth. "She'll turn many a head as she gets older. You can count on that."

"Right."

It hardly took a moment for both kids to refuel and then dash toward the barn to continue exploring, after Tug had agreed to show Lester a good place near the house to look for frogs some evening, and Sammy had gotten him to agree to spend some time meeting the dolls she'd brought along but had left at the hotel.

"Well, Dad, what do you think? Cassie asked. Clint and his family had just left for their hotel. The house was suddenly very ordinary and quiet. The chatter had stopped. No more jokes. No more questions.

Her dad had told more stories than she thought

he knew. Sammy had been able to nuzzle right into a small corner of his chair. If the young girl was not off exploring, she was chattering non-stop with Tug. Cassie hadn't seen her father so freely energized for a very long time. Laughter must truly be good for the soul.

And Lester spent a considerable amount of time cataloging her riding trophies in his mind. He wanted to hear the story behind each of them. Silver Hawk had remained rather quiet, but obviously took in everything that was happening. Cassie knew Clint was pleased. He was proud of his children, and rightly so.

But they did need a mother.

Her father answered. "What do I think? It was a fine meal. The day was hot, but not as muggy as yesterday."

"Dad! What about Clint, Lester, Sammy, Silver Hawk? What do you think about them?"

"Oh, them." Tug's lips twitched. "They're quite a family. They can laugh together. That little one is a real jewel. She'll turn some fellow's heart someday." He paused, his eyes twinkling. "Seriously, Cass, there's no question they love you. And you're good with them. But do you love him? Is he the man you want to chase dreams with?"

Not waiting for her reply, he continued, "Because if you do, then tell him. It's a lot easier chasing dreams when you have a partner to share ups and downs."

"Thanks," said Cassie, bending to kiss her

father's cheek. "There's another person in Clint's family I'd like you to meet someday — his grandmother. Somehow, I think the two of you have much in common. Both of you are romantic philosophers."

It thrilled her to see the gleam in her father's eye. Being around the kids had been good for him.

Would he talk to her now about a pain they both shared deeply? It mattered; she knew it did. How could she even think about becoming an instant mother without ever having had one?

She took a deep breath and let it out slowly. "Tell me about her. Why didn't she want to be my mother?" Her throat constricted. She watched her father's eyes cloud over; his fingers automatically clenched.

"Why are you asking after all these years?" He gasped for air.

Alarmed, Cassie said, "I don't want to hurt you, Dad. We don't have to talk about her."

"No. No, you're right, we've got to talk about her. It's way past time. I think I understand why, now. You're not like her, Cass." He sighed deeply, no doubt thinking back to a much earlier time. "When you were little, there wasn't much we could tell you other than your mother wouldn't be coming back. Your aunt thought it best if we just ignored the past and moved on. That was easier for me, too. Looking back, I'm not sure it was best for you."

"You did what you thought was best. I'm not questioning that. I just want to know more about

206

her. I've only seen one picture of her. How did you meet? What did she want out of life?" Cassie's voice cracked. "Did she love me?"

"Ah, in her own way, she loved you very much," Tug responded. "Maybe she didn't know how to love you better. Maybe I should have done more to help her.

"I thought I would be a bachelor until I met your mother. I was almost twice her age. She was young and pretty.

"I never knew why she thought I was such a good catch. Guess she was runnin' from a home life that wasn't good. They expected her to raise her younger brothers and sisters, and there was a slew of 'em. Abigail did most of the diaperin' and cookin'. Her father was some kind of a traveling salesman. I seldom saw him. Her mother seemed more hooked on soap operas than anything else."

"That sounds like a harsh existence." Cassie absently twirled strands of hair around her fingers.

"Yeah, I imagine my lifestyle of haulin' from track to track was romantic at first. We had a whirlwind relationship. Two months after we met, we got married. A month later she was pregnant with you. And then reality sank in. For both of us.

"She stayed with me on the road until she was six months along. Then I brought her back here. Your aunt watched over her like a hawk. I don't expect Abigail liked that one bit. You were born, and for a while she seemed thrilled with you and with the family."

"So what went wrong? What happened to drive her away?"

Tug stared at Cassie's trophies on the shelf. "I'm not sure what to tell you. I knew she was gettin' more and more unhappy. She made sure she didn't get pregnant again. She said she didn't want so many kids around her that she'd feel like a slave, yet she still seemed to care for you."

"Well, something must have soured her on me."

Tug continued on as if he hadn't heard her. "Whatever glamour she found travelin' with me on the road quickly faded. She didn't like stayin' here by herself. There was no one to run interference with your aunt. Both women had red-hot tempers.

"The downhill slide started slowly, I think. But the spark that first sizzled so hot between Abigail and me turned as cold as black ice." Tug paused, then added softly, "I got word from your aunt that Abigail would bring you down to the living room or kitchen to leave with her, and then be gone for hours. Then it was days. Sometimes she'd come back drunker than a skunk. Then she'd forget to even to tell Lizzy she was leaving. First your aunt would know about it was hearin' you screamin' from your upstairs bedroom."

Cassie's jaw dropped. "I didn't know."

"You were too young to remember, thank goodness. I tried to get through to her, but she said I loved my horses more than her. I don't know, maybe she was right...She was so young and beautiful. You have her beauty, you know? Finally, she just disappeared." He choked on his emotion. "I don't know why she left, but I'm so glad she didn't take you with her."

Cassie moved to hold her father's hands. "I didn't mean to put you through a lot of pain, making you remember like that."

"It's okay. We should have talked about it years ago. But you didn't ask. And I wasn't about to bring it up on my own. But Cassie..." He looked at her a long time, as if he wanted to touch her soul. "You certainly have your mother's blood in your veins as well as my own. You have her beauty, no doubt about that. But you have so much more than she did. You give of yourself freely. You can be patient, even in spite of that fiery temper of yours."

Cassie nodded, watching through teary eyes, waiting while he put together what he wanted her to hear.

"You will make a super mother. Hell, you've been a mother to all those delinquent kids at the group home. Lester and Sammy could never find a better mother. If you love the man, don't let your mother stand in the way of your dreams. She had her own and chased them in her own way. Now it's your turn."

The morning chores at the track were finished. Driving back to the farm, Cassie clutched the steering wheel of the pickup tightly and glanced over at her passenger. Clint seemed engrossed with the passing billboards. She figured by this time she should be able to read him fairly well, yet she felt like she hardly knew him. He volunteered little about himself and responded to her questions with adequate but certainly not revealing answers.

"So what was it like growing up on the reservation?"

Clint turned and looked at her blankly. "Huh?"

"What was growing up like for you? You know that I bounced from track to track and that my mother walked out on us when I was young. You know that my aunt filled in the best she could. But I hardly know a thing about your childhood. I like your mom and grandmother a lot."

"Not much to tell." Clint shrugged. "I didn't grow up on the reservation, although much of my social life revolved around it. I had my share of bad and good. My sister and I were well loved." Clint smiled. "My Mom is such a great cook it's amazing I'm not roly-poly. Grandmother made sure we learned the *old ways,* as she put it. I did the vision quest thing and learned about my place in the grand scheme of things."

"So what about your father? How did your mom and dad meet?"

Clint's features clouded. He turned away again to watch the Chicago suburbs whiz by. "My father was a geologist with one of the gas and oil companies sent in to determine whether it would be profitable for the tribe to drill. He fell in love with the high desert plateau."

Cassie nodded. She could understand that.

"The story goes that he met my mother at a community dance. And theirs was a fantasy courtship. Love at first sight, both said." He grimaced, shifting his weight in the seat. "That might have been true for them, but not for their families."

"They didn't like the idea of them marrying."

Clint laughed bitterly. "That's putting it mildly. His parents threatened to disown him if he married beneath his station. Her family warned her of all kinds of bad happenings if she married outside her race."

"But they ignored family threats and advice?"

"Yeah, to everyone's dismay. They ran off to Reno and married."

After prolonged silence, Cassie asked, "So what happened then?"

"My mother's family came to accept my father with reluctance, but at least they accepted him."

"And your father's?" Cassie kept her eyes on the road, but listened closely.

"Well, let's put it this way. I've never met any grandparents or any other relative on that side of the family. Don't even know if any of them are still alive."

Cassie cringed. "That's terrible. I'm so sorry."

"Yeah, guess we both know something about rejection."

"But did your father grow to resent his adopted family?"

"No, not in the least. I think it might have been

211

a relief for him to get away from his own. He became quite successful with the ranch and with the stock market. His knowledge about oil and gas put him in an excellent position to take advantage of the oil crisis and down markets of the early seventies. He was well positioned when things bounced back. Very well positioned. That's when he started dabbling in race horses, first quarter horses and then thoroughbreds.

"It was a natural progression, I guess. We'd always had horses. I rode in front of one of my parents long before I could walk. There were always reservation horse races and rodeos to take part in. My sister and I have taken the horseracing business much further than Dad ever envisioned, but he got us started."

"And he died young."

"Yeah. The doctor said it was a sudden heart attack." Clint's voice faltered. "Nothing could've been done."

"And you miss him."

"So what do you think Lester and Sammy have cajoled out of your father this morning? They're experts at getting people to do things they never intended."

"They sure are." Cassie peeked over at him. His cheek muscles remained taut. The conversation about his father was concluded. What had he left out?

"So how much money should I bet when Hope runs next?" Ashton Brookings asked. "Are we still

212

playing cops and robbers?"

Clint gave Cassie a questioning look before responding in a low tone. "I wouldn't suggest betting the house."

He'd immediately liked Cassie's long time friend. The woman's dark chocolate skin nearly glowed and her refreshing humor seemed to be without bounds. He knew her questions were in jest, but a cafe near the racetrack where most of the regular Friday lunch crowd had some connection with the track or the backside was hardly the place to discuss or joke about playing detective or wondering about who was conspiring to throw races or drug horses.

Beside him, Cassie flinched and shook her head sadly. Clint brushed her shoulder with his.

"We still don't know about the other," Cassie whispered in hushed tones, tipping her head toward nearby folks.

"Oh," said Ashton, glancing around at the other tables, "sorry, I didn't think about being overhead. I'm generally more careful." She picked at her salad briefly before asking, "So tell me, Clint, about Utah. I've never been there. Is it as conservative as we hear?"

"I doubt the state will break any liberalism records," Clint began. "No casinos. No betting. There are folks who believe it's their responsibility to look out for the morality of others. Yet there's much more diversity than many expect to find. While there are very few blacks, there is a strong Chicano community. And of course my people were present in the area long before any white man made it across the mountains. Do you like mountains?"

"Sure," Ashton said. "I've been to the Smokies, and to the Green Mountains of Vermont. I haven't traveled west yet."

"Then you haven't seen mountains yet." Clint chuckled. "Many of our peaks are snowcapped until the middle of summer. The fall can be spectacular when the color line creeps down the cliffs and the draws. If you like canyons, we have plenty. If you like desert, we have a lot of that, too. You know what I miss most, though, is being able to see for as far as the eye can see."

"It's expansive," Cassie chimed in. "I felt like my eyeballs were going to stretch and burst. It didn't seem like anything stood in the way to stop them from straining."

Clint chased ketchup across his plate with a French fry. "So you're a social worker like Cass?"

"Yeah, I work with kids getting into trouble with the law. Your world sounds like another planet to me," Ashton said. "I'd like to get some of our project kids to see something like that. They think their world ends four blocks in any direction."

"The place may look quite different, but we share the same problems," he confided. "I work with some of the local kids, trying to keep them out of the grasp of the legal system."

"That's right. Cassie told me you've done some work with kids." Ashton shook her head. "You two do have a lot in common. But it still stretches my mind how you blend horses and social service."

"Maybe we'll have to work harder on that," Clint said, resting his hand on Cassie's knee.

Cassie blushed, but took no action to remove his hand.

"Maybe I should be bringing some kids out to your farm, Cass. Is there magic in those horses?"

"I don't know about that. But you're welcome to bring as many as you want. Certainly there are professionals who argue strongly for the therapeutic value of kids being around animals."

"It's something to think about." Ashton checked her watch. "I'm going to have to run. Gotta get back downtown soon. Am I going to get to meet your kids on this trip, Clint? I've heard a lot about them. They sound like a couple precious imps."

Clint laughed, glancing quickly at Cassie. "They are that. Sure. They're going to be here for over a week. We don't fly back to Utah until a week from next Tuesday."

"Why don't you plan on coming out to the farm for a picnic supper this Sunday?" Cassie said. "I'll see if Traci and Susan can come, too. Lester and Sammy will have a great time. Just don't let them wheedle you into doing something you don't want to do."

Showing a lot of white teeth, Ashton asked, "Is that what you're afraid of, Cass?"

Cassie looked at Clint in horror. Her breathing

215

faltered. Speechless, she stared back at Ashton.

"It's okay, girl," Ashton said softly, placing her hand on top of Cassie's. A half dozen bracelets jangled. "It's okay to be afraid sometimes. It makes you human." Directing her gaze at Clint, she added, "Cassie O'Hanlon was always known as the tough-skinned one in grad school. You could put her in the ghetto, in the detox center, in the home for unwed mothers, and she'd tough it out emotionally.

"She needs someone to share her innermost self with...without being hurt." Smiling genuinely, Ashton said, "I hope you're the man who can do that. But if you hurt her, I'll have to find my way out to that desolate territory they call Utah and shoot me up a ranch."

Gracefully, the woman stood to leave. "See you two on Sunday. Nice meeting you, Clint." Ashton waved and headed for the exit.

Clint leaned back in the booth and howled."Damn," he said, "I think you're surrounded by an army of admirers who don't flinch at warning strangers that you're special and deserve special treatment. Fortunately, I happen to agree with them."

Looking like she wanted to protest, Cassie chose not to. "A little pampering, from time to time, is okay," she admitted. She stuck out her chin. "Just don't forget that I'm quite capable of taking care of myself, with or without a man."

"Now how could I ever forget that?"

"Just see that you don't."

216

"Do the kids really scare you, Cassidy?" Clint asked seriously.

Cassie inhaled sharply before answering. "They are the most lovable creatures. And they scare me nearly to death."

"I want to go see the submarine!" Lester shouted.

"No. No! The doll collection. Please, can't we go see the dolls?" Samantha begged, tugging on Cassie's hand.

"Dolls. Yuck!" Lester groaned.

Glancing quickly at Clint for some kind of direction, Cassie found nothing but a broad smile. How had she become the tour guide and decision-maker?

It had seemed like a simple thing to do...the right thing to do. The Museum of Science and Industry had a little bit of everything. She now admitted it had a lot of everything and there was no way they could see it all.

Silver Hawk had begged off this tour to spend some time with the horses and to take a break from these kids possessed by boundless energy. Now Cassie could better appreciate why a break was needed. She needed one, and they'd only been at it for two hours.

"We can do both. The submarine exit is on the way to the doll collection, so let's do the submarine first and then the dolls," she suggested. "Okay?"

She picked Sammy up as an extra incentive for

217

waiting, and the little girl immediately wound her fingers through Cassie's hair.

"Okay, but don't forget," Sammy warned.

Cassie looked to Clint for some relief.

Grinning, he remarked, "You do that so well. I'll bet you took a course on mediation." Leaning over, he pecked her cheek while disentangling his daughter from thick strands of auburn hair.

"Actually," he offered lamely, "why don't we get something to eat first."

"All right!" both children responded in unison.

"That way we can sit down for awhile," Clint whispered in Cassie's ear.

Cassie chuckled. "You do that so well. You must have taken a course on bribery."

"It works. That's what counts."

After they'd made their way to the food kiosk, Cassie watched happily as the kids tore into their hot dogs. She'd never had a tastier hamburger. How had she become so famished?

Sitting down felt so good. The energy of a six and eight year old amazed her. And it seemed very odd not to be at the track on a Saturday morning. But she and Clint had decided that they needed time to be alone with the kids.

Actually, Lester and Sammy had made that decision, now that she remembered right, and the grownups concurred. Neither she nor Clint had horses running that weekend, so they'd turned their care over to a couple grooms. And here they were surrounded by noise and smiles, with a pout

218

or two thrown in now and then.

She loved it. Yet she was keenly aware of being the visitor. She was the part-time stand-in for a parent. What would it be like to have that role full-time? Her body temperature dropped two degrees.

"Are you okay, Cassie?" Sammy asked, frowning. "You look like your soda went down the wrong tube. That happens to me when I drink too fast."

Cassie blushed at being caught by a six year old, but she wasn't about to share her thoughts. "No, I'm fine. Maybe you're right. Maybe I was drinking too fast."

CHAPTER TEN

"How about your social work stuff?" Clint inquired, straddling a straight-backed chair in Cassie's loft apartment, his long legs stretched out before him. "Could someone be steamed enough at you because you wrote them up or maybe recommended jail time or argued to keep an abusive guy away from his wife?"

Cassie's brows arched in mild frustration. Ever since their mid-afternoon return from the museum, Clint seemed preoccupied with figuring out who was drugging Hope.

She welcomed the quiet. Silver Hawk and her father were watching the children. Cassie felt like her brain was fried and wasn't sure she really wanted to use their alone time playing detective.

And Clint was now sleuthing in an area she hadn't given much thought to, even though he'd mentioned it earlier. It was simply too farfetched to expect to find such a link. Nobody at the home was out to get her. At least, she hoped that was true.

"I certainly can't think of anyone with a grudge."

"But it's possible."

"I suppose anything is possible." She frowned and stood. Beginning to pace, she offered, "I can't remember everyone I've crossed swords with in

221

the last year or so."

"If you don't mind, maybe we should drop by the group home. Staff may have heard something but not made a connection or thought anything of it. Besides, I'd kind of like to see where you hang your hat when you're not training horses."

Cassie paused her pacing to stand before Clint. "Okay, I guess there's nothing wrong with running by there, but I don't think we're going to find out anything helpful. I still don't know how anyone would put Cassie O'Hanlon the social worker together with Cassie O'Hanlon the horse trainer."

With the flash of an arm Clint grabbed her about the waist and plopped her down on his lap. Pulling on a long tendril of auburn hair, he said with a laugh, "This hair might be the first clue, my lady. You do stand out, you know."

After studying her for a long minute, he continued, "No, you don't have that picture of yourself, do you? Sometimes you boggle my mind. You seem to think you're as drab as Madam Librarian in the *Music Man*, while any red blooded male knows you are much more striking, like Julia Roberts in *Pretty Woman*."

"You!" Cassie exclaimed, pummeling her admirer softly.

He pulled her head down and lightly touched his lips to hers.

"'Tis a one track mind you have, Mr. Travers," she muttered, separating his lips with her tongue. The kiss continued, long and mutual. Cassie loved the feel of his muscled thighs, of his arousal rising against her bottom, of his lips, which tasted equally safe and dangerous.

Breaking the kiss, Clint groaned impatiently, "Enough sleuthing for one day. Do we have time?"

She laughed, framing his chin between finger and thumb. "This is the first time we've been alone since you brought the kids to Chicago. There's time. We'll make time. Silver Hawk will keep the kids at the house. And Dad is probably having a blast telling of some adventure that's improved by the remembering and the retelling."

Clint brushed the back of his fingers across her warming cheek. "It has been so long. How shall we begin?"

He took the lead by running his tongue along her cheekbone and then nuzzling her nape.

"A nice start," she moaned, clasping her hands behind his back. "Ah, yes, it's been far too long."

His tongue eased its way to her ear lobe. She scrunched her toes as Clint tenderly washed her ear, inside and out. At the same time, she became aware of fingers working on her blouse buttons. She helped unbutton the last two as his fingers traced a line over the top of her bra cup. Her skin heated rapidly. In response, she squirmed on his lap, purposefully rubbing her crotch along the expanding length of his shaft. Even through several layers of clothing, she felt his cock pulsing to meet her movements.

Clint groaned. "Hold still," he ordered. "You

don't want this to end before we've started, do you?"

Cassie laughed. *Of course not.* Yet she enjoyed this power over him. But any semblance of control was illusionary, for her bubbling heat reacted acutely to his teasing and his adoration.

The bra gave way beneath his practiced hands. He palmed each breast. Then he ducked to greet one with his mouth. Cassie nearly corkscrewed off his lap. He held her tight, running his tongue around the orb, ever so close but never quite touching its thickening tip. She scrunched forward, trying to thrust more of her breast into his mouth while grinding her pussy harder against his crotch, but Clint wouldn't yield.

In a war of wills, she finally caved in, allowing him his love torture. Just when she could stand no more, his tongue caressed a nipple. He pressed the aching flesh inward as if it were a button. It might as well have been. She soared through a misty universe seeking completion, embracing it under his adept guidance.

He waited for her body to stop shaking. His muscles relaxed as hers stilled. He had no way of knowing that her soul was vibrating at its very core. "My god, my god," she groaned, "why do I waste so much energy trying to resist you?"

Not knowing she'd spoken aloud, Cassie was startled by his response. "Because you think too much. At least when we make love, you allow yourself to feel."

She hauled herself off his lap even though she

felt like she carried the weight of an anvil. "Don't let me think, then. Come on, lover. This bed has never had a man in it."

- o -

"Wait," Clint said, grabbing Cassie's hand. "I want to finish undressing you."

"That's fine," she replied, standing before the bed and reaching for his belt, "and it looks like you could use some help, too. Somebody appears to be trapped."

Clint let her pull his zipper down and shove his Levis over his hips. He kicked the pants aside and her hands were inside his boxers, pulling them off and grabbing his cock at the same time. She'd driven him nearly crazy before sliding back and forth on his lap. Now she'd really entered the danger zone.

He grabbed her hand to still her stroking. He kissed her nose. "You're still ahead of me. Why don't you work on the shirt with both hands while I figure out what's holding this skirt together?

Chuckling, Cassie said, "You might want to look for a side zipper and hook. That's right. I'll see what I can do with this shirt. Men's shirts always seem to button backwards."

Tugging her skirt and panties down at the same time, Clint dispatched with them quickly. His chest tightened as he cupped her bare pussy in the palm of one hand. He'd never grow tired of that initial sensation of exuberance when he felt her inner heat warming his palm. "You're already sopping wet."

"What did you expect?" she murmured against his bare chest. "I've been looking forward to this for days. If you want to determine my temperature, you might want to slip a finger or two in."

He didn't need a second invitation. Placing one hand on her butt to help steady her, he slid one finger and then two into her wetness.

"Yes," she mumbled.

"God, you're on fire down there."

"More," she moaned, squirming against him.

With three fingers in her, Cassie rose on her toes and began rocking against them.

He felt her entire body tighten.

"Don't make me do this alone," she grunted, grinding against his fingers. "Finger-fuck me. Deep."

"Yes, Ma'am." Clint flexed his fingers deep, drew back and sank them deeper.

"Yes." Cassie wrapped her arms around him and held on tight. "Do me. Hurry. I need to come. Make me come, Clint. Make me come."

Curling his fingers, Clint found her internal button. Within seconds, she crashed against him. He only waited for her breathing to settle slightly before withdrawing his fingers.

Her eyelids fluttered open as if to protest.

He lifted her easily. While she clung to his shoulders, he maneuvered her hips until his stiff cock found her opening.

"Yes," she moaned.

With a single thrust, Clint entered her to the hilt. "Jesus," he groaned. "So hot."

"So big. You fill me so good."

"Keep your arms around me tight and your legs loose. That's right." Cupping an ass cheek in each hand, Clint began to slide her back and forth along the full length of his cock.

"Oh, wow." Cassie shuddered and giggled. "I'm your push-me pull-me toy. You feel so good."

"Me? I've missed this. I've missed you." Clint kissed the top of her head and slowed his movements. "Perhaps we should take this to the bed. No, don't move—let me."

Carefully he waddled the few feet to the bed. She wasn't helping any by sinking her teeth into his shoulder.

"My he-man," she said, wiggling her frame against his.

He settled her butt on the bed without breaking their connection and resumed sliding in and out of her.

She raised her legs high in the air. "Welcome home. Give him to me, I want all of him."

"Christ, woman, you turn me on like no other." Clint arched his back as Cassie raked her fingernails up and down his spine.

"Don't wait. Don't hold back. Ride me like you would a runaway mare."

Heeding her advice, Clint began rocking back and forth. He swore her inner temperature rose a hundred degrees. Smiling as her green eyes rounded wide, loving what they reflected, he whispered, "It's good to be home. I don't want to ever leave."

His voice choked. Shaking his head, ridding himself of a sudden wave of melancholy, he moved deeper into the woman he loved with every ounce of passion he could marshal.

She caressed his cheek, then fell back against the pillows and closed her eyes. He resolutely probed her internal volcano. Her inner muscles tightened. He gathered speed. She matched his pace, bucking up to meet him thrust for thrust. "Soon. Soon. Soon," she cried out. "Don't hold back. Fill me."

Clint moved beyond thinking, beyond remembering. He hurtled onward like a wayward tornado. After all the teasing, after all the foreplay, after all the days of waiting, he sensed his surge cresting, threatening to explode the circuits of his brain. He came in waves and then in spurts.

She raised her hips, accepting, demanding. "Give it all to me. Don't leave anything."

Her words were like spurs urging him on and on. His body had no mind, only this endless drive for completion. Each time he thought he was finished, his hips drove forward again, giving her more than he thought he had. He quaked, flexing his hips long after motion was necessary. Out of breath, out of energy, he collapsed, covering her. His tears graced her breasts. Her arms and legs folded around him, holding him in place.

Fully dressed, Cassie sat on the bed next to a sleeping Clint, dragging a hawk feather slowly across his chin and down his chest.

Clint opened his eyes and snickered. His hand snaked out quickly and captured the feather, keeping her from moving it any lower. "No need getting me riled up again. By the looks of you, it must be about time to head up to the house."

Making a long face, Cassie replied, "I'd rather stay here and play in our little bordello, but," she added lightly, "there are other responsibilities."

"Guess you're right." Clint paused. "What we just shared...incredible."

"I know." Cassie didn't like the catch in her voice. She wasn't ready to elaborate on how incredible their lovemaking had been for her — or how it had opened her heart. Would she ever be the same? Were there other worlds yet to be explored? She'd soared so high and so far, maybe she'd seen them all. And then she'd been relentless, pushing Clint over the edge, beyond *his* comfort zone. He'd been so deep. She could still feel him pulsing in her depths. She hugged herself, thankful she was on the pill. "I've never been fucked so thoroughly, not even by you."

He shook his head. "I've never had a woman take me to that place before. I didn't know if you were ever going to let me stop. And that was more than a thorough fucking."

"For both of us. I'm glad. I hope you are, too."

Pulling the sheet up over his body, Clint sighed. "I don't know what the tears were about. I'm not that type. I only remember tears on three other occasions. When my dad died. When my wife died. And when I was able to save the life of a young colt that the vet had given up on. No one ever saw me cry...before now."

Cassie sat on the edge of the bed and traced a finger across the sheet covering his chest. "That makes it even more special. I've been crying a lot more lately, myself."

"Maybe it's a sign." Clint placed her hand firmly between his. "I don't want to lose you, Cassidy. I love you. I want us to share these kinds of moments, and all the other kinds, forever."

Cassie struggled to fend off the wave of panic suddenly washing over her. No way—she could never be a mother, ever.

"Where are you at, Cass? On us?"

His tone was insistent. He wanted a declaration she couldn't give. She rubbed her sweaty palms on her shorts. Couldn't he just be satisfied with what they had? Why did it even have to have a name?

"This is no damn fling, Cassie. You got to know that by now. We're way beyond that."

"I'm keenly aware of that." Could he see her panic? Caught between this man she didn't want to lose and a deep shame she hoped he'd never discover, Cassie couldn't find words. Finally, she said, "That doesn't make things easier. Sometimes I feel like I'm mired in quicksand."

Clint recoiled as if she'd slapped him.

Cassie flinched. "Please don't be angry—you mean so much to me, already, and the kids, too. I just don't know how it would ever work."

She stroked his hand. "Clint, you're moving too fast for me. I'm not ready for more. Not now." She felt her voice constrict. "I don't know if I ever will be—but I'm working on it. I hope that's enough, for now."

Clint sighed and his expression softened. "We've got time, Cassie. It can work. If we want it badly enough."

The phone rang.

"Okay," Cassie said into the phone, "we'll be right there. Thanks for the afternoon. See you shortly."

"That was Silver Hawk," she said, shifting her attention back to Clint. "Supper's about ready. And she claims we owe her one."

"I'm sure she does," Clint drawled. "I'll get dressed."

Cassie watched him climb out of bed and reach for his clothes still scattered across the floor. Was this an opportunity? "Tell me about the children's mother. You said her death was one of the three times you cried. You must have loved her dearly."

He pulled a dark tee shirt over his upper torso and cast her a wary glance. "Yes, I loved her very much. I thought the moon and sun rose to bless her daily."

Cassie nodded. "Was she a full blood Ute?"

"No. She was actually a little less than half Shoshoni. And then all those other things white

231

folks tend to be," he added, grinning a lopsided smile. "Julie was from the Wind River area in Wyoming. We met in college."

"In college?"

"Yes, I went to college. At Weber State."

"What did you study?"

"I have a degree in criminal justice. Thought maybe I wanted to be a detective, but I much prefer horses."

Cassie's brow creased. "Well, I'll be. Why don't you ever tell me these things? Why do I have to pry your life story out of you?"

"I just figured when you wanted to know, you'd ask."

"Damn, now I have so many questions, but we have to go to supper or Silver Hawk will send out flares and come in search of us. Don't think you're getting off easy though, bud. You are really fair game now. I'll write my questions down on paper. And I won't be put off until I get some answers. A detective?" she bantered, running a brush haphazardly through her hair. "I don't think we would've met if you'd followed that route."

"There, you see? Now you know why I didn't. Another question answered."

"So that's why you're so suspicious and seem to know something about investigating a crime."

"I imagine I'm naturally suspicious. I do have an old college buddy who runs a small private detective agency here in Chicago. We may want to tap into his skills at some point. He'd love to help. He's always wanted me to be some kind of silent partner. So far I've resisted the temptation. I'm not sure horses and detective work mix."

"About as well as social work and horses, I suppose," Cassie quipped. "Actually, right now we seem to need to be a little of everything."

"That's often the case. I'm game for whatever as long as *lovers* is included in that list."

Giving him one last hug, Cassie said, "Okay, wise guy, enough for now. I think a couple kids may be feeling neglected. Let's go see how firmly the two hellions have Dad wrapped around their little fingers."

Clint laced his fingers through hers and grazed her lips with his. "I'm pleased you're not threatened by Julie."

"Why should I be? She's still the children's mother. I wouldn't want anything or anyone to diminish her in their eyes."

"And you wonder why I love you?" Clint patted her rump as they made their way down the loft stairs. "Woman, you're remarkable."

Giggling, Cassie raced happily down the steps. How could this be wrong for her — or for them?

After the last dessert was eaten, after Clint had carried a sleeping Sammy to the car and taken his family back to the hotel, Cassie collapsed on the living room sofa. "Wow! What a day!" she said to her father. "The silence is soothing to the ears. How did you manage it?"

"The nap helped. Maybe I hear too much silence as a rule, being here by myself most of the time," he said with a sly look. "You're gonna have you hands full with them two. But I do hope you'll want another one or two."

"Dad!" Cassie slouched lower on the sofa. "Everybody seems to be trying to make my mind up for me," she complained. "It's my decision."

"I know, girl. I didn't mean to pressure you. But you are so good with Clint and the kids." Tug chuckled lightly. "And I'm not getting any younger. Would like to know that Irish temper of yours is being passed along before I die."

Cassie scowled. "Right, no pressure. None at all." She moaned and rubbed the back of her neck, watching her father's dismay spread across his face. "It's all right, Dad. I love you anyway."

She closed her eyes and leaned back into the comfort of the worn sofa. It had been a very good day. Her dad was right—she really did enjoy the kids.

And detective Travers? No wonder he was so deliberate in seeking clues. She'd agreed to go by the group home with him Monday morning. She wasn't sure how she felt about that. She'd been back only twice since she took leave. Would the kids at the home feel betrayed by her absence? Would she want to go back sooner than expected?

She still had more than another six weeks of leave. Sometimes she wished she had a crystal ball. How would she feel about her job by then? Cripes, how would she feel about anything in another six weeks?

CHAPTER ELEVEN

"Nice location for your office," Clint said Monday morning, sidestepping dog excrement as they made their way down the sidewalk to Cassie's place of work.

Cassie glanced around the familiar setting. The lot adjacent to her building sat vacant with bald tires, an old remnant of a box spring, and a variety of rusted cans strewn about. Its centerpiece was a burnt-out 1968 Impala. Papers of all shapes and colors were blown up against a chain link fence that obviously kept no one out or in.

"I didn't say this would be a scenic tour," Cassie quipped as she climbed the steps ahead of him. She knew the large two-story house needed some cosmetic repair, but it was kept up well enough. Its owners leased out the building while trying not to put too much money into it. They hoped gentrification would get to them soon.

As soon as Cassie stepped through the door, she was assailed by familiar scents and sounds. The place always smelled mildly of disinfectant, of too many bodies, especially in the summertime, and of some sort of pasta cooking in the kitchen. The hum of the place was the same. Bickering could be heard from upstairs, the crack of billiard balls came from downstairs, and tone-deaf Mrs. Hampton, in charge of the kitchen, droned along on an old gospel tune.

Cassie and Clint made it no further than past the long second-hand leather sofa before being accosted by a deafening scream. "Cassie! You're back! I need to talk to you."

A gangly young woman hugged Cassie until both gasped for air.

"It's good to see you too, Daisy. I'm just back on a visit today," Cassie said, separating herself from the girl's long arms. The girl looked even thinner than usual, and she'd been underweight back in the spring.

"Oh, no. We need you here. Raul can be mean without you around." The young girl looked bereft as she slouched before them in a white tank top and tattered bib overalls. Neither shoes nor socks adorned her feet. Apparently not knowing quite where to put her hands, she stuffed them inside her overalls.

Cassie smiled. "Now, I doubt that a lot. Maybe I'm just a softy."

"Well, you listen better. And you don't punish us for what others do."

"Daisy, you know that depends on how the group is taking responsibility. It's good to see you, but I can't stay and talk. I've got to see Raul about some things. Quickly, though, tell me how you're doing with summer school?"

"I was kicked out," the girl complained, spitting out the words. Her eyes focused on the floor. "They didn't like me."

"So that's why you're hanging out here. Do

they have you working on your basic math skills? Is anyone helping you with your spelling? You have to get ready for the fall."

"Yeah, that's happening. But it's a pain in the butt. Maybe I won't be here much longer. You know my sister's been married almost a year now. They should be settled soon."

"You never know," Cassie said gently. "Things change. We have to be prepared for things not to work quite like we hope they will."

The girl frowned and then shook her head, shrugging off Cassie's words. Beaming a bright smile, Daisy turned her attention to Clint. "Who's your friend, Ms. O'Hanlon?

"This is Mr. Travers, Daisy, and you can wipe that sloppy grin off your face. He's none of your business."

"Yes, ma'am," Daisy replied. She ducked away, still smiling, obviously having found out exactly what she wanted to know. "See yah."

"Smartass kid!" Cassie groused. But she did miss the repartee. It was good to be back in this crazy environment. Then she remembered why they'd come. "Guess we'd better get downstairs and talk to Raul. I'd like to be out of here before lunch is served and more of the kids straggle in."

- o -

Raul Hernandez sat at his desk with papers strewn every which way. Piles of papers took up more floor space than anything else, making the

237

small office feel even more cramped. As soon as he saw Cassie enter, he jumped up to hug her. "So when are you coming back?"

His voice had an enticing quality. Clint watched the shorter man's easy smile. Laughter danced in his eyes. Clint decided he liked the fellow, and he didn't often make such quick decisions about people. He wondered about the rusty ship's bell that sat on a small bookcase with books stacked on top of one another instead of side by side. And he was curious why the man had chosen to hang on his wall a black and white print of Don Quixote tilting at windmills. The picture, itself, hung at a rakish angle.

Cassie broke the embrace. "I'm due back in October."

"We need you now."

"I'll be back in October."

Gesturing toward a couple wooden chairs, he said, "Just set those reports on the floor somewhere. So who is this dude?

"Raul, I'd like you to meet a friend of mind, Clint Travers. Clint is from Utah and is in the horse business."

Clint reached across the desk and the two men shook hands, each quietly assessing the other. "Cass has told me a lot about you," Clint said. "Most of which is good."

"Better be. Welcome to our home away from home."

"Tell me, how are things going?" Cassie inquired eagerly. "Are we full? How are the kids doing? Tell me about Lucinda, Ricki, Rex."

Clint gave Cassie a sharp look. She really did miss this place. That had been evident when she'd been accosted by the tall thin girl upstairs, who could have been anywhere between fourteen and twenty-four. Clearly, Cassie was loved and respected. Would she ever want to give up this world?

"More of the same, here," Raul was saying. "Auditors—too damn many auditors." He hefted a stack of papers to prove his point. "Grant auditors. State auditors. County auditors. Fiscal auditors. Program auditors. Building auditors. The list is endless. And we're supposed to be teaching kids about trust?

"We're full at an even dozen. Eight boys and four girls. We continue fighting with the state to keep them from overloading us. Lucinda got pregnant while on a home visit. That's not too surprising. She's going to keep the baby. Children's Services says she should give it up. At fifteen, she's too young to be a mother, they claim." He lifted and dropped his shoulders. "She's not too young to get pregnant."

Cassie sighed. "So much for all the talking and instruction on abstinence and birth control."

"Rex was sent to St. Charles for armed robbery. He'll very likely finish serving his time as an adult. He finally got what he wanted—to be in the big time.

"Ricki is our success story of the quarter." Raul's tone took on the pride of a pleased father.

"He's doing well at U of I. He's taking a half-time load while working part-time. He should be eligible for a good scholarship after this first year of proving what he can do, even though his high school record was poor. He wants to be a social worker. Can you believe that?"

"Yeah, I can believe it." Cassie turned to Clint. "It's the Rickis of the world, who make something of themselves despite the projects, the drugs, and the crime, that help us deal with the pain of losing the Rexes."

Clint nodded. He knew something about that. The same stories could have been shared about kids he'd known on the reservation.

"So, young lady, what's on your mind? I doubt you came by to show off this gorgeous workplace to your friend. And apparently you're not yet ready to dust off your desk and get back to work." Raul stroked his mustache.

Before she could speak, Raul addressed Clint, "Oh, by the way Clint, I'm a happily married man with four kids. Thought I better get that settled. You're a lot bigger than me."

Clint smiled easily.

"Men!" Cassie snapped. "All right, you've had your fun. We've had some problems at the track. Clint thought it might be tied into a kid or a family I've worked with in the past."

"Somebody's been drugging a horse Cassie is working with," Clint said. "We were just wondering if anyone has heard of a former resident having a grudge against her."

Raul shook his head. "Everybody likes Cassie. She has a good way about her. She can get a kid to change his ways without putting him down."

"How about when she went on sabbatical?" Clint probed. "Sometimes kids take that personally."

"Yeah, you got a point there. You know something about this kind of work."

Clint watched the man stroke his mustache and draw a deep breath as he thought through the names of kids.

"Sure, there were tears," Raul said at last. "Maybe...Harold was very angry when you left."

Cassie nodded. "I thought he'd get over it quickly enough. We spent a lot of time preparing him for the transition."

"It went on for days." Raul moved papers from one side of his desk to the other. There was pain in his eyes when he glanced back up. "He tore up some games in the day room, ripped apart some of his own personal items, and wrote *bitch* on your office door. As you might expect, he received a series of consequences for his behavior." Raul shrugged. "Within two weeks he seemed to have gotten over his anger. You were just one more adult who passed through his short life."

Cassie squeezed her shoulders and scowled.

"So where is Harold now?" Clint asked. "Can we talk with him?"

Hernandez shrugged, palms upward. "Don't know. He left here in June. Once they're out, we don't hear any more from them. He could be

241

anywhere."

"Great."

"I doubt he has any connection with the track, though. He's an urban kid."

Chuckling, Cassie said, "And so are about half the people who work on shedrow."

"You got me there. Afraid I don't know much about horses, or the track for that matter, but I do like to go out and bet on the ponies now and then. But I imagine you're right. Not all the folks who work there are natural cowboys. So, how are you liking it, Cass? Are those four legged beasts going to lure you away from us, or what?"

Clint tried not to smile as Cassie took her time responding to her boss' question.

"I can't deny some of it's very satisfying. I love working with horses. But being a full-time trainer is a tough life for anyone, especially for a woman."

Clint knew she was purposefully avoiding eye contact with him.

"No, this is my career," Cassie continued. "I do miss the kids and the crises. It's hard to imagine not being a social worker. It's what I've trained to do."

"My friend, you'll use your social work skill whatever you do and wherever you are," Raul said. He gave Cassie a quizzical look. "I want you back, but I trust you'll follow your heart, and that will be right for everyone."

Cassie's neck turned crimson.

Clint coughed — it hadn't taken Raul long to pick up on Cassie's indecisiveness.

"Well, thanks anyway," Cassie mumbled. "We'd best be going. You have a mountain of work to do and we have some horses to see to."

"Sorry I can't be more helpful," Hernandez said, rising to his feet.

"That's okay," Clint interjected. "You've been very helpful. We can take it from here."

"Hey," Hernandez shouted from his office doorway. Cassie turned at the top of the stairs to listen. "You haven't called with a hot tip yet. Remember, I'm a poor man who would welcome a long shot coming in."

Smiling, Cassie called back, "Keep your money in your pocket. I don't know a thing about handicapping horses. I only train them."

- o -

Walking down the stoop, Cassie thought of Harold. She couldn't prevent a nagging tingling sensation from creeping down her legs. Could the villain at the core of the drugging mess really be Harold? It had to be somebody at the track who was getting to Hope. She hadn't seen Harold since she'd gone on leave. But the young boy was sixteen, and could have a job anywhere at the track.

"So, you miss the place," Clint said, making their way to the car.

Cassie knew he'd made an assessment. It was a statement, not a question. She looked curiously at him, wondering what he was really thinking and what he really wanted to ask. "I miss it. At least part of it. I miss seeing light bulbs come on when a kid finally gets it. I miss having them come back to show off their first paycheck or some decent grades. I don't miss seeing them move deeper into the system. Or learning that one of my former kids endangered a life. I imagine I miss the pace some. There's always a crisis happening. You're needed every moment of the day."

"Sounds like you're describing parenting."

Faltering slightly, Cassie whispered, "I suppose you may be right."

"So why did you choose to be a social worker?"

Cassie laughed. "How much time do you have?"

"A lifetime."

Cassie felt her cheeks burn. "I wanted to be in a position to help people help themselves. I guess I especially wanted to help kids stay out of trouble. My childhood wasn't done by the textbook, you know, but I was loved and supported, even if I didn't have a mom. It was important for me to help other kids like myself. To help them feel loved and to know that they could be loved and loving and could study and work hard and be whatever they wanted to be."

"So you are a dreamer."

"Of course I am," she said, poking him in the side. "That's not a banner headline at this point in our relationship."

"No, but it's one of the many aspects about you that I have come to love very, very much."

Cassie fumbled with the remote to unlock the car.

Getting into the passenger side of the car, Clint changed the subject. "I think we should check up on this Harold kid. I can have my private detective buddy do a run on him."

Cassie nodded. "Okay, if you think it's necessary. But I can't imagine he'd know enough to drug Hope."

"We can't rule him out without checking. He only has to know someone who can do the job for him. My friend is good. If the kid is tied into your troubles, we'll know about it soon."

"Not soon enough," Cassie groaned, merging into traffic.

"Hope is coming along real nice. She'll be primed for Saturday's race," Silver Hawk said, admiring the sleek filly moving fluidly about the large paddock.

"Yeah, it's only Tuesday, but I'm already anxious about Saturday," Cassie replied, leaning against the white fence boards. The horse looked like she didn't have a care in the world. Cassie was envious. "I'll probably take her to the track on Friday to reintroduce her to the racing surface. And then bring her back here so we can keep an eye on her. Thank goodness Hope trailers easily."

Unlike Hope, Cassie carried a burden of worries. Her father's health seemed to benefit from all the extra attention, yet he had a long ways to go before being in a position to do much but sit

245

and watch the world go by.

She'd appreciated Silver Hawk's help with the horses as well as with the kids. Yet, she still felt uncomfortable around the woman. Whenever Cassie looked her, Clint's sister seemed to be scrutinizing her.

Cassie heaved a sigh. Maybe her women's group was right. Maybe she was simply suffering from too much intense self-analysis of late. Maybe it was best to sort of let things happen. She shook her head. She needed to be much more in control of herself than that.

"I don't remember when I've had more horse under me," Silver Hawk said. "She moves like a natural athlete. Thanks for giving me an opportunity to exercise her this morning. I hope, for your father's sake, we can nail the guy who's trying to destroy his dream."

"Yeah, me too," Cassie said wistfully. Somehow it didn't surprise her that Clint's sister connected so easily with her father and his dream. After all, she was a woman who had lived and worked with horses full time probably from the time she could ride. "This may be his last chance. I don't see any more *Cassie's Hopes* in the stable. Dad refuses to go out and buy a contender. And I don't know how many more seasons he has for this game."

"None of us knows that," agreed the bronze-skinned woman, glancing thoughtfully at the early morning sun. "The past we can't change, and the future remains a blur. We only have this day."

A soft breeze tossed strands of long ebony hair

across Silver Hawk's face, briefly obscuring her features.

"Yeah," Cassie responded, "sometimes I wish I had a crystal ball to see past tomorrow. But I don't, and I can't."

"And what about Clint?" Silver Hawk asked, dropping her voice low. "How many more seasons does he have without the woman he loves? Without you?"

Cassie stared at the smug questioner and then shook her head. "Damn, I thought Indian women were supposed to be indirect."

Silver Hawk laughed easily. Propping a foot on the first fence rail, she replied, "Some are, some aren't. But then you certainly know about the dangers of stereotypes. Maybe it's my years at Berkeley. Maybe I don't want to play at being extra polite." She paused.

"My brother loves you." Silver Hawk turned toward Cassie and folded her arms across her mid-section. "That, I know. So do the kids. Now that I've seen you with him and with Lester and Sammy, I know that you love them too. You may be hiding that fact from yourself, I don't know. You are good for him, and I expect he is good for you." Silver Hawk raised an eyebrow. "So what's the problem?"

Cassie struggled to find her voice. Idly, she tugged on a blouse sleeve. She couldn't find the right words to form an answer.

"What's the hang up, Ms. Social Worker? With many white women, it might be the color of our skin," Silver Hawk said caustically. Her voice softened. "But somehow I don't think that's got anything to do with it for you."

"No, that's not it at all," Cassie stammered, taking a step a back.

"I know that," Silver Hawk hastened to respond. "So what is it?"

"I'm not even certain what it is," Cassie finally confessed, fighting back tears. "I'm scared, I know that."

"Is it the kids? They think you're very spectacular."

"That's part of it. They're darlings. And I know they want a mother, but I'm not sure I'm up for handling that kind of responsibility."

Silver Hawk nodded, but said nothing.

Both women watched a mare in the neighboring paddock arch its neck and reach down to nuzzle a spindly-legged foal.

"There's so much at stake," Cassie said, wrapping her arms tightly around her torso. "It's not just me. It's not just me and Clint. It's not just the kids. There's his family. There's Dad. How could we pull it all off, if we wanted to? Where would we live? What about my career? What of the future? Will I throw everything away only to be rejected again?"

"Ah," Silver Hawk said. "We never know how much to risk for the unknown."

"I've gone through a lot to get what I have. What I have may not be much in the eyes of many. But it's mine, and it's safe."

"We don't go out of our way to seek pain. You have much to share with my brother, with his kids, with all of us." Silver Hawk flashed a hopeful smile. "But it is not a one way street. He — they, we — have much to share in return."

Silver Hawk paused and looked to the west. "I'd guess about now, Grandmother would remind us that we are not alone in all of this. Great Spirit has a plan. We often cannot see it clearly. Sometimes we can only feel our way along the path."

Cassie closed her eyes, remembering the bent elderly woman. "How do you explain your grandmother?"

Silver Hawk looked sharply at Cassie and her brow crinkled. Then her eyes, her entire body convulsed with laughter. "I don't try to explain Grandmother. She is inexplicable. She is simply Grandmother, and I accept her and love her as such. You can, too, if you wish. Grandmother has blessed you; you are one of us. What you do with that, only you can decide. Only you can discern your own path."

Cassie moved to hug Silver Hawk. How wrong she had been about her initially. Here was a woman she could trust, could lean on if necessary. But would she ever be able to trust the invisible path? How could she trust something she couldn't hold in her hands?

"Thank you, Silver Hawk," Cassie whispered, clutching the woman tightly. "I'll try to remember your words."

"I've been doing some research," Clint announced later that afternoon, placing his laptop computer on the desk in Cassie's loft apartment. "Maybe this will shed some light on who's behind the drugging."

As the machine booted up humming and flickering, Cassie stepped closer to see what Clint was pulling up on the screen.

"As you know, the *Daily Racing Form* maintains a record of every race a horse has run, along with names of other horses, jockeys and trainers, in addition, of course, to the names of winners and so on," Clint said. "I've checked every race Cassie's Hope has run. Excluding the Wyoming races, four trainers have had horses in each race she has entered. And in each race there were six jockeys in common. Look. Here's a list of trainers, and next to it is the list of jocks. Any reactions?"

Cassie stared at the familiar names. She shook her head, pursing her lips. "Louie Picard and Earl Sheraton have been long time friends of Dad's and mine. I hardly know Troy Jackson, but others claim he's honest as the day is long."

Shrugging, she groaned at the last name. "Harrington's an ass, but I don't think he would go out of his way to hurt me. And the jocks? They've all ridden for me in the last few months. Can't say much at all about them. They ride, and I pay them."

"Yeah, I didn't think it would be that simple," Clint grunted. "Still, it may prove to be useful information. These are the people with the most access and probably the most to gain from throwing a race. Besides owners and bettors, of course.

"Eight owners have run against you on at least two or more occasions. Anything surprise you on this list?" Clint asked, pressing a button to bring up the owner list.

Again, Cassie studied the names. "Nope. It's a combination of folks we've known forever and a few new faces. But I've no reason to suspect one person over the other, or any at all."

"I'll try the names out on your father tomorrow morning and see if any name jogs a memory. I'm still guessing that this has more to do with your dad or you than with the filly."

"What do you mean?"

Pushing away from the desk, Clint grimaced. "Your dad's been in this business a long time. He's bound to have made some enemies here and there. Or maybe it's somebody who doesn't like the idea of a woman trainer starting off with a stakes contender."

"I've wondered enough about that," she responded cautiously. "Maybe it's someone who doesn't want a woman trainer around, period."

"Has anyone been ragging on you, giving you a hard time for working at the track?"

"Not unless you count Harrington."

"Why have you ruled him out from suspicion?" Clint's expression blended surprise with accusation.

She blushed, remembering that Harrington didn't trust Clint. Would the two men be friends if it weren't for her? Probably. They had more in common than either cared to admit, including an overly protective posture toward women.

"Well?"

A corner of her mouth turned up. "It's not what you're thinking. I know he was interested in me, but I set him straight about that. I guess I don't think he'd stoop so low as to drug a horse."

"Don't be so sure," Clint countered. "He didn't seem very pleased to have another man nosing about trying to find out what was going on with your Hope..." He paused. "Harrington stays on the list." His voice rose. "Okay?"

"Fine! Both you guys seem to suffer from an excessive amount of male testosterone."

"Now, what the hell does that mean?"

"Never mind," she said, turning to march across the small loft room. She was both annoyed and flattered by his display of jealousy.

"You know, what you and I have is very rare," Clint said, his voice rising a bit. "And it will work if we both let it."

Cassie tensed. She knew he meant it would work if she let it happen. "Clint, you promised you wouldn't pressure me."

"Well, it would work," he said, ignoring her plea. "We could use this place as our base. Your dad is too frail for us to think about any other arrangement. The kids could go to school here and then maybe spend their summers with their grandmother and great-grandmother. They will want to continue teaching them the ways of our people. But there's nothing to stop us, if we decide it's what we want."

Cassie closed her eyes. He was so determined to work out the practical difficulties — did she dare tell him how terrified she was by the vision of being a wife and mother? She swallowed.

"You could keep your job, whichever one you choose — social worker or horse trainer. I can do my work from here with periodic commutes to the ranch. Silver Hawk could manage things at the ranch nicely and I could continue to travel to the sales. It would all work. Can't you see that?"

She chewed her trembling lower lip. "I don't want to hurt you or anyone else — but I can't see it. Not yet. And I don't know if I'll ever be able to see it. You're not playing fair, Clint Travers. You're not playing fair at all. You bring the kids here. You have everything worked out." She turned her back on him. "Well, I don't. And I'm not ready to do that kind of practical thinking."

Cassie turned to watch him shove his papers in his briefcase. Why had he pushed, after his promise not to pressure?

He exhaled through pursed lips and said, "You've got your meeting with your girlfriends tonight. That's good. Perhaps we need a little break from each other. Damn, I want all of this horse drugging stuff done so we can concentrate on where we're going."

Cassie's skin crawled as a wave of panic

washed over her. The sooner they finished their investigation, the sooner she'd have to sort herself out. Would Clint try to force her to make some big decisions before she was ready? Her shoulders drooped. Trying to keep any telltale sign of emotion from her voice, she responded, "Maybe a little separation would be good for us. Things are tumbling awfully fast."

The pain on his face nearly crushed her. She placed her arms around him. Pressing her hands against his neck, she rose to meet his lips. She brushed them lightly. He made no attempt to deepen the kiss. Pulling away, she whispered, "I'll miss you. But we need a little space. How about breakfast tomorrow morning at The Country Café near the track?"

"Fine. I'll be there."

He stalked out the door. She closed the door softly behind him, turned and leaned against it. Had she made a mistake? Should she have insisted on sorting things out now and not run the risk of them festering? They both would have to trust the process.

How many times had she said that to other people having relationship problems? She needed more time. But time was running out.

CHAPTER TWELVE

"Cassie, I know you're in a quandary, but maybe we can start with a simple question," Susan said. "Do you love him?"

Wrapping her arms tightly around her body, Cassie sat with a leg tucked under her on Traci Steele's love seat. It was Tuesday evening. She and her three friends sat in a circle in the living room of Traci's upscale Near North high-rise apartment overlooking Lake Michigan. While her own living standard was considerably lower than that of her lawyer friend, this was her life — urban, sophisticated, sleek, cosmopolitan.

Not able to give Susan a quick answer, Cassie stood and walked to the floor-to-ceiling windows overlooking the lake. She wasn't ignoring her friends, and they knew it. They honored her need for silence and space. Her situation with Clint and his kids had been the focus of the evening. After a brief check in from everyone over the soup and salad dinner, the group had turned to Cassie. This was her night, and they were there to support her in any way she wanted.

She saw lights blinking on a ship probably several miles out from the shoreline. She wondered if it was coming or going.

Cassie turned to face her friends. Each watched her attentively, but no one made an effort to speak. They must look like a strange quartet to the outside observer. Susan. Prim and proper Susan, dressed in a stylish pink and white pantsuit, as if she had stepped out of the pages of a designer catalogue. Ashton. Ashton of the golden hoop earrings and longish red fingernails. The dark skinned woman wore a wraparound skirt and a silk blouse and there was always that ever present captivating smile, as if she was aware of a secret and just about ready to share it. Traci. High cheek bones, long tan legs. White shorts and an old Harvard sweatshirt gave her an air of cool understated beauty, matching her personality. And Cassie, herself, stood there before them in jeans, comfortable riding boots and a baby blue tank top. What an odd assortment of friends. And yet how right they were for each other. They'd cried together and laughed together. They'd lifted each other up and were also quite capable of holding each other accountable.

Taking a deep breath, Cassie shoved her hands in her back pockets. "Okay," she began, "it's not going to surprise you that I do love him."

"Well, hurrah!" Susan squealed.

"Good for you, Cass," Traci said.

"I'm glad you can admit it to yourself," Ashton chimed in, lifting her glass of wine.

"But now what?" Cassie groaned, slumping back down on the love seat. "It's one thing to love him. It's another to talk about marriage, which I know he wants. And it's very much another matter entirely to consider being an instant mother."

"Ah," sighed Ashton, "we're back to the old bugaboo of instant motherhood."

"Yes."

"But the kids are so cute," Susan said. "We all enjoyed them so much at the picnic Sunday. Sammy is a delight and Lester is such a little man. How can you resist them?"

Cassie studied Susan for a moment. It was less than two months since Susan had thought Dirk Johnson was perfect for her. Now she was convinced motherhood was just right? "The kids are great. They're not necessarily the angels you saw at the farm on Sunday, but they're great kids. The problem isn't them — it's me."

"What do you mean?" Traci asked. "Spell it out. I'm failing to understand the dilemma here. You love the guy. The kids are great. So you get married and live happily ever after. And we hope you'll continue to come to our group."

"Oh, I'll always be part of this group, no matter what happens." Cassie sat silently for a long while, tugging on the hem of her tank top. When she looked up, her vision was clouded by tears. She caught Ashton's eye. "You remember when we studied childhood development...the theory goes that a child will develop naturally and well if it has a *good enough* mother." Tears spilled down her cheeks. "I'm not sure that I can be a good enough mother."

"What?" Susan and Traci gasped in unison.

Ashton got up, sat next to Cassie, and draped

an arm around her. "You know, girl, I've known you for some six years or so. You sometimes surprise me with what you have to say. I admit I was a bit shocked when you left your job to go train that horse. I supported you then, and I still do. But what you just said is the biggest crock of bull that I've heard from you or anybody else. You're a natural mother. I certainly didn't hear Lester or Sammy complaining. Where did you get this idea of not being a good enough mother?"

"I don't know. I guess it's always been there. And the kids only know me a little, and then part-time. And they want a mother so badly, I doubt they're the best judges."

"I think you're wrong about that," Susan said. "Kids may be the *best* judge. I always thought I had good parents. Some of my friends thought they had poor parents, and from what I could see they were probably right."

Traci uncrossed her legs and leaned forward. "Cassie, we've been friends for a long time — since college. We've helped each other through a lot of thick and thin and I've never had an inkling how you felt about motherhood. If we're going to be helpful, I think you've got to tell us more. We can't just change your mind by saying *well of course* you'd make a super mom, even though we know you would. So what gives? Where is this coming from?"

"Well, what about you Traci? Your mother died when you were young. How have you learned to be a good mother?"

"I don't know where I learned it. I don't even know that I will be a good mother, but not knowing won't keep me from trying if the right man ever shows up." Traci stood up to retrieve the wine bottle and fill glasses. "Is that what this is all about? You didn't have a mother through most of your childhood, and therefore you question your own ability to be a mother?"

Cassie grimaced. "Your mother died, Traci. Mine walked away—abandoned me and my father. How do you ever shake that? Her blood runs through my veins. How can I be certain I will do a better job? And I never want to do to a child what she did to me."

"Wow. That is a load," Ashton said. "No wonder you're shaking like a leaf. Maybe I would too, if I had your experience. I didn't. I was surrounded by loving parents and a large extended family, but I don't know if that'll make me a better parent. And when the time comes, I hope to share that role with a father. Clint strikes me as a fine father, loving yet capable of saying *no* when necessary, and doing so in a kind manner."

"Oh, Clint is a fabulous father. That makes it even worse. Maybe I won't live up to his expectations of a mother."

"Your dad loves you very much," Susan said, with her own eyes tearing up. "I only knew your aunt briefly, but she seemed to care for you a lot."

"She did the best she could. She never had any kids of her own, so I guess I was kind of the experiment. We both learned together, I imagine.

As far as Dad goes, I know he loves me. And he's probably taught me more about caring for living things than anyone, but he wasn't a mother."

"What about your group home work?" Traci asked. "When I've been by there to see you, some of them called you Mama Cass. And I doubt they ever heard of the *Mamas and the Papas*. The kids seem to respond very well to you."

"Don't get me wrong," Cassie said sharply. "I'm a damn good kid worker. But that's different. I get to go home when the day is done. The kids move on with their lives. I'm just a blip on their life screens. It's a different level of commitment."

"Ah, the *C* word," Ashton chided gently. "I wondered when we would get around to it. Commitment! Oh, my god, commitment. Yeah, parenting is a long term commitment—for parents who stay together and for parents who split. But not for your mother. She just ran away. Funny, usually it's the kids who we think of as the runaways, but your mother definitely was a runaway.

"Are you a runaway, Cassie? Have you ever run from anything important in your entire life? How many daughters or sons would have run from your father as hard and fast as they could when he asked them to take a leave of absence to help him chase a long-held dream?

"How many folks, including social workers and many a mom, would have run away from sixteen year old Janice when she got pregnant, thumbed her nose at the system, and told everyone to bug out of her life? You hung in there. She wasn't able to drive you away. And in the end you were a huge help getting her out of the projects and into a situation where she could make something out of life for herself and for her daughter. You helped her become more than a good enough mom. So what are you running away from? That's what I want to know. And I'm prepared to sit here as long as it takes to find out."

Cassie nodded and stood. Again she walked to window. All she could see now was driving rain. It had its own beauty, but she longed for that late night view of the familiar harbor lights. Ashton was right. She was running, or at least in danger of running.

Her childhood hadn't been terribly unhappy. True, there was a lot of traveling from place to place. Her father could have left her behind, but he didn't. He'd kept her with him as much as he could and had provided well for her needs. And her aunt had kept a home for all of them. She was never one Cassie felt comfortable confiding in, but then not all mothers probably were, either. She'd always been able to talk with her dad. And he usually had a good listening ear. When she was down, he would always find some Irish tale to cheer her up. When she was elated, he usually found time to celebrate with her. And when a horse won, he would twirl his little girl about as if the best possible thing in the world had just happened for both of them.

There was no question that she'd had an

inadequate mother, regardless of what her dad might now say. Even so, she'd grown up in a far from inadequate family. She'd been taught values and resiliency, how to dream and how to work hard, how to laugh and how to love. Maybe it was time to name the beast and move on.

She walked back to join her friends. With her hands clenched at her hips, she said, "You're right. I've been running. Running away from myself, as if that's even possible. I *am* scared of being like my mother. But you've helped me see that's not inevitable." A trace of a smile crossed her lips. "It may not even be likely.

"So I'll quit running. I'll try to turn around and face it, whatever that means. But I'm still scared. And I don't know what's going to come of all of this. But you've given me much to think about." She paused. "Thanks. Thanks for everything."

As was their custom, her friends quickly surrounded her in a circle hug. Tears were matched with laughter.

- o -

By mid-morning Wednesday, Clint sat in a comfortable chair on the O'Hanlon farmhouse porch swapping stories and dreams with Tug O'Hanlon. Cassie had called him just before midnight Tuesday, after picking up her phone messages on her return from Chicago. "Raul asked if I can come in first thing in the morning. They just found Daisy and pumped her stomach — she tried to kill herself. I think I'd better go. This could take most of the day. Can we do breakfast Thursday instead?"

So they'd agreed to meet at the track kitchen for breakfast the following morning. He didn't question her decision at all. He would have done the same. Seldom had the group home staff called during her leave, but this was one of those exceptional days.

Clint regretted that it had to be on his time. He also was uneasy about the strained words they'd exchanged the day before. He usually thought of himself as a patient man, a very patient man. But he'd recently discovered that jealousy could flow very hot through his veins. He'd never felt that way about any woman, not even his children's mother.

Although he enjoyed talking with Cassie's father, he didn't like being separated from Cassie for even a few hours. Soon he'd be going back to the ranch, and then all they would have would be the telephone and e-mail. He fidgeted, wondering how she was handling the trauma of her day.

"So you think if we bring in some of the California breeding lines, we'll strengthen our foals?" asked the older man, scrunched up on the edge of his seat.

"Given the breeding history you've told me about, it should," Clint reasoned, dragging his attention back to the white-haired man across from him. Discussing horses would at least provide a welcome distraction from worrying

263

about Cassie. "A. P. Indy and his lines should add some vigor to your foal crops. Could give you some interesting nicks in the future."

Sipping his coffee, Clint leaned back and glanced with approval at the greenery of the yard and pastures stretching out from the dull red barn. "If you'd want," he offered, "I could represent you at the Barretts Fall Sale in October. There'll likely be some fine yearlings and well bred broodmares coming through the ring there."

Tug smiled. Scratching his chin thoughtfully, he confided, "I kinda always wanted to do that someday. Never been much for sales. I like to grow my own. But I'm gettin' long in years for growin' much. Maybe Cassie'd like to work with some better quality horses."

Looking at the other man sharply, Clint raised his eyebrows. "You don't think this is just a six month thing with Cass, do you?"

"Maybe, maybe not." The old man ran a hand up and down his arm. He hesitated. "My daughter's still tryin' to find herself. This life is in her blood just as surely as an A. P. Indy filly is going to show stamina and distance. I'll put my money on my girl takin' this racing stable to a new plateau." He stopped long enough for Clint to blink. "You wanna take that bet?"

"Not at all," Clint said. He wasn't sure he liked what the old man had in mind. If Cassie really took a strong interest in a horse training career, would that make it easier for them to forge their future together? Or more difficult?

264

Answers remained hazy. But it was very clear her dad was as crafty and cagey as his own grandmother. Both were forces not to be underestimated. There were moments when he, too, believed that horses were in Cassie's blood, even if she wasn't ready to own that fact.

"Whatever Cassie winds up doing, we have to nab whoever's trying to mess it up for her," Clint said, refocusing their conversation on something they could do something about.

"You're right about that." The old man nodded apprehensively.

Getting up from his chair, Clint suggested, "Let's go into the kitchen table where we can spread papers out for you to look at. I've been compiling a number of lists. Maybe something will pop out at you."

"Sounds fine to me," Tug muttered, "I need a coffee refill anyway."

Clint studied the older man as he eyeballed the lists. Cassie's father might still be recovering from a stroke, but there wasn't anything wrong with his mind. He ran a finger down each list, pausing over a name now and then. He cussed at a few and smiled at others. Clearly, he was reliving old friendships and old enmities, and that was precisely what Clint had hoped for. Maybe something helpful would emerge from prodding those memories.

"So, you don't know of any old scores to be settled, or trainers who are simply jealous, or jocks who thought they were treated unfairly? No name jumps out from those lists of trainers, jockeys and owners?"

"Nope, nothin' rings a bell," Tug said, handing the sheets of paper back to Clint. "I coulda missed somethin', but I don't think this thing is personal." His voice thickened. "Someone just doesn't wanna compete against one of the best horses on the backstretch."

"Yeah, guess so," Clint said, draining his cup of coffee. "I think we'll know for sure soon enough."

"What's your plan?" Tug leaned forward over the kitchen table. "I knew you'd come up with somethin'."

"I've checked with the stewards. They've agreed for us to have two video cameras trained on the paddock area and on the filly throughout the post parade and at the starting gate. It took some persuading, but they realize that track detectives are known by almost everyone at the track except the casual bettor. We'll be less obvious. I'll be very surprised if we come up empty. Of course, there may be no attempt to drug the horse on Saturday. They may wait until the Land of Lincoln."

Tug shook his head. "No, I think they'll try. It's a feelin', I suppose. Almost like the challenge to get away with it is bigger than the result. Sort of like a bettor or a trainer keeps bettin' or pushin' a horse 'cause they don't think they can lose."

"You may be right. This may be about things we haven't even considered. Somebody is going a long way to see that a horse doesn't perform well. Not in just one race. It's like they want to destroy the horse's career."

The old man laughed and then wheezed. He struggled to catch his breath and then lifted his coffee cup in a mock toasting gesture. "Sort of like that backstabbin' Harrington tryin' to get Cassie to believe you were behind it all. He'd like to put his brand on Cass, but that'll never happen."

"What!" Clint exclaimed. A sudden chill filled the room. "Cassie thought I drugged the horse? I wasn't even here."

He felt the blood leave his face and stood to catch his breath. Backing against the kitchen sink, rubbing his brow with taut fingers, he gasped for air. "She really thought I did it?"

"Only briefly, until I set her straight. Well," Tug backpedaled, "I doubt if she actually ever believed it. Though Harrington told her you didn't have to be here to do it. You could've paid someone to do the dirty work. He said you might be tryin' to stop her from trainin' horses so she would go away with you."

The old man coughed loudly. "Course, I pointed out to Cass that Harrington could have the exact same motivation, make her fail so he could take over our horses and come to the aid of a fair lady in distress."

Tug scowled at Clint. "Now, I don't for a minute believe Cass really thought you were behind all our troubles."

Clint hardly heard Tug's efforts to qualify his

267

earlier words. A wave of hurt and rage washed through his body. His chest collapsed and his brain could not put two coherent thoughts together. He glanced down at his quivering hands.

"Thank you, Mr. O'Hanlon," Clint mumbled through clenched teeth. "I've got to get out of here."

- o -

Cassie sat in the visitor's lounge hugging the young slim girl tightly to her body. After Daisy's stomach had been pumped of enough amphetamines to kill her, she'd been transferred to a secure residential treatment center.

In spite of how much Raul had teased Cassie about coming back to the group home before her leave was up, he'd seldom called on her, even in times of serious crises during the past several weeks. But Daisy's case had gone beyond serious, and Cassie was one of the few people who had a relationship with the girl that might make a difference. He and Cassie had always discounted Daisy's contention that her half sister would eventually want her to come live with her.

Cassie had heard that fantasy from the moment the waif of a girl had stepped through the doorway over a year before. "As soon as Maxine is settled in, I'm out of here," was the story. And no amount of reasoning could dissuade her from that notion. She'd clung to it like a life preserver.

Raul said the call had come in around six

o'clock the prior evening. Daisy's sister didn't want to hear from her again. They hadn't lived together since their grandmother died. Maxine was getting on with her life, and she expected Daisy to do the same, one way or the other.

Daisy had gone berserk, screaming, pulling the phone out of the wall and dashing out of the house. The evening staff were unable to locate her. The police had been called.

Finally, long after dark, Daisy had been found lying face up in the grass near the intersection of Forty Seventh Street and Lake Shore Drive, rain pelting her unconscious body. She was lucky she hadn't died of hypothermia. Ironically, maybe the drugs had kept her body humming enough to resist the chill.

Now Raul had finally gone home to get some much needed rest. Daisy was certainly safe where she was. And she would likely be there under observation for at least thirty days. Cassie had already gotten a commitment from her to cooperate with staff. The suicide attempt was a cry for help. Now the question was whether Daisy would accept the help given her.

"You knew all along, didn't you?" Daisy sobbed softly. "That Maxine wouldn't take me in."

"Not for sure." Cassie said, rubbing the girl's back. "But I was afraid that might happen. That's why I talked so much to you about thinking through all your options."

"But I didn't listen."

"No, not much."

"Guess I've really made a mess of things this time."

"I'm just happy they found you in time. We need to look ahead, not back." Cassie's own words jarred her like alarms from a dozen clocks. What nonsense. Hadn't that advice been at the core of many of her own difficulties? People who loved her didn't want to talk about the past, so it just hung there like a large millstone around her neck. No, she would do better than that by Daisy.

"What I just said — about not looking back — that was wrong. You'll need to look into your past to understand what went wrong last night. But you don't have to remain mired down by it, either. We all have to look at our demons, maybe name them, maybe make peace with them, and then move on. Do you understand what I'm trying to say?"

The girl nodded. "I think so. Will you help me do that? Try to understand what happened, and move on."

"Of course I will. And Raul will help. And the folks working here will also help. The important thing to know right now is that you are not alone. You have a lot of people who care about you and love you."

"I feel so stupid," Daisy said, glancing away from Cassie. "Maybe I knew all along that Maxine wouldn't take me. Maybe I just didn't want to believe. Maybe I was afraid to believe."

Daisy scrunched her thin legs up against her chest and wrapped her arms around them, holding herself rigid. "Stupid. Not just alone, but really dumb. Embarrassed. I didn't know what to do. I didn't think. I know I raged and made a big scene. I just wanted out of there, big time. Just away, where no one could see me or would tell me *I told you so.*"

"That had to be a terrible time for you. It must have been a night of pure terror." Cassie smiled softly and held the girl's hands. "And all that you say about knowing and not wanting to believe may be true. But it's not important to figure it all out at once. You've got plenty of time. Let's not try to press it. You're not alone. You're safe. You're loved. And you want to get your life together. That's a very good start."

"So after this place, will they send me to another foster home, or can I go back to the group home with you and Raul?" The girl's voice rose with a modicum of hope.

Cassie shuddered. She wished she could tell Daisy what she wanted to hear, but she couldn't. "To be honest, I'm not sure. It's far too early to tell. You're fifteen. It's unlikely the court will allow you to live on your own. Perhaps we could get approval to start working with you toward some kind of supported emancipation when you're sixteen. But I'm sure there must be some foster parents out there who would love to have a girl like you."

"Right. Fat chance of that." Daisy's face fell. "Like only those who want the money would take me. I'd rather stay at the home with you guys. All I want is to be some place where people care for

271

each other."

"I know, honey," Cassie said, lifting the girl's chin up so she could look her in the eye. "I promise that I will do what I can to make sure that happens. Will you promise to do your best to be honest with the folks around here and work on your stuff? They will likely give you a lot of tests. Don't play games with them. Let's get you back on your feet and out of here so you can get on with putting your life together. Okay?"

"'Kay, I'll do my best," Daisy whispered, a slight grin crossing her lips.

"Good, that's all anyone can hope for. Come give me another hug. It looks like this nice young fellow is here to talk with you," Cassie said, nodding in the direction of a counselor. "Staff will probably keep you quite busy for awhile. I'll check in on you in a day or two. People here have Raul's number and mine. If you need to talk to one of us, don't hesitate to call. You take care."

"Yeah, you too."

- o -

"I want them on the next plane back to Salt Lake." Clint kept his voice calm and level with great effort but refused to meet his sister's gaze in the Palmer House suite.

"Aren't you overreacting some?" Silver Hawk asked. "Your pain is obvious. But have you talked to Cass? Have you heard her side of the story? Have you given her a chance to explain?"

272

"There's nothing to explain," Clint responded coldly.

"I'm supposed to run one of the video cameras on Saturday, remember?" Silver Hawk stood her ground.

"I'll hire someone. We'll catch the bastard." He closed his hands into fists and opened them slowly. "I want to see her face when she learns that it's not me who's drugging her damn horse."

"I don't think that's going to shock her," his sister said, hands on her hips. "I know the mood you're in. You're hurt and confused, and you've shut down. Don't do something stupid that you'll regret for the rest of your life. You've got an incredible woman ready to love you. Don't throw her away by being a stubborn ass."

Absently, Clint ran a hand through his hair. "Thought you didn't like her."

"I told you that wasn't true. I just didn't know her. Now I do, maybe better than you." Silver Hawk arched an eyebrow. "Apparently, much better than you. You're letting hurt and rage blind you to your own heart."

"Enough of this!" Clint declared. "You don't understand. It's a matter of honor. Let's get the kids packed."

"We don't want to go," Lester said tearfully. He and his sister had been listening from the other side of the adjoining bedroom door, and now they stood in the open doorway.

Sammy ran toward Clint and threw her arms around his legs. "Don't make us go away. Ms.

Cassie is a good woman. She wouldn't hurt you, Daddy. She gives warm hugs."

Clint knelt on one knee, holding a child in each arm. He didn't like seeing their tears, but they were young. "I'm sorry, kids," he said, more gruffly than he intended. "I wouldn't have brought you out here if I'd known this was going to happen. You're too young to understand. Someday maybe I can do a better job of helping you with that. But now you'll have to trust me. It's best that you go back home to Grandmother. Your aunt will see that you get there safely. I'll be home just as soon as I can."

"But..." both children protested.

"No, there will be no debating this," Clint said firmly, standing abruptly. "Now run along. There's a lot to be done to get you on one of the afternoon flights."

Clint walked toward the bathroom trying to ignore the sobs coming from his children, who threw stuff into their duffel bags haphazardly. He also worked at avoiding the frigid stare of his sister. Why didn't anyone understand what he was going through?

The woman with whom he'd hoped to live out his life couldn't trust him — she'd played him for a fool. And now his own family was turning against him.

CHAPTER THIRTEEN

After a half eaten supper, Cassie sat down to write in her journal. Her life was in such a turmoil she didn't know which problem to try to solve first. Daisy had been on her mind ever since she'd left the care facility. The young girl had a rough road ahead of her, but with proper support, she would make it.

The youngster had demonstrated resilience and courage over and over again. Would the court let her stay at the group home? The cost of services there was much more expensive than in a foster home. Cassie hoped she could stay long enough for them to develop a good transition plan. Daisy would need some help, probably a lot of help.

While she'd been feeding the horses before supper, a wild question had popped in her mind. *If I wasn't working at the group home, would I apply to be foster parent for Daisy? It would only be a two year commitment or so.* Cassie remembered laughing at that thought. If she became the girl's foster mother, it would be a lifelong commitment, and she knew it.

The idea niggled at her. She scribbled in her journal.

Apartment. She quickly put a line through that. Her Chicago apartment was almost too small for one person, let alone two.

McHenry farm. Yes, she could imagine living there, particularly if she didn't have to commute into the city every day. And there were plenty of social work jobs out in this area, too.

Utah.

Utah! "My goodness," Cassie gasped, her hands flying to her mouth. She hadn't thought much of Clint in the midst of Daisy's crisis.

She recalled Ashton's words, *What are you running from?* Had she been running from commitment? And yet here she was, considering at least the remote possibility of turning her life upside down for a girl who had little hope. If she could even fantasize about taking Daisy into her life, why not Sammy and Lester?

God, there was so much to resolve. Was she really a woman of courage? Was Clint really the right man? She knew the answer to that: *yes!*

What about being an instant mother? She wasn't her mother. She knew that now. There was no genetic rule saying she had to repeat her mother's mistakes.

The image of Daisy lying unconscious in the rain fixed in her mind. She never wanted anything remotely like that to happen to Lester or Sammy. They wanted and needed the same thing Daisy did—a place where people cared for one another. She needed that, herself.

Cassie thought back to her work with a yearling in the round pen earlier in the week and a sudden insight hit her. To train a horse, you had to have some basic knowledge, but the good trainer

276

listened and responded to the animal with her heart. The same could be said for raising children. She knew the basics. But more importantly, she already responded to Lester and Sammy with her heart. She would never be their mother, but she could be a very good step-mom.

Tears formed in Cassie's eyes and her fingers cramped from gripping the pen so hard. Why had it taken her so long to see what apparently so many others had seen for some time? She loved him with her total being. And she loved his children. They could make a future together. They *had* to.

She reached for the phone and then saw how late it was. She would sleep on her discovery and tell Clint in person at breakfast.

Although she was exhausted, Cassie's mind continued to whirl, keeping sleep at bay. The night seemed long already, and it wasn't even midnight.

As she reached for the romance novel on her bed stand, Cassie heard a vehicle winding its way down the driveway. Was something wrong at the track? Had Daisy had another crisis? In either case, someone would have called. Then she recognized Clint's truck and a thrill pulsed through her body. Already, she could feel dampness between her inner thighs.

Rushing to the door, she held it open and watched Clint climb the stairs two at a time. "Welcome, my midnight lover. Am I ever pleased to see you," she sang out in what she hoped was her most sultry voice.

Without speaking a word, Clint brushed by her outstretched arms, stepped to the center of room, turned, and glowered at her. His dark eyes were colder than ice. His nostrils flared. His tightly compressed lips contained no evidence of love. His hands flexed in and out of balled fists.

Cassie closed the door, involuntarily pressing her backside against it. "You look terrible. What's wrong?" she squeaked, aware of the trace of fear in her voice.

He said nothing.

"Let me hold you," she offered, breaking the heavy silence and stepping toward him.

She backed up immediately when his arms flew out to keep her at a distance. Her own anger began to flicker. "If you're not going to tell me what's wrong, how am I supposed to help?"

"You, help? That's a cruel joke."

The silence was deafening, but Cassie waited.

"So," he said tightly, "you've got it all figured out. You think I'm the man behind drugging the filly."

"What?" Cassie's hands clenched together, grinding at the terrible growing knot in her stomach. "That's silly. I'd never believe that. Who told you that?"

"Your father believes he had to dissuade you from that possibility." Clint's voice was flat and emotionless. "Another man—Harrington—appears to have more influence over you than good sense."

"That's not true," Cassie protested, finding her

voice at last. A cold dread seeped through her pores. She could see their future, or their lack of one, written so plainly on his face.

"Don't lie to me." He took a step forward. She could feel the hard steel of his anger. And she began to catch a glimmer of his overwhelming sense of betrayal.

Be calm, she told herself. *Let the anger wash over you. He doesn't mean to hurt you.* "It's true that Harrington was suspicious about you, but I told him that was nonsense."

"Your dad didn't seem to hear it that way."

Would he believe anything she said? He'd already called her a liar. "Dad and I were sharing hypotheses. I told him what Ed said. That's all." Trying to break the tension, Cassie eased from under his stare to sit in a chair next to the bed. Her legs were shaking so hard she had to sit down, no matter how he might interpret her behavior.

"And I was a hypothesis?"

Cassie quickly tired of his rage. He wouldn't hurt her physically, but he seemed to be doing everything in his power to destroy whatever they might have had between them. Was he listening to her at all? Did he want out that badly?

"There was a kernel of a possibility that you wanted me so much you could do something that devious," she said softly, trying not to provoke him further, but desperately wanting him to understand the quandary she'd been in. She had despaired for Hope—and for her father's dream. Clint had left for Utah. Looking back, she knew

279

she'd been more than a little vulnerable to Harrington's suggestions. But Clint's reaction was going beyond the pale.

"That dastardly, don't you mean?" He stepped to her chair, leaned over, and lifted her chin. "I don't need a woman, any woman, bad enough to drug a horse."

He stepped back quickly, as if he'd touched a hot stove. "Lady, I don't know what game you've been playing with me, but it's over. I thought whatever else happened, we trusted each other, had something we could build on. I see I've been sorely mistaken."

"So...it's over," Cassie said cautiously.

"That's what you wanted all along, isn't it?" His steely gaze froze her in place. "You've wanted out of this relationship all along, and didn't have the guts to say so."

"That's not true." How many times could she say that? Had he heard anything she said? "What about the kids? Do I at least get to say goodbye to them? Or am I to be placed in a dungeon, to recite my litany of sins?" Surprisingly emotionally intact, Cassie folded her hands and held them politely in her lap.

"The kids are back in Utah by now," he said with an air of smugness. "They left this afternoon. They didn't need to say goodbye."

"You bastard!" Cassie leapt off the chair. "You go out of your way so I can get close to your family, and then you just pull the rug out from everyone."

She faced him squarely. "What are you doing here, Mr. Travers? Why aren't you back in Utah? Did you enjoy pulling legs off of insects when you were a kid? I don't need this shit!"

Pushing up the sleeves of her Bears shirt, she said coldly, "And I'm not going to take it from you, or anyone else. You can get out of here right now and out of my life forever. Thank you very much." Cassie marched toward the door and swung it open wide.

"Not quite yet, but not soon enough, you can be assured," Clint retorted. "There's some unfinished business. I won't leave until I clear my name. There will be two video cameras on your horse Saturday. I'll be operating one of them."

"I don't need your help, goddammit!" Cassie stood her ground, still holding the door wide open. "I want you out of my life, now."

"It's not lady's choice this time," Clint said evenly, his eyelids narrowing to slits. "Believe me, I'm not doing this to help you. I'm doing it to regain my honor."

"Honor. That's about the dumbest thing I've heard yet." Cassie rolled her eyes skyward. "I can assure you, you've really handled this whole fiasco in a most honorable way."

Clint stepped over the threshold. "You probably don't know much about honor, but it's something very important to me. I'll be there on Saturday. You can count on that."

He reached for the door. "Better watch out, lady. If you're drugging your own horse, the

281

cameras won't lie." He closed the door behind him.

Cassie's book crashed against the wood frame.

Too devastated and resentful to cry, Cassie lay on her bed trying to feel something positive about the man who had just stormed out of the loft. No such feelings came.

How could he think she believed he was trying to bring her down — and why wouldn't he listen? She understood part of his sense of betrayal, but his anger went far beyond that.

What about honor? She'd honored him more than any man. She'd honored him with her body. She'd honored him with her love. She'd honored him with her trust. But he didn't see it that way. And then her tears began to flow.

He'd been so quick to judge, giving her no chance to explain. And he'd sent the kids away, as if she were some kind of demon. Now she'd never be able to hold those children and watch them grow.

The bed was covered with tissues before Cassie resolved to get on top of things. If he wanted to be so damn stubborn, fine. They'd catch the culprit who'd been drugging Hope and go their separate ways. That was the way he wanted it. That was the way she wanted it.

She'd been getting along quite fine before she'd ever met the damn cowboy. She would simply go back to where things were before she met him.

She threw two pillows across the bedroom as

she flashed on Clint's parting accusation — that she might be drugging Hope herself. "The nerve of that stupid, stubborn son of a bitch who thinks he's so damn honorable. We'll see about honor. The Irish know something about honor, too. We don't confuse it with spiteful pride."

Feeling like some sort of zombie, Cassie went through the motions the next morning of supervising her horses' exercise at the track and then at the farm. She tried to stay busy. She tried to keep her mind from functioning.

At ten o'clock, the barn phone rang, intruding on her desire to be alone. Never knowing if there was a problem with a horse at the track or with Daisy, she had no choice but to answer.

Could it be that he was calling to apologize? "Fat chance of that happening," she muttered, making her way down the barn aisle toward the phone in the tack room.

"Hello," she mumbled into the receiver, slumping against the small desk.

"Is that you, Cassie?"

The feminine voice slowly penetrated Cassie's fog.

"Yeah, it's me," she sighed.

"What's wrong?" Traci Steele asked. "You sound like you shouldn't be out of bed."

"Just not a good day," Cassie said, not wanting to disclose the real cause of her depression. "How are you?"

"Don't try to change the subject," chastised the

283

voice on the other end of the line. "We've been buds for too long. Something bad has happened. It's not your father?"

"No."

"Did you have an argument with Clint?"

Silence filled the airwaves.

"That's it! Isn't it? Tell me, Cass."

"It's over," Cassie said. "He thinks I believe he's the one behind drugging Hope. I couldn't change his mind. He stormed out of here late last night."

Traci waited patiently.

"Traci, he sent the kids back home without letting them say good-bye to me." Cassie sobbed. "Why couldn't he at least let me say good-bye?"

"Cass, listen to me," Traci said emphatically. "I'm coming right out to pick you up. Change into a loose fitting blouse, shorts, and tennis shoes. Make sure you have your bathing suit on underneath it.

"Pampered decadence is what I'm aiming for. We'll spend the rest of the day on Dad's sailboat. We were out over the week-end and everything is shipshape. I'll arrange for catered food so we won't have to bother much with lunch or dinner. If you want to talk, that's great. If you just want to sit back and feel the movement of the boat that will be fine too."

"I can't…"

"Nonsense, you're not going to get much done there moping around. You don't have to go through this alone. I insist."

Cassie recognized the determination in the other woman's voice. She knew she'd be doing the same thing if the tables were turned.

"I thought I was the social worker," she protested. "You're supposed to be an uncaring lawyer."

"Right. Go get showered and I'll be there in forty-five minutes."

"What about your appointments? Your work?"

"You're my only appointment. See you."

Cassie held the phone in her hand. Again she wept. She cried for Clint and herself, for the kids, and for friendship.

Nearing the harbor, Cassie decided there were at least a number of good reasons for having a rich friend. Traci had been her pal since college days. Her father was a well known and well-heeled lawyer with offices in the loop. He specialized in corporate law.

Glancing over at her tall, dark haired friend, Cassie wondered when Traci would finally take the initiative to break away from her father and do what she wanted to do. Traci wanted to practice criminal law, and one of the best ways to begin would be working in the county prosecutor's office.

Strangely, her friend was often more stubborn than she herself, yet Traci found it extremely difficult to challenge the wishes of her father. He'd wanted a son, but got a daughter. He wanted an heir to his practice, but she wanted something different. Cassie knew Traci loved her father a lot, perhaps too much. Someday there would be a reckoning between the two of them. That would be a good day for everyone else to duck.

"Here we are," Traci announced, smiling confidently. "What great weather for sailing. A gentle breeze, but no strong wind and plenty of sunshine. Though it'll be a lot cooler out on the water than here."

Conversation was sparse as the two women prepared for their sail. Cassie appreciated that.

Traci maneuvered the thirty-foot sailboat through the harbor toward the open lake. Cassie, sitting to one side of the boom and feeling rather unneeded, smiled at her friend's efficient movements. There was no wasted effort. It was as if her legal mind had *to do* lists for sailing, and each task was being checked off in order.

At last they were under sail. They skimmed across the water with very little resistance. There wasn't much for Cassie to do but breathe deeply and watch the Chicago skyline recede. "Watch your head," Traci commanded, "we're going to change direction."

Cassie ducked as the boom came across overhead.

"All right, we'll tack this line for awhile," Traci said. "Once we're out a ways, we can drift, and I'll go below to get the food out."

"Won't you let me do something?"

Traci gave her a whimsical smile. "You just sit here and take in the sunshine and the lake breeze.

I'll take care of the rest. Do you need more sunscreen?"

"Thanks." Cassie opened the offered bottle and rubbed more oil into her skin. Leaning back, she closed her eyes and let the sun bake the lotion into her heated pores. She felt like she was sizzling. Relaxed for the first time in hours, she dozed off as Traci puttered below.

"Bet you could use some nourishment," Traci said half an hour later.

Soft sounds of Celtic music drifted into Cassie's awareness and she labored to open her eyelids. When she did, she saw that Traci had deposited a platter of food on a deck table. Her stomach growled. She hadn't eaten anything since last night's half-eaten dinner.

With the corners of her mouth turned up, Cassie said, "You really did things up royally, didn't you?"

"Well," her friend admitted, "I never can remember if one feeds a cold and starves a fever or vice versa, but I do know you feed with care a broken heart."

Cassie nodded agreement and reached for the boiled jumbo shrimp. There were apple slices, carrots, cauliflower, mushrooms and a variety of dips. If this was lunch, she wondered what the catered dinner would be. "I see you're going to feed me healthy."

"Of course," replied Traci. "No man is worth getting fat over."

Cassie looked blankly at her friend and then laughed. It felt good to laugh. Laughter could cure most anything.

"So. Do you want to talk about it? It might help."

"I know. And I really appreciate all that you're doing, Traci. You're a treasure."

Before she drowned again in her own tears, Cassie provided a blow by blow description of her midnight encounter with Clint Travers. Oddly, hearing herself recount the event provided some emotional distance. To her surprise, she had no tears until she spoke about him sending the kids home without letting them say good-bye.

"Sounds like you've been to hell and back!" Traci said.

Cassie nodded, fighting back the tears. She hugged herself. Traci moved to put an arm around her.

Sobbing, Cassie keened, "What must they think of me? Lester and Sammy. They don't deserve to be hurt by our pride and stupidity."

"Kids are more resilient than we think. Look at me. Look at you. I'm sorry they might be sad and not understand, but it seems to me that the pivotal piece here is you and your rancher friend. Do you see any hope?"

"None. His honor, his pride is much bigger than us."

"Hmm. Keep in mind," Traci chided gently, "that you're seldom in short supply when it comes to honor and pride."

Cassie gave her friend a half smile and a nod. "I know. But this is different. He won't come back. That's for sure."

"Then how are you going to put him behind you and move on?"

"I don't know." Cassie became sharply aware of the agonizing frustration in her voice. Numbness paralyzed her body and mind. She hated not knowing which way to turn. She'd had no warning — it all happened just when everything seemed so full of promise and hope.

"I know I'll move on in time," she continued. "I always do. The timing was all wrong. First he wanted to get closer, and I ran away from him and from thinking about being a mother. I can't believe it fell apart just when I decided I *could* take on being a mother. He never gave me time to tell him that when he stormed into my apartment."

Traci handed Cassie a tissue.

Cassie blew her nose loudly. Damn, she wished she'd never met the man. That she'd never gone to Wyoming. That she'd never agreed to train Hope.

She shook her head vigorously. She couldn't lie to herself. Even though it wasn't going anywhere now, meeting Clint Travers and working with Hope had been exciting, and she wouldn't want to have missed either. Even with all the pain.

Wincing with a new realization, Cassie resumed, "The problem is, it isn't over. He's going to stay around until we catch whoever is drugging Hope. He'll be scathing to be around. I should just pull Hope from the race, but I can't do that. That would be the end of Dad's dream."

Stretching her long legs out, Traci ventured, "I expect you deserve that shot as much as anyone, Cass. You've put your heart and soul into that horse. I don't pretend to understand why, but I know it's important to you, and I'll support you any way I can."

"I know you will. There's not much anyone can do. All the cards are on the table. The game just has to be played out to its conclusion."

"I wonder about that. In my work, just as in yours I assume, when two parties have a blow up, usually each person thinks they've been crystal clear in communicating, while they have not completely heard the other. You may think all the cards were on the table, but if Clint was here, he'd probably say some were face down."

Cassie shrugged offhandedly, somewhat annoyed that her friend probably had her finger on something. Maybe she should have been quicker when she saw him climbing the stairs. Quicker to declare her love. And to say how much she wanted to mother his children.

But she'd been surprised by his coming to her in the middle of the night, and she'd hesitated and played sultry instead. And then it was too late. He assumed she was using him. She hadn't been able to penetrate his anger and hurt. Oh well, it didn't matter now.

"How about a nap? We can swim later in the afternoon, if you like," Traci suggested.

Welcoming Traci's effort to provide her with

more down time, Cassie readily agreed.

In only minutes, Cassie put on more lotion, rolled over on to her stomach, and luxuriated in the warm caress of the sun. It wasn't the caress she remembered best, but it would have to do.

She lay there thankful for the skipper of this little excursion. Traci had done exactly what was needed. She'd plied her with ample sunshine, food, and silence. She'd also gotten her to tell her story. And while Traci seldom gave direct advice, she was usually quite insightful.

The lawyer typically shied away from examining feelings, keeping her own under tight restraint. Although they knew each other well, Cassie remained curious about what must smolder beneath Traci's often icy exterior. But today she'd provided just the right balm for Cassie's wounds.

The sun was disappearing in the west before they began to sail back to the harbor. Still hurting but refreshed, Cassie knew she could deal with whatever came her way. The next few days wouldn't be easy, but she would make it through them.

"The blood red sun setting behind the skyline makes the city look like it's on fire," Traci said, redirecting Cassie's attention. "It's a sight I've seen over and over again, but I'm awed by it each time."

Amused, Cassie allowed herself to remember with gentleness the bent old woman who had named her Fire Woman. What would Clint's grandmother make of this debacle?

Meanwhile, Clint had been busy. He'd moved out of the Palmer house early in the morning. There was no need for such spaciousness or luxury since the kids were gone. And he wouldn't be bringing any woman there.

He'd moved into an economy hotel near the track. The place offered horsemen's specials.

By noon he'd returned the rental car and picked up his truck from the track. When he left this time, and he hoped to God it would be soon, he would transport his horses back to Utah. There was no reason to leave them in Chicago. He wasn't coming back.

Numb, he drove his pickup north on I-94. He wasn't headed anywhere in particular. He just needed to get out of Chicago...away from her and everything that reminded him of her.

Even with the pedal pressed to the floor, his pickup had a hard time doing eighty. Fence posts blurred. He wished memories could blur as readily.

Crossing the Wisconsin border, Clint slowed down to seventy. The state patrol was famous for nabbing out of state speeders. Even in his dazed sense of reality, he knew he didn't want to be pulled over.

It wasn't the fine he was worried about. He might not be able to maintain a civil attitude with a cop, and that could only spell trouble. And his cup overflowed with enough trouble already.

When he saw signs indicating Milwaukee was only twenty miles ahead, he muttered aloud, "Damn, I don't need another city."

He took the first exit west and found himself shortly driving through rolling green hills.

He'd really believed she was the one. She'd given him new life. And then she'd snuffed it out like it hadn't mattered a whit. He wished to hell he hadn't exposed his kids to the red-haired devil.

The worst part was that he'd have to be around her until they found the bastard who was drugging the horse.

Glancing at the gas gauge, Clint saw the needle hovering near empty. He pulled into the next small town gas station and got out and stretched. In addition to filling the tank, he picked up a ham and cheese sandwich and a Sprite.

The middle aged buxom woman at the cash register smiled warmly and accepted his credit card, ignoring his glower.

"My, you've come a long ways," she said, waiting for his card to clear. "We don't get many folks here from Utah."

"I bet."

The woman asked, "Is it as beautiful as I hear? I've never seen the mountains."

"It's pretty, all right," Clint replied.

After signing the credit slip, he grabbed his bag to leave, then hesitated. "Is there any place around her where one can get some peace and quiet?"

Nonplused, the clerk ran her fingers through her mousy brown hair. "There's a motel on the outskirts of town."

"I'm not looking for a bed," Clint interrupted. "Is there any country around to walk in, any vistas to see?"

"Sounds like you're homesick."

Clint ignored that comment.

"We don't have views like you're used to," the woman said, "but if you take that road you came in on two miles out of town and turn on County Road A, you'll go through some pretty country. It's called the Kettle Moraine, left behind by the glaciers."

"Thanks," Clint muttered.

Within twenty minutes, the woman's words had come true. He could breathe again. Very few houses were around. Initially, he drove through thick woods, and then he'd come upon an open meadow, and then the scenery would turn quickly to woods again. And it was all gently rolling. The kettles and the moraines, he imagined.

At one turn-off, he pulled over to stretch his legs and watch the waterfowl come and go on a marshy lake—mallards, wood ducks, Canadian Geese, and further off to his right a blue heron stood in the water near the marsh's edge. They seemed so sure of themselves, whether they were finding a place to land or a place to feed.

The sounds were soothing. Ducks quacking. Geese honking. He could also make out the cry of redwinged blackbirds and the call of a kingfisher. In the midst of his misery, life went on whether he wanted it to or not, whether he was ready or not.

Sitting on the edge of a knoll, Clint dozed off to sleep. It was a fitful sleep as a nude woman with rich auburn hair chased him naked across the deep green grass of rolling hills. When he stopped to take the woman into his open arms, she'd vanish only to reappear some distance away. They chased each other, but failed to ever touch. The green of the landscape dazzled his eyes. It was a lush land, matching the disposition of the comely redhead. He knew it was Ireland, though he'd never been there before.

He awoke as the blood red sun nestled close to the western horizon, leaving its flames etched across the sky. Those flames stretched over his head.

His heart clinched. Fire Woman. Hah. He wondered what his grandmother would make of her now. He'd been scalded by her fire, that was for sure. Never again. Never ever.

Disgusted with himself, he had to admit that while the woman had lied to him over and over, she had never spoken those three words he'd wanted to hear so badly. At least she hadn't gone that far. He wished to hell *he* hadn't.

Determined to protect himself from the fickle smoldering redhead for as long as it took to catch a crook, Clint walked to his truck to begin his trek back to the Windy City.

"I tell you I'm goin' out to see her work over the track." Tug O'Hanlon glared. "Either you can take me along, or I'll call a cab, but you can damn well count on me bein' there."

"Dad," Cassie protested. She was about to trailer Hope from the farm to the track for a light workout so the filly could get reacquainted with the track conditions and its surroundings. She certainly hadn't expected company, especially her father.

"Don't *Dad* me. I don't care what the doctor says. This may be my last chance at havin' a real good horse. I gotta be certain we're doin' everything we can. Maybe she just don't like the track surface. Maybe she's got somethin' botherin' her that no one else can see. I've been around horses a long time, Cass. Sometimes they talk to me in ways others don't hear."

"But what if…" Cassie fought the tears forming in her eyes.

Tug responded with a dry chuckle. "None of us are gonna live forever, girl. If I had my choice I'd die at the track anyway, but I don't think you're gonna get rid of me that quick. You can't deny me this chance to help. You don't know what it feels like to sit here day after day helpless, lettin' you do all the work, tryin' to figure out a way to keep a finger in the pot. You need me. Hope needs me. I'm comin' along to watch how she takes to the surface."

Exasperated, Cassie threw up her hands in defeat. When had she been able to deny him of late? No doubt he'd been scheming for days trying to come up with a convincing argument to get to the track.

Particularly now that Travers was working only to protect his damn honor, her dad wanted to be more involved. There was no question he missed the life at the track. But...

But, she couldn't stop him. If she went without him, he'd call a cab as soon as she was out of sight. At least if he was with her, she'd be able to keep an eye on him.

"Okay, you win. As usual." She smiled weakly as the frail man beamed. She hoped his excitement would carry him through the morning without killing him.

Sitting in his wheelchair at the edge of the track, Tug O'Hanlon lowered his binoculars. "She's good. Damn good. You've done a fine job with her, Cass. I'm proud of both of you."

"Yeah, well we haven't done much to earn that pride on race day now, have we?" Cassie fidgeted with her hands and shifted her weight from foot to foot. There was too much worry for pride. The outing seemed to have actually perked up her dad, but then when would he crash? He must be running on pure adrenaline. Hope did look good, but she always looked good in the morning hours.

And then there was the dark figure of a man hunched over the rail a hundred yards away watching his own horses work. How could he stand being in the same place she was? How dare he work his horses at the same time she worked hers? Well, Travers could stay there until he turned to stone, for all she cared. She would simply go about her business and ignore him.

"I'm even more convinced that Travers is right," she heard her dad continue. "Somebody's gettin' to the horse. The track surface isn't botherin' her. She looks as sharp as a tack."

"I see you brought the expert out this morning," Ed Harrington said, joining them at the fence. "Good to see you, Tug. Maybe you can figure out what's wrong with that damn filly."

"Dunno," Tug groused, "seems like there may be a number of theories, but no one can really get to the bottom of it. How you been doin', Harrington? Understand you can't keep your nose in your own business any more than ever."

"I'm okay. It's not the same without you here. The stories sound too true. Few can stretch a story quite like you, Tug."

Tug smiled easily. Struggling, he lifted his right hand. "I've missed you all, too."

"Well, look what the cat drug in, pardner." Louie Picard knelt beside Tug's wheelchair and laid a gnarled hand atop those of his old friend.

"Uh, oh," Harrington joshed, "now the stories will start thick and heavy."

"Nonsense," Tug complained. "Louie and I have been going at it for decades and I don't think either one of us ever stretched the truth."

Cassie laughed along with the rest. There were no two guys more noted for storytelling on the Chicago circuit than her father and Louie Picard.

"It's good to see you, old friend," Louie said. "It's been pretty boring out here without you. Though Cass has been filling in real good."

"Yeah," Tug replied, with more than a little pride, "she's a chip off the old block."

"So do you think this chestnut filly is the dream you've been chasing all these years? She's a beaut, that's for sure."

Tug coughed while Cassie moved quickly to pull the blanket more snuggly around him. "Don't know," he said at last, "but she's sure got a lot of potential." He paused for breath. "So how's your string doin', Louie? They keepin' you in oats?"

"Okay, we win some and we lose some, but that's better than not trying."

Tug grimaced. "Expect I've heard you say that a thousand times, old friend, but you don't really know what it means until you can't come out to shedrow on a daily basis...This is a precious life we all share." Brushing dirt from the corner of his eye, he added, "Don't ever forget it."

With effort, he turned to Cassie. "Best you wheel me back before I make a fool of myself. Take care, boys."

"You too," Ed and Louie replied. Each headed toward their respective barns.

The phone rang, as Louie had expected. He sighed heavily and then picked it up on the third ring. "Yeah."

"Louie, you know what to do."

"Yeah."

"Don't screw up. This is a big one."

"Have I ever?"

"How about at Sportsman's in 92?"

Louie scowled. He'd tried to forget that mistake.

"I don't want the filly killed, Louie. Just slowed down."

"Right. Don't worry, I'll get it done."

"Will your grandson graduate at the winter graduation?"

"You know he will."

"I know. Just don't *you* forget. I'll be watching."

CHAPTER FOURTEEN

It was a muggy, hazy August Saturday in Chicago. The weatherman had predicted ninety-eight degrees with the humidity lagging only slightly behind. Not a good day for human or beast.

Pausing in front of the portable fans she'd brought along from the farm, Cassie pulled the thin blouse fabric away from her skin, seeking any modicum of relief. She'd set up the fans to try and keep Hope cool and relaxed until it was time to walk to the saddling paddock. They'd been at the track for two hours to give the horse some time to acclimate from the trailer ride in.

The breeze, what there was, might have been blistering hot, but the air between her and the man slouched against the stable wall staring at her with raw contempt couldn't have been colder if they were on an arctic ice sheet.

He'd said nothing other than to inform her that the video cameras and operators were in place. She'd expected he'd be behind the cameras, but it was clear he wasn't going to let either the horse or its trainer out of his sight. His constant glare did little to inspire confidence, but damn if she would show any sign of weakness. She tried to go about the business of preparing for the race as if nothing bothered her or the horse.

It was so important not to let Hope feel her own anxiety. Maybe there would be no attempt to get at Hope this time. Cassie didn't believe that for one minute.

"How's the horse, Cass?" Ed Harrington asked gruffly. "Suppose you think criminals are lurking all over the place."

"She's fine, Ed. She should do well today," Cassie responded evenly, hoping the man would gracefully move on down shedrow.

"Well, well," Harrington said, acknowledging Clint's presence, "if it isn't the cowboy from the wild, wild west."

Clint turned his head away from Harrington and spat. Otherwise he made no response to the man's jibe.

"Cat got your tongue? Heard from a groom that you're hauling your horses back to Utah next week." He grinned boldly, triumph filling his eyes. "Can't stand the competition, huh? That's okay, cowboy. Chicagoans are a breed unto themselves. We know how to race the best horses and how to take care of our women," Harrington taunted. "Looks like you'll be needing more help than you thought, Cass."

"Don't count on it," Cassie replied tartly.

Clint moved smoothly from the stable wall to stand directly in front of the trainer. "I think the lady would like you to move on, mister."

"Are you trying to make me move?" asked a red faced Harrington.

"Nah, wouldn't want to force you to do

302

anything. Certainly a Chicagoan should know when he's not wanted."

Harrington stared hard at Clint, clearly measuring his options. "Okay, you win, cowboy. But we'll see who wins on the track." As he turned to walk away he added, "And we'll see who wins the girl in the long run."

"*The girl*," Cassie sputtered. "Who the hell does he think he is?"

"Your next lover, no doubt," Clint said tersely. "He's well aware of a vacancy. At least he didn't go anywhere near the horse. Not yet, anyway."

Over the public address system came the announcement to bring horses for race five to the paddock.

- o -

Staying on alert, Clint walked beside Hope as Cassie led her toward the saddling area. He let his gaze dart about, taking in everything around them. Nothing seemed out of place. Hope seemed relaxed. The unexpected didn't seem to be happening. He'd put money on an attempt being made. Someone felt so strongly about keeping Hope from performing that he couldn't let the horse get away with a clean race.

The saddling went smoothly. Clint saw nothing unusual from the paddock judge or attendants. A groom led Hope out to the paddock circle and began walking her around.

The jockeys came out from the jockeys' room.

Cassie hefted the jockey into the saddle. The horse behind her reared. Louie Picard came over to put his arm around Cassie, wishing her luck. Earl Sheraton stepped between horses to shake Cassie's hand, also wishing her luck. Harrington passed by to wish her horse a good trip. This was not uncommon. Trainers competed with each other, but they also looked out for each other. None wanted a horse to be hurt. Clint scowled. At least that was the code. He studied the paddock crowd. Someone in this bunch didn't care one whit about jeopardizing a horse.

Shrugging, he headed for the stands. He hadn't seen anything, but he really hadn't expected to. There was simply too much confusion in the paddock area to see everything.

But the cam recorders would, if they covered the appropriate angles. He hadn't bothered to look, but he knew Cassie followed him carrying another set of binoculars. Both mounted the stairway quickly.

Both saw the same thing. They watched a horse who had started the post parade up on her toes and eager to race slowly flatten out along the backstretch, before the horses ever even came close to the starting gate.

"They got to her," Cass whispered, her voice laced with despair.

"Yeah, they sure did," he said, keeping his voice even. "Now we can get to the bottom of this." He let the binoculars drop to his chest and started to leave.

"You're not going to watch the race?"

"No need to. I've got what I want."

"You wanted her to be drugged, didn't you?" Cassie accused, brushing stray strands of hair from her forehead.

"Of course, otherwise I'd have to stay or come back until she *was* drugged," he responded. "I can't clear myself until I find the bastard who's behind all of this."

"You don't care about Hope. You don't care about Dad's dream. You just care about yourself."

Clint grabbed her wrist. "Listen carefully. Very carefully. I do care about the horse and about your dad. But I've also learned the hard way that my caring can be misplaced and trampled on…

"I'll bring the videos by the farm this evening. We'll look at them on your dad's VCR. Another set of eyes that knows the people and the inner workings of tracks and horses may be helpful." Without waiting for a response, he walked toward the stairs.

- o -

Cassie watched the man skulk away. Even his resolute determination could not hide his brokenness. He looked drained of energy and spirit. His vulnerability shook her to the core. Until now, she hadn't really realized how badly he was hurting. Cassie wiped tears from her eyes in time to watch Hope run gamely across the finish line in fifth place.

The three of them, Cassie, her father and Clint, hunkered in the farmhouse living room in front of Tug's VCR, running and rerunning the tapes of Cassie Hope's movements from the time she stepped into the paddock area until leaving the gate at the start of the race.

The tension in the room would dull a knife. Very few words were exchanged between Cassie and Clint. Tug's attempts at conversation were rebuffed. Cassie sat on the couch leaning forward, resting her chin on her hands, watching the screen intently. Clint was down on his knees close to the TV glaring at the screen, as if demanding it prove him innocent.

On the second run through, Clint felt they'd missed something. He wanted to go frame by frame. It was a painstaking effort, but it needed to be done.

Cassie's eyes blurred from focusing so hard. She looked away and then quickly back. "There!" she shouted. "Back it up. I thought I saw something, like a shadow."

The picture in the frame showed the jockey ready to be hoisted up atop Hope. It was that moment when trainers and owners were wishing jockeys and each other well. There was Cassie doing just that, giving last minute instructions to the jockey. And there beside her in the shadows was a man who had just finished the same with his rider. Just prior to greeting Cassie with a smile and a hug, his right palm had brushed Hope's near hip. It was a brief instant, but it could have been enough.

The frozen picture frame did not lie. Clearly visible, in a flicker of real time, was the friendship ring that a child had given a man as a token of trust and love.

"Oh my god!" Cassie cried out, collapsing against the sofa.

"That son of a bitch!" gasped a startled Tug O'Hanlon.

"What? Who is it?" Clint asked, through compressed lips not taking his eyes off the screen.

"Louie Picard. One of Dad's longest friends. He's wearing the friendship ring I gave him when I was ten years old."

"Damn."

"But we don't really know that that one tap on Hope's hip is it. Do we?" she asked, not wanting to believe.

"We can continue to look frame by frame," Clint said icily, "but I'd bet my ranch we've found the bastard. We don't have time to set up another trap for him. The next race is the Land of Lincoln. We'll just have to confront him. Maybe we can smoke him out of his hole."

"Just be careful," Tug O'Hanlon advised, frowning sourly. "This smells to high heaven. I don't doubt it was Louie. But he wouldn't do it on his own. I can't believe that. Somebody's behind him."

The next morning, Cassie and Clint found

Louie Picard on shedrow filling a water bucket and invited him to a private room inside the track kitchen, with the promise that he would be surprised by what they had to share with him.

Immediately wary, Louie declined grumpily, "I don't have time for surprises. I'm too old for 'em." Returning to his work, he tried to ignore the two intruders.

"Come on, Louie. Just for me." Cassie put her arm on his shoulder, trying to be as sweet as she could, hating every second of it. *This is the man who betrayed me. Why? Why Hope?*

Clint gripped the man's other arm with less tenderness. Louie went along grudgingly, apparently not wanting to make a scene and draw a crowd.

"Have a seat, Louie," Clint instructed roughly, closing the door to the small room containing a few chairs and a television with a VCR. "We've got a video we think you might find fascinating, if not downright revealing. We'd kind of like you to interpret it for us. Turn it on, Cass."

Cassie pushed the button. The saddling paddock with all the horses being saddled for the previous day's race number five came in clearly. In the number three stall, Cassie saddled Hope. In the number four stall, Louie was doing the same with his horse. The grooms walked their horses around the circle for a few minutes until the paddock judge called riders up.

Louie fidgeted and started to noticeably perspire. The tape showed Cassie helping the jock mount Hope. Breathing heavily, Louie groaned, "That's enough. I don't need to see any more."

Cassie pushed the stop button and slowly let out a trapped breath. She stood gawking at Louie, feeling like a stricken little girl betrayed by a best friend. To her amazement, she saw a couple tears working their way down the man's weathered cheeks. Cassie shook her head, trying to keep her own in check.

"Why?" she asked. "Why my horse?"

Scrunching up in his chair, Louie said, "Wasn't nothin' personal with you, honey."

"Don't call me honey, dammit." Cassie gripped the back of a chair for support, her knuckles whitening.

"Okay," Louie responded painfully. "It didn't have nothin' to do with you, or even your horse."

"I don't understand." Cassie ran her fingers furiously through her hair. She rubbed her nose and sighed deeply. "It sure as hell was personal. You were ruining Hope's chances. You were trashing Dad's dream. You made me look like a fucking idiot."

"Cassie," Clint hissed, "let him tell his story. Give him some space."

"Yeah, I know," she said, unable to meet the eyes of her old friend. "Okay, go ahead."

"It goes back a long ways. Back to the sixties, long before you was even born, girl." He paused to light an old stogy. "Your daddy was beginning to make a name for himself as an up and coming trainer hereabouts. The mob took notice."

"The mob?" Cassie squeaked.

The old man nodded. "One day your dad had the favorite for the featured race. They didn't want that horse to win. Your dad wouldn't throw the race. The boys lost a lot of money that day. Twice more they came to your old man. Each time, he refused to help." Louie stopped talking to cough harshly.

Cassie's entire body shook. She could never imagine her stubborn father taking orders from anyone. But the mob?

"So," Clint prompted, "they came to you for help."

"Yeah," Picard grunted, wiping a hand on his dirty jeans. "You don't turn your back on 'em and just walk away. They don't always kill people or break legs like in the gangster movies, but they have their ways. From that point on your dad ran a lot of horses, some good horses, but never a real contender. Never the kind of horse he wanted and sometimes thought he had."

"You," Cassie accused, her facial features tightening in horror. "You made sure those horses wouldn't win. You, his best friend."

"Who better to do it, from the mob's point of view? It was easy," Louie acknowledged, casting a lopsided grin. "Your dad seldom had a big winner here in the Chicago area anyway. They didn't take his job away from him; they just made sure he'd never reach his dream."

"How cruel."

"Maybe."

"Now what?" Cassie asked, looking at Clint.

"We've got some options, I suppose," Clint began, moving to turn off the humming VCR. "We could turn him over to the police. We could take what we have to the track stewards. Louie would certainly be banned from tracks for life. The question mark in all of this is the mob. Will they simply replace Louie? And will they pass the curse from father to daughter? I think for the moment we ought to sit tight. Louie's situation is precarious enough — I doubt he's going to want to attract mob attention at the moment."

The door to the small room opened and closed behind a slight older woman with graying auburn hair. "You've taken the fall long enough, Louie." She walked toward the man sitting stiffly in his chair. "That was quite a concoction about the mob. Almost began to believe it myself."

She directed her attention to Cassie and Clint. "You two are good. You may think it strange that that pleases me. But I've sought revenge against your father all these years. I can't say it's been thrilling — but I've never harbored ill feelings against you, Cassidy."

Cassie's eyes bulged. Her heart stopped. *Don't faint. Hold on.*

The woman laughed thinly. "You look like you're seeing a ghost. Maybe you are. Can't blame you. It's not like I've been around much. Oh, I've watched you from a distance zillions of times, but you never saw me. Or when you did, you never made the connection. Yes, I am your mother."

"Jesus," Clint muttered.

"Why?" Cassie managed to say in a squeaky voice.

"Why? I imagine that's a lot of questions. Until yesterday, I guess I'd never forgiven your father for taking you from me."

"He didn't take me. You left!"

Cassie's mother nodded. "True. But I had no choice. I learned too late that I couldn't bounce around following him from track to track. And the farm became my prison, with your aunt as my jailor. It was unbearable.

"I couldn't afford to take you with me — you'll never know the countless times I regretted not doing so. But your aunt, for all her ill feelings toward me, was a good mother to you — probably better than I'd ever have been."

"But you're my mother. How could you?"

"I'm not going to spend a lot time defending my actions, and there's a lot I'm never going to tell you. I wish I'd done some things different. I should have come forward much earlier and maybe carved out some space for me in your life. But I didn't. I can't rewrite history."

"So," she said directing her attention to Clint, "What do you plan to do about me and Louie?"

"That's up to Cassie," Clint said. "But I'm curious why now. Why did you come forward now? Louie was covering for you. Clearly you've earned his loyalty over the years."

"Louie didn't deserve carrying this burden alone. I take full responsibility for his actions, as

312

well as my own. Maybe I'm just tired of being bitter. After awhile it becomes a cancer. Then — then I saw your father in the stands. In the wheelchair. He's a broken man. I don't want any more part of it. "

"It sounded like more than that."

"You listen well, young man. I watched you and Cassidy and your two young ones at the museum and in the park. You were all so excited and babbling you never noticed an old woman walking by or standing by a tree looking for birds.

"It broke my heart again. To realize what I'd missed by running away so many years ago. I gathered from Louie that my daughter questions her own ability to be a mother."

She turned her gaze to Cassie. "I'm not expecting your forgiveness, Cassidy. I won't even ask for it. I'm not expecting to saunter back into your life. But I do want to make one thing very clear. Yes, you are my daughter. My blood flows through you. But you are not like me. I've seen you with your kids outside the group home. I've seen you with Mr. Travers' kids. No, you're not like me.

"You're stronger, much more confident. You're much more comfortable being with children. When they hug you, you hug them back — you don't worry about crushing them or being crushed by them. You're more playful than I could ever be — guess you get that from Tug. I do like to think you got some things from me. Your beauty, even your temper. I urge you not to make the mistakes I

313

made. Risk being in love. Risk being a mother.

"I've said enough. You've been very quiet, Cassidy. What do you want to do with Louie and me?"

Cassie shook her head. How could she think straight? Her mother? Good god, her mother had been behind so much disappointment, so many tears. Did she really have any idea?

"We won't prosecute," she said, looking at Clint.

He nodded.

"I'll take you at your word that it's over. At this point, I'm not inclined to explain it all to Dad. This could prompt another stroke. We'll figure out something to tell him." Cassie stared at her mother through teary eyes. "I don't know what else to say. Or what you want."

"That's fine," her mother said. "This has to be a huge shock. I do appreciate not having to talk with the police."

She nodded at Clint. "If there's nothing else, I guess it's time for me to make another exit." She pinched the bridge of her nose. "I do wish you happiness, Cassidy. I always have. Come on, Louie. Let's leave now."

Louie Picard walked ahead of Cassie's mother and opened the door. They both walked out. Louie closed the door softly behind them.

The shaking started as soon as she heard the soft click of the door latch. She couldn't stop shaking. She couldn't even slow the trembles. Cassie allowed Clint to gather her in his arms. She

314

shook and cried for a very long time. He combed her hair with his fingers.

At last Cassie began to relax. She stepped out of his arms, walked over to the VCR, and removed the tape. Doing something — anything — helped.

She turned to face Clint. "This is going to take awhile to sort out."

"I can imagine," Clint said. "I'll return the VCR to the office and be on my way."

Could this day get any worse? She didn't have enough energy to deal with her mother's betrayal, and now she had Clint staring her down as if she were some alien. "So that's it."

"That's it." Clint's voice was gruff. "I've got responsibilities waiting in Utah."

Cassie nodded, turned, and slowly made her way to the doorway through which her mother had just exited.

A week later, with her morning chores finished, Cassie sat alone on the porch steps. It was like her roller coaster ride had bottomed out and stayed there — stuck. Her mother, again. And Louie Picard had betrayed a childhood trust. Clint Travers had chewed her up and spat her out like unwanted fat. Even her dad seemed to hold her more responsible for that ill-fated relationship than he did Clint.

Her father missed the Utahan. *So what?* she fumed. He could pick up the phone and call the man, if he wanted to. She wasn't about to do that.

The soul wrenching sound of a mourning dove

shattered her awareness. Unwanted tears yielded to the bird's call. Was the bird wailing over the loss of a mate?

Cassie hugged herself. She had to get on top of things. She needed a plan. "Stop analyzing. Start living," she muttered, tossing a pebble across the yard.

That evening she would meet her friends for dinner. It could be a dicey get-together. Susan would cheer. Now she'd be able to fix her up with an appropriate cosmopolitan man. Traci knew the story and no doubt would continue being supportive. Ashton wouldn't ask many questions. She'd listen. Cassie felt guilty for having avoided the woman who had admired the man from Utah. No doubt, Ashton would find a private opportunity to grill her about the breakup.

But before all of that, before dinner, on her way to the restaurant, she would stop at an exquisite little bath and oils store on the near North Side and pick up some of the most expensive items they had. Tonight she would pamper herself with the best bubble bath ever imagined.

And then. The Land of Lincoln was rapidly approaching. One more week and it would be over...one way or the other. Cassie trusted the next week would be better in some ways. She would be so busy and so focused on the race she wouldn't have time to think about betrayal.

As she rose to enter the house, she paused, realizing her plan had said nothing about social work. She was due back at work in only a matter of weeks. She grimaced—her grand plan extended to all of one week.

Chuckling, she said aloud, "Better than one day at a time." How often had she advised folks to take it one day or one step at a time? Well, tonight would be the first step, and then the next week would be a gigantic leap. She could not see further down the path. And that had to be okay, at least for the moment.

Thankfully the restaurant lighting was dim. Some might find the soft light romantic; Cassie found it protective, like a hazy fog. Maybe the puffiness around her eyes would be less visible. She'd waited until after the entrees arrived to make her announcement. She appreciated that Traci had made no attempt to pre-empt her, but then Traci was a lawyer and seemed to know how to wait and bide her time.

Determined not to break down, Cassie sat up straight, clasped her hands at her waist, and spoke slowly. "It's over. Clint and the kids are back in Utah. It was a summer fling after all."

She tried to ignore the shock on Susan's face and the immediate concern on Ashton's.

"Is this the reason for the message on my machine telling me not to bother to come and see Hope race last Saturday?" Ashton asked. "These last few days have been so filled with crises at work, I haven't even had time to follow up."

"It wouldn't have been much fun. Mr. Travers was hell bent for leather protecting his honor." She gulped. "Dad let it out that a trainer friend at the track suggested to me that Clint might be the culprit drugging Hope. Clint went berserk—he never let me explain that I didn't believe the man. He sent the kids back home immediately without letting me say goodbye and then he almost accused me of drugging my own horse."

"Oh," Susan gasped, "my goodness."

"Yeah, well, he can sit on his damn high desert ranch and dry up like a prune, as far as I care."

"Did you catch the fellow causing all the problems for your horse?" Traci asked.

Cassie flinched and looked away. "Yeah. It was my mother and one of Dad's oldest friends. She didn't want him to reach his dreams because he had thwarted hers. Can you believe it?"

"Your mother!" Ashton exclaimed. "You've got to be dying inside."

Cassie shrugged. "Apparently, she's been around more than I ever knew. Graduations. Outside the group home. She saw me and Clint and the kids at the museum. That might have played into her coming forward once we were onto Louie. Pretty weird, huh. But that's how it is."

"Boy," Susan said, "that gives new meaning to being wary of a woman who thinks she's been wronged."

"So," Traci asked, "what are you going to do about them—your mother and your dad's old friend? They did commit several crimes, apparently over many years."

"Nothing. They won't try anything again. We didn't tell Dad that my mother was behind it. That seemed more than he needed to bear. He accepted a story that Louie told us about mob involvement.

Cassie picked up a fork, only to place it back down on the table. "Funny, I always wondered what happened to my mother, what she looked like, what she might think of me now. She stood there so cool, almost serene. She said something about bitterness being a cancer." Cassie shook her head. "I refuse to let bitterness eat at me — whether it's about my mother, or about Clint, or about anything else. It's not worth it."

Traci skimmed fingers over Cassie's hand. "Maybe your mother helped you after all."

Cassie winced "Maybe she did."

"Well, doesn't that beat all," Ashton declared. "No wonder you weren't able to get Hope to perform at her ability. So you got your horse back, but you've lost the man."

Cassie reached for her glass of water, nodded and remained quiet. No words could express her sense of desolation.

"I've got a cousin I'd like you to meet, Cass," Susan said, with a huge warm smile. "He's into art and theater. Jason is in corporate sales. He has a big office in the Loop."

Cassie started shaking her head before her friend even finished speaking. "No, not now. I'm too busy," she responded demurely. That was all she needed — another male to contend with. No way. Now was not the time. Maybe never.

319

"But..."

"No, it's over. That's all there is to it. I don't need a replacement man. And I don't want to talk about it anymore, especially here." She picked up her fork in an attempt to eat.

"When do you think you'll move back to your North Side apartment?" Traci asked, twirling linguini around her fork.

Cassie went blank. She hadn't given that any thought. Why not? "I haven't planned that far ahead. There are several weeks left on my leave of absence. We have to get past the Land of Lincoln Stakes before I can think much about any kind of future."

"You better start thinking and taking control of your own life pretty soon," Susan chided. "Life is too short to let others run it for you."

Cassie focused on the ice cubes floating in her water glass. "Doesn't anyone else have a life to talk about? Why is it always me we're picking on?"

"Now girl, don't go getting defensive," Ashton said, resting a hand on Cassie's arm. "We're just concerned for you. But what about Cassie's Hope? Will she win on Labor Day Weekend? That's what I want to know. I plan on being there, and I've saved up a little stash to use as my betting poke."

At last Cassie had something to smile about, and she did so brilliantly. "There are no guarantees in horse racing, but I think Hope has a great chance to win. And you should get some fairly good odds on her. Just don't blame me if she loses," she added with a twinkle in her eye.

Luxurious. Heavenly. Romantic. Cassie lifted large globs of bath suds with her palm and blew them into the air. She had been in the tub for nearly an hour, letting cool water drain while adding hot. This was a superb idea. Pampering needed to be done with no sense of time.

She would not rush. In fact, for the first night in recent memory, she wouldn't even set an alarm. An assistant would take care of the animals at the track, and she'd placed extra hay out for those at the farm. If she didn't awaken until mid-morning, that would be all right. What a concept.

Later, as she patted herself dry with a huge terry cloth towel, a wave of loneliness nearly brought Cassie to her knees. Tears spontaneously threatened to overwhelm her mellow mood. Looking in the mirror, she stood stock still, chagrined by the sunken eyes looking back at her. Was she really that bad off? Letting the towel drop to the floor, she realized she'd lost some weight over the last two weeks. Her dad had been harping at her about eating like a bird. But she didn't have much of an appetite. And what woman couldn't stand to lose a few pounds?

Her lips turned downward as she brushed her fingers against her heaving breasts. It was the wrong thing do. Immediately, sensations of other fingers, of his fingers caressing those nipples flashed through her muscle memory.

"Damn," she grumbled, "can't I even touch

321

myself without thinking of him? He's gone. Get out of my loft. Get out my life," she shouted to memories. Kneading her forehead, she tried to prevent a headache from developing into a full-fledged head splitter.

Cassie flipped off the light switch, crawled under the covers without even taking the time to put on her Bears night shirt, and hugged herself into a tight ball. She couldn't stop the sobbing. She couldn't stop the flood of memories — of his touch, his words of hope, his kids' innocent love, of a future she'd finally been prepared to embrace.

They'd nearly made it happen. She had finally convinced herself that she could be the mother her mother wasn't. She'd been willing to take the risks of looking at career and living options. She'd been ready to declare her love just as Clint had done. And then.

Everything had gone up in smoke.

Would she ever be able to pull herself together again? So much had changed. She'd opened herself to a kind of pain that had no mercy. Never again. She'd gird herself with some sort of emotional Teflon that would resist leaps of passion, that would protect her from unwanted romantic intrusions, and that would guard her from men with good looks and sweet words.

Mercifully, sleep overtook her.

Without aid of an alarm clock, she was up by five-thirty. It was dawn when she entered the barn. Cassie took a deep satisfying breath. Smells of hay, straw, leather, and horse co-mingled, soothing her pain from the night before.

"This is good," she murmured. "Horses will do the best they can whenever they have a chance. They don't get blown apart by emotional land mines."

- o -

Fifteen hundred miles away, Clint Travers was convinced he could forget the red-haired minx, if his family would just let him. As he carried another bale of hay from the wagon to the pole barn that already held several hundred bales, he couldn't keep the faces of his family from haunting his every step. There was no escaping their ire and disappointment.

His sister hadn't spoken over a dozen words to him since he'd returned to the ranch. She just glared at him, as if trying to cast a spell.

Lester and Sammy asked questions he ignored. They had placed a picture of Cassie on the mantle along with souvenirs collected in Chicago. It looked like a damn shrine. But he wasn't going to let it bother him. He could make them take it down, but he wouldn't stoop that low.

When he entered his mother's house, she'd only pursed her lips and said, "You're back." That was it, he thought grimly. Fortunately, he'd been able to avoid his grandmother so far.

Clint stopped at the truck to retrieve a jug of water. Taking off his hat, he rinsed his face and neck, then took a few sips. He still fumed every time he thought of the woman not trusting him — not trusting *them*. If she'd had more faith in him, they wouldn't be in this mess. Well, he wasn't in a mess really. That was the past. He just hadn't found a way to disconnect, to move on.

Maybe he should go into town and party some. Even the thought tasted like stale beer. He wasn't ready for partying yet. He certainly wasn't ready to get involved with another woman. Maybe never. Horses were more reliable — and when they were startled or angry, they'd only try to kick you. They wouldn't destroy your dignity and your honor.

Looking up from his truck, Clint groaned. "Here comes trouble. Well, let's get it over with." His bent-over grandmother picked her way slowly but steadily along the rutted driveway toward her destination. There was no doubt that *he* was her destination.

"Nice day, Grandmother," Clint said casually in greeting. "It's good to see you."

"Humph," she retorted. "So good I have to walk miles to see if you are still alive."

He ignored her sense of drama, sure that as usual she'd been able to hitch a ride to the road a mile from his driveway. "If you'd get a phone, you could've called."

"Don't change the subject," the old weathered woman declared. "So, tell me about Fire Woman."

"There's nothing to tell." Clint stiffened, crawling into his defensive shell.

324

"Don't try avoiding me. You can't do it. Never have, never will. I want to know what happened between the two of you. Everybody else here has told me how unhappy they are. But you have not sought me out. I want to know. You will tell me. Now." After one of the longest speeches in her life, Clint's grandmother waited without shifting a muscle.

Frowning, Clint knew there was no way to escape. "Okay, Grandmother. Sometimes you can be quite frustrating, you know."

"I'm quite sure of that," she said without smiling.

Clint took her through the story the best he could. He left out the lovemaking parts. Even she didn't need to know about that. By the time he finished, he was leaning against the front fender of the truck, much more relaxed than he'd expected. It was his turn to wait.

His grandmother didn't respond immediately. She looked steadily toward the eastern horizon before speaking. "Do you love Fire Woman?"

Shifting his weight uncomfortably, Clint chose his words carefully. "I did. I surely did. But not anymore. No, I don't love her anymore."

"That's too bad." Looking deep into his soul, the old woman spoke softly, "She loves you."

"Come on, Grandmother. How do you know that? She never said that. She tried to bring dishonor to me, and through me, to the family. I'd think you'd be on my side on this one."

The old woman chuckled. "If you truly thought

325

that, I expect you would have come to see me...I saw Fire Woman last night in a small bedroom over a stable. She was weeping big tears. Her heart was crying for you. She loves you." The words were spoken matter-of-factly. There was no need to dress them up.

Clint didn't want to believe. He refused to believe. "That can't be, Grandmother. You must have been dreaming."

"Humph. You should hear yourself, Grandson," the elder woman chided. "You have lost your bearings. How do you know she doesn't love you?"

"That's easy. She never once uttered those words."

Again, his grandmother studied the eastern sky before replying. "You did not hear those words with your ears, but did you listen with your heart?" The woman thumped her heart with an open palm. "When she lay upon your chest after making love, did you not hear those words from her heart, speaking to your heart?"

"Grandmother," Clint protested.

The old woman raised her hand to still her grandson. "Because I am old, you think I do not know the ways of love. I never forget. Somehow you have lost your way. You are confusing pride with honor. How honorable were your actions over the last two weeks?"

Clint refused to answer.

"I can see that talking to you is a waste of my time. You don't really know you're lost." Her features relaxed. "When you do, Grandson, come and see me. It's never too late to do the right thing, to be truly honorable."

Angry and confused, Clint stood and watched the elderly woman begin to walk away. After taking several steps she turned and asked, "When you come to my house, tell me how bears survive in the big city. Tell me about the Chicago Bears."

Wrinkling his brow, Clint shook his head in disbelief. The Chicago Bears? How could his grandmother have seen Cassie's night shirt?

CHAPTER FIFTEEN

Labor Day in Chicago ushered in a crisp cold front. Fall was definitely in the air. Race fans came to Arlington Park in large numbers. Because of the holiday, five of the nine races on the card would be stakes races. Some of finest horses in the midwest would be featured. A few had shipped in from California and New York. The crowd was jubilant, filled with anticipation.

Cassie wished she could be so carefree. The big day had finally arrived. There wasn't anything else she could think to do. Standing back in Hope's stall to admire the filly once again, she smiled grimly. "We've come a long ways girl, through thick and thin. Now it's all up to you." The horse whinnied in response with a gleam in her eye, as if she knew the importance of the day.

Time dragged by slowly. Cassie's Hope would race in the seventh race, a feature race for fillies at one mile. The specter of Cassie's mother and Louie still hung over this race.

Pulling herself together, Cassie reminded herself to think positively. *Don't give off the wrong vibes to the horse. Give her all the support she needs.* Cassie chuckled. Some of that advice was good social work, some had come from her father, and some came from the lips of Clint Travers. Damn, another train of thought she wanted to abort immediately.

Mercifully, horses for the seventh race were called to the paddock for check-in and saddling. To Cassie's relief, Hope pranced to the paddock, seemingly ready to carry the O'Hanlon colors to victory. She found her own spirits picking up with those of the horse.

The saddling went without complication. As she helped Jessica Wilder into the saddle, Cassie reminded her, "We don't really know what her best running style is because of the drugs. Just let her run her own race. If she wants to run up front, okay. Off the pace likely would be better. Just don't let her drop too far back. There's a lot of speed in this race."

Cassie watched the jockey guide the horse from the floral garden paddock area to the pathway leading under the stands to the track. Trying to hold onto her scrambling nerves, Cassie flung the lead rope over her shoulder and made her way to the box seats, where she knew she'd find her father with Ashton, Susan and Traci. She was so thrilled his doctor had finally relented and let her dad come. He was no doubt entertaining her female friends with the guile and wit of a true horseman. It was race day, and Tug O'Hanlon was never better than on race day.

"Here she comes now," Tug said, spying his daughter threading her way through the crowd. "Hope looks good," he offered as she entered the box.

"She's as ready as she'll ever be. Hi, guys," Cassie sputtered anxiously, "glad you could make it." Gesturing toward her father, she added, "Has he given you any trouble?"

"Not at all." Traci smiled broadly, pushing dark hair away from her face. "He seems to enjoy having three nurses taking care of his every need."

"I'll bet he does."

Cassie settled uneasily into a chair while focusing binoculars on the backstretch where Hope and the other horses continued to warm up for the race. This was the horse who ran in Wyoming. She pranced up on her toes, alert, and had that rocking gait which was a sure sign of readiness.

Ten horses and riders entered the starting gate right in front of the stands. Cassie's heart was in her throat. She saw her dad breathe deeply, trying to relax. Her friends, catching the tension of the moment, fell silent. Hope looked so beautiful, so much like the race horse she was bred to be.

The start was clean. Going around the first turn, Jessica Wilder allowed Hope to run easily without encouragement. The filly fell in behind the leaders, running in fourth. She maintained that position throughout much of the backstretch. As they neared the far turn, two horses moved up on the outside of Hope.

Cassie froze. This was the first real test. Would the filly crumple under the pressure, or would she dig in? Without hesitation, Hope matched the pace of the horse trying to pass her. Two of the lead horses ran out of gas and were dropping back. Expertly, Jessica maneuvered her mount slightly to avoid being boxed in.

As they rounded the turn at the top of the homestretch, Hope inched up alongside the leader, along with the horse on her outside. It was clear to Cassie that unless something went dreadfully wrong, it was now a three horse race. At the sixteenth pole, the horse that had been leading all the way faltered, leaving Hope and the outside horse dueling toward the finish line.

It was the kind of tight finish that fans adored and that gave owners and trainers acid stomachs. Stride for stride, the two horses made their way down the home stretch. The horse on the outside bobbled slightly, as if gasping for air. For a moment, Cassie felt like she could see into the heart of her horse as Hope charged forward, like a champion, with powerful, unrelenting strides. She crossed the finish line barely a nose ahead of her closest competitor.

With tears flowing, Cassie hugged her father, who also freely shed his own tears. "She did it, Dad! You did it. The big horse."

"You did it, child," sobbed her father. "You did it, with your perseverance and skill. And with a touch of Irish Luck," he added, grinning sheepishly.

Ignoring the photo finish sign, everybody knew who had won. Cassie dashed toward the track to greet her horse and lead her into the winner's circle. The girls would bring her father.

As she attached the lead rope to Hope's bridle, she ran her hand over the filly's sweaty heated flesh and knew in that instant that she'd never experienced a more precious moment in her life.

Jessica Wilder brought her back to the present. "She ran a great race, Cass. You've got a real race horse here."

"Thanks," Cassie replied, reaching up to grip the jock's outstretched hand. "And thanks for keeping her out of trouble out there."

"Yeah."

While Cassie held the filly steady in the winner's circle, track personnel presented the Land of Lincoln Stakes trophy to her dad and placed a green and white blanket across Hope's withers. Pride overran Cassie's heart as she watched her father's broad smile. How long had he waited for that moment?

As Cassie began to lead Hope out of the winner's circle, Ashton pulled on her sleeve. "Is it okay if I tag along? I've got the barn pass you arranged for," she said, showing her the laminated badge.

Cassie smiled ruefully. "Sure, come along. Traci and Susan can take Dad back. It'll be awhile, though. First we have to take Hope to the test barn, and then cool her out before taking her home. It might be a couple hours or more."

"That's okay with me. Don't have anything better to do. Boy, what a day for you, Cass. What a day!"

"Yeah, it's outstanding all right," Cassie said,

leading the horse toward the test barn. "Now if Hope can cooperate and give them a urine specimen quickly, this won't take too long. Sometimes horses are so keyed up, it takes awhile. But this is part of what keeps racing clean...testing winners for drugs. Usually, they also test another horse or two in each race randomly. Hope was never randomly chosen before, or maybe we would've known about Louie and my mother earlier."

Shaking her head, Cassie muttered, "But I don't want to dwell on them now. Damn, didn't she run a great race!"

Ashton smiled in response. "Yeah, she did. But truthfully, the only way I know is that she won. And I did well at the betting window." Rattling the several gold bracelets decorating her left arm, the woman hooted, "I may have to go back to the jewelry store on Monday. Boy, I've never seen your dad so excited. He's sure proud of what you've accomplished."

Cassie nodded, tearing up.

Once the filly was loaded for the trip home, Cassie took one last look around the stable area and the track. This was a life she'd been around for so long. She'd rejected it once — now it was coursing through her body like the lifeblood it had become. At times like this it was difficult to recall her other life, her job, her delinquents.

Was Raul right? Had the four legged beasts lured her away? His words echoed in her memory:

You'll use your social work skills wherever you are.

Cassie stifled a sob. Why couldn't that obstinate cowboy be here today? How the kids would have loved the race and standing in the winner's circle at Arlington Park. She shook her head sadly. That was the past. She started up the engine.

There was a loud banging against the side of the trailer. Glancing in her mirror, Cassie scowled. Ed Harrington was trying to get her attention before she pulled out. She knew she should just put the pedal to the floor and go home. But she didn't.

She looked out the open window and there he stood with his hat off, looking uncharacteristically contrite.

"Can I speak with you for a minute, Cass? It's important." He nodded toward Ashton and said, "Sorry to interrupt."

Cassie hesitated and then smiled. Nothing could ruin this glorious day. Not even Harrington. "Sure," she said, "what's on your mind?"

"Can we talk in private," the man whispered through nearly closed lips.

"Oh, okay." She shut off the engine, opened the door, got out of the cab and walked to the rear of the trailer, all the time wondering what kind of problem the blond trainer was going to lay on her this time.

"Okay, spit it out, Harrington. I don't have all day." She knew she was being rude, but she was more than a little irritated by his melodramatic intrigue.

335

Harrington furrowed his brow and sighed. "I just wanted to congratulate you on a real fine win, Cassie. You did a great job with Hope and it paid off big time."

"Oh—well thank you, Ed," she replied, flustered by his praise. "I am pleased to hear you say that. You're right, this is certainly one of the happiest days of my life."

"I also wanted you to know that I'm sorry I've been ragging on you so much." He winced, as if in great pain. "I can't quite explain it. I know I'm no great shakes of a man, but I'm usually not such an ass, either."

Cassie felt her cheeks redden. The man was genuinely sorry. She could tell that. But now what was she supposed to do? She certainly didn't not want to lead him on.

Playing it straight was best. Crossing her arms, she said, "Your apology is accepted, Ed. I've always respected you as a trainer, or I wouldn't have worked with you as closely as I have these last several months. You're damn good at what you do."

"Thanks."

"But don't go to thinking that there's anything now or ever will be anything personal between us. It's just not going to happen."

Ed surprised her by smiling easily. "Don't worry, Cass. I'm clear on that point. But I would like to continue our professional relationship, with fewer sparks."

"That sounds fine with me," Cassie concurred.

"Well, I'd best be going home."

"There is one more thing."

"What's that?"

Shifting his weight uncomfortably, Ed stammered, "I'm sorry if I caused you trouble with your Utah rancher."

Cassie's eyes sprang wide.

"But I really was afraid he was behind all your difficulties with the horse. It seemed quite logical to me. I wasn't just trying to cause problems. And I was shocked to hear that it had been old Louie all along."

Giving him a half smile, Cassie said, "Yes, that was a shock for Dad, too. And I'm sure it did seem reasonable to you that Clint might be behind it all." She wiped the back of her hand across her brow. "Whatever happened between me and Travers isn't your fault. It was bound to happen. It's just the kind of people we are. Now, I really must be going. There's going to be some serious celebrating tonight. I probably won't see you for a day or two."

"Thanks for listening. Thanks for understanding," Harrington mumbled. He turned to head back toward shedrow. "Congratulations again, and good luck."

"Yeah."

Stepping back into the cab, Cassie was pleased he'd stopped her. They did need to clear the air, and now that was done. Another event to celebrate on this day of celebrations.

"You hear any of that?" she asked.

"If the man wants to have a quiet conversation with a lady, he ought to get a softer voice," Ashton chuckled. "Seems like he had his tail between his legs."

"Harrington is an odd sort of man. Basically, I think he's a decent fellow with an oversized ego. But he is a damn good trainer."

"I bet that gravelly voice attracts women, too."

"So I've heard," Cassie said, pulling the trailer out into traffic.

As Cassie maneuvered through streets making her way toward the interstate, the chatter between the two of them stopped. Once they pulled on the main highway, Ashton asked, "What are you going to do about him, Cass?"

"About who?" Cassie answered, frowning, unsuccessful in masking her annoyance.

Ashton laughed. "About the man who hangs over this day. About the man who said he loved you and you were slow to believe. About the man who clutches your soul, whether you like it or not, girl."

"Nothing," Cass whispered faintly. "He doesn't ever want to see me again."

"Don't you think he'll call and congratulate you on Hope's victory? Certainly, he'll learn of it."

"He could've watched it on satellite, if he wanted to. But he'll never call. Ashton, I can't tell you how absolutely stone-walled he went when he thought I suspected him of drugging Hope. He was so shut down, I don't think he heard anything I said."

Ashton chuckled, pulling down the visor to keep out the glare of the late afternoon sun. "It does sound like he lost it. But when I met him, he struck me as a basically calm and steady kind of guy. Sounds like he was great with his kids, and he was so obviously in love with you. I don't think that kind of love can dissolve in one night. I suspect he's embarrassed and as plagued about what to do next as you are."

Cassie shrugged. Keeping her eyes on the traffic, she mumbled, "It's over. That's about all there is to say."

"I've never seen you give up like this, Cass. You'd told me what he won't do. What do you hope will happen with Clint?"

"I don't know." Cassie turned sharply to her friend. "I honestly don't know. And don't try to be my social worker, Ashton. I don't like it one bit."

Shifting her attention back to the road, Cassie felt the tension ebb from her body. "I'm sorry. I know you care, and I appreciate you so much. I imagine I've put a lot of things on hold until after the Lincoln. Dad has finally reached a longtime dream—though I doubt that will be enough for him now.

"Once horses and horseracing get in your blood, there's always the push for more. Can you make it to the next level? Can you improve the breed another notch? You watch the little foals running around the paddock and you can't help but wonder which of them will be the next big horse." Cassie laughed at herself. "I guess it's true you've got to be a dreamer to work with racehorses. But what a great dream to pursue."

"That's what's happening to you, isn't it?" Ashton's eyes went wide. "You want more. You want to pursue the dream further. Cassie's Hope is only a beginning."

"I do," Cassie confessed, feeling goose bumps gather on her arms. "I'm still shocked by my own response to being there today in that winner's circle. I've stood there with my father on many occasions, but not like today. Not having trained a horse with some promise to a point where she could not only contend but win against stiff competition.

"You're right. I don't know how I can go back to my old world. It seems so mundane, now. I'd love to be able to breed horses like Dad does. We'd sell some and race some, but always attempting to improve the breed."

"Isn't that what Clint Travers does?" asked Ashton innocently.

Cassie hit the brake. The trailer swerved. She managed to straighten things out before causing an accident. She glared through the windshield, wishing for the turn-off for the farm to appear. She loved Ashton deeply. They'd been friends for years, but she didn't want to delve into her feelings about horses or about Clint Travers.

As they turned into the driveway, Ashton stopped humming a popular tune. "I want you to know, Cass that this has been a very special day for me too. I am so thrilled for you and your dad."

340

She chuckled. "If you make this your career, I'm going to have to get some books and read up on betting. It was fantastic standing with you in that winner's circle. And I can certainly understand why you'd like to replicate that moment over and over again."

Cassie welcomed the lighter mood. "Maybe you might want to buy into a horse. Nothing is better than being an owner of the horse in that circle set aside for winners."

A slow smile crept across Ashton's face. "You know, I think you're onto something there. I could do that. And we could continue chasing some dreams together. I think I'd like that."

After turning off the ignition but before getting out, Cassie clasped her friend's hand. "And I do appreciate your concern and your insights, Ashton. I'll always value our friendship."

"You better, girl," Ashton teased. "Because I'll be watching."

The party was already in full swing when Cassie and Ashton entered the house. Glasses of champagne had appeared from somewhere. Her father probably shouldn't be drinking any, but Cassie knew it would be futile to try and stop him. Instead, she joined in the celebration.

They took their glasses into the living room where her dad sat in his most comfortable chair. He didn't look any worse off for having spent much of the day away from the house. Actually, he had a little more color than usual.

Lifting his glass in salute, he announced, "And here comes the best damn trainer at the track. Congratulations, honey."

"Thanks," she retorted, "but I have a long ways to go before that happens."

"Your dad has been glowing about your achievements ever since we left the track," Susan bubbled. "He has more stories about you than I bet you even know."

Cassie winced. "I wouldn't doubt that one bit. But then I wouldn't believe most of them, either. Remember, you're listening to an Irish horse trainer. Listen to everything with a block of salt."

"Now, Cass," Tug protested, reaching for her hand.

She allowed herself to be pulled down so she was sitting on the floor beside him. This was good. How long had it been since they shared such happiness?

"Tell us," Traci prodded with a laugh, "about the time you and your dad slept in a horse trailer overnight to save money down in Oklahoma and the police came by."

"He didn't," Cassie scolded glaring at her father.

"Well, now we've lived a rich life, girl. These young ones haven't seen or done half of what you've done. Isn't it a shame?"

Tears rolled down Cassie's cheeks. She knew what he said was true. She'd been ashamed of much of her childhood. But he was right. They'd had a rich life in spite of a reluctant mother. And damn, she was going to celebrate. She lifted her empty glass and didn't notice who filled it.

"You chased the dream and won," she said happily. "How does it feel, Dad? How does it really feel?"

She watched him turn serious. The jokes and storytelling were over, at least for the moment. He was reaching for something special and she wanted to hear it.

"It's hard to find the right words," he began. "Maybe I don't know what they are."

Four women waited for him. No one tried to rush him.

"We've been through so much. The good and the bad. I guess the dream probably cost us your mother. No, don't try to tell me otherwise, girl," he said before his daughter could speak. "We've been in and out of a lot of towns and tracks looking for just the right horse. I'm just so pleased that we raised Hope from a foal. And that you could take the time to train her. You don't know how special that has been for me. It's like the two of you have been learning and growing together. I expect she's taught you a thing or two."

Cassie nodded in agreement. Her tears matched his.

"That's the way it ought to be between a horse and trainer." Tug reached for his large bandanna and blew his nose. "Well, this is good. No denying that. But now," he winked at his listeners, "we've gotta conjure up another dream. How about the Kentucky Derby?"

The women were stunned.

"Well, you gotta have dreams to live, don't you?" Looking around he sputtered, "My glass is empty. Is anybody gonna do anything about it?"

Chuckling, Ashton did the honors and whispered to Cassie, "Where did he get *his* social work degree?"

- o -

With satisfaction and relief, Clint Travers watched the replay of the Land of Lincoln Stakes on his TV fed by a satellite dish. He'd known all along the horse was damn good. The way she raced so patiently only underscored her ability to pace herself. She could have a very good four-year-old campaign if anybody cared enough to race her. He sure hoped Harrington didn't have that opportunity.

"There she is," Sammy shrieked, running to the large screen TV to point out Cassie shaking the jockey's hand. The camera followed Cassie leading her horse in circles waiting for the final results to be posted. Then they all watched as she led Hope into the winner's circle. It was hard to tell who was smiling most, Cassie or her father. Clint was pleased to see the old codger had made it to the race. He looked healthier than he'd ever seen him.

His heart lurched when he saw her lean over to kiss her father. "Damn," he mumbled.

"When are we going to see her again?" Lester demanded. "We never had a chance to say

344

goodbye."

Clint shook his head at his son's sense of unfairness. He'd have to learn things didn't always work out the way one hoped.

Sammy crawled up into her father's lap. "I want to graduate Cassie. Can't we call her up?"

"No, I don't think that would be very good idea," Clint said, wishing his daughter would forget about the woman.

"Well, I'm going to graduate her." Sammy stubbornly dropped to the floor. "Aunt Silver Hawk, you'll help me write a letter, won't you?"

"Sure, I will," she sighed, scowling defiantly at her brother. "I'm sure Cassie will be pleased to know that you're happy for her."

Blurred by a mixture of emotions he could not define, Clint lurched to his feet and fled the house, rushing to the stable, where he usually could regain his balance.

Shortly he was working a young filly through her paces. Even in the round pen, he couldn't escape the nagging feeling that he was not entirely finished with the woman on the TV screen. His grandmother's words continued to haunt him, for he knew he could not easily dismiss the old woman. And the kids certainly had not accepted his claim that he was through with Cassie. Sometimes he'd like to wring his sister's neck, but he supposed it wasn't a terrible thing for Sammy to write her congratulations to Cassie. He had to admit that he was proud of what she'd accomplished with Hope. But damn if he would tell her that.

Later, as he was putting away tack, he was none too pleased to see Silver Hawk entering the stable.

"The horse ran a good race today," his sister volunteered, plopping herself down on a bale of hay.

"She ran the kind of race I thought she could. It was a good win."

"Cassie looked happy."

"Most winners do."

Silver Hawk nodded, looked away and then back to give her brother a withering glare as only she could.

Watching her emotions ebb and flow, Clint thought, and not for the first time, that his sister had received a stronger gene pool from his grandmother than he had, and that it wasn't fair. Both of them could be mysterious, undaunting, and incredibly damning.

"So," Silver Hawk began, tossing her braids over her shoulders as if she were preparing for war, "when are you going deal with the mess you've made?"

"What mess?" he growled.

"You know what I mean. Cassie. The kids. Yourself. Our family. Pick anyone," she said, "they all seem to be intertwined, like a wet lariat."

"Time will take care of things," Clint said, none too gently. "It doesn't require meddling from anyone else."

346

"Okay. I give up. You win," the young woman said sadly. "I'm not blaming you completely. I'm sure Cassie has to own her share of the burden here. But the kids shouldn't." Silver Hawk's voice rose uncharacteristically. "They're hurt because they gave of themselves freely with no strings attached."

Clint continued to glare, but knew it was useless to interrupt.

"Somehow you have to help them get through this," his sister pleaded, "however you and Cassie resolve things."

"They're resolved!"

"Like hell they are," Silver Hawk hissed, jumping up from the hay bale. "And Lester and Sammy only feel rejected and hurt. You didn't let them say goodbye, and you haven't even tried to explain anything to them so they might have a chance of understanding and getting beyond the pain. This thing between you and Fire Woman is bigger than either one of you. When are you going to wake up and see that and do something about it?"

"Fire Woman." Clint lurched away from the stall wall. "That's a crock." He started to walk away ending the conversation.

But his sister was not yet done.

"I'm going to saddle my horse and pack some food. I'll be gone two, maybe as many as four days. Deal with your kids while I'm gone." With that injunction, she spun on her heel and stalked off.

Clint felt faint. He'd never exchanged such ugly words with his sister. They'd had moments of disagreement, but nothing like this. Was she right? Had he been running away so hard and fast that he ignored the needs of his own kids?

Before the children's bedtime, Clint sat in the middle of the couch in his family room with Lester on his left and Sammy on his right. Silver Hawk's plea rang in his head like an incessant car alarm. Sharp pain resided behind his right eye. His palms were sweaty, reminding him of his childhood when he'd had to tell his father he had to stay after at school or had failed to make the honor roll.

He tried to stay focused. The words on the book open on his lap blurred. Wasn't he supposed to be reading to his children? They had been peering at the colorful pictures as he read *Alexander And The Terrible, Horrible, No Good, Very Bad Day*. And then he had stopped reading. Words and sounds escaped him. Somewhere deep in the recesses of his mind he was aware that this was not going well at all.

Lester examined his father with concern. "What's wrong, Dad? You sort of look like Alexander."

Pulling on her father's shirt sleeve, Sammy asked, "Are you going to read more?" She checked the picture again. "That's not the end, Daddy."

"No, that's not the end," Clint acknowledged, relieved at finding his voice. Laying the book on the coffee table, he placed an arm around each of his children. "You know, you two are more precious than anything to me."

"Even gold!" exclaimed Sammy wide-eyed.

"Yes, even gold." He chuckled. "And I owe each of you an apology."

Both children sat perfectly still, eyeing their father closely. Even they knew apology meant saying *I'm sorry*, and that was a very difficult thing to do.

"It's about Cassie," he volunteered.

Lester let out a breath and nodded knowingly.

Sammy whispered, "Oh." She tucked her feet under her so she could sit on them.

"Look," Clint said, breathing hard, "I was very upset that day I sent you home from Chicago. Cassie and I had a big fight."

Sammy leaned away from him and pursed her lips. "Like when Tommy pulls my braids," she interrupted, "and I smack him over the head with my book bag?"

"Well, sort of." Clint swallowed and tried to continue. "Looking back on it, I should have had your aunt take you by the farm so you could've said goodbye to Ms. O'Hanlon."

Agreeing, Lester offered, "That would have helped some."

"I didn't want to say goodbye," Sammy cried, her lower lip trembling. "I didn't want to go."

As he lifted his daughter onto his lap, Clint's voice cracked. "Look, little one, I don't know how to explain this to you any better. I thought I loved Cassie, but it turns out she didn't love me. So I

349

can't put a band-aid on the hurt and make it go away. It just hurts…for you, for me, for all of us."

"For Cassie, too?"

Clint frowned his exasperation. "I don't know about that."

"Can we go back and find out?" Sammy asked, her small voice rising with hope.

"No, we won't be doing that."

Lester crossed his arms and pouted. "I think we should be allowed to visit Cassie. It's only fair. Divorced kids do that."

Groaning loudly, his father complained, "How did I ever raise you two to be so independent?"

Giving him a toothy smile, Lester said, "Because you love us so much."

Clint nodded, trying to see through watery eyes.

"Daddy, I think you made a huge 'stake," Sammy whined, moving to kneel on the couch to eye at her father directly. Her eyes snapped with a mixture of emotions that Clint did not want to decipher. "Cassie loves all of us. I know she does."

His shoulders slumped. He'd made little progress in making peace with his children. But all was not lost. He still was the parent.

"It's time for pee-jays," he announced gruffly.

"Already?" Lester hooted.

"It's past bedtime."

As his kids scampered off to get ready for bed, Clint wondered if they would ever understand what happened in Chicago. Would he ever understand himself?

CHAPTER SIXTEEN

The morning was bright and crisp as Cassie made her way by the junk strewn lot toward the group home. September was half gone; but what a turning point month it had already been. Her spirits were up. She walked slowly, unsure how her decision would be received inside the house.

She found Raul in his usual place: ensconced in his office, half hidden behind stacks of paper, scribbling feverishly on a yellow pad.

Dotting a sentence firmly, Raul looked up to see Cassie standing in the doorway. "Welcome stranger. You look worried."

Cassie couldn't decide whether to sit or remain standing.

"So, you've decided not to come back," Raul said, leaning back in his chair, clasping his hands behind his head.

"How did you know?" Cassie sat across from him, feeling like a stray cat.

"At times your face is a newspaper, Cass. Don't worry about it. We'll miss you, but we'll be fine. None of us are indispensable."

Taking a couple breaths, Cassie struggled to explain. Raul was her friend, and she wanted him to understand. "I'm not sure I can adequately explain it. But it's something I have to do. The horses are in my blood in ways I never realized

351

before."

"That's not surprising. You were raised with them. You were probably at a race track before you could crawl."

"No doubt about that. I hate leaving you in the lurch, though."

"We've had six months to prepare. When you were here with the Utahan, I expected this decision. Is he part of it?"

"Hardly." Cassie rubbed her temples gently, fighting a headache. "He's out of the picture entirely."

"I'm sorry. I rather liked the man. So that really makes this a pure horse decision, right?"

"Yep." Cassie gave Raul a half smile. "I'm not leaving you for another man. I just need to be with the horses, at least for now."

"There'll be other men, if you'll allow them in your life. And haven't I always said you'll do social work wherever you are? We may leave one job for another, but we don't leave the doing of social work."

"You're a real gem, Raul." Cassie stood and beamed with much relief. "It's been great working with you. I guess I'd better find Daisy and let her know what's happening."

"Don't worry too much about the girl. She'll bounce back okay. She's come a long way in the last couple of weeks."

Cassie hesitated. "I'd like to stay in contact with her, if you think that would be all right."

"All right! I think that's fantastic. She can use

every friend she can get." Raul rushed around the desk to hug his former employee.

She clung to him, hoping she'd made the right decision. She knew it was, but she'd still miss this man.

Raul stepped back and said quietly, "You know, you'd make a hell of a foster-mom, Cassie."

"Are you a mind reader, or what?" Cassie took a deep breath. "It's possible. I don't want to say anything like that to Daisy. She's had too many hopes that haven't turned out. But I'm seriously considering it."

"You know you have my support, whatever you decide."

Cassie found Daisy sitting on the steps leading from the first floor to the second.

"I heard you were here," the girl said tentatively. "You're not coming back, are you?"

Hurriedly, Cassie took the gangly girl into her arms. Sobbing, matching the sobs of Daisy, Cassie muttered, "How come everyone knows what I'm doing today before I can tell them?"

"It just shows," Daisy whispered. "I'm going to miss you terribly." Her body shuddered.

"Maybe not," said Cassie, sitting on the floor by the teenager. "My not working here may actually mean we can spend more time together, if you want."

"Really!"

Cassie quickly held up a hand, not wanting Daisy to over interpret what she intended. "I thought you might like to come out to the farm now and then. And maybe to shedrow."

She was heartened to see the girl's eyes round in surprise. "If you get along well with the horses, we could maybe find you something to do out there, like being a part-time assistant groom. I'd pay you for your work, of course."

"Oh, you wouldn't have to pay me," Daisy squealed, bouncing up and down. "I'd work for free. Does that mean I could stay overnight sometimes?"

"Absolutely."

Daisy glanced away shyly and then turned back with a tiny smile and tears streaming down her cheeks. "I think I may be happier with you not working here."

September had been a month packed with excitement, Cassie wrote in her journal at the beginning of October. She was a full time horse trainer. She loved the look of those words on her journal page.

More than that, she and her dad were going to expand their broodmare operation. Leaving social work had been a gigantic step, but she felt good about it. She expected Daisy to be with her at least a couple weekends a month. Soon, she'd have to decide about taking Daisy on as foster child. The state wouldn't continue supporting her stay at the group home much longer.

Cassie smiled at her entry. Who was she kidding? That decision was already made. She should start the paper work and get on with it.

To mark this major new life change, Cassie had changed her appearance dramatically. She'd decided that all that long hair just got in the way, whether in the barn, in the round pen, or at the track. After much deliberation, she'd had her hair shaped in a bob, leaving her neck bare.

Glancing at the mirror as she wrote, she remained quite pleased with that decision, too. Shorter hair seemed to make her appear taller, perhaps even more sophisticated. At minimum, the hair style gave her a fresh look for a new direction. And it was definitely a brand new day.

As she reached up to play with it momentarily, her hand stalled. She wondered how it would feel for a man to do that. Her exposed neck was extremely sensitive to touch. Cassie shivered, allowing herself to pleasantly ponder fingers other than hers grazing that smooth skin.

During September, she'd also received a note printed in bold letters from Sammy congratulating her on Hope's victory. The little girl's words had wrenched Cassie's heart in a dozen different ways. She'd written back thanking her young friend for the letter, asking her about school, but making no promises.

Laying her pen aside, Cassie reread her journal for the month. It surely had been a decisive time. She did feel good about those decisions, and about how her life was taking shape. But something was missing. She knew that without question.

She grimaced at the mirror, wondering what

Clint would think of her recent life choices. He'd probably not look at her twice with short hair.

So be it. She didn't wear her hair a certain way for any man. Had she cut it to celebrate her new career, or had she done it to spite him?

No matter, it was done. A woman had every right to determine how she wanted to look. Pressing her lips in a mock kiss at the mirror, she mumbled, "And I do like the new me."

Still, she wondered if he would.

Cassie returned from the track the next morning around eleven to find her father sitting at the kitchen table with several books and papers strewn across its surface.

With a twinkle in his eyes, Tug greeted his daughter, "Hi Cass, thought you'd never get here. Sit down. Got somethin' to show you."

After pouring a cup of steaming coffee, Cassie warily pulled out a chair and sat down. She'd seen that shrewd furtive look on his face many times before. "Now what are you up to? Haven't you done about enough scheming and planning for a year?"

"Hardly," the old man said, leaning back in his chair. "There's still almost a quarter of a year left. And we're just now comin' into that dreamin' season for horse folks."

Nodding, Cassie knew what he was referring to. No matter how disappointing the prior season might have been, many trainers and owners spent the winter months plotting and dreaming for the coming year.

"I want you to go to the Barretts Fall Sale in California to buy us some quality horses." Her father smiled, his wire rimmed reading glasses sliding down his nose.

"California!" Cassie gasped. "Why there? I thought you didn't want to go out and buy contenders. I've got horses to race here. That could take weeks." Her reservations and objections tumbled out of her mouth.

"Whoa there, young lady," her dad responded with a bemused look. Forming a tent with his fingers, he continued, "Why California? Because they have breedin' lines that we don't see much of here in the mid-west. I've been studyin' the Barretts catalogue now for three weeks. *After* you decided to work with horses full-time, by the way."

"I'm not talkin' about buyin' two year olds in trainin' who are ready to go to the track. I want us to buy a couple broodmares and a couple yearlings. I'd like you to go over the hip numbers I've tagged as possibles." Tug offered her the sales catalogue.

Blowing bangs off her forehead, Cassie said, "And you think this is more important than staying to race the string we have currently consigned to us."

"Cass, you need to be involved with contenders like Hope. I don't see any horse in our current crop who's gonna come near that level over the next couple years. We—you—need to plan for the

357

future. This makes good horse sense, to bring some new blood into our breeding line."

Cassie nodded. Her dad had always wanted to be a breeder first and trainer second. Now, he had that chance.

"Okay," Tug said, "I want to get into the A.P. Indy line; his offspring show a lot of stamina and are bred for distance. There are four broodmares in the sale that are daughters or granddaughters of his. If you agree, I want you to go after the two you think are best conformed. You have as good an eye for a horse as I do, girl. Don't hold back on dollars. We're not gonna go all that way and get skunked."

"No, I don't suppose so."

"Then there are eight yearlings carrying that same bloodline. You pick the best male of the group and the second best yearling, male or female.

"I've done a lot of talkin'. What do you think?" Her dad leaned back and eyed her.

Arching her eyebrows, Cassie grimaced. "It looks like you've got it pretty well decided."

"That's not at all true," Tug disagreed, "and you know it." The old man chuckled. "You just don't like to think I can get by without you that long. We need your on-site expertise at the sale to make the best possible selections. And I want you to go over this catalogue with as much care as I have. Read up on the A.P. Indy line. Do your own research."

"I'm not second guessing what you want to do.

Truth be known, I'm pleased with the confidence you're placing in me. We're no doubt talking about a fair amount of money here." Cassie tried to duck away from his intense, hopeful stare. "It's just that I'm not sure I want to be away from you and the horses—from here—for that long. This will take the better part of a month."

"Nonsense. Hell, girl. You don't have to drive all that way. We'll fly you out. We can afford to ship the horses back."

With her cheeks warming swiftly, Cassie went on the offensive to keep her father from cornering her. "How come you've all of a sudden become enamored with California horses? Have you been talking to Travers?"

Tug O'Hanlon coughed loudly. "Well, of course, while he was here we talked a lot about breedin' lines and about horses I hadn't heard much about, me being here in the middle of the country. He did tell me about the Barretts Fall Sale. That's it."

Tug filled their coffee cups. "You know, kid, I don't know if he'll be at the sale, but if you stay active in the thoroughbred world at the level you want to, then you'll run into him at some point. You might as well prepare for it."

Squaring her shoulders, rising to the bait, Cassie snorted, "If it happens, I can handle it. Clint Travers is not going to make me be a captive of Chicago. Horses are my business, and I go wherever that business takes me."

"That's my girl," Tug chuckled. "'An O'Hanlon

ain't afraid of nothin."

- o -

Sitting in his truck in front of his grandmother's house, Clint rested his throbbing head on the steering wheel. Where had he made the wrong turn? Wherever he turned, no matter how busy he stayed, no matter how much he drank, he could not escape the woman his family called Fire Woman. Was it about honor? Was it about pride? Was it about something deeper than all of that? He no longer knew what to do. He was stuck. He was lost.

The days had dragged by. His sister gave him little slack. The kids were doing well in school, but at home they failed to have that spark that was so uniquely theirs. They seldom asked him to join in their play.

Sundays had always been a fun gathering day for the family, whether at his house, or his mother's, or his grandmother's. Now a kind of dullness washed over everyone. Laughter, when it happened, was no longer spontaneous. It seemed forced. His mother was always polite and caring, but she seldom asked anymore about how he was doing. His grandmother had not spoken to him of anything important since that day weeks before in his driveway. She'd hardly noticed he was alive.

He felt responsible for the fragmentation of his family, yet he could not figure out how to make things whole again. Try as hard as he could, he

360

could not see a way out of the morass. He was not only lost, he was stuck, mired deep in a mud he feared was gradually turning into quicksand.

"It took you long enough to come in," Mrs. Littlefield observed when her grandson stepped through the doorway.

"It was a hard decision. I didn't know if you'd want to see me," he drawled, slouched over with Stetson in hand.

"Humph. You didn't know if you wanted to be found." His grandmother gestured toward a chair.

Without quite knowing how it happened, Clint sat at the ancient wooden kitchen table with his hands firmly wrapped around a hot thick cup of coffee. His grandmother's coffee always had body. No one ever described it as weak. After scrutinizing his cup for what seemed like an eternity, he looked at his grandmother's wrinkled face. "You were right about not wanting to be found. But now I'm here. I've decided to be found. Now what, Grandmother?"

"What hurts most?" she asked, watching closely every nuance of reaction her grandson made.

He thought long and hard about her question. It wasn't new. How many times had he asked the same question in the past weeks? Not able to avoid his grandmother's penetrating stare, he answered the best he could. "The fear of not being found. The fear of rejection, I guess."

"You're not certain?"

361

"Yeah, I'm certain."

"That's not surprising," his grandmother said, buttering a piece of toast. "The way your father treated you. You walked around afraid of what might happen next."

Clint stared at his grandmother blankly. How did she know? He'd loved his father, but he'd also feared him. He'd done everything he could to live up to his father's high expectations, to win his praise, to bring honor to the family. But he always came up a little short. As a child, as a teenager, as a young adult, he lived in fear of his father, of his father laughing at his failures, or of being rejected for not adequately measuring up.

And then the man died before Clint could prove himself. He'd never been quite good enough in the shadow of his father. He'd never told a soul about those fears. He never realized anyone else knew, until today.

Yet this gnarled woman with strands of gray shooting through otherwise black hair and with more gum than teeth showing when she smiled — his grandmother — had known all along. Gradually, it dawned on him that she'd been there through those difficult years, helping him accept himself without ever asking him to name those fears, and without undercutting his love for his father.

Now, with the stakes so high, she challenged him to look inside himself and not shrink from what he might discover. He realized, then, that she was encouraging him to find himself.

"I didn't know you knew," he mumbled at last.

"It wasn't that difficult to see." The old woman shook her head. "I never could understand why. Maybe he thought he had to be extra hard on you because you were of mixed blood. In his mind, maybe he was doing his best to prepare you for a tough world."

"Maybe."

"What next? What hurts most next?" The elder woman wanted to know.

Clint's eyes focused sharply on the salt and pepper shakers. He nodded, recognizing a truth that he had been coming to but had not quite named. "The fear of losing her, of her rejecting me," he said, his voice cracking.

"Ah, you have come a long ways already, my Grandson." His grandmother placed a weathered hand over his. Her touch felt surprisingly warm. "You're beginning to see how the past colors the present."

"But I don't know what to do next. I can't just crawl back to her like some wounded animal...I don't know how to get her back."

"No, you don't have to do that, but only fools are afraid of admitting their mistakes."

Silence hung heavy in the small once-yellow kitchen. A clock ticked loudly, time refusing to stand still.

"I guess I should call her," Clint volunteered at last.

Smiling weakly at her grandson, Mrs. Littlefield shook her head. "To listen to another person, to truly speak to another, you must be in that person's presence. Go to her, my Grandson. Let your heart do the speaking. Let your heart do the listening. You are a good man. You will be fine. Trust your heart."

Clint fought back the mist clouding his vision. He nodded silently. After talking with Tug O'Hanlon a few days earlier, he'd initially decided not to go to the October Barretts sale. Now it seemed like a good idea to go. He no longer wanted to avoid the woman of fire. At least Barretts would be neutral ground for them to meet.

"Thanks, Grandmother." Standing to leave, Clint reached in his pocket, retrieved a small pouch of tobacco and placed it on the table. "Thank you for helping me rediscover who I am."

Feeling much lighter than he had for weeks, Clint Travers whistled as he walked to his pickup. Once again he had a purpose and sense of direction.

He would not allow the specter of his father to control his life. He had tried so hard to earn that man's love.

But now he had to find her. He knew she would show up at Barretts. Whether the fire woman would accept his apology or not, he had to tell her that he was sorry for mistrusting her and for letting his own fears force him to run from her. Did she ever think of him?

Cassie surveyed the sales area. Barretts, on the edge of the Los Angeles County Fairgrounds in Pomona, was a horseman's paradise. Row upon row of stalls, building after building housed thoroughbreds with fine breeding and considerable promise for racing. Attendants would bring an animal out into an open area to walk and trot for prospective bidders. All eyes tried to detect that telltale flaw that would derail a horse from reaching its potential. Buyers compared one entry against another trying to decide what weaknesses in conformation they would accept. Everyone knew the perfect horse did not exist; yet, everyone looked for that horse.

As Cassie evaluated a bay yearling being led away from her by an attendant, she heard a familiar low voice.

"Nice looking filly," Clint Travers said softly.

Her toes curled immediately. Without taking her eyes off the yearling, she responded caustically, "It's not a filly, Travers. It's a colt. Have you gone blind as well as nuts?"

"I wasn't commenting on the animal."

"Oh." She felt her face flush. "Thanks for showing me the colt," she said, dismissing the attendant leading the bay. "He's real nice. He's got a lot of potential."

"I'm curious," Clint queried, "were you talking about the colt or about me?"

"Could be," Cassie responded, ducking her

eyes from his intense stare.

"Look, this is kind of a hard place to have a conversation. Can I buy you a cup of coffee? Or do you have more yearlings to look at?"

"No, that was the last one. The ones I'm interested in will come through the auction ring mid-afternoon. I do have a few broodmares to check out before tomorrow morning." Trying to keep her composure bland, she said, "I've always got time for a cup of coffee."

Walking toward the canteen, they shared comments about the yearlings of interest to each of them. Both gave a sigh of relief when they realized they would not be bidding against each other.

After sitting down at a corner table with their coffee and rolls, Cassie shared how she'd ranked the eight yearlings based on conformation and breeding and elicited Clint's evaluation. Cassie glanced from her notes to Clint, whose gaze was fixed on her. She looked back at her notes. This was surreal. How long could they carry on this very professional conversation before talking about what really mattered? Maybe now was the time. Neither one of them had said a thing for an entire minute. She'd never experienced such an enveloping silence. Who would go first? It had to be him. He was the one who had stormed out on her.

"Your dad said you've made a career change. That's huge," Clint said, taking the last bite of his cinnamon roll.

"Yeah," she responded shyly. At least that was

more personal. Damn, he was handsome in a white shirt and jeans. His deeply tanned skin seemed even sexier against the starched white. "I wasn't aware how much it was in my blood until Hope ran the Lincoln. I do want to thank you for all your help. We couldn't have done it without you."

Before she started to slobber, she brought herself up short. "Say, did my dad know you were going to be here? Is he trying to play some kind of god in all of this?"

Clint spoke up quickly, "No, no, he actually thought I wasn't coming. I'd planned on being here until I heard you were coming. Then I changed my mind." Clint looked away.

"What made you change your mind again?" Cassie asked hesitantly, holding her breath.

He smiled briefly. "I realized I was lost. And I had a long talk with my grandmother. She's always been in your corner, you know. The whole damn family is." Clint shook his head. He hesitated and then forged on. "Grandmother doesn't give a lot of direct advice. But you learn a lot just talking to her."

Cassie smiled. "How is your family, Clint? How are Sammy and Lester, your mother, Silver Hawk, your grandmother? I miss them."

"I had hoped you might stop on the way back and find out for yourself," he replied cautiously. "Other than the fact that they all think I'm a jerk, everyone seems quite fine."

Coughing on the coffee she'd been swallowing,

Cassie stared hard at the flustered dark haired man who seemed suddenly very ill at ease. She wished she could read his mind. Had his family been putting him through hell all of this time? Still, discomfort with kids and relatives would not be enough on which to form a renewed relationship.

"Look," Clint suggested, regaining control and checking his watch, "we both have other horses to evaluate. I have to get over to the auction ring soon. But can we have dinner this evening? There's so much to say, and so little time."

"Sure," she said, reaching for the bill. "I've got a lot I want to tell you too, but we do have other responsibilities."

Her body simmered. He did say he'd been a jerk, right? At least they agreed on something. But there wasn't time to pursue that line further. "We're on for dinner, but right now I've got to get focused. Wouldn't want to spend thousands of dollars without a clear mind."

Matching Clint's strides toward the stables, Cassie's step was lighter than it had been since before leaving Chicago. Nothing was settled. Much had been left unsaid. Yet much had been said with the eyes, with body language, with the heart. She trusted they could at least talk honestly with each other before the day was finished.

- o -

Feeling like a soaring eagle, Clint glanced down

at the sleek redhead walking beside him. He let go of a deep breath he'd been unaware of holding since he'd seen Cassie checking out the bay yearling. She'd looked so lovely, even with short hair.

It was growing on him. He liked the way the new look set off the ivory skin of her neck. He could easily imagine running his lips up and down that bare skin. Too easily, he could visualize her in something other than that conservative yellow dress she wore. In no way did it do justice to the body he'd memorized square inch by square inch.

They hadn't cleaned up all their emotional garbage, but this might yet be the red-letter day he'd hoped for.

- o -

Cassie sat on the edge of an aisle chair in the fifth row of cushioned seats at Barretts' plush carpeted and paneled pavilion. Awed by the atmosphere, she nervously fingered the pages of the tattered sales catalogue she and her father had spent hours poring over. She'd been to horse auctions before, but never one like this, where a half dozen auctioneers and floor men were dressed in tuxedos, and where bids often were measured in the hundreds of thousands of dollars. The place reeked of money — the kind of money she and her father didn't have, even after selling a piece of the farm..

"Don't be paralyzed by the richness of the place," Clint counseled, sitting on her left. "A lot of these animals will sell for under thirty thousand. Hell, by late afternoon some will go for less than two. But you didn't come this far to pick those up. It's usually the first fifty or so hip numbers that attract the big buyers and the largest dollars."

Nodding, Cassie welcomed his advice. She wasn't about to let the tension between them get in the way now. After all, he did this for a living. She rummaged in her purse until she found the package of antacids.

An attendant led out Hip Number 52 onto the raised podium. The dark bay yearling colt looked tremendous under the lights. Cassie hoped the bidding wouldn't push the animal beyond her price range. The opening bid was seventy-five hundred. Her shaking hand raised the bid a thousand. She didn't have to do more than twitch to stay in the bidding game once she was identified by a floor man as a bidder.

Rapidly, the bidding moved to thirty-five thousand. Longer time lapses between bids occurred as bidders reconsidered just how far they would go for Hip Number 52, but with so many lots of horses to be sold, the auctioneers would not wait very long. Decisions to spend large sums of money were made in seconds, not minutes. At forty-five thousand the bidding stopped. The gavel fell.

"Sold to the pretty young lady in the fifth row,"

the affable auctioneer announced.

Cassie tried not to jump up and shout. She wanted to do a victory lap. But instead, she waited impatiently for the floor man to bring over the purchase slip for her to verify and sign. Damn, she'd just spent more than her old annual salary on a yearling and a dream.

Grabbing her hand, Clint whispered, "You did great. Real cool down the stretch. I can see we're going to have to do this often."

"Yeah, well how come I'm shaking like a leaf before gale-force winds?"

He smiled at her lazily. "That's normal. You're having an adrenaline rush in the midst of some fierce competition."

After picking up Hip Number 68, a nicely conformed yearling filly for twenty-two thousand five hundred, Cassie was ready to call it a day. Once she'd signed the slip, she got up to leave, then sat quickly sat back down, aware that Clint hadn't made a move to follow.

"You haven't done any bidding," she told Clint. "I don't want to offend you, but I've got to get out of here. I've got to go see those two yearlings I just bought."

"Cassie," he said, watching the handlers lead in another horse, "I know you've got to double check that those yearlings are okay. And you have to go look at them and wonder what you missed when evaluating them on paper and in the flesh. Run along and check them out. There's something I need to see about before leaving. Meet me back here at five and we'll find a place to eat."

"Sounds fine to me," Cass whispered. "Thanks for understanding."

As she stepped through the swinging doors of the pavilion, she leaned heavily against the wall, clutching her stomach, hoping passersby wouldn't notice her trying to catch her breath and steady her nerves. What a day, what a day, she wanted to shout. Two beautiful yearlings and the possibility of getting her man back in her life.

Would he really listen to her? They'd been quite calm in the canteen, given the circumstances. But what about when they were alone, away from the horse crowd? Would he be honest with her? Could they trust each other enough to let go of the past and look to the future?

Uneasily, Cassie pushed herself away from the wall to check on her horses. Her spirits lifted again when she walked along the horse stalls. If nothing else, she had two very fine prospects to take back to the farm. The trip had already been worthwhile.

CHAPTER SEVENTEEN

"I'm sure I'm repeating myself."

Clint grinned at Cassie sticking her fork into a tender piece of prime rib while still chattering about her purchases. Horses were so in her blood.

"But I have to pinch myself now and then to think that I stayed in the bidding for the bay colt. Thank god, we stopped when we did. I don't think I would have gone much more than another five thousand."

They sat in a candlelit curtained alcove at an upscale restaurant. Unlike at lunch, neither noise nor stares of other patrons threatened to intrude.

"You did real fine," Clint said, with a little hint of pride. "Once, though, I thought you were going to go over and clobber that guy in the loud green sport coat."

"Well, he looked at me with such disdain. Like I didn't belong." Cassie pouted. "I didn't like him one bit."

"Some folks think they can intimidate anybody, especially a woman."

"Hah, a lot some folks know," she retorted. "And that beautiful little filly. I still can't believe I stole her for such a low price. Both of them looked fantastic. I expect to buy a couple broodmares tomorrow to go along with them. What about you? You're not going to drive back to Utah with an empty trailer are you?"

"No, while you were checking out your yearlings, I was dickering with the buyer of Hip Number 12. I offered him ten thousand more than the original purchase price and he took it."

"Hip Number 12," Cassie muttered, brushing back wisps of hair from her ear. "That filly sold for a hundred thousand, easy."

He loved watching Cassie with her mouth open. Cute. It made her look cute. "You have a good memory."

"You bought a horse plus made reservations for this luxury setting? You've been a busy boy. What else have you been up to?"

"It's not uncommon at these auctions for a horse to change hands a couple times before it actually leaves the premises. A lot of folks are in this to make a quick profit. This guy made ten thousand, a ten percent profit, without lifting a finger, buying a bag of oats, or taking a risk. He's happy and I'm happy. That's what makes for good horse trading."

Clint sliced another tender piece of meat. Knowing they couldn't avoid discussing the topic weighing on them like reinforced concrete any longer, he decided to go for broke. "We've got to talk about us, you know."

"I know," she said weakly.

He put his fork down on the tablecloth and sighed deeply. "I told you earlier about going to see my grandmother. She was very helpful." He chuckled. "You might not be surprised to learn

374

that she came by one day to tell me to come and see her once I realized I was totally lost."

Wiping a tear from the corner of her eye, Cassie nodded. "That's not hard to fathom."

"Anyway, I've felt lower than a snake for some time about what I did to you. What I did to the kids. To all of us. Now, I'm aware I was battling fears of losing you and being rejected by you. In the end, I guess I thought I wouldn't measure up. You were taking so long to decide. I panicked."

He paused to sip some water. "You see, I had to reject you before you walked out on me. It was so uncharacteristic of me to declare my love before knowing where you were. I was certain you were using suspicions of my involvement in drugging your horse as a way of rejecting me."

Cassie shook her head. Tears pooled in her eyes.

"I now know I was dealing with stuff I'd learned from my father as a child." Even to him, his words sounded hollow, divorced from feeling. "You see, I never quite measured up. I had learned that love was earned, meted out in small bits as a reward for good behavior...

"Anyway, I had to at least see you and apologize for distrusting you, for hurting you. I'm so sorry, Cassidy. You were the best thing to happen to me in years, and I threw you over like it meant nothing." Clint paused. His shoulders slumped. "I was wrong."

Cassie reached into her purse for a tissue. Gingerly, she reached across the table to wipe his tears away, then dabbed at her own. "I can't tell you it didn't hurt terribly. You wouldn't listen. It was like I was a non-person. I made a pledge to myself that I would never forgive you."

She chuckled softly. "Yet, here I am. Oh, I was still raging at you when I left Chicago. But somewhere along the way—maybe flying over Utah—I rediscovered my heart, what is really important and what I really want. You are not the easiest person to love, Mr. Travers. But I seem to be up to the task."

His heart pounded into overdrive.

"The irony is that I ran from you, too," she added in a soft voice. "I ran from your declaration of love. I didn't know if I could be a good mother. I knew loving you would be a terribly wrenching thing for my life. I wasn't at all sure that I wanted to take the risk to really love. And when I decided...the day I decided to make that leap, to acknowledge and completely express that love, you showed up at my door in the middle of the night accusing me of betraying your trust and your honor."

For long moments Clint met Cassie's gaze, unable to respond with words. The yellow flame of the tiny centerpiece candle flickered in the breeze of the air conditioner.

Clint wet his lips and broke the silence. "I love you, Cassidy O'Hanlon. I always will." He swallowed and waited.

Cassie smiled radiantly and murmured, "And I love you. And always will."

"Then we ought to be able to figure out a way of building a future together. Don't you agree?" he said, again holding his breath.

"We ought to." Cassie chewed on her trembling lower lip. "If we can commit to listen to each other — and when we think things are going awry, to stop and ask how we're doing. Then we'll have a viable future."

Cassie laughed out loud, her eyes snapping playfully. "Remember what your grandmother advised me…the message you gave me from her: *Tell Fire Woman to trust only her heart. Not what she sees or hears. Only her heart.*"

He closed his eyes briefly. "Yeah, I remember."

"Well, it was a very long flight out here from Chicago." Moving aside her plate, she placed her elbows on the table and spoke quietly. "When I left, I dreaded the possibility that I might bump into you here. I cussed you out in all the ways I could think of. By the time I landed, I was hoping you would be here. That we might have one more chance."

Clint could have watched her eyes sparkle and dance all night long. He had no doubt they'd have as many chances as it took.

"Maybe I needed that time alone." Cassie sighed, interlacing her fingers. "Anyway, I tried to take your grandmother's advice and listen to my heart. Maybe I needed a lot of quiet, solitary time before I could hear what my heart was speaking. For in my heart, I know we belong together. Somehow, we have to work it out."

377

"We'll work it out," he responded confidently, reaching for her hand. "We have to."

"Would you two like some dessert?" asked the waiter, pulling back the alcove curtain.

Cassie replied quickly, "Why not? I'll have the New York cheese cake."

"Make that two," Clint said. "And could you bring us another bottle of wine?"

"Sure. I'll bring it right out."

"You're not trying to get me drunk, are you, Travers?" Cassie quipped. "Get the lady drunk and work your wiles on her."

"That's a thought, but I'm not in a rush," he drawled, clinking his glass against hers. "The night is long, but we do have to be back in the pavilion by the morning to catch up with your broodmares. You want to get the best you can afford."

Cassie brought the wine glass to her lips. "This is your world, isn't it? You don't bat an eye dealing with these high prices. You're a much more sophisticated fellow than you like to project at the Downs or at the ranch."

Shaking his head, Clint gave her his best boyish smile. "I don't know about that. I do okay, I suppose, but I much prefer working with a yearling in a round pen or taking a two year old out to a training track.

"Still, I'll probably be able to make a fifty percent profit on Hip Number 12, if not more. This world gets crazy at times. I sometimes can't believe what people are willing to spend. Yet, we might decide to have you race her. Or, given her breeding, she would make an excellent broodmare for the ranch or for the McHenry farm. You know she's a chestnut. Reminds me a lot of Cassie's Hope."

- o -

Cassie watched Clint carefully, sensing he was switching the conversation back again to a much more intimate level. They'd enjoyed sharing dreams about the yearlings and had playfully skirted issues that still remained between them. But no longer. Those earlier declarations of love weren't going to be enough.

He wanted more than that. So did she. Here we go, she sighed, as goose bumps scurried to find a safe place on her arms.

"You know, Cassidy, I've only loved one other woman," Clint said. "She was the mother of my children. I don't take love lightly at all."

"I know you don't," Cassie murmured, trying not to roll the napkin into a tight ball.

"I want you to marry me," he declared simply. The flash of desire in his eyes made her knees go weak. "I want you to be a mother for Lester and Sammy. I want you to be the mother of our children yet to be born."

Cassie's heartbeat stopped and then leaped of its own accord. Her vision fogged over.

"I love you, Cassidy. Will you marry me? Will you dream with me?" Clint asked, reaching across the table the table to stroke her cheek lightly.

She'd waited through a lot of agony to hear that question. Now she wanted to savor it, but there was no time for that. The corners of her mouth turned up happily. She reached across the table to interlace her fingers with his. Her voice was calm and exuded strength. Her words were uttered without hesitation. "I love you, Clint. Yes, I will marry you. I want us to chase dreams together. I want to be the mother of our children."

She leaned over to brush her lips across his. He chewed lightly on her lower lip and then let her sit back.

Cassie choked more out. "I want you take me to my room now, Mr. Travers. I want to touch my man all over. I want you to touch me all over. I want to love and be loved."

"You'll get no argument from me on that, my lady," Clint said, scrawling his signature on the credit card slip.

Much later, she luxuriated in his touch, in his feel. As soon as they'd reached her room, they'd made love fast and furious. They'd been in a pell-mell rush, as if to close the distance that had separated them for weeks. That had been bone crushingly fantastic. This was delightfully sweet.

Intertwined side by side, facing each other, his cock filling her completely, they hardly moved, yet she sensed another wave building from deep within. He laved a hardened nipple. She ran her nails lightly across his back. His fingers grazed her bare nape, as if trying to memorize its texture and indentations. Subtle movements flickered back and forth. Her pussy clenched around his shaft, causing him to groan. She watched his eyes follow her hand as she reached between them to graze her clit. She blew him a kiss, knowing how much that simple gesture turned him on. He swelled deep within her.

"Now," she heard him say hoarsely. She braced herself for the final charge.

"Faster," she murmured. "Fuck me. Love me."

The wave enveloped her. She crested as he released. Not wanting him to withdraw anytime soon, she hooked a leg around his butt and held him in place. He lurched into her one more time, depositing more of his essence. She hugged him tightly.

At last she let herself bask in the afterglow of lovemaking—and in the six dozen yellow long-stem roses that had greeted her on returning to her room. Clint had spent a very busy afternoon.

Again, she felt him busy himself by nibbling the base of her throat. Would she ever grow tired of his loving attention? Never.

"You know," she said, "you haven't commented on my hair. Are you disappointed I had it cut?"

"Nonsense," Clint murmured. "You'd be beautiful if you were bald."

Cassie giggled. "I don't think I'll try that anytime soon. But do you like it? It would take some time to grow it back, but I would."

"No. I like it a lot," he confided. "The long hair made you appear sultry and I loved playing with it, but this style actually makes you look, if anything, breezier and even sexier. And it's much easier get to this sensitive skin."

He laced her neck with butterfly kisses; her skin drank deeply of his wet caresses.

"That feels so good. I think I'll keep my hair short, at least for awhile.

Moments later, Clint asked, "Cassie, did you ever show the kids your Bears night-shirt?"

"That old thing? Goodness, no," Cassie said scowling. "Why in the world do you ask that?"

"Oh, just wondering."

Surprised but not disappointed, Cassie felt Clint's cock harden once again. She squeezed him, letting him know she was still there, still wanting. They might not get any sleep tonight, but there would be many more nights for that.

Late on Thursday, Cassie's spirits surged wildly. She sat alongside Clint in his pickup. They were pulling into his ranch driveway. His recent purchases were in the trailer they hauled behind them, and her horses were being vanned to Chicago.

Clint brought the rig to a stop. Lester tugged at the passenger door handle. Sammy stood by him with arms held wide waiting for a hug. Happily, Cassie jumped down to hug both of them. *Her* children. She held nothing back. They'd share a lot of joys and a lot of pains. At times she'd mess up, but even that would be okay. They would all learn to grow together, and she knew the entire family would be there to help her.

Silver Hawk stepped closer. Cassie rose to greet the woman with a warm embrace.

"Welcome back, Cass," Silver Hawk said. "I knew you wouldn't let my idiot brother screw things up for good. But it sure has taken some time."

Cassie could not contain her smile. "Well, we both contributed to making it look pretty bleak there for awhile, and we both worked hard to get it back together."

"No matter." Silver Hawk shrugged. "You're here, and that's what counts."

"When's the wedding?" Lester asked, pulling on Cassie's hand to get her attention.

"You, young man," Cassie chided, "are going to have to have more patience with women. But ther your father took years to learn such patience," she quipped as Clint joined his family. "I guess there's hope for you. Yes, we have discussed the wedding."

"Hurrah!" both children screamed.

Behind the children, Silver Hawk nodded her head, beaming brightly.

"We'd like it to be in December," Cassie said. "Lester, would you mind if we don't do it in Chicago? If we get married there, I don't think Grandmother Littlefield would be able to come. We really think she needs to be there."

"Me too. She's got to be there," Lester agreed.

"But can your dad come out?"

Cassie put an arm around the boy, appreciating his concern. "Yes, we'll fly him out along with my three girlfriends. He's doing much better now than when you last saw him. And the girls will take good care of him."

"Then where will the wedding be?" Lester persisted.

"Probably in Salt Lake City. Then we can all make a holiday of it." She winked at Clint. She didn't need to go into all the details of their planning. Clint didn't particularly want to get married in the church where he'd wedded his first wife, so they'd decided on Salt Lake.

- o -

Later that afternoon, Clint took his family by his mother's house to share their news. He was not at all surprised to see the matriarch of the family, his grandmother, sitting at the kitchen table when they entered.

His mother greeted Cassie by clasping her hands between her own. "Welcome, Ms. O'Hanlon. It is good to see you."

"Oh, thank you so much," Cassie cried out, seemingly unable to stop grinning. "It's great to be here."

"So you two finally found each other," Mrs. Littlefield said. "It's about time. I'm not getting any younger."

"Grandmother," Clint admonished.

384

"No, you are all here," the old woman said. "That can only mean one thing. And your marriage makes me very happy."

Clint cleared his throat to speak.

"No," Mrs. Littlefield said, holding up her hand, "I am not finished." She looked around at all the smiling faces, and her eyes sparkled. "You all sometimes think I'm a little touched in the head. Now don't shake your heads. I know so. But it don't matter. It's a gift of age.

"Fire Woman, I bring a present for you. Wear it on your wedding day. It would please this old woman much." Reaching down the front of her dress, Mrs. Littlefield brought forth a carefully tissue wrapped object.

The old woman held in her hands the most beautiful blue sapphire and silver necklace Cassie had ever seen. Her eyes blurred with tears of awe and joy.

"It was handmade generations ago by my great-grandfather," the elder woman said with pride, handing the gift to Cassie. "I knew it was yours when I first saw you. She who wears this will be charmed through the years with a loving family who will walk with her though pain and much joy."

EPILOGUE

Cassidy O'Hanlon Travers sat beside her husband at their wedding reception table surrounded by family and friends. At least for the moment, all was perfect with the world.

It'd been the kind of wedding she'd hoped for. The pastor had been thrilled to plan a wedding ceremony with them. Turned out he was an avid horse racing fan and was very pleased when he opened the envelope Clint had pressed in his hand to find not only his fee, but also two season passes to the following summer's races at Wyoming Downs. His lovely wife had played Cassie's favorite wedding music on the organ.

The church's small chapel, decorated for the Christmas season, turned out to be a charming, inspirational setting for the wedding. Just the right size for their small gathering.

Looking around the table, fingering the blue sapphire hanging on its silver chain about her neck, Cassie treasured the feel of family. Her dad had come, along with Ashton, Traci and Susan. Clint's mother, grandmother and sister were there as well as several cousins, aunts and uncles she'd just met. And of course, Lester sat on his dad's left and Sammy sat next to her. A toasty comforting warmth infused her body. She smiled at her father, who stood and lifted his wine glass for the umpteenth toast of the evening.

"We've toasted the bride and groom and everybody present," began her father, "but I want to propose a toast to one who isn't here. You see, all of this started with a little chestnut filly named Cassie's Hope. I propose a toast to Cassie's Hope, who never gave up when the going got tough."

"Hear, hear," was the response as each person raised a glass.

"And," Cassie added, "here's to dreams that refuse to die."

All present cheered loudly and clapped their hands.

- o -

The End

About the Author

Adriana Kraft is the pen name for a husband/wife team writing sizzling romantic suspense and erotic romance. The award-winning pair has published over thirty romance novels and novellas to outstanding reviews. Long and Short Reviews: *"scorching hot...refreshing...something to read when you want straight up hotness."* Romance Junkies: *"filled with warmth, blazing hot sex, well-developed characters...not for the faint of heart."* Romantic pairings include straight m/f, lesbian, bisexual, ménage and polyamory, in both contemporary and paranormal settings.

We hope you enjoyed *Cassie's Hope*, and we love hearing from readers! You can find all our links at our website:

http://adrianakraft.com

Adriana Kraft

When It's Time to Heat Things Up

BOOK LIST

SERIES

RIDERS UP Romantic Suspense novels
Book One *Cassie's Hope*
Book Two *Heat Wave*
Book Three *Detour Ahead*
Book Four *Willow Smoke* (forthcoming, January, 2015)

SWINGING GAMES Erotic Romance novellas
Book One *Anticipation*
Book Two *Hook-Ups*
Book Three *A Tempting Taste*
Book Four *Complexities*
Book Five *The Adventure Continue*
Book Six *Who's the Coach?*
Book Seven *Dare to Adventure*
Book Eight *Pushing the Limits*
Book Nine *Too Close for Comfort*
Book Ten *Triple Play*
Book Eleven *Summer's End*
Book Twelve *Foursomes and More…*

COLORS OF THE NIGHT Erotic Romance novels
Book One *Colors of the Night*
Book Two *Aria Returns*

PURGATORY POINT Erotic Romance novels
Book One *The Mistress of Purgatory Point*
Book Two *Return to Purgatory Point*

THE DIARY Erotic Romance novels
Book One *The Diary*
Book Two *Writing Skin*

STAND ALONE NOVELS AND NOVELLAS

The Heist Romantic Suspense novel
The Unmasking Romantic Suspense novel
Cherry Tune-Up Erotic Romance novella
The Reunion Erotic Romance novel
Atlantis Woman Found Erotic Romance novella
The Best Man Erotic Romance novel
Santa's Boss Erotic Romance novella
Through the Mirror Erotic Romance novella
Sheila's Prenups Erotic Romance novella
Full Circle Erotic Romance novella

SHORT STORIES IN ANTHOLOGIES
Accidental Contact, in *Sapphic Planet*
A Taste of Ginger, in *The Cougar Book*

www.ingramcontent.com/pod-product-compliance
Lightning Source LLC
Chambersburg PA
CBHW072108250626
47159CB00007B/2357